AGAINST THE LAW

A Selection of Recent Titles by Jay Brandon

The Edward Hall Series

AGAINST THE LAW *

The Chris Sinclair Series

ANGEL OF DEATH
AFTERIMAGE
SLIVER MOON
GRUDGE MATCH
RUNNING WITH THE DEAD

* *available from Severn House*

AGAINST THE LAW

Jay Brandon

Severn House Large Print
London & New York

This first large print edition published 2018
in Great Britain and the USA by
SEVERN HOUSE PUBLISHERS LTD of
Eardley House, 4 Uxbridge Street, London W8 7SY.
First world regular print edition published 2018 by
Severn House Publishers Ltd.

British Library Cataloguing in Publication Data
A CIP catalogue record for this title is available from the British Library.

ISBN-13: 9780727829160

Severn House Publishers support the Forest Stewardship Council™
[FSC™], the leading international forest certification organisation. All
our titles that are printed on FSC certified paper carry the FSC logo.

FSC
MIX
Paper from
responsible sources
www.fsc.org   FSC® C013056

Typeset by Palimpsest Book Production Ltd.,
Falkirk, Stirlingshire, Scotland.
Printed and bound in Great Britain by
T J International, Padstow, Cornwall.

This, like one of my favorite earlier books, is dedicated to Elizabeth and Sam.

And for Becky.

One

Edward was enjoying watching dusk erase the buildings and thinking about getting another beer, when he faintly heard his phone ringing. He felt only a mild curiosity about who might be calling, but then the front door opened and Mike leaned out and tossed the phone at him.

'You might want to take this,' he said. 'I already accepted the call.'

Accepted the call? What did that mean?

But then the recorded voice said, 'Hold for the inmate call.'

Edward sat upright with a strange swirl of dread and nostalgia suddenly roiling his stomach.

'Edward?'

'Amy? What are you doing calling from the jail?'

'I'm in it, Eddie. Booked in. This is my one call. You know, the famous one call? Tell me I didn't waste it.' He recognized the panic in her voice, knew it intimately.

'Of course you didn't. What in the world, Amy? What did you get arrested for?'

She started crying. He stood up and walked into the house, through his roommate Mike's concerned stare and into his bedroom. *Don't let them see you cry,* Edward thought. Don't show the other inmates any sign of vulnerability. Cons may have few other life skills, but they knew how to zero in on the weak. Maybe the

1

rules were different on the women's side, but he doubted it.

'Edward, can you get me a lawyer, a really good one? I figure you'd know the best.'

'Of course. You know I will, Amy. But what the hell? I need to prepare the lawyer for something. What's the charge?'

She hiccupped and her crying paused. In a tiny voice that reminded him of Amy as a child, she said, 'Murder?'

'My God. I'll be right there.'

After he got dressed Edward dug an old address book out of a drawer. On his way out he said to Mike, 'Stay close to your phone, OK? I may need you.'

'Sure. What's up?'

'My sister's been arrested for murder.'

They kept him waiting nearly half an hour, on the attorney's side of the visitor's booth of the Harris County Detention Center. He wasn't on Amy's visitors' list – she didn't have one yet – but he'd gotten in by showing his bar card, which felt very strange. Good thing he hadn't followed his first inclination after being disbarred, to cut it up into little pieces and throw it into Buffalo Bayou.

Amy looked like hell. That was no surprise, almost everybody did after the arrest and booking process, but what interested him was the way she looked like hell. Her eyes were wild, not only red but darting around, and her hands shook when she put them on the counter in front of her, on the other side of the thick plastic. Check, check. Standard signs. But her hair was beautiful. Higher

2

on her head than he remembered, thick and lovely, brown like his own but with red highlights and obviously coiffed. Her mouth still showed traces of lipstick, though of course the jail had confiscated her jewelry. She must have looked great a short time ago.

'Thank you for coming, Edward. I didn't know if they'd let you see me.'

'They did. As your lawyer. For now. Saturday night, Amy, not that easy to get in touch with lawyers right now.'

'You're here as my lawyer . . . But didn't you get – you know – disbarred?'

'Yes. You know what? They don't have a ceremony and strip off your pinstriped suit and break your briefcase in half.' He held up his bar card. 'They don't take the card away. And some people here still remember me fondly.'

'So you're impersonating a lawyer?'

'Are we going to talk about my crimes? Which one of us is free to walk out of here? No, let's talk about you, Dr Amy. What happened?'

His harshness was deliberate. You often had to do that with clients, especially ones in jail.

She recovered herself a little, so it had worked. Her eyes skittering away from his, she said, 'Is this covered by attorney-client privilege? You know, when you're not actually – an attorney?'

'Let's say it's covered by the brother-sister privilege. Do you think I'd betray you?'

There was an awkward pause.

In a calm, reassuring voice, Edward said, 'Amy. I would never tell anything you asked me not to tell. No matter what. OK?'

3

She finally looked at him. Something in his face made her sit up straighter and nod. 'OK.'

'Who did they arrest you for killing?'

She maintained eye contact, to her credit. 'Paul.'

That didn't come as a great surprise. Somehow he'd figured.

'What makes them think you killed him?' Sometimes you jumped right into the ultimate question with a client, usually you circled around it.

'I guess I'm the natural suspect, right, the estranged wife? Plus, I found his body.'

Edward managed not to wince. Estranged was supposed to mean not seeing each other, so if Amy had been there, well, he understood why police had questioned the situation.

His silence had the same effect as a question. Amy leaned forward, hands flat on the countertop, with that urgency to make her listener understand that cops count on when trying to get a confession.

'Yes, we'd been seeing each other again. I hadn't told anyone because I didn't want to put that pressure on us. As a matter of fact, we were supposed to make our public debut tonight. There was a medical awards dinner. Paul was nominated. He asked me to go with him. Not suggested we go together. Asked me out.' She dimpled slightly, enough for her brother to see how much that had meant to her. Which meant Paul was still the love of her life, maybe.

On the other hand, that's who murderers usually kill.

'So you went to his house. That's when you found him? Was he supposed to pick you up and when he didn't show you went over there?'

4

'No, I went to his place. We'd planned to meet there. He said he didn't want to sit in my living room waiting for me to be ready. So I went over there. The door was unlocked, but I knocked anyway, just to be polite. That's when I heard the shot.'

'You actually heard it?'

She nodded, her head going up and down in tiny bobs. 'I panicked. I didn't recognize it at first. I thought his stove had exploded. It scared me. I just stayed out there for a minute. Then I opened the door and called his name. I thought I heard the back door close. That's when I smelled it. Gunsmoke. Did you know that's a real thing? I had no idea. But I smelled it. It's still in my nostrils.'

She was still panicked, words skittering out of her mouth, but Edward didn't say anything to calm her. Sometimes this initial gush carried the best information, unfiltered by a screening brain.

'So then I ran. I dropped my purse and my wrap and I ran to the back of the house. The smell got stronger. He was in the bedroom, on the floor. It looked like he'd fallen back on the bed and slid off. I turned his body over. He'd been shot. He was still alive, Edward. He looked at me. He couldn't speak, but his eyes were so frightened. Then they just glazed over. I was screaming his name, I think. I started doing chest compressions, but that was just making him gush more blood. I saw his phone on the nightstand and called 911. I just left the line open while I tried to revive him. I was yelling at them, telling them to hurry. I couldn't remember the address right then, but of course they had it, from the phone.'

So they'd been able to place her at the scene

5

at the time of his death. And she'd undoubtedly been covered with blood when police arrived. No wonder she'd gotten arrested.

'I kept working. I think I had him back at one point, I'm pretty sure I did, but by the time EMS came—'

'Amy. Look at me.'

She did, coming back from a long distance. He looked levelly into her eyes and asked, 'Was the gun there?'

She nodded. 'Right there on the floor. I kicked it out of the way to get to Paul.'

Please tell me you didn't pick up the murder weapon. 'Was that the only time you touched it?'

'Yes. I didn't even see it again. I'd kicked it under the bed. That's where police found it.'

So it looked like a clumsy attempt to hide it. Again, he couldn't fault the detective who'd arrested her.

'What about the door closing? Did you follow up on that?'

'I was trying to save his life, Edward. I was trying to bring my husband back from the dead. No, I didn't run to the back door and look out.' Edward didn't respond and she calmed down a bit. 'I was sort of trying to listen with one part of my mind, but I didn't hear a car starting up or anything. I guess the killer just ran across the backyard and over the fence to the alley.'

'Any idea who that might have been?'

'I haven't even thought about it. I've been replaying what happened, wondering what I could have done differently. If I'd just managed to get

6

his heart beating again for five minutes. EMS were on their way. If I'd had a defibrillator . . .'

It may have been true that she'd been trying to save him. It must have been horrible for her, a medical doctor, to feel that life so close at hand and not be able to grab it and force it back into Paul's body. To see the man you loved lying there, looking almost like he had when he was alive, his last panicked look begging you to bring him back and you helpless to do it. But that didn't mean she hadn't shot him, having second thoughts after committing a murder was very common.

And cops thought linearly. If you couldn't give them another suspect, the investigation never went in any other direction, except deeper into why their one suspect must have committed the crime. He was being Amy's lawyer now. It was his job to think better than she could at this moment.

'Do you have any ideas?'

She looked at him blankly and he knew she didn't understand the question. But before he could even draw breath to rephrase it, Amy pulled herself together. Her eyes focused. She'd always had the best concentration in the family, even better than their father's. When she was a girl he imagined he could actually see the thought bubble forming over her head, her will to understand was so strong.

'No,' she said. 'I have no idea. We'd been separated for nearly six months; I don't even know who Paul's friends were lately. What he was into.'

Edward steeled himself to be her lawyer, not a brother sparing her feelings. 'Had he been dating someone else before you?'

7

She shrugged. 'Of course he was. He was a doctor in the big city, separated from his wife. Do the math. There could have been women waiting for years to fling themselves at him. But I don't know details.'

He waited, watching her while thinking himself. What else would police want to know? What might they have read into the scene? If she'd told them why she was there, they would have started trying to discredit that story already.

He realized he was thinking like a prosecutor, adopting the cop's viewpoint, trying to figure out why evidence would be admissible rather than otherwise, thinking of ways to discredit the client's story rather than supporting it. Interesting. He'd been away from the game long enough that he'd reverted to his roots, his early training as a prosecutor. The years of overlay of being a defense lawyer had fallen away. Not a good thing, if he was going to take care of his sister.

But it was her story that set off this response. It was so easy to pick apart.

All right, then. Let's beef it up.

Amy's eyes remained distant. She was still in that bedroom. Edward did the meanest thing he could have done in that situation. He said her name.

'Amy.'

She looked sharply at him, eyes widening. Even replaying the scene of her dying husband was preferable to the current reality; this sordid, cold cinder block room, the thick plastic between them smudged with handprints of desperation.

'How long had you and Paul been going out together again?'

8

'Three weeks. I can tell you the date. It was our anniversary.'

'Your anniversary's in June.' It was March now.

'Yes, I know, Edward.' She spoke reprovingly, as if she were the one who got to criticize his answer. 'This was the anniversary of our first – a different anniversary.' She didn't quite blush, though her mouth closed down to as thin a line as it could. Amy stared straight at him. Again he could see the girl she'd been, the playful teenager with a secret she wouldn't keep for long.

'OK, so three weeks. Was it usually like this, you going to his place, or would he pick you up?'

'Neither, at first. We'd meet at a restaurant or bar. Places where we'd never gone before. Then he came and picked me up a couple of times. Tonight was only the second time I'd been to his house, almost as if he didn't want me to know where it was. The secret lair. The fortress of solitude.' She smiled. Sitting on that plastic chair, in her thin jail coverall, she actually smiled at having penetrated his defenses.

'Who else knew you and Paul were seeing each other again?'

She shook her head. 'Nobody.'

'Amy. You haven't kept a secret for three weeks in your life. And this was a big deal. Who did you talk to about it? Jean? Roy?' He was shooting in the dark, trying to remember names.

'I'm not sixteen any more, Eddie. I don't have best friends. I have colleagues and I have old friends I don't have time to see any more. What about you? Who did you call when you first got—? Sorry, that was mean.'

9

Her apologizing to him in this situation was so absurd he had no answer. He reverted to lawyer talk.

'OK, what other clues might you have left? Was it a new dress you were wearing tonight?' She nodded. 'Where'd you buy it?'

'Lord and Taylor's. The Galleria. It's beautiful, Edward. It's a little off the shoulder, deep blue—'

'Do you still have the receipt?'

'Yes. In my desk drawer at home.'

'Anything else new for the occasion? Earrings? Perfume?'

Her mouth went small again, but she opened it to say, 'Underwear. Victoria's Secret.' Her eyes were flat, daring him to say something.

Edward went on quickly. 'OK. Good. The details support your story. Is there any other hint that might say what tonight was? A diary? Note to yourself? Facebook?'

She shook her head, then stopped. 'Wait. Yes. It's in my appointment calendar on my desk at home. Just Paul's name and an asterisk. Oh, and his new address on a page about a week earlier, from the first time I went there.'

That combined with the fact that the awards dinner was happening tonight should help.

'OK. Amy, here's my most important question so far. Is there anything incriminating at your house? Anything at all, even something a dumb cop might misinterpret to mean you were making plans to kill your husband? Or not even plans, but that you might be mad at him, or the conflicts had escalated? Anything at all like that. Think very hard about this.'

He watched her face and could tell she wasn't doing what he'd asked, thinking hard. She was barely putting any thought into his questions at all. Excellent expression. He wished he could capture it. It wasn't the face of a murderer trying to remember anything that might give her away.

Then she frowned. Her face changed completely. Maybe someone else wouldn't notice, but he'd known her face her whole life. A guilty thought had just crossed her mind. Then she shook her head.

'No. Nothing,' she said. 'There couldn't be, because I had no thought of killing him. Never had. I didn't.'

'Is there another gun in the house?'

'No. I've never owned one.'

'OK, here's what I want you to do.' He got a legal pad from his briefcase and wrote hurriedly on it, including the date and a signature line. 'This is written consent to search your house. I want to give it to police, so they can search the place before you get out of here, before you've had a chance to hide anything you might have left behind. So they'll find the appointment book and the receipts themselves. They prefer finding evidence themselves to having the defense hand it to them. I want to do this now. OK?'

He couldn't get out of the lifelong habit of treating Amy like a little sister, but she was smart, probably smarter than Edward. Amy understood all the implications, but she nodded. Because this was a lawyer's visiting booth, there was a slot at the bottom of the thick plastic. Edward slid the one sheet through it, followed by his pen. Amy read quickly and signed without hesitating.

11

But as she did, she said, 'We all have secrets, Edward.'

She looked up at him, clear-eyed and unrepentant. What guilt was she both acknowledging and shrugging off? What would police find? Evidence of another man? Just something embarrassing that she'd prefer her brother not know? Edward hoped it was something as inconsequential as sex toys.

'OK. I need to move fast. They're probably already trying to get a warrant.'

'What about me? Don't leave me here. God, Edward, you have no idea—'

He looked at her sharply and she remembered to whom she was talking. But her panic only escalated. She tried to reach him, putting her fingers through that narrow slot.

'Then you know better than anyone. I've got to get out of here. That holding cell, God, I thought I was going to die or be raped or drowned in the horrible toilet.'

'They'll put you in another cell soon. It'll be better. I've got work to do on the outside, Amy. I can't stay here just so you get your own little private booth. Don't worry, I'll get you out as fast as I can. You've already been booked, that's what slows down the release process, so that's good. You've seen a magistrate, right? Did he set a bond?'

She nodded. 'Two hundred thousand dollars. It didn't seem like she put any thought into it at all. It was if she was just following a chart or something.'

'She was. The bond schedule. OK. The bond

12

fee is ten percent. Do you have twenty thousand dollars? That you have access to right now? Or you can wait in here. Monday I can probably get your bond reduced, even make it a personal recognizance bond. Or you could put up a cash bond for the whole amount and get it back at the end. Do you want—?'

Again, her wide eyes and reaching hands answered him and stopped him. He slowed down and said, 'OK. So do you have the money?'

'Of course. But getting it tonight? I can't. Not without—'

Telling their parents. He knew what she was thinking. As if this was going to remain secret long.

'OK. I'll take care of it.'

'You will? You can? How? Do you have—?'

'Just let me work, OK, Dr Amy? Damn it, look what time it is. I've got to go.' He shrugged on his jacket and stood quickly. 'Is there anything else, Amy? Anything I need to know?'

'I loved him, Edward. More than ever. Going to this dinner tonight, it was like every prom and date I ever had rolled into one, but better, because I loved him and I knew he loved me still too and we were going to make it. I was so happy standing on that porch. Just before I heard the shot.'

This was obviously a declaration she wanted to make, but not exactly useful to Edward at the moment. He, by contrast, stood there a moment longer so he could give her information she could use, on the other side of that door.

'Amy. Keep your head down. Don't look them in the eye. Keep everything inside yourself. Don't look weak, but don't engage. If they force themselves on you, use what you've got. Tell them you're a doctor. They won't be able to stop themselves from saying, "Say, Doc, I've got this rash," or "cough", or "sick mother" or something. Diagnose if you want. Or tell them you're about to get out and ask if they want you to take a message to anybody on the outside. They all want to get messages out. OK? You can do this.'

She stood up. She faced him and nodded, her face almost dead, then said, 'And when I get out we need to look into that little tremor you've got in your left hand. It suggests hypertension. Take an aspirin tonight.'

She gave him a tiny wink, taking him back in time again. He nodded at her and hurried out, heading for his phone that he'd had to check at the counter.

Two

His first call was to the police, its homicide division; a number he was surprised he still remembered. Edward got lucky and got through to a night detective he knew slightly. The detective seemed to remember him better, which could be good but maybe not.

'Detective Skinner, you're assigned to the investigation into the death of Dr Paul Shilling? The arrest of his wife, Dr Amy Hall?'

'Yeah, it's mine. What about it?'

'Do you know she's my sister? Well, she is. I've just come from seeing her. I have her signed consent for you to search her home. I will meet you there and let you in, but it has to be right away. I want it searched before she gets released, which will be soon.'

Detective Skinner, to his credit, obviously understood. Edward wanted his sister's house searched, so the record would show it was while she was still in jail, having had no time to hide evidence. So he was offering the detective an easy, quick way in, but asking for a small favor in return.

'I don't think she'll get out before we get a warrant, which we're in the process of right now. I think I'd rather wait for the official piece of paper.'

'This is official. But OK, you wait. I'm on my way to her house now and I've got a key. So I'll be inside when you get there.'

15

'Hold on, hold on.' Skinner reconsidered quickly; Edward could almost hear his thoughts through the phone.

People become cops for two reasons: they genuinely want to help people or they want to tool people around with impunity. The split probably wasn't fifty-fifty. Detective Skinner seemed to fall into the second camp. His immediate instinct had been to give nothing to the lawyer, not even a fair trade. Now Edward had bullied back. He figured the detective was trying to figure some way to screw him, like send a uniform over there to prevent Edward's entering, but there was no authority to keep Edward from getting in.

So the cop accepted the offer. 'OK. I'll meet you over there. On the outside. What's the address?'

Edward gave it to him. 'I may be a few minutes behind you. I have to arrange bail first.'

'OK. I'll wait there.'

Edward hung up and looked around. He was standing in front of the Harris County Detention Center and could feel its bulk behind him. Across the street, the sights were impressive in their own way. It was bail bondsman city over there. Every little office, house or trailer was a bail company, all in prime locations, all offering the same price structure. And all open for business twenty-four hours a day, with garish neon signs advertising that fact. It looked like a tiny Las Vegas for the accused over there.

All of them, of course, wanted cash up front, which he didn't have. Edward gave a full two minutes of thought to his next phone call.

Lawyers can make bail bonds; the lawyers who

16

have registered property with the county, such as certificates of deposit or real estate. Then the lawyers could make bonds up to the value of that registered property. They would do so for the usual ten percent fees, which the lawyer kept. There were several lawyers who made more money from having a few rent houses and CDs registered with the county than they did from practicing law. Edward stood there in the waves of liquid light from the neon signs and tried to think which one he should call.

Finally his decision was made for him, by which one had his home number listed in directory assistance. The lawyer answered on the fourth ring, as Edward was about to give up.

'Hello, Pete. This is Edward Hall. Hope I'm not interrupting anything.'

They kept the small talk mercifully brief. They weren't friends, just colleagues who could talk like professionals.

'I'd like you to keep this to yourself, Pete. My sister's in jail for murder. Her name is Amy Shilling. The victim is her estranged husband, except they had started to see each other again. Supposed to be going together to a medical awards dinner, instead she found him dying on his bedroom floor. So, of course, got herself arrested.'

'Cops,' Pete answered disgustedly. Coming upon a bereaved widow and having no other thought except to arrest her.

'Yeah. So she's in jail on a Saturday night with a two hundred thousand dollar bond. And terrified. I can get you the ten percent Monday. Can you help me?'

There was a pause of a second, two, three, long enough for Edward to realize the night was growing colder. Houston in March, not normally remotely wintery, but tonight's air carried a chill.

'Sure,' Pete said in his ear. Not the easy, automatic offer of help from a friend, but the end result of a calculation tinged by acquaintanceship. 'Yeah, Ed, I can do it.'

'Thanks, Pete.'

But of course Pete should be thanking Edward, because Pete would get to keep the twenty thousand dollar fee. Edward had just handed out his first big favor in this case.

'I'll be right down.'

Coming down to the jail on a Saturday night was a favor in return, but not a twenty thousand dollar favor.

The search of Amy's house was uneventful. The detective had brought a couple of evidence techs to do the actual work. Edward told him about the desk appointment calendar and the receipt for the dress, but didn't go inside. That would give the cop more confidence that Edward wasn't trying to hide anything. It was also a small kindness to Amy, not to be part of this intrusion into her privacy. If she had other secrets the search would reveal, as she'd hinted, at least only strangers would find them. As he walked away, Edward wondered if he was making a mistake. There was no handbook for this kind of thing. It sometimes surprised him that, no matter how much experience one had, new situations still jumped up in every case. And this was a case, whatever else it might be.

He realized he was very tired and hadn't eaten tonight. He headed home and fell immediately into bed, but slept fitfully, expecting his phone to ring. It didn't.

It had taken until closer to dawn than midnight to get Amy bonded out of jail. She hadn't called because she'd gone home exhausted, to find that her house had been searched and only very clumsily reassembled, but too tired to care. She slept into Sunday afternoon.

Edward didn't have another significant conversation with his sister until two days later. By that time the story had exploded, as they say, in the media. Married doctors, both prominent in their fields, one arrested for killing the other. Poor people killed each other every weekend and barely made page five of the metro section, but when the players were successful and well off, it made the front page. Amy had dealt with that and had talked to their parents. Edward stayed away from all that. Besides, he didn't think his presence would help with their parents. It would look even more clearly as if his sister had fallen into the black sheep status into which Edward had been the trailblazer. The Daniel Boone of disgrace.

Instead he gave her the names of the three best criminal defense lawyers he knew, two smart, experienced men, one aggressive, one more of a good old boy, and also an up-and-coming younger woman, with a great track record in trial already and who knew how to play the press. He assumed Amy would choose her but, after that first meeting, Amy wanted to keep her appointments with the other two. She didn't say why. She did surprise him by asking him to come to the third meeting with her.

'For protection?' he asked on the phone.

'To translate. The first two said you're very good, by the way. They said it was a shame you couldn't . . . you know.'

'OK.' He shrugged off the compliments, which the lawyers had had no choice but to make to his sister. 'I'll come with you if you want, Amy.'

So he found himself on the client side of the desk in a law office. This one belonged to Don Hudson, a fifty-something former prosecutor and long-time defense lawyer, who seemed to be godfather to all the judges' children and drinking buddies with the most important prosecutors. Edward didn't know how Don could have time for a personal life, but saw that the wall behind Don's desk featured at least a dozen pictures of him with his wife and children. No law books in here, just a desk that was a table with no storage space. The desk surface was mostly clear. In front of Don were a legal pad and a pen, but he never touched them. He sat and listened, with his clear-eyed gaze. His greeting to Amy had been pleasant but remote, his handshake with Edward friendlier. He didn't seem to mind having Edward there, waving away his apology then concentrating on Amy. He hardly broke his gaze at her face during the entire interview.

They weren't ten minutes into it before Edward saw the problem. He had contributed to it himself, with his first jailhouse conversation with his sister. She had been open and emotional with

20

him, but he was family. By now she had regained her protective reticence.

Retelling her story for at least the sixth or seventh time, Amy's answers were rote. She knew what the lawyer was going to ask and which details were significant. *Why did you pick up the gun? When did you hear the back door close? Are you sure he knew you were coming to his house?*

She answered automatically, beginning her answers before the lawyer finished the question. Don Hudson nodded sometimes during her recitals, but never smiled.

He also never challenged her story. Never asked if she was lying, never leaned across the desk to say: *You know why the cops think you shot him, don't you? You know why you're the natural suspect, right?* Lawyers had different theories on that issue. Most experienced ones never ask new clients: Did you do it? They ask something very neutral like: What happened? Some, Edward knew, started by telling the client the possible defenses, then asking her to tell the story, so the client could decide whether to fit her version of the story around one of those defenses.

Edward had always felt, though, that he himself was the first judge and jury a prospective new client faced. He would stop the tale to say he didn't find it believable, if that was the case. This practice of his had caused a few people to walk out of his office abruptly. All of them, he took small satisfaction in noting, ended up getting convicted.

When Amy stopped talking Don asked her a couple of more questions, one about the gun, one about how far in advance her date with her husband that night had been made.

'OK, then,' he concluded. With a glance at Edward he added, 'I don't know how much you know about the process . . .'

Amy stood up abruptly. 'If you don't mind, I'd appreciate it if you'd discuss my case with my brother and let him relay your thoughts to me.'

'That's very unusual.'

Edward leaned out of his chair, trying to catch her eyes. 'Amy—'

'Please, Edward? I'm not up to this anymore right now. Thanks.'

She hurried to the door and out, in a slight flutter of skirt and heels. When the lawyers were alone, with the door closed behind her, Don sat back and said,

'Did I offend?'

'No, Don. She's just feeling a little overwhelmed, I think. Maybe the reality of having to deal with this just set in, when she knew she was going to hire you.'

'Is she?'

'Sure. I think. I would. So what do you think? What will you do?'

Edward saw the slight hesitation as Don made the calculation. Normally he wouldn't talk to a family member, but the client had specifically authorized him to do so and the family member was someone the lawyer had known for years, who could speak the language. So he answered.

'You know what I'll do. Talk to the prosecutor as soon as possible. They probably haven't even gotten the case from the cops yet, but it will undoubtedly be a family violence case, so one of maybe three prosecutors. Maybe even go to the top and talk to the first assistant. In the meantime develop defenses. Distraught over the divorce; I hope to God he cheated on her and we can prove it. Sudden passion, maybe? I have to go over her story with her again, pressing harder this time. I hope you know that.'

Edward said, 'What about that closing back door? And the fact that Amy says she was on the front porch when she heard the shot fired?'

The lawyer mused for a few seconds. 'Just have to check out the scene, you know. Talk to all the neighbors and get my investigator to find if there was anybody else hanging around. It would be nice if someone heard the shot and saw Amy on the porch at the same time, but what are the chances of that? As for the back door . . .' He shook his head. 'That's a nice touch, maybe it can give us some traction with the D.A. or a jury, but it's a little too, I don't know, fanciful? Without some evidence to back it up.

'Anyway, I'd talk to the prosecutors as soon as possible. Wouldn't ask for an offer too soon – we don't want that to be set in stone – but pretty soon. Just to consider, while we evaluate the case. You know what I mean.'

Edward nodded. Alternatives. That's one thing a good lawyer offered a client. The client makes the choices.

Don smiled for the first time that hour. 'It's a shame you can't handle it yourself, Edward. Or can you? Did you fix that little problem with the bar?'

'Yeah, I paid my tab.'

Don chuckled. 'Well, you're a damned good lawyer. Look forward to running into you in the courthouse again really soon.'

Edward took the obligatory compliment in stride and repressed the little shudder the thought of re-entering that building produced in him.

Over coffee a block away, Amy said, 'Isn't it strange how this thing has dispossessed me from my life already? Normally I'd want to go to my office to talk about this, or even home, but I still feel stalked by the press at the house and in the office I'd imagine my staff listening at the door. God, I hate this.'

On the other hand, you're alive, he thought, but didn't say it.

'So what do you think? I didn't see your other interviews, but Don is damned good, not just in court but behind the scenes. I'm a little surprised you didn't want to go with Michelle right away.'

Amy stopped him with a little hand gesture. She closed her eyes, showing how tired she was. She'd dressed up nicely for this interview, in a business-ready dress, no jewelry, but enough makeup to hide the redness around her eyes. But not their puffiness. He suddenly saw that she was exhausted and that she'd been crying. None of that had come across in the lawyer's office, where she'd been stiff and formal and apparently unfeeling: the perfect defendant, from a prosecutor's perspective. The cold-blooded killer, sitting there coldly staring.

'No, I didn't hire Michelle,' Amy said slowly. 'And I wasn't that crazy about your friend just now, either.'

He wondered if Amy's problem was what he had suggested to Don, that she was reluctant to hire a lawyer because that would signal that her prosecution was beginning for real. She couldn't bring herself to pull the trigger, so to speak.

'Look, Amy, you're going to have to—'

'I know. I'm not in denial, Edward. This is a reality I have to confront. You know what weird thing I keep thinking? I have to do this for Paul, too. Someone killed him. It wasn't me. Who's looking for that murderer? Not the police. They've decided on me. I know that. I've never had to think about it before, but I see how they work. They settle like flies on the closest piece of dropped sandwich and don't go looking for something else.'

Good metaphor, Edward thought. Amy, at only the beginning of her first exposure to the justice system, had seen what it had taken him a long time to learn.

'It's just like doctors,' she continued. 'If you go to one with a cough and he discovers you have bronchitis, he doesn't check for lung cancer, too. Take the easiest, most obvious diagnosis and move on. So I have to be free to find that killer. I have to prove I didn't kill Paul so police or someone will start looking for the person who did.'

'But you need a good lawyer to help you do that, Amy. I can't—'

'I know, Eddie.' She put her hand over his. Hers was warm and a little moist. 'You've been wonderful. More than I could have asked for. I love you.'

He turned his hand to squeeze hers, reflecting how different it was when Amy called him by a nickname than when other people did. He had never introduced himself as anything other than Edward. When an acquaintance called him something else, it was embracing a shared intimate past that had never existed. But Amy had called him Eddie when they were children, especially when she was very young. Her voice changed when she said it. He heard her inquisitive, questioning, vulnerable past calling to him.

'Love you too, baby girl.'

'So of course you know I'm going to ask you one more favor. I'll pick a lawyer, very soon, but can you go to the first court setting with me? Just show me around. I'm sorry, Edward, but I need you.'

He started to say no automatically, to tell her she needed her lawyer chosen by then, so that lawyer could start representing her right away, in the first discussion with the prosecutor. But that wasn't really true. Nothing happened at the first setting. It was doubtful even that the prosecutor who responded to that docket call would be the eventual trial prosecutor. The first setting had very little significance.

He just nodded. Didn't bother to reiterate that she had to accept the reality of what she was facing. Court would do that for her soon enough.

She looked so happy when she smiled at him. An observer might have thought they'd just gotten engaged. And he wondered if it was because she was innocent or because she thought she'd convinced her brother she was.

'When is it?' he asked.

Three

The Harris County Criminal Justice Center was maybe twenty years old, built in the middle of downtown Houston to take the criminal cases out of the civil courthouse. The volume of criminal cases in Texas' largest city seemed to have lifted the building from the ground, inflating it further and further until it was a twenty story glass and steel skyscraper. The staircases weren't easily accessible and the building's elevators were so overwhelmed by the traffic that there were bailiffs who did nothing else but point out available cars and sometimes push people into them. The wait to get to an upper floor could be half an hour. Once you got up there you felt trapped. *The Criminal Justice Center*, the joke among lawyers went, *only twenty minutes from downtown Houston.*

The courtrooms were all interior rooms with no views. They had the same view: pews, the railing, counsel tables, the judge's bench, the jury box. There was no central aisle to the front, as in traditional courtrooms. The aisles were on the sides. And every room the same. They were interchangeable, subtly conveying to the defendants that they were too. Soon your case would be done, those cold rooms said, and a hundred more would take your place.

Edward had told Amy to come an hour before

her nine o'clock docket call. He met her in the parking lot and guided her through the melee of people getting onto the elevators, which was still much, much less crowded than it would be as the hour came closer. Defendants were notoriously late arrivals. If they could follow rules, they wouldn't be here in the first place.

Edward no longer had the ID that would get him special treatment, but one bailiff, an older, oddly cheerful black woman, gave him attorney's privileges and pushed him ahead of people into an elevator anyway. Edward nodded his thanks and pulled Amy in with him just as the doors were closing.

It was unusual to have the luxury of sitting with Amy in the courtroom, helping her ease into the system and giving much longer explanations than usual of the process. Normally, even if he only had one setting, he would have been up there looking at the case file and trying to create a rapport with the prosecutor, maybe even joking with the judge over coffee back in chambers. No client had ever gotten such undivided attention from him. He continued to hold her hand and so could feel her tension building. It jumped a couple of levels when they brought in the prisoners in their orange jumpsuits, their shackles making them shuffle their way into the jury box, where they sat and waited for their lawyers. Some looked out at the audience, seeking family members or friends. Others tried very hard to pretend they weren't there. Edward remembered being taken into custody in a courtroom identical to this one, just after his no contest plea, sitting in that jury box with his hands cuffed, waiting for the bailiff to take him back to the holdover cell. He remembered the anger, regret and resentment but, most of all, the embarrassment. Seeing normal life – the life he'd just had – going on without him. The shame at having been demoted from player in the criminal justice system to its product. Just that quickly.

For Amy it would be much more than the three years Edward had gotten, if things took the course they usually did in these courts. Her grip on his hand was becoming painful. He didn't even try to reassure her.

When the judge emerged Edward was surprised, then mad at himself for his surprise. He'd heard about Cynthia's appointment, about the same time he'd been released on parole. Cynthia Miles, thirty-four, had been a prosecutor with a reputation for preparing a case so tightly it seldom went to trial. She would have been an attractive appointment for the governor when this bench came open: a tough prosecutor, African-American, poised, pretty, with a great smile, but also the coldest stare in the building if someone overstepped. She had a wide forehead, prominent brown eyes and rounded cheeks over an expressive mouth.

Judge Miles took her seat on the high bench without looking out, immediately turning her attention to the docket sheet in front of her, scanning for names of lawyers she knew or defendants whose names had become familiar because they'd spent too long on her docket.

'You know her?' Amy whispered.

29

'Little bit.'

Time moved in jerks and starts after that, seeming to crawl as other defendants' names were called and their lawyers made brief responses to the judge or longer explanations of why the case wasn't ready to be resolved. Judge Miles showed no emotion other than mild irritation and that was when greeting a lawyer like an old friend. Edward saw that was the best one could hope for when she was dealing with her cases, just as when she'd been a prosecutor.

Abruptly, Amy's name was called. It was clear from Cynthia's neutral tone that 'Amy Shilling' meant nothing to her. Amy jumped to her feet, still holding her brother's hand.

'Here, Your Honor.'

'Ms Shilling, do you have an attorney?'

'Yes, Your Honor.' She pulled Edward's hand upward and he, startled, quickly obeyed the implied command, standing next to her. Then he turned his attention forward, to where the judge had set down her docket sheet and leveled a steady gaze at him.

'Mr Hall.'

'Good morning, Your Honor.'

'Good morning. You're here with Ms Shilling?'

'She's my sister, Your Honor.'

'Ah. Well, approach the bench after the docket, please.'

'Yes, Your Honor.'

He sat back down, bemused by how quickly he'd fallen back into the habit of automatically saying yes and using the honorific to everything a judge said. *Are you ready for trial, Mr Hall? Yes, Your Honor. Are you going to help me move this docket,*

Mr Hall? Yes, Your Honor. I'm going to have my bailiff punch you in the face now, Mr Hall. Is that acceptable to you? Yes, Your Honor.

But he quickly turned his stare on his sister.

'Amy, what the hell—?'

'Please, Edward. Just today, OK? We'll talk after, OK?'

'We damned sure will.'

He sat next to her, wondering what the hell she was thinking, wanting to take her out into the hall to talk to her, or slap her, but also anchored to the spot by the life of the courtroom. It moved around him, the court clerk swearing defendants in, to ask if they were indigent and so deserved a free lawyer, and the bailiffs watchful, checking their lists, because usually one or another of the defendants had picked up a new charge and an arrest warrant since their last setting. Most of all Edward, watched the judge, Cynthia Miles, who never looked up from her paperwork and certainly never in his direction.

'Amy,' he said urgently under his breath. 'You have to make a decision about who you're going to hire.'

She didn't say anything. Her hand remained in his, squeezing hard. It seemed a small hand, almost as small as when she'd put it into his when they went to the zoo or a museum, or when they heard a sudden noise at home.

'Amy—'

'Shh. Tell me what's going on.'

Edward looked around. He could tell almost immediately. The lawyer talking earnestly to his client, who sat cuffed in the jury box, was probably

31

on the hook to go to trial today if he couldn't talk his guy into taking whatever deal had been offered. Edward could tell from their postures, the lawyer leaning in more and more urgently, the defendant answering back, looking reasonable from this distance but probably spouting crazy like worms slithering out of his mouth. It was always a bad sign when the client talked back. They should just listen and nod.

One of the prosecutors was talking to a defense lawyer, the young prosecutor nodding but not paying much attention. The other prosecutor, older than the other, sat at ease, leaning back. The prosecutor didn't know yet which case he'd be trying and didn't much care, since all trials went mostly the same way, with the prosecution winning. It made those kids think they were good lawyers, that winning.

Edward whispered some of this to Amy.

'What makes you think they must be going to trial?'

'Because they do every week. There are too many cases not to. Don't try things and the case-load just gets unmanageable. Besides, from the way the judge is—'

Edward looked at Cynthia on the bench. And the judge raised her eyes to him. He remembered she'd told him to approach after the docket call.

'Oh, sorry, wait here, Amy.'

He jumped up and hurried down the aisle. He put one hand on the swinging gate and went through it easily. Nothing happened. Only lawyers were supposed to come into this part of the courtroom, but there was no alarm system. Edward

32

walked into the lawyers' realm as easily as he had for ten years. He hurried up to the bench. Cynthia Miles' face was only a few inches higher than his, but the distance seemed huge. It was his first time to see her in a robe.

No, second. For a moment he was back in a memory, but he erased it quickly, hoping it hadn't shown on his face. It was impossible to tell from Cynthia's calm, nearly blank expression whether she'd read anything from him.

'Mr Hall.'

'Judge.'

'It's good to see you. How long have you been back practicing?'

'I'm not really, Your Honor. I have a job. Non-legal. But my sister needs some help and she asked me—'

'Yes, she does. I see that.' The judge glanced down again at her docket sheet, which told her what Amy was charged with. Cynthia returned her calm gaze to Edward. 'Some kind of mistake?'

'Yes, Judge. She's a doctor. So was her husband. She was the one to find his body, so police – you know.'

'Yes.'

Edward looked for nuances in Cynthia's expression, maybe in the way she turned her head or tilted her shoulders. But she gave nothing away. She seemed so placid no one would have thought there might be another layer to their relationship.

'I guess I'll be seeing some of you then, eh?' she added.

'I suppose so, Your Honor.'

She smiled ever so slightly, a dismissal. Edward

bowed his head minutely and turned away. The older prosecutor glanced at him, but with very little interest. Edward didn't know either of these two. He'd been gone three years, which could be a generation in the D.A.'s office with its revolving door. Edward stopped and said to him, 'Amy Shilling. First appearance.'

The prosecutor nodded. 'Not indicted yet. Out on bond. Just get another setting from the clerk.' Just as Edward was about to step away, he added, 'So she's your sister?'

Edward nodded. The prosecutor shrugged one shoulder and made a small clicking noise with his tongue. Edward knew what he was saying. Stupid idea, representing a relative. Having skin in the game made for some bad lawyering. Edward nodded back.

'That wasn't so hard, was it?' Amy asked once they were outside. 'The hardest part was getting up to the courtroom and then back down again.'

Yes, Edward thought, *getting out again could be the hardest part of going to the courthouse.* But he didn't say anything. Amy was scared enough. She looked lighthearted now, though. He understood her relief.

She asked him to get coffee, but after they'd walked for a block they realized it was a beautiful spring day. Trees were budding out in flowers and the grass was that thick, lush green of Houston, before the summer heat had singed or wilted any of it. So they just continued to walk.

'Amy, look. I understand this smiling you're doing. I understand you're almost skipping along the sidewalk. You just stepped into the belly of the beast and managed to walk out again. Believe me, I know exactly how you're feeling. It seems easy. But it gets harder and harder. A good lawyer can do some of his best work here at the front end of the case. You need to hire—'

'What would a good lawyer do now?' Amy asked.

'Do you think I'm that stupid?' Edward stopped walking, taking her elbow to stop her too. 'You think I'm going to start talking to you about how I'd represent you and I'll get excited and think "I can do this" and you'll look up to me with your big blue eyes and say, "Help me, Edward," and we'll be off on our big adventure? You think that's how it's going to work? No, Amy. I cannot practice law. I wouldn't represent you if I could. It's a terrible idea.'

'Edward.'

'What is the matter with you, Amy? If someone came to you with a lump somewhere would you advise them to ignore it? So why won't you hire a lawyer? Is it money? Because I could probably—'

'It's not money. It's this, Edward. You were there for my last lawyer interview. What did he start telling me immediately after I'd finished telling him my story?'

'The steps in defending you. What he'd do. Which was excellent advice, by the way. You need—'

'Edward.' She stopped him again and looked very seriously at him from those pleading blue eyes. 'He started talking to me about plea bargains. Reducing my sentence. Talking about my inevitable conviction.'

'You have to deal with those—'

'They were all like that, Edward. He was the best of the lot, actually. He seemed to pay some slight attention to my defense. But they all think I'm guilty, Edward, from before I come in. And nothing I say makes them doubt that conclusion for an instant. They're used to representing guilty people, that's what they assume I am, and that's how they deal with their cases. They give very little or no thought to planning an actual defense. They don't know how.'

'We've all had innocent clients, Amy,' Edward said, whilst thinking *they are giant pains in the ass*. There was nothing worse for a lawyer than believing in your client's innocence. Because Amy was right, the system was going to treat them all the same way; the very rare, irregular-shaped pebble of an innocent person rolled right along the conveyor belt with the other peas, heading for the can.

Amy continued as if he hadn't spoken. 'They all think I'm guilty because they only know me as a client. We didn't meet before. We didn't go to school together. They only know me as a woman accused of murdering her husband. And charges like that are nearly always true, so that's what they think. They only know me in relation to this crime. I need a lawyer who knows me, Edward. I need one who really believes, who knows in his heart, that I'm innocent.' A crease appeared between her eyes as she continued to look at his face. 'You do, don't you?'

Of course he did. Didn't he? Sweet little Amy, his baby sister, she couldn't kill a man, could she?

Well, no, not a generic man. But her estranged husband, who might have done who knows what to unhinge her?

Edward had known such cases.

But this wasn't a case. This was his sister.

Edward's roommate, Mike, came home late in the afternoon to find Edward lying face down on the sofa. It was something Edward had done since law school. Face down on the sofa, arms at his sides, his face resting on a little pillow that only covered his eyes, not his mouth. It was a way of blotting out the world while he concentrated on something. Edward did it to put himself and a problem alone together in a dark, dark room, with no door out.

It wasn't the least bit restful.

But it did allow him to focus. When he had the toughest problems of all, he'd add a pillow that he'd hold around the back of his head, covering up his ears as well. In the cave of his thoughts, he nearly always came up with a solution. He'd missed this in prison, where you couldn't afford to let go of your senses or show the world your back.

Edward hadn't covered up his ears today, because he wanted to hear Mike come in. But he didn't stir as he heard the back door open and close.

'You OK?' Mike asked the inanimate lump on the couch.

'Why do you ask?' came Edward's muffled voice.

Mike laughed. A minute later Edward sat up to see Mike sitting across the room watching him, beer bottle in hand. Mike was thin, edging into middle age, and if someone didn't notice his wrists or forearms, or his knotted hands, he could take Mike for being slight. He had a face for blending into the woodwork, with hooded brown eyes and no particularly prominent features. But he could hold a stare better than anyone Edward had ever known. Mike had a way of looking at someone without moving and with no expression, patient and non-judgmental. During Mike's twenty years as a cop – the last twelve as a homicide detective – he had extracted many a confession from a sullen inmate with that unmoving, neutral stare.

Edward said, 'Amy wants me to represent her.'

'Hmm.' A sound that didn't require Mike to move his tongue or his eyes.

'I took her to three damned good lawyers, but apparently they failed to impress. She wants me.'

'Hmm,' Mike said again, but this time added, 'She must have bought your shit over the years about being the best lawyer in Texas.'

'I never said that.'

Mike just looked at him.

'Hell, I don't even think that. Well . . .'

Mike chuckled.

'That's not her reason, though. She says other lawyers all think she's guilty and I don't. She wants someone representing her who believes her.'

'And do you?'

That was one of the things Edward had been asking himself as he lay face down on the sofa. He hadn't seen Amy and Paul together enough to have any insight about their relationship. The drama of their separation had happened during his gap time. So the only way to judge the question was to decide what he thought his sister was capable of doing. He still thought of her as the little sister, coming to him with her problems. But Amy had not only gotten through the tough years of medical school and graduated near the top of her class; she seemed able to live with the burden of a famous father in her own chosen profession. Edward couldn't imagine her pointing a gun at a person, let alone pulling the trigger. But anyone is capable of anything under the right – or wrong – circumstances. And no one can drive someone to murder like a spouse.

'Of course,' Edward said.

Mike gave him a skeptical look. 'Well, you could certainly do it. You always did take pride in your trial skills.'

'It's not about that. It's not completely about that. There's something else, but Amy thinks I believe in her more than any other lawyer would.'

'And what value does that have in trial? You'd still be committing a crime, right?'

'Oh yes, no question of that.'

Edward would be screwed. At some point the parole board would find out he'd been practicing law without a license and his parole would be revoked. He'd probably be prosecuted for the new offense and his chance of actually ever being licensed to practice law again would decline to: *Are you kidding*?

But his sister was charged with murder. If he could save her, he would.

'So you want to help?' Edward asked his roommate.

39

'Help put you back in prison? Sure. That's what I did for twenty years, put felons back in the pen. Sure, Edward, I'll help. Just tell me one thing.'

In retirement from the police force, Mike had been a private investigator for three years now. Though he was still getting used to the idea of working on behalf of someone charged with a crime instead of against them, he was good at it.

'What?' Edward asked.

'What's your real reason for wanting to represent your sister?'

'I already told you.' And Edward gave his room-mate a stare as level and unemotional as his own. Mike seemed to accept it, shrugging again before getting up and heading back to his bedroom.

The honest stare was completely false. In the cave of his thoughts, Edward had realized why he should represent Amy, the advantage he had over every other lawyer – every real lawyer – in the world. That's what had convinced him to do such an idiotic thing.

He thought he was off to a good start in his re-entry into the legal world, getting away with a lie like that stare.

Four

A lawyer only ever has one real client: himself. Even while doing your best to take care of your clients, in every case you have to take care of yourself too. Some of those clients are going to turn on you later, say you were incompetent or drunk or gave away their secrets. You do things for the client, but you document what you did for yourself. Write down your time spent; make notes on what you told the client. Have him sign a letter saying he's rejecting certain advice. That's not for the client's benefit. It's for you.

Because of those conflicting interests, there's always at least a slight distance between the lawyer and the client. Except in those few cases of that crazed, true-believer lawyer, who knows he and the client are one and everything the lawyer does and thinks and breathes and eats is for the client. Those are the ones most likely to have the clients throw them under the bus later.

Edward wouldn't be able to keep that careful distance in this case. Even signing onto it would be throwing away his own future for his sister. And what if he lost, as criminal defense lawyers nearly always do? He would be destroying his relationship with the sister he'd tried to save. How could he go and see her in prison, knowing he'd helped put her there? How could she ever forgive him? Nor would the rest of the family ever understand or forgive him.

But, he asked himself, would walking away be any better? If another lawyer took the case and lost – the most probable outcome – Amy would always think her big brother could have saved her but wouldn't.

So Edward had good reasons for taking up this insane task. But those weren't the decisive ones. He had two advantages that no licensed attorney, no other person he knew, could have. First was the fact that he *was* unlicensed. If he lost the trial and then revealed his undocumented status, it would be a potential ground for reversal on appeal.

But the primary reason, the one that drove him running the next day until he was exhausted, was his secret shared past with the judge. He and Cynthia had known each other slightly when they were both in the D.A.'s office; she a new baby prosecutor, he already feeling like a veteran trial lawyer after three years in the office. They had tried one of her first jury trials together, when he was supervising her, teaching her and evaluating her skills. Cynthia was very tightly buttoned-up, always carefully dressed in a suit even on non-trial days, when some prosecutors would come to work in jeans. She was fresh-faced, very pretty and obviously determined to be a killer prosecutor. She never talked about her personal life, never went for a drink after work with the others. Cynthia got to work early, did her job and left promptly at five o'clock, as if her real life was waiting for her impatiently.

But in that trial, Edward had noticed a reckless streak in her. At first he thought she didn't know the rules of evidence or procedure, but that wasn't it. Cynthia seemed to know the rules – she could look them up quickly and quote them to the judge when the occasion called for it – but she tried to skirt them. She would force the opposing lawyer to object or she would inject inadmissible evidence into the trial if he didn't. It must have been exhausting for the defense lawyer, who not only had to be alert with every question Cynthia asked, but had to make the split-second decision whether to object at all. The defense lawyer had known that, by making repeated objections, he'd make the jury think he was trying to keep something from them and by extension that he knew his client was guilty.

Edward had watched her performance with fascination. Cynthia remained tightly controlled, her face emotionless as she asked increasingly outrageous questions. She tried to elicit hearsay, irrelevant emotional information, even privileged information. 'Objection,' the defense lawyer said again and again, with increasing weariness. Within an hour he didn't even have to say the basis for his objection, as old Judge Morrison repeatedly sustained them, instructing the jury to ignore what they had just heard.

Edward almost told her to tone it down, but then decided to give the baby prosecutor her head, sitting back and marveling. After all, it was only a DWI, a misdemeanor, so the stakes weren't very high. He stayed in his seat as the defense lawyer asked to approach the bench. He and Cynthia went up there and inclined their heads toward the judge, who obviously then instructed her to knock it off. Cynthia didn't even give him the courtesy of nodding before she resumed her seat and went right back to it.

This performance culminated when the defendant took the stand as the last witness. His lawyer kept questioning him on increasingly irrelevant details, obviously reluctant to hand him over to the shark-like prosecutor, but he finally had no choice.

Her first question on cross-examination to the defendant was, 'How did your lawyer instruct you to behave in trial? Did he tell you to sit up straight, look at the jury, even stutter a little when you—?'

'*Objection!*' the defense lawyer almost screamed. It had taken him a couple of seconds to leap to his feet; he was so taken aback by her questions. Quivering, he said, 'These questions invade the attorney-client privilege, Your Honor. They're also irrelevant. They have nothing to do with whether my client is guilty or innocent.'

'I sustain both objections,' the judge said, his ponderous stare on Cynthia Miles. 'Ladies and gentlemen of the jury, you are to disregard those questions. The prosecutor is not allowed to inquire into what has been said between the defendant and his lawyer. The defense's relevancy objection is also well taken. A good lawyer will instruct his client how to behave in trial whatever he thinks of the client's guilt or innocence. Young lady . . .' He turned back to Cynthia, with the cold stare of a lion trying to decide if he's hungry enough to go after that little gazelle. '. . . watch yourself.'

'Thank you for those instructions, Your Honor,' defense counsel said. 'But I must also ask for a mistrial now. I believe the prosecutor's questions through the entire trial have so tainted this jury that my client can no longer receive a fair trial.'

'That will be denied,' Judge Morrison said, then beckoned all the lawyers up to him, pointedly including Edward. He leaned toward them and in a barely lowered voice said, 'The next such request will very likely be granted. Mr Hall, are you just here as a spectator?'

'No, Your Honor. Thank you, sir. I will instruct my colleague.'

Cynthia said nothing, no apology, no explanation. As they walked back to their table Edward said quietly, 'You heard the man. You can knock it off now. I'm sufficiently impressed.'

She said nothing. With her back very straight, she lowered herself into her seat and did not ask another objectionable question for the rest of the trial. But, by that time, Cynthia had both the defendant and his lawyer so flustered that the red-faced defendant couldn't answer a simple question without stammering. Edward had seldom seen a defendant look so guilty. And Cynthia gently guided him right off the cliff, into admissions of his guilt he didn't know he was making. For example, that he was driving because he thought his friend was too drunk to do so and that they'd been out celebrating a recent promotion. (When one is out celebrating with a drunken friend, one tends to be drunk too.) By the end, all that mattered

45

was the way Cynthia had made him look, not only like a liar, but with his red face and incoherent replies, like a drunk.

'That was impressive,' Edward had said to Cynthia after her guilty verdict. 'But I think you should apologize to the judge.'

Cynthia had turned to him with genuine curiosity. Edward was struck again by how pretty she was, with her eyes wide and her head held high.

'Why?' she asked. 'I was just doing my job and he was doing his.'

'OK.' Edward had shrugged. 'But Judge Morrison might have it in for you for a long time after today.'

'What could he possibly do to me?' Cynthia asked calmly, then reassembled her file and walked away, while Edward stared.

But that wasn't his last or most memorable encounter with Cynthia Miles, prosecutor.

Edward and Cynthia never again tried a case together, but they did oppose each other several years later, when he was a defense lawyer and Cynthia had risen rapidly to become a first chair felony prosecutor. She shook hands with him before the potential jurors came in, but gave no hint they'd ever known each other in any other roles.

Edward was a high-flying defense lawyer by then, having won a couple of well-publicized trials, so his fee had gone up and he had a steady stream of clients. His suit was Armani, his shoes Ferragamo, his hair cut to precisely the most flattering length.

He flew high in other ways, too. Edward no longer

represented shoplifters or thugs. He had developed a clientele used to the finer things in life, including the best lawyers. Some of them liked to share: expensive dinners, women, habits. Edward enjoyed – that was the word – the lifestyle of a successful, single trial attorney.

But that didn't affect his trial performance. His client today was a man in his late twenties, on the verge of moving into middle management in his organization, but who had made the blunder of becoming personally involved in one more sale. Unfortunately, it was to an undercover police officer. Fortunately, Edward's client hadn't personally handed anything over to the officer or accepted anything from him. He had just been in the room. Also good for Edward's case, the undercover officer had some problems of his own, some in his personnel file, some Edward's investigator had discovered, that even the cop's supervisors and the prosecutors didn't know about. It was going to be fun.

It was a hard and well-fought trial, not just with aggressive lawyers, but thoughtful ones. Cynthia had greatly tempered her earlier fierceness. She seldom asked an objectionable question now, so sometimes she could slip one by, because the defense counsel wasn't poised to hear it. She'd learned it was more effective to be a sniper than a shotgunner. She knew the weakness of her case was the undercover detective, who had cleaned up for the trial in a suit and tie, but still had a scruffy look about him. And red, tired eyes, Edward was happy to note. He looked dissipated, as if coming off a binge.

But Cynthia was waiting for Edward whenever he got close to devastating her witness, objecting to hearsay or making an objection that would be denied, but in the process told her witness what his answer should be. Before that, in her own questioning of the witness, she'd gone into some of his indiscretions herself, such as his three-day suspension for claiming to be on the job, when he was really elsewhere. The detective testified that he'd been taking care of a sick parent. Edward had other information, which he would bring out in his own turn.

So it was satisfying work, trying a case against Cynthia. As usual, shortly into the trial, Edward forgot the client sitting by his side. This was a dance with his opponent.

Toward the end of the detective's testimony, Cynthia handed the witness a paper bag and asked him to identify it.

'This is the substance the defendant's partner sold me,' the officer said. Edward objected that there was no evidence his client was partners with the actual salesperson and was sustained. But in the next moment he forgot that, as the detective opened the bag and took out a smaller plastic bag; a gallon-size storage bag almost filled with white powder.

Everyone in the courtroom had seen this in movies and TV shows, this Gold Medal flour size batch of supposed cocaine. But very few of them had seen it in real life, up close. It had a texture Edward recognized, a weight composed of more than the grams it weighed. He knew what it could do. Edward's nostrils flared from

48

twenty feet away. He could swear he could smell it. Taste it.

Afraid of giving himself away, he tore his eyes from the bag and they fastened on the prosecutor, standing there because she had handed the evidence to the detective. So she was much closer to the coke. Edward saw that she had paused too, staring at the white powder. Cynthia's nostrils were flared too.

Ah ha, he thought.

But then time and the trial continued. As she walked back to her seat, Edward saw her run her finger across her lips; a finger on the hand that had held the bag. She resumed her questioning professionally, but something had gone out of her performance. Cynthia was distracted now.

So was he. But when the prosecution rested, Edward called his witnesses, putting on evidence of indiscretions the detective had committed that were yet unknown to his commanding officers. Edward had asked the officer during his cross-examination if he had set up Edward's client, because they were rivals for the same woman.

'That's ridiculous,' the officer had replied. 'I would never do something like that.'

Which had been exactly the answer Edward had hoped for. It was broad enough – 'never' being the key word – that it allowed Edward to put on evidence that the detective had done exactly that. He called two young men to testify that the officer had planted evidence on them after he'd called their girlfriends for dates. The prosecution would claim these were lies to cover up their guilt, but in one case Edward produced the girlfriend, too, to corroborate the story.

This didn't really prove anything that had happened or hadn't in Edward's case, but it made the detective look sleazy and worse, a liar.

Cynthia did a good job on Edward's client on cross, when the time finally came, but the young man had been coached for long hours and held up well. He had a legitimate job, a college degree, a mortgage. He could appear to be a solid citizen when he needed to do so. After both sides rested and the jury had been excused, the veteran trial judge, who was very friendly toward Edward and obviously respectful of Cynthia, shook his head and muttered, 'Close.'

Yes, it was. A close, well-executed contest. Edward and Cynthia shook hands sincerely. She looked at him slyly.

'Wishing you hadn't taught me so well?'

'You taught yourself, lady. You're better than I ever was.'

'I don't know about that.'

They looked back toward the front of the courtroom, where the court reporter was collecting the exhibits. She picked up the prime exhibit, now back in its paper bag, as casually as if it was a child's lunch. Edward stared. Cynthia, beside him, was looking that way too.

They argued the case that afternoon and it went to the jury about four o'clock. At 5:30 the judge called them back and asked if they wanted to keep deliberating. The foreman shook his head.

'We have a lot to talk about.'

Which sounded hopeful to Edward. The judge

dismissed them for the evening. The courtroom relaxed, like an airliner decompressing, as the jurors filed out. Edward's client shook his hand and left, maybe to celebrate his last night of freedom for a while.

'Good job,' Cynthia said again to Edward, then hurried out. Courtroom personnel were shutting down the room. By six it would be dark, and everyone gone home. In fact, he could feel how much the building had emptied out already. The halls of justice are not open late.

By 6:30 of that day – three years ago now – that whole floor of the building and, in fact, most of the Justice Center was darkened. There were security lights on every floor, but the courtroom was dark. So was the hallway behind it that led to the court offices and jury rooms. Edward emerged from one of those jury rooms, looked up and down the hall, and came out quietly. No longer wearing a tie or his suit jacket, he walked swiftly and silently down the hall. At the door to the court offices he hesitated, then put his hand on the knob and turned it ever so quietly. The door was locked, but hadn't been pushed all the way closed. A clerk in a hurry to get home must not have pulled it tight. It opened at Edward's touch.

He didn't think he'd made any noise as he entered the outer office, the one where two clerks sat during the day. The room was empty and dark now, with that peculiar waiting emptiness of a room that bustled with people during the workday. Edward crossed it, heading for the court reporter's office. Farther down the interior hall of the court offices, the judge's chamber was dark.

But the court reporter's door, to his surprise, was slightly ajar. And sounds came from within.

Damn it. The court reporter must be working late, preparing another record for an appeal. Or maybe just on the phone with her boyfriend, but he didn't hear a voice and the office was dark. Was the court reporter working in the dark?

Edward didn't have enough information. He needed to turn around and hurry out, down the hall and out of the building. But he still had that smell in his nostrils, that taste on his tongue, like the aftermath of a burn. He needed to salve it. That need was greater than his need for self-protection.

He pushed the door open ever so slightly more. There was light in the office after all, but not the overhead light. He pushed the door open more. This was crazy, but he had a hunch. If it was the court reporter, he'd claim he had forgotten something and ask if she had picked it up for him.

But it wasn't the court reporter in the reporter's office. When Edward stuck his head around the corner, he saw a woman's back as she knelt in front of a cabinet against the wall. The woman wore a crisp white blouse that stood out under her black hair. Her brown fingers were working at the cabinet's lock with something Edward couldn't identify, but that wasn't a key.

Edward must have made some noise, or maybe the first intruder's caution just kicked in. She turned and looked at him. The light came from a penlight she held in her mouth. But Edward could still see her features behind the light.

Cynthia Miles dropped the flashlight and stood up quickly.

'I lost my purse,' she said quickly. 'I thought maybe Gloria put it away for me.'

Obviously a line she had ready.

'Uh huh,' Edward answered. 'Why didn't she just look in the purse, find out whose it was, and call you?' As Cynthia started to stammer out more of an answer, Edward gestured her aside. 'Let me,' he said quietly. He took a set of lock picks from his pocket. As he bent to perform the job she'd been trying to do, he said over his shoulder to Cynthia, 'A burglary client who couldn't pay his bill traded me a couple of lessons instead. Said they might come in handy.'

Cynthia's voice came hoarsely. 'Must not have been a very good burglar if he didn't have enough money to pay a lawyer.'

Edward stood up and opened the metal cabinet door. 'Maybe my skills are better than his.'

He looked at Cynthia and gestured at the interior of the cabinet. Their heads bent together as they peered inside.

'I don't see a purse,' he said.

For a long moment they remained silent and motionless. Deciding whether to trust each other, how far to go. But that hunger was strong. And they both came to the same solution at the same time.

'I think we have a duty to the justice system to make sure the evidence is authentic,' Edward whispered.

Cynthia nodded. 'Field test it.'

That was the solution. If they both did it they'd be partners, neither would have something to hold over the other's head. They reached in together and pulled out the paper bag. Edward held it open and let Cynthia pull out the laden plastic bag, slowly, the way some children open the first present of Christmas morning.

She carried it carefully to the desk and opened it. They both bent toward it, inhaling like connoisseurs sniffing the slowly swirling wine. Then Edward pulled from his pocket a tiny spoon. It was gold, ostentatious, a gift.

But Cynthia stopped him as he started to reach into the bag. She, it turned out, had brought her own razor blade and a small hand mirror. She pushed back a paper on the desk to reveal them. Edward understood. Once he'd produced his own paraphernalia, Cynthia was willing to show him hers.

She raked out some of the coke with the razor, then expertly swept it into four lines, each about two inches long.

'I assume since he's your client he gets the good stuff,' she said softly.

She pulled from her pocket a dollar bill already rolled up, bent at the waist with the elegance of a gymnast and sniffed up the first line. Then she handed the bill to Edward. When he brought the bill close to his face he saw it wasn't a dollar, it was a hundred. Cynthia *was* experienced. But he'd seen that already. He bent and inhaled his own first line, then wiped up the tiny bit of residue and rubbed it on his lips.

The two of them stood with their heads slightly back and their eyes closed, with what looked like reverence. Edward was the first to break it, with a deep sigh. Cynthia didn't move. She was savoring. Her face in repose was lovely in a way he hadn't seen before, with classic lines from her cheeks all the way down her neck. With her hair falling down behind her, she could have been Cleopatra.

Or that could have been the cocaine talking. It didn't matter a bit. Edward felt great, beyond great, and breaking the law with a beautiful woman only enhanced the experience.

After a minute or two, Cynthia bent without even opening her eyes and inhaled the third line. Eyes still closed, she passed the rolled-up bill to Edward. He sniffed up the final line and the feeling returned, the feeling of being smart, powerful, brilliant, invulnerable. He and Cynthia dropped into the two visitors' chairs in front of the desk. Edward was looking at her when she finally opened her eyes, a languorous smile spreading until it illuminated her whole face. She shook her head in wonder and said, 'I wish we could smoke in here.'

'Can't,' Edward said. 'It's against the rules.'

That set them off on a laughing jag that went on and on, until they were shushing each other like children creeping downstairs long past their bedtime.

After another minute Cynthia said, 'That's good. Should probably quit now.'

Edward nodded. 'Yep.'

But they sat. It wasn't long before Cynthia looked at him, her smile changing.

'They'll never miss it,' Edward said, reaching for the bag.

Like her, he laid out four lines. Nobody ever did only one. That first rush always came with a beckoning finger that asked you back for the second kiss.

He'd laid out longer lines than she had. Cynthia gave him a look, but then bent again for the first sniff. This time he watched her before indulging himself. Watched her lean back in her chair, watched her skin flush, her smile begin to encompass her whole face, watched until her shoulders widened and her eyes opened. The smile remained in place and her eyes fastened on his, so she looked like a woman in love. She didn't even question his staring at her.

Edward bent and inhaled his own line. When he opened his eyes he saw that Cynthia had unbuttoned the top buttons of her white blouse, down to where her cleavage began. She looked like an executive on her second drink after work. He continued to look at her face. She looked back.

They each took one more hit. This one made Edward analytical, or what passed for analytical in the current setting. Cocaine was the best drug ever invented. It turned on all the pleasure sensors, made him feel smart, assured, confident that he was the first person who would live forever, get rich and be universally adored.

But how did it do that? He felt so great. Well, damned good. Not bad.

The pleasure ebbed that quickly. An afterglow of the rush remained, but he could no longer capture what had made him feel so good. A minute after sniffing up the line, he couldn't begin to describe how the cocaine made him feel. Only the desire remained.

Cynthia was watching him, tapping the razor

blade on the mirror. Her lips parted, but she didn't speak. Edward looked back at her. Cynthia still looked beautiful to him, at least that feeling hadn't swirled away. Especially with her top blouse buttons undone, her lips parted, her eyes with that gleam. Red, red lips. For a long moment his gaze lingered there.

They were sitting in adjoining chairs. At some point they had turned them to face each other. He didn't even remember doing that. Still staring, he bent toward her. Cynthia remained leaning back and he suddenly felt unsure. But then her smile widened. He had to move forward in his chair for his face to reach hers. Without otherwise touching her, he brought his lips slowly to hers. She didn't duck or evade. Her mouth remained slightly open. So were Edward's eyes as their lips touched. Cynthia's were exquisitely soft. He lingered on them for a long minute, another. One of them moaned. He couldn't have said which. It was like something between them, born of their joining. Edward reached for her.

Cynthia did stop him then, but gently. He leaned back, puzzled. Was she calling a halt? But Cynthia still smiled at him and that smile had turned intimate, not quite a smirk. She reached for the bag of cocaine again and Edward had a moment's jealousy. She preferred the drug. Well, he couldn't blame her for that.

Cynthia picked up the little spoon he'd left on the desk, and scooped out as much white powder as the small implement could hold. She brought it toward her nose, then stopped. Still looking him in the eyes, still smiling, she carefully dropped the cocaine onto the top of one of her breasts, so it formed a small pile where the breast just protruded from her blouse. Then she waved a hand in his direction.

Edward's eyes widened. He gave her a questioning look.

'Hurry up, man, before I lose my balance.'

So he bent quickly then and inhaled the cocaine, not using the rolled-up bill, just going close enough to her skin to sniff. So he inhaled Cynthia at the same time, an earthy but sweet smell that was more heady than the coke. Then, of course, he licked the residue off her breast. Then, of course, let his tongue explore. Cynthia reached under him to undo more buttons. Edward pulled back just enough to discover that her bra fastened in front. It unfastened easily, in spite of the slight tremble of his hand.

Cynthia inhaled with a sound of relief as her bra opened. Her breasts were magnificent, smaller than he'd expected but wonderfully shaped. Edward returned his mouth to them. Cynthia breathed even more deeply.

That was the last inhibition. From there it turned into an old-fashioned sex romp. Twenty minutes later they were naked and had moved to the couch in the judge's office. Still in the kissing and touching stage. Edward's tongue was in Cynthia's navel, which she seemed to enjoy, and he was trying to decide what direction to take from there, when she gently pulled him up to where he could see her face. There were cocaine traces around her mouth. She was looking past Edward, with the wildest gleam of all in her eyes.

She was looking at a coatrack beside the office door. Hanging on it was the judge's robe.

When their eyes met Edward's had widened again. But Cynthia nodded at him and she was impossible to refuse. She rose, took his hand and pulled him upright too. As she advanced Edward walked very close behind her, touching her, which made Cynthia giggle.

They took one more hit, no, two, in the court reporter's office, then tiptoed to the door out to the hall. Edward had his hands on her continuously now.

'Come on,' she whispered, and Edward did one of the stupidest things he'd ever done. He followed Cynthia, naked, out into the hall. It was only a few steps to the door of the courtroom, but they seemed to take forever. Cynthia opened that door too. She was a prosecutor, in the justice center every day, and probably felt a greater sense of ownership of it. Edward marveled at how confidently she moved in just her skin.

The courtroom was dim, with security lights under the railing of the jury box. Cynthia walked up two steps to stand behind the bench, next to the judge's chair. She turned and Edward caught up to her. They kissed again then, their bodies touching at full length. Then Cynthia stepped back and with a mischievous grin drew on the robe. She zipped it up carefully and presented herself to him with spread arms. Edward smiled and shook his head, but in wonderment, not denial.

So it was that he was the first person in the world to see Cynthia Miles in a judge's robe. And out of it. Anyone entering the courtroom from the outer hall a few minutes later would have seen what appeared to be a judge sitting on the bench. Cynthia even had a gavel in her hand. Edward was out of sight, under the bench.

'Oh, God, yes,' Cynthia groaned. Edward pushed her chair back and rose. Cynthia stood up too, for the first time looking slightly uncertain. Then Edward stepped aside and she grinned and leaned forward, resting her forearms on the bench. Edward positioned himself behind her and lifted the robe, until it was above her waist. Moments later he achieved the fantasy of many a lawyer before him. And maybe of a few judges.

That wasn't the end of the evening, but it was the highlight. From the courtroom they went back to the judge's office and couch, stopping off again at the court reporter's desk. The cocaine was significantly diminished now, but they didn't notice. The couch in the judge's office was black leather, so Cynthia, naked again, looked lighter skinned on it. She seemed to like the texture, too, writhing on it like a cat. Edward loved the combination of textures too. He couldn't seem to get enough of her and Cynthia obviously felt the same way.

They were on their way back out to the court reporter's office when they heard a sound. It froze them. A moment later it became clear it was the sound of footsteps in the hall.

To their credit, the lovers moved very quickly. Edward closed the plastic bag, stuck it back in the paper one and shoved them into the cabinet. He closed the metal door as quietly as he could, made sure it was locked. By the time he turned back around Cynthia had wiped up all the spillage. She was rushing into her clothes at the same time. Edward pulled on his pants.

And the door from the hallway opened.

It was a guard, of course. He didn't call out, which led Edward to believe he already knew someone was there. The justice center would have security, of course, maybe video surveillance. Edward and Cynthia looked at each other, twin portraits of alarm. She had frozen again.

Edward made a split-second decision. Cynthia looked so scared. A protective instinct he didn't know he had kicked in. Maybe they could pull it off, maybe he should kiss her, let the bailiff find them that way. A big laugh for everyone. An embarrassment, nothing more. But in putting away the cocaine Edward had noticed how much lighter a load it was. The court reporter or someone else would surely notice in the morning. And maybe the bailiff wouldn't even be fooled. This was undoubtedly not the first time someone had tried to break into an evidence locker.

Edward gathered up his clothes and stepped out into the interior hall that ran through the offices. Cynthia reached for him, but he shook her off. He shot one last glance back over his shoulder and saw her pleading eyes, enormous in the dimness. Then he turned and ran.

Luckily, the bailiff had stepped into another office, the court coordinator's, so Edward was able to run past him. He got to the hallway door and bolted out. He ran down this dim back corridor with the guard's shouts in his ears.

Edward made noise himself, wanting to make sure he was pursued. He turned the corner and made it to the door out into the main, public hallway. Edward had hope then. He might actually get away, hide in a men's room, finish getting dressed, walk out coolly. But the bailiff was close behind him and he had a radio. Edward got to the junction, looked around for an emergency exit, couldn't find one. Frantically he pressed the elevator buttons, but that was silly. The bailiff came around the corner at a walk.

So those damned slow elevators got him.

Five

By the time Edward and the security guard had gotten back to the court offices they were empty. So Edward's plan had worked: Cynthia got away.

He and she were never alone together again. Or almost never. As Edward's criminal case worked its way through the system, Cynthia stayed in the D.A.'s office. She didn't prosecute him herself, but she didn't intervene, either. He didn't blame her. If she implicated herself now, his sacrifice would have been useless. Edward stayed away from her at least as much as she avoided him.

One day, though, they found themselves walking toward each other down that narrow back corridor. Cynthia stopped, her face going toward pale. Her hands began to tremble. Edward kept walking, planning just to pass her by. But as he did Cynthia grabbed his hand, holding him in place. Edward turned to her, but she wouldn't or couldn't look at him.

Eyes closed, shoulders shaking, she said in a fierce whisper, 'I'm sorry, I'm sorry, I'm sorry.'

'It was my decision,' he said, and walked on down the hall.

The justice system couldn't quite decide what to do with him. The detective of course found the missing cocaine the next day, but they couldn't charge him with possession of cocaine, since he'd never taken it out of the room where it started.

So they ended up charging him with burglary of a building, punishable by up to twenty years in prison. Normally a lawyer with Edward's completely clean record would have gotten probation. Two unique aspects of his crime stopped that. The first was the target of the crime – not only the Justice Center but the justice system itself – and the fact that Edward had taken advantage of his position as an officer of the court to steal evidence from the system. The second was that the judge, whose court offices he'd romped in with Cynthia, made it known he wouldn't tolerate a lighter sentence and anyone who offered Edward one or any judge who assessed it, would have an enemy for life. The judge had held office for twenty years and was thought to have some power over voters, so his threat carried weight.

And Edward couldn't afford to take the case to trial. Jurors given the chance to sentence a lawyer would probably give him worse than probation.

So he accepted a plea bargain offer of three years in prison, did two, had been out for a year, and had now seen Cynthia Miles in a judge's robe for the second time. As he'd stood in her courtroom looking up at her, Edward had hardly felt the irony. The courtroom was too formal a setting in the daylight, full of people. And Cynthia hadn't given him a wink or a kind word or any sort of secret signal. Not even a sympathetic gaze. She'd only looked directly at him for a second or two and that had been more a look of assessment. Probably wondering how Edward felt toward her.

He hadn't heard anything from her for more than three years. By the time he was sentenced, Cynthia had moved higher in the office and had kept her distance from him for months. Not a note, not crossed paths. If she was arguing for leniency for him behind the scenes, he didn't hear about it. And, of course, there was nothing from her during his time in prison and since. He had suspected that the only way Cynthia could deal with what had happened to him would be by forgetting he existed. How could she have gotten through even one of the seven hundred plus nights he'd spent on a prison bunk if she thought of him there?

Now that he'd returned, walking right into her courtroom, Cynthia was in a delicate position. If she recused herself from his sister's case, people would ask why. No one knew of her being any closer to Edward than any of the other judges were. Of course she couldn't explain, not even some fake explanation about a secret friendship they'd shared, because she'd need Edward to back her up on that and they shouldn't even communicate right now.

On the other hand, if she stayed on the case and Edward involved himself in the defense, she had to worry about what she would do if he tried to blackmail her, either overtly or just by his appearance in the case. It was a very delicate position and, oddly enough, Edward felt sympathetic. She hadn't done one thing for him in spite of his sacrificing his career and two years of his life for her, but he still felt a trace of that protective urge that had driven him half-naked out into the hallway in the first place.

One ironic aspect of the whole debacle was that Edward's client, the one charged with possession of all that cocaine, was found not guilty by the jury the next morning while Edward was bonding out of jail. So he was on a winning streak as a trial lawyer. He'd beaten Cynthia in court.

Edward's thoughts were back on his sister the next day when his phone rang.

'Hi,' Edward said familiarly.

'Hi,' Linda answered. 'I haven't called because I didn't know—'

'I know.'

She didn't know what to say about his sister's arrest. Amy's troubles, of course, had been splashed all over the front page and even the TV stations had covered it.

'You going to come see me soon, Teddy?'

Linda was one of the very few other people from whom he'd tolerate a nickname, mainly because she'd made it up herself and she didn't let anyone else know about it.

'I will,' he said. 'I've been thinking about you. I just need . . . I'm kind of caught up in all this mess.'

There was a brief silence, after which she said, 'I figured.'

'I'll call you tonight,' he said.

'If you have time. I just wanted you to know I was thinking about you.'

'Thanks. I'm thinking of you too, Linda.'

And she clicked off. Edward dropped his phone in the cup holder beside him. Sometimes he hated phones. The conversations that gave the illusion of contact but really just emphasized the distance between the talkers.

The next call was worse in some ways, from Amy. After very brief greetings she said, 'Mom and Dad would like to see you.'

'So what are you, their social secretary?'

'Edward—'

'Sorry, Amy, sorry. I just . . . If they're going to issue a summons, it could at least be a little more personal.'

'It's not like that, Eddie. They just knew I'd be talking to you anyway. Mom says she came by to see you, but you weren't home.'

That could be true. He was out a lot. But they have these things now called phones. His mother didn't like them. She communicated in the old-fashioned ways of southern women, with little touches and expressions, in which a sentence could have an entirely different meaning if her head was cocked one direction rather than the other.

'OK. When?'

'Tonight at eight? Dinner at their house?'

Edward shook his head. 'I'll come at seven for drinks. Y'all can have dinner afterwards and talk about me. The family tradition.'

'Eddie,' she said reprovingly.

'Sorry, Amy. It's not your fault. It's just . . . you know how it is.'

'I do.'

* * *

A little while later, he was driving into River Oaks; the most exclusive neighborhood in Houston, old brick or stone mansions on large lots. Edward had been eight when they'd moved here. His younger sister remembered only the River Oaks place as their family home. Edward could remember living in a much smaller house when it was only him and his parents, when his father was doing his residency. Edward had loved that little neighborhood: kids in every house, spilling out into the front yards at any given time, mongrel dogs in the backyards, pick-up soccer and basketball games, playing hide and seek, tag, sometimes running into the street without looking. A girl two houses down had kissed him and the boy across the street had punched him, unrelated events but he could still feel both physical sensations.

Edward pulled up to the address. Amy thought of this place as home, Edward felt sure, but for him it still seemed new and not quite permanent. Edward, as the oldest, felt more transient.

He stood on the front porch and rang the bell. In moments his mother opened the door and looked at him with her head tilted and puzzlement creasing her forehead.

'Edward! What are you doing ringing the bell? Why didn't you just come in?'

'Hi, Mom.' He kissed her cheek. 'How have you been?'

'Well fine, until all this business with Amy, of course. Come in, come in. Everybody's here.'

Edward looked at his mother for a few seconds. Beverly Hall was a thin fifty-eight-year-old, but looking as much younger as weekly massages, a personal trainer and regular spas could accomplish – except in her neck and her hands, which showed her age in spite of everything. Edward inhaled.

As they stepped into the living room his mother said, 'Would you like a drink?'

God, yes. 'No, thanks. Maybe later.' The convicted coke fiend needed to display some control.

The rest of his family was in the living room, a high-ceilinged room twenty feet wide and thirty deep, with tall windows on the far side. Marshall Hall stood in the center of the room with a drink in his hand. Dr Hall, like his wife, gave the appearance of being tall by maintaining an erect posture at all times. He looked the same as ever, his weight kept down, his gray hair mostly still in place. Dr Hall had a straight nose that he could peer down when necessary, a broad forehead and a thin-lipped mouth.

His distinguished, slightly forbidding appearance suited his place in the world. Dr Hall was a specialist, an internist who had become the leading diagnostician in the city, possibly the state. Patients came to him from as far as Saudi Arabia. Awards and pictures with celebrity clients lined his office walls in his medical building.

He was beloved in his world, but in private let leak to his family his true opinions. Very quiet, cutting remarks about everyone he knew. At first the children felt special because he let them in on these observations. But Edward later realized that his father probably did the same thing with other people about his children. Secretly criticizing is an addiction; you can't restrict it.

Dr Hall said, 'Hello, son,' and came toward him. They didn't shake hands and they weren't huggers, but Dr Hall clasped Edward's shoulder for a moment.

'Hello, Dad. How have you been?'

'Good, good. Well enough. Worried about Amy, of course. Do they make these false arrests very often? Now I doubt every criminal case I've ever read about, where I just presumed the arrested people were guilty. Now I wonder.'

So innocence was the prevailing theory in the Hall household. Good, he supposed, except it didn't prepare the family for what usually followed an arrest: trial and conviction.

'Well, cops are no more competent than doctors, Dad. Probably less so.'

Nobody laughed. On the other hand, nobody looked shocked, either. They'd 'put up with Edward's sense of humor for years,' as his mother put it.

Edward went to Amy and gave her a brief hug. In this setting she looked younger than when he'd seen her recently and rather embarrassed at being the occasion for the occasion. Amy didn't have a drink either. The only two people in the family who'd ever been arrested had to keep their hands clean.

Dr Hall said, 'Amy tells us she wants you to represent her, Edward. Can you even do that?'

So they were going to get right to it.

'No, I can't.'

'Eddie—'

'I can't, Amy. I don't even know why you want me to. It's suicidal.'

'Is it?' their mother asked. 'You always had a good trial record, Edward.'

He couldn't believe everyone wanted him to do this.

'She needs a real lawyer, Mom. I'm not that anymore.'

'Well, you have the same skills you had,' his father said. 'I'm not advocating one way or another, I'm just getting the facts straight,' his father answered his son's surprised expression.

'Would you recommend a surgeon who hadn't performed a surgery in three years and had spent most of that time in prison?' Edward asked him.

'I don't think I can give a blanket answer to that,' Dr Hall said slowly. 'It would depend on what I knew about the surgeon, what kind of skills he'd demonstrated before the hiatus.'

Edward couldn't think of anything else to say. This wasn't how he'd expected this meeting to go. This was probably the most flattering his father had ever been about Edward's legal career.

Mrs Hall said, 'I just want what's best for Amy.' She sounded more forceful than she usually did. 'And this family, of course,' she trailed off.

'I want what's best for Amy too,' Edward said quietly. 'Why don't we talk about her?'

Edward's father was still looking at him. 'All right, tell us about her, Edward. Her legal situation, I mean.'

'In a way, it's too soon to tell. She was arrested because she was at the scene with the victim's blood all over her and she's his estranged wife. In that situation that person is going to get arrested nine times out of nine. That doesn't automatically—'

'Really? Police just make these assumptions, so an innocent person has to spend a night in jail?'

'Mom, please. I'm not defending the investigation. I'm just telling you how things happen. The problem is not that that's how the investigation started, it's if—'

'That's where it stops,' his father said. 'Yes. Once you've made one diagnosis you stop checking for anything else. Amy passed on your analogy. Which is quite good. So what do we do?'

Amy said, 'If the cops aren't doing their job—'

'Then you hire a private investigator,' Mrs Hall said. 'Right? We have to.'

Edward was struck more forcefully than he ever had been that this was a smart family. They were discussing a specialized subject unfamiliar to them, but he didn't have to explain at much length.

'Yes. We have to hire private investigators. Amy and I have already talked about that. The problem with that is that prosecutors have relationships with police officers, it's the natural course of things for a police investigation—'

'To lead directly into the District Attorney's Office,' Amy said. 'And they don't give the same weight to something a private detective brings them.'

'Not nearly,' Edward affirmed. 'But if the investigators uncover solid evidence, something you can put in front of the D.A., it's hard to ignore that.'

There was a time when Edward, at the height

of his cowboy *chutzpah* as a trial lawyer, would have kept such evidence to himself until trial, when he could spring it and hope for a win. But that was too risky here. The goal was to avert trial altogether.

'Sounds like a process that needs to start right away,' Dr Hall said judiciously. 'But we have one other advantage. Your relationships with these people: the prosecutors, even the judge. You know them from before, don't you? They'll listen to you.'

'There are other lawyers with equally good relationships in the system. Even better ones, because they've kept them up for the last three years. And they'd have the advantage of sounding more objective, talking about a client who's not a relative.'

'Yes, but who had paid them a great deal to defend her,' his mother said. She had come even closer, until she put her hand on Edward's arm and held it there. 'You sound more sincere because you know her.'

They were all looking at him. Edward felt those stares like summer sun beginning to burn his skin, but he continued to look only at Amy. He felt he knew everything she'd been thinking, but she'd barely spoken. He wanted to ask her to say something, but he could tell from her expression that's exactly what she didn't want. Amy had reverse-aged since he'd seen her last. Here in her family she was no longer the smart, accomplished professional. She looked more like a girl. A frightened girl.

* * *

73

What struck Edward, as he drove away from this family meeting, was what they hadn't discussed. The facts of Amy's case, for one. Everyone had just assumed, or at least seemed to assume, that she was innocent and that Edward could prove that if he exerted himself to the full extent of his ability.

The other un-broached topic – the elephant in the room so big they were all inside it – was that he was not a lawyer anymore. He didn't have a law license and wasn't legally entitled to appear in a courtroom on behalf of a client.

As Edward drove he tried to think his way around that problem. He could do the early stuff for Amy certainly: talk to the prosecutors, oversee the defense's private investigation, spin legal theories. If the case came to trial, he could talk her into hiring an actual lawyer, while Edward sat in on the defense as an advisor.

Or he could just continue to fake it, pretend to be the lawyer he used to be and let everyone think he still was. That way led to disaster for Edward himself, but that didn't matter. It was also crazy, but that was irrelevant for the moment too. He wondered suddenly why he hadn't just said, *I can't do it. It's not legal*?

There was one thing that had kept him from saying those words. Amy's eyes. Amy relentlessly focused on him during the whole discussion. She had been pleading with him. Edward tried to remember if anyone else's need for him had ever been so apparent.

But maybe it was her own secret behind that liquid stare. Amy had something else to tell

74

him, something she wouldn't share with anyone else.

Mike said, 'You've got to get her to talk to me.'
'I know, Mike.'
They sat in the living room of the house they shared. It was very much a bachelor pad. Edward sat on the sofa that was at least third-hand. Mike had pulled over his favorite chair, which he might have been hauling around ever since his divorce; a padded monstrous recliner of some manufactured material that didn't even make an effort at pretending to be leather. Worn carpet on the floor might, at one time, have been white but now there was no telling. The blessing of familiarity was that they didn't notice their surroundings.

Mike tossed a manila folder onto the coffee table. 'That's my investigation file. See what I've got after two weeks.'

Edward opened it and found what he'd expected: police reports. Firstly, one by the initial patrol officer on the scene, then supplemental reports by detectives who'd followed up by the actual investigation, such as it had been. They noted that Amy had refused to talk to them, which was smart but didn't look like what an innocent person would do.

'I talked to the neighbors myself,' Mike said. 'The ones the cops talked to plus more. I looked for surveillance videos from somewhere close by, maybe a gas station, but there wasn't any place close enough. It was just a house on a street, a few blocks off Richmond. And nobody saw anything. One neighbor saw Amy on the front porch, two heard something that might have been a gunshot, but nobody's clear on the time. Nobody had ever seen your sister there before.'

'She said they were trying to keep it discreet.'

'Yeah, well, they succeeded.'

Left unspoken was what Mike would have said about any other client. *Or maybe nobody ever saw her there, because she was never there before that day. Maybe she's lying.* Edward heard it.

'So now we've got to find another suspect,' Mike continued. 'I know it, you know it. No one obvious presents themselves so far, so I need to start digging deeper. The victim's bank accounts, credit card statements—'

'Paul. The victim's name is Paul Shilling. He was my brother-in-law for four years.'

'Those are two of the few things I do know. I've got lots of other questions. Did he go out, did he have girlfriends? Maybe one with a jealous boyfriend? Or was it financial? Did he owe the wrong person?'

Edward tried to think. He'd known Paul well enough to play tennis with him, have a couple of just-guys lunches, but never a close talk. Paul had seemed to him often preoccupied, ready to move on to the next thing.

'How about professional?' Mike suggested.

'Professional jealousy,' Edward offered. 'Paul was a medical researcher; he could have been involved in any number of projects with other doctors. Maybe someone thought he took too much credit or wanted to take more than they deserved themselves.'

76

'Sounds a little TV-movie-ish to be a real motive.' Mike shrugged.

'We're talking stuff that could lead to a Nobel Prize. And I'm not saying it was a calculated murder. Maybe an argument, tempers get out of hand . . .'

'He was shot, Edward. It wasn't a situation where someone punched him and he fell and hit his head.'

'Yes, but it was his gun, it was already there. Maybe he had it out for some reason when this colleague dropped by unexpectedly—'

'Yes, just sitting there cleaning his gun, while waiting for his estranged wife to show up to go to this gala. I can picture it.'

'OK, it was planned then. They were on their way to an awards dinner, don't forget, Paul was getting some kind of award. That could stir jealousy if someone else thought he deserved some of the credit and wasn't getting it.'

'Most of the time when someone gets killed it's by someone with whom they're intimately related. I like a jealous lover much better, if we can find—'

'I prefer women myself,' Edward said.

Mike laughed. But bringing up the topic of women brought Amy to mind. They sat there thinking the same thing, that the estranged wife was always the most likely suspect.

'And your sister keeps dodging me. Claims other appointments, she's busy with her practice, blah blah. In my experience,' Mike said carefully, sitting back, 'an innocent person accused of a crime is eager to talk to the investigator. She wants to convince everybody. I grant you, I don't

77

have that much experience of working for an innocent suspect, but still. She's hiding something, and she doesn't want to share it with me. You need to talk to her.'

Edward let the useless paper fall back into the file.

'I know,' he said.

Edward later realized he and Mike had forgotten the victim in all this planning. But Paul Shilling had been part of his family for four years, part of their lives much longer than that. He and Amy had started dating in medical school, had gotten married while residents. As a student, Paul had worked with Dr Hall as his research assistant. They had continued that association after Paul graduated. The research became more important, as evidenced by the award Paul was supposed to receive the night of his killing. That had been for independent work of his own, not something to do with their father. Edward didn't know enough about it to know whether it was important, but the award seemed to answer that.

For that matter, he knew very little about the nature of Amy's and Paul's marriage. That had evolved mostly during the time Edward had been estranged from the family.

Someone had felt strongly enough about Paul to kill him. If not Amy, someone else. Edward had a lot of work to do; getting to know about his family member's life posthumously, after it was too late to know him as a person.

* * *

Edward knew he needed to talk to Amy very soon. There was something she didn't want him or anyone else to know, and he had to approach that delicately. But he learned Amy's secret a different way, from the prosecution.

Amy's indictment, when it came, was a shock of the horrifying variety. The D.A. didn't indict her for plain murder. The indictment charged she had caused the death of Paul Shilling in the course of committing burglary of his home.

'*Burglary?*' Amy shouted over the phone. 'Burglary? That's ridiculous. I was *invited*. The door was *unlocked*. He was expecting me.'

If only we could prove that, her brother thought.

'Oh, my God, Edward, capital murder? This is insane. Are they—? Are they going to ask for a death sentence?'

'No. I'm sure not. They couldn't possibly go that far. Even this charge is ridiculous. I'm going to go talk to the prosecutor, find out how this craziness happened. It's probably just something they did as a bargaining tool. I'm sure I can argue them back down.' Back down to *murder*, he thought wildly. The stakes had changed radically. 'Don't worry,' he added lamely.

'What do you want me to do?' Amy's voice was a little girl's again.

'Just sit tight. Let me see what I can do.'

'OK.' Her voice was so tiny he could barely hear her.

It felt so strange to walk back into the District Attorney's offices. Edward had been here many times, starting with when he'd worked in this office for five years. Walking those halls today, he remembered that feeling of being at the center of power, learning details of investigations, holding power over the lives of hundreds of defendants – but so casually that the young assistant DA's could joke about a defendant's stunned expression, when a jury came back with a sentence three times higher than anyone had expected. Actual years the dumbass defendant would spend in prison, but a joke to the prosecutors.

But the real feeling of power here didn't come from that insider knowledge or the ability to make or deny plea bargain offers that would alter entire families' lives. It was the power of confidence in one's own abilities that permeated these offices. Nearly every prosecutor was a trial lawyer, in court every day, going to trial every week. Trial work was a very specialized skill. You could plot out the course of a trial long before the first potential juror was questioned, which required devising long-term strategies very much like battles, but a trial never followed that well-thought-out course. There were always surprises: unknown defense witnesses to cross-examine, rulings by trial judges excluding important evidence, a prosecution witness telling a story to the jury differently from what she'd ever told the prosecutor. And the trial prosecutor had to deal with those unexpected developments. The best of them became quite expert at that. Never letting a jury see you flustered, never losing sight of the goal of conviction.

Of course they all knew who the best trial lawyers in their office were and there was constant effort to change or maintain those rankings. But part of being a great prosecutor was projecting an air of indifference, as if unaware of any competition, playing a different game at a different level from everyone else.

By the time Edward left he had been one of those elite. He had walked at ease through these halls, usually with a little smile on his way to court. A fellow prosecutor he dated for a while mentioned that smile to him one day; one night, actually, while they were in bed. She found that smile attractive, though some people might take it for arrogance. 'You look like you're having fun. Like you have a secret you can't wait to surprise someone with. Or like you're on your way to take a test you know you're going to ace. It's sexy.' She'd whispered the last sentence, then demonstrated how his smile excited her. Edward remained grateful to her for this observation. He'd known about the self-confidence, felt that every day, but the smile told him something else. It was fun. He loved his work, yes, but it also gave him a sense of who he was.

Now he was back and all those senses – competition, confidence, whirring brains trying to think three steps ahead of other smart lawyers – churned around him in this building.

When he walked into David Galindo's office, David was on the phone, waving a hand for Edward to enter while drawling into the handset, 'I'm sure the client doesn't like the offer, Cindy. If he liked it, it would be a pretty weak offer, wouldn't it? And I don't have a weak case . . . Well, if you can prove that, good on you . . . OK. See you in court. Hello, Edward.'

81

David didn't rise or offer his hand. David was lanky and tall, wore suits well. He was usually a languid presence, as if he weren't putting any effort into thought. But his trial record showed otherwise. He and Edward had been rising through the ranks of the D.A.'s office at the same levels when Edward worked here. Edward had been promoted to felony first but then David, after an impressive trial win, had jumped ahead of him. A while after that they had made first chair simultaneously, a draw. Not long after that Edward had left the competition behind to enter private practice. David was a senior prosecutor now, a veteran with an impressive string of trial wins. From the ease with which he lounged, David enjoyed his position very much.

He did give his former colleague the courtesy of looking straight at him, saying, 'Man, I am sorry.'

'Thanks, David.'

David shook his head. 'Prison. I couldn't believe that shit. Prison time for a lawyer? For a little low-level screw-up like you did? I couldn't believe they worked so hard to turn it into a burglary. Make it a little possession case, a misdemeanor; maybe even let you keep your license while you're on probation. That's what I told people. Anyway, man, I'm sorry.'

'Thanks,' Edward repeated. 'And now this,' he added, shifting topics.

'Now this,' David agreed. He had Amy's file on the desk in front of him. It was surprisingly thick, much more so than Edward would have thought.

'What the hell, David? Capital murder? Seriously?'

David sounded apologetic. 'Well, you know, high profile doctor victim, investigation on the front page for days . . .' He got up and closed his office door. When he returned to his desk he kept his voice low.

'Edward. If you repeat any of this I'll say you're lying and I'll be believed. But here's what's going on. It's playing to the public. It's the appearance of equal justice. This decision was made at the top. Julia decided' – Julia Lipscomb, the three-term District Attorney of Harris County – 'we have to make this a capital murder and seek a death sentence. It's about—'

'Death?' Edward felt his voice skittering higher.

David held out a placating hand. 'You'll win at punishment, of course. No jury's going to give your sister a death sentence. But we have to ask for it. Look.' He leaned back a little. 'If I seek a death sentence against a twenty-year-old poor black kid, who shot a convenience store clerk without really meaning for it to come out that way, how can I not against an educated rich white woman who planned and carried out an execution methodically?'

'Execution?' Edward sat stunned.

But David was hurrying relentlessly on. 'That's what I mean about equal justice. This office can't keep the public's trust if it looks like our decisions are based on bad reasons, like race or social class. We have to be just as hard on people like your sister.'

'Everybody knows our decisions are based on race and social class.'

83

'But we can't give anybody proof of it,' David answered. He sat back in silence for a moment, maybe waiting for Edward to bring him some counterargument, but Edward couldn't find anything to say. His mind couldn't recover from the essential fact. Knowing the District Attorney's Office was implacably determined to ask for a death sentence left him limp in his chair.

'You couldn't possibly have any punishment evidence,' he finally mustered. In the punishment phase of a capital murder trial the prosecution had to prove the defendant was likely to commit future acts of violence. The State tried to do that by showing other criminal acts the defendant had committed. They didn't have any evidence like that against Amy. She'd never been arrested before.

'But we do,' David said. He wasn't gloating. He sounded sad, continuing to give an old friend one piece of bad news after another. He waved a hand at his file, indicating its thickness. 'When it came to committing burglaries, this wasn't your sister's first rodeo. Far from it.'

He offered the file to Edward, who opened it and leafed slowly through the pages. There was a tab labelled: Other Offenses. Edward turned straight to that and found a series of police reports about burglaries, from as much as ten years earlier, all with an unknown suspect.

'Here's the bottom line, Edward; Amy's a serial burglar. She's been breaking into her friends' houses for years. These cases were all unsolved until she was arrested and her fingerprints got put into the system. Then the computer started pinging like crazy. Now, some of these we couldn't prove as burglaries. I mean, they were her friends, like I said; her fingerprints naturally would have been there. But not in some of the spots where the prints were found, like on the floor under a bed or on the jewelry case. Or in a house where the owner said Amy hadn't been inside in months before the burglary.

'She probably did it for kicks at first. But the point is, when she needed to slip into her estranged husband's house and kill him, she had the skills to do it. So we do have punishment evidence.

'But like I say, you'll win at punishment,' David continued, waving a hand generously. 'She's not a danger to anyone, as long as you're not her cheating husband. We know about the other cases, but I'm not even sure you could call them burglaries. It doesn't look like she ever stole anything. So they're just trespassing cases. No one's going to give her a death sentence for that. Maybe she wasn't a great person to have as a friend, but not dangerous.'

Mad, bad and dangerous to know, Edward thought irrelevantly. Someone's description of Lord Byron. No, Amy wasn't that. But she wasn't the sister he'd thought he knew well, either.

'You know you'll lose at punishment, but you're still going to ask for a death sentence,' Edward said, still hearing that hollow tone in his voice.

'I have to, Edward. You know that. It's not personal.'

Edward looked at him and David shrugged, an acknowledgment of the inanity of his last remark.

There was one more exchange on Edward's way out.

As David walked him through the halls he said, 'Are you really going to try this thing yourself? Didn't you have some problem with the bar?'

'Yeah. I paid my tab.'

David laughed. 'Served out a probation of your license suspension already, or something like that?'

'Yeah,' Edward said again, whilst thinking, *something like that. But actually nothing like that at all.*

Six

Later, when Edward began thinking clearly, he was struck in retrospect by David's offhand remark about Amy's 'cheating husband.' Did he have some evidence of that? Had infidelity by Paul caused the breakup of Amy's marriage? If so, that was a motive for the murder, one of the best.

So forget capital murder, forget these other crimes. This case still came down to Edward having to prove that Amy hadn't murdered her husband. Even though they were in the process of divorce and she was found next to his body, with his blood all over her and the murder weapon a few feet away.

That was probably why he and David hadn't talked about the case itself. It still looked like a lay-down for the prosecution. And maybe there was a good reason for that. Maybe no alternative theory worked because police had arrested the right suspect. Edward sat and thought hard about that. If this was any other client, if he was still a lawyer, he'd have acknowledged her likely guilt by now.

So he needed to look at those other cases. Once Edward started looking through the police reports and witness statements David had given him, Edward found himself fascinated. The burglaries

87

seemed unmotivated and without pattern. One couple – Edward vaguely recognized their names as being friends of Amy's – had called police to report that they'd returned from a weekend trip to find someone had entered their home and apparently stayed there for some time. How did they know? Because the wife was a secret smoker and the burglar had found her hidden cache of cigarettes and smoked several, leaving the butts and ashes in a cereal bowl on a coffee table. The couple also felt someone had been in their bed, because of the rumpled state of the sheets, which was not how they had left them. From that one, Edward even picked up a hint that the homeowners suspected sexual activity in their absence. As if a degenerate Goldilocks had broken in to spread her vices around their home.

It was easy to see why police hadn't pursued that case. Burglary was entering a home with the intent of committing a felony or a theft inside. If someone just broke into a building without intending to do anything illegal inside – say to get out of the rain – that wasn't a burglary. It was what David had called it, trespassing. In the case of depraved Goldilocks, she hadn't stolen anything, unless you could count the cigarettes.

The one that seemed most like a burglary had happened three years ago, while Edward was serving his prison sentence. Someone had gotten into a River Oaks home near Edward's parents' home and taken a set of 1920s era stemware. Then a couple of weeks later had gifted those glasses, anonymously, to the couple's eldest daughter as a wedding present. This time it seemed as if some version of Robin Hood had been at work. The crime made no sense. The daughter, opening her presents in front of her family, had exclaimed over the glasses, her mother had recognized them, and the daughter dutifully returned them on the spot. Net loss: zero. Edward puzzled over that one for long minutes, but couldn't make any sense of it.

Others were just as random. He couldn't see the connection to Amy at all. For this crap they were going to seek a death sentence? *But they might be able to get one.* Reading through the reports, Edward realized he'd been subconsciously constructing a profile of a sociopath, a serial criminal with no regard not only for law but for her friends' feelings. Burglary was a violation. It made the victim feel not just unsafe in his own home, but as if it was no longer quite his. Aside from whatever the burglar took, it was a theft of part of the victim's identity. Someone who did it again and again, even just as a joke, felt no compassion, no empathy for her victims. Victims who were friends of hers, or at least acquaintances.

They weren't horrible crimes in themselves, but they showed disregard for other people. That defined a sociopath. And once that serial criminal had committed murder during one of those burglaries – the ultimate violation – wasn't it likely she would do it again? She didn't have a sense of other people's feelings; she didn't really see them as human, so why not snuff out another one if he crossed her?

He found himself afraid to call his sister. Not

just because he had such bad news for her, but also because Edward wasn't sure he knew her any more. This was what mere accusation like this could do. Portray someone as a completely different person from what even an intimate had always thought her. That was one reason for accusing a defendant of every little thing he'd ever done. Each little deviation from the norm made him that much more unknowable, more beyond the pale of our lives. Edward was afraid to call his sister's number, not knowing who might answer.

Dusk found him knocking on the door of a nice little white frame house in the Heights, a neighborhood near downtown but with a small-town feeling. In recent times, it had become gentrified, many of the homes restored to their Victorian-cottage original appearances. This was one about halfway up the scale: small, with a little front porch comfortably holding two white rocking chairs and flowers planted close to the house. Edward knocked on the door and waited.

'Hi,' Linda said, surprise in her tone. 'Knocking? What's up? Why didn't you just come in?'

'It's your house. I didn't want to—'

'Well, it's yours too, Teddy. At least I thought so.'

'Wait a minute,' he said as she was turning away. 'Let me look at you.'

He held her shoulders and did just that. A grin took possession of Linda's face, spreading her full lips, lifting her cheeks, adding a glint to her eyes. The eyes were brown, with long lashes, her face surrounded by wavy brown hair.

90

She had the same smile every time he looked at her full on like this. Edward smiled back. After a few seconds Linda ducked her head.

'How you stare,' she murmured.

They went inside. There was music playing quietly. Edward could never quite identify Linda's music, but he loved it. Sometimes it was classical, especially classical guitar. Sometimes the voice of a woman he'd almost, but not quite, recognize. He took her in his arms, swaying a little as if dancing. She was a perfect size, almost Edward's equal in height. Linda leaned her head on his shoulder. He didn't want to leave ever again. He didn't even want to talk. Talking would bring the world in. He just wanted to be here, with her.

But that wasn't possible for long of course.

After a while he said, 'Do you want to go to dinner? Have a date night?'

'Sure,' Linda said, as if it was a silly question. 'But we don't need to go out. Come onna my kitchen,' she added, with a different grin at him.

He had known Linda for years, as a friend of a friend, someone he'd seen at parties. She was a paralegal for someone he knew, so he sometimes saw her in business situations as well. They'd always been friendly, but when Edward went to prison she turned out to be more than that. She wrote to him regularly and, once in a while, sent him a care package of homemade cookies or a book from a writer she knew he liked. She even came to visit him once, sitting shyly on the other side of the mesh, picking up the phone with such timid curiosity it was clear she'd never been inside a prison before. Edward had been embarrassed for her to see him there, after knowing him in a suit or as the life of a party after three or four drinks. But he also appreciated her kindness. So many people with whom he'd thought he was much better friends had dropped him entirely once the doors had clanged shut behind him.

She was waiting for him in the parking lot the day he got out. He came stumbling into the sunlight, his paper bag of possessions in his hand, free for the first time in two years, relieved, terrified. The world looked so big. The parking lot across from the prison was an expanse of asphalt the size of a football field. A few scraggly trees bordered it. He hadn't touched a tree in forever.

Edward was wearing the suit pants, white shirt and black dress shoes he'd been wearing in court when he was taken into custody. His hard soles crunched on the caliche underfoot. He hadn't arranged a ride. Hadn't even told his family the exact day he was getting released. He'd had the vague idea he would take a bus into Houston, which was only thirty miles from his unit.

Someone had gotten out of a car on the far side of the parking lot, the roof of the car shimmering in the Texas sun. She raised a hand in greeting. The glare was so intense he could barely make out that it was a woman. Edward waved back, thinking his sister had found him.

But then Linda stepped out of the glare. She had been such a peripheral part of his life that seeing her brought much of it back abruptly. He almost felt himself standing in a parking lot near the courthouse. Linda waved and he walked toward her.

'Are you—?'

'I'm here for you, silly,' she said, put her arms around him and kissed him. It seemed to take a long time for her to step back. When she did she wore the biggest smile he had ever seen. Her eyes sparkled, her dark red lipstick was a little smeared. Linda was very fair, with light brown hair streaked with highlights in front, hanging down past her cheeks. She wore a simple blue dress that changed the color of her eyes a little and, now that she'd kissed him, she had pink spots on her cheeks. In profile she looked shy, her eyelashes fluttering.

Once he was in the passenger seat she pulled out confidently.

'How did you—?'

'I called the prison administration and pretended I was working for your lawyer. I know exactly how to do that.'

At the exit Linda stopped, put the car in park and turned in the seat.

'I had a feeling you wouldn't have anyone from your family meeting you. Or anyone else. If you had, I would have just watched. But I wanted to be here for backup.'

'How could you have known that?'

'Edward. I know what you're like. You'd be embarrassed. You don't want them to see you like this, ex-con not used to the world yet. You want to return to your parents in – I don't think splendor is the word, but something like that. Looking like nothing's changed. Probably already with a job.'

He wondered how she could possibly know that much about him, when he hadn't even known it himself. This time Linda just looked back at him, her mouth pursed but twitching a little playfully.

It was dusk by the time they drove into the outskirts of Houston. They had talked non-stop the whole way, about her work and of course about Edward's time inside. Linda already knew enough from his letters that she could ask questions about specific people and nod knowingly as he talked.

'Where to?' she asked casually.

'I have a friend who said I could crash with him.'

'Mike?' Linda guessed. At Edward's nod she added, 'But you haven't talked to him yet.'

He shook his head.

'How about something to eat first?' she asked casually.

She took him to a café on the edge of Montrose, with white tablecloths and a bound wine menu. In Edward's white shirt and black shoes and Linda's versatile blue dress they were dressed perfectly for the place.

When a waiter came Linda folded her hands under her chin and said, 'Do you want a drink?' Edward actually thought about it for a few seconds. This was the perfect time to restart his life, make himself a better person, starting with remaining as sober as he'd been for two years.

'Absolutely,' he said.

Over dinner they stopped talking about prison or law. Linda guided him away from that world so gently he didn't even realize it. Instead she got him to make plans. No law license, no law

94

practice. What else did he know? Nothing. He'd spent his adult life being a lawyer, then being a prisoner of the law.

'Well, what skills do you have that would translate?'

Edward put down his fork and looked at her. 'Are you interviewing me?'

She smiled at him, that glowing smile. 'Aren't I doing it well? Isn't this good practice?'

He laughed. 'So, Mr Hall,' she continued with mock seriousness. 'You established rapport with clients . . .'

'Sometimes.'

'Always. Or convinced them you had. You persuaded judges and juries . . .'

'On my good days. I guess what I did was sell my knowledge. Of the law, but more of the system. The courthouse is scary if you're in danger of being kept there. I was a good guide. I knew all the ways out.'

'You sold yourself,' Linda said, leaning toward him. She put her hand over his. 'In a good way. You created confidence in you. You could do that with something else.'

He watched her. Linda must have thought he was thinking about her advice. But what he was thinking about was her hand on his and back to that kiss in the parking lot.

After dinner, which was long and included a bottle of wine, she took him home, to the pretty little house in the Heights. It looked so homey Edward just sat in the driveway looking at it. He could picture it inside, the pastel colors, the whites, the space, the lightness of everything.

'You want to come in and call your friend?'
'Sure.'
But inside he just stood in her living room. It was nearly as he'd pictured, clean but not pristine, hardwood floor with an area rug softening it, an irregular shape like a puddle the glass coffee table might have dripped if it melted.
'There's a phone in the kitchen.'
'Thank you.'
But they both just stayed there. She was looking at him, he at her. Linda's stare only looked puzzled for a moment, then it softened. Her mouth lengthened, her lips long and lush. Edward felt dirty by comparison. She looked so fresh. Edward felt sure he still had a layer of prison dust on him.

Then she stepped toward him and tilted her head as if in inquiry. Edward took the one step remaining between them and bent toward her as she lifted her lips to his. This kiss was different from her greeting, deeper, a landscape of lips, exploring, questioning and answering. It went on and on before her mouth opened more and he found his arms were around her, hers around his waist. His hands moved down, down her firm arms to her waist, feeling her hip bones, then he lifted his arms again and held her tightly against him. She pressed her leg against his.

They made it to the bedroom. They were both barefoot by that time and Edward had lost his shirt. Linda had kissed his chest after she removed it, making him shiver. The bedroom was as lovely as the living room, the queen-sized bed made with a white coverlet, extra pillows across it.

Edward stood quite still on the threshold of that lovely room.

'Are you sure?'

'No,' Linda said, 'I'm having second thoughts,' and reached back for her zipper. He hurried to help.

In bed, naked, they held each other for a long time, running their hands up and down each other's bodies. Edward felt oddly virginal and Linda had some residual shyness in spite of her bold talk and stares. But when he separated her legs with his hand so he could stroke the underside of her thigh, she shuddered, closed her eyes and said, 'Now.'

After he entered her he just lay still, on top of her, feeling that amazing interior world as if for the first time.

'God,' Linda breathed.

'You can call me Edward.' He risked the joke and luckily Linda laughed which caused a whole new chain of sensations and started them moving.

Later, spent, breathing deeply, still looking into each other's eyes, she wiped a tear from his eye he hadn't known was there. He kissed her. Linda grabbed him, held him tightly against her.

'This is what I wanted,' she whispered fiercely. 'I wasn't being nice. I was being naughty.'

She wouldn't let him go, refused to be the one-night stand celebration. She invited him to dinner at her house, introduced him to some of her friends at a happy hour. He had hung onto Linda just as tightly as she attached to him, showing up on her doorstep late in the evening, needing someone to hold as he fell down into sleep, needing her specifically, knowing she would cling to him just as tightly, wanting that, absolutely having to have that. Sometimes he felt no connection to anything or anyone else.

Once he found his job selling security software to companies, making pretty good money for a single man with few living expenses, he took Linda out regularly and nicely. She could make an occasion out of very little, because she liked dressing up and when she did she'd have a secretive smile of amusement at her own happiness. Her secret purring joy made her a lighter weight on his arm. They could laugh and talk for hours.

The one disagreement between them, and it was rather huge, was that she wanted to meet his family. She had wanted to meet them early on and he could have done it then, except that Edward wasn't seeing his family himself. He and the family had had the big celebratory dinner in one of the nicest restaurants in Houston a few days after his release and, after that, his mother called him once a week or so. He met Amy for drinks two or three times. But there was no regularity to his family life. He wasn't drawn back in.

When he tried to explain that to Linda he couldn't, or she couldn't understand.

'You feel like they're judging you all the time?' she'd asked.

'Well, they are. But that's always been true. But now I'm judging them back. Sort of. They're wondering how they failed to teach me their values, while I'm thinking I just want to develop my own. I'm out of the commune. I don't drink the Hall family Kool-Aid anymore.'

'Can you just say what you mean, Teddy, instead of giving me these sayings? I want to understand, but—'

'I mean I'm not only trying not to worry about the fact that I'm not living up to their standards, but to forget that I ever knew their standards at all.' Because once upon a time he had. He had been the firstborn, the one who did everything right, who seemed like a worthy heir to his esteemed parents. It was one of the narratives of their family story, that they could count on Edward, that someday he would have a place in the world as prestigious as his father's.

Edward had already strayed from that storyline when he'd left the D.A.'s office, not to go into a big firm doing respected work, but into the semi-criminal underworld of criminal defense work, as his parents saw it. They stopped asking him about his cases. He stopped telling them stories about lunch with the murderer and drinks with drug dealers, sometimes celebrating Edward's having secured their continued freedoms. Even before his arrest he'd seen his family less and less.

But Linda only knew him post-prison, when a reason for keeping her from meeting his family seemed obvious to her.

No, it's that they're not good enough for you, was what he wanted to say, knowing what bullshit that would sound like. He wanted her and the life they might someday have to himself. He didn't want them being woven into the family

99

narrative. But Linda continued to believe only one thing about his reluctance to introduce her to them; she wasn't good enough, so he was embarrassed by her.

He introduced her to everyone else he knew, including old friends he looked up just for that purpose. *See, here's one of my friends from prep school, a snotty rich kid and I'm happy to introduce you to him with my arm around your shoulders.* Perhaps those meetings mollified Linda, perhaps she just let it go. Generally she was one of the happiest people he'd ever known. She worked at her job, laughed with her friends and performed undeserved acts of kindness that made her happy. Her sunny nature was one of the great joys in being with her.

So what Edward greatly preferred, and what Linda mostly let him have, was the illusion that the two of them constituted their own family, complete. Edward had even proposed marriage once and Linda had put him off so gently she hadn't answered at all. Edward came and went from her house and it sometimes seemed Linda was as happy to see him go as to see him in her bed.

One change in the last few weeks was that they talked about his family again. Linda was the first person with whom he shared the new news about his sister, for example.

She had a view of the news he hadn't considered.

'I don't see what difference it makes,' Linda said, frowning to concentrate. March had passed into April. The high temperature of the day had been ninety. Linda wore cut-offs she'd probably had since high school and a T-shirt from Colorado; she wore no bra underneath, so the Colorado shirt seemed to feature a view of the Rockies.

'So she goes into her friends' houses sometimes when they're not there. So what?'

'It makes her a criminal, see? It lets them argue that killing her husband wasn't just a one-time fit of rage that doesn't show her character at all. She's someone who has no regard for any laws or anyone's feelings.'

'Why? Did she break anything? Did she take anything valuable? You said they have her finger-prints on a jewelry case, but no jewelry was missing. She just looked at it. She was just curious.'

'It's a series of crimes,' Edward repeated, wonder-ing how she could not get that significance.

'Sounds more like a sickness to me.'

That was interesting. A sickness? Edward saw everything differently for a moment. Was there something wrong with Amy? What psychological deprivation made her unable to resist breaking into the houses of people she knew? Was this a strange strain of something like kleptomania? What led to that? A sort of emptiness that could never be filled? That quickly, he saw his sister completely differ-ently from the way he always had. What kind of sad, deprived person was she? In the moment of Linda's remark the whole story had changed, which was good. The prime goal of criminal defense was changing the narrative. The prosecu-tion's story line was always simple: depraved killer (rapist, robber, whatever) acts without restraint on her own desires, heedless that the act will deprive her victim of his life. To counter that, the

101

defense needed to change, in jurors' minds, the simple view of the act. Change the identity of the murderer or the character of the victim, or just the circumstances. Make the act a mistake, or self-defense, or an uncontrollable impulse.

He had to get Amy psychologically evaluated, by someone very good. Because whatever else she was, his sister was a very smart woman with medical training. Could anyone catch up to her on the twisty pathways of her mind?

'Edward?'

He realized Linda had said his name more than once. He blinked at her, coming back into her living room.

'Where did you go? Is that how it happens?'

'How what happens?' But he knew what she meant. Was that how he went absent when inspiration struck? 'That was good,' he said. 'What you said about Amy. Good insight. Thanks, babe. You're hired.'

Linda smiled. He smiled back. He leaned forward and their mouths eased into each other. But Edward was still living at a slight remove. Still turning over what Linda had said. He was looking forward to seeing Amy again, seeing if he saw her differently in real life now he knew this secret of hers.

Linda watched him with a secret smile of contentment, thinking she'd gained her own insight. Wondering how many people had seen Edward in moments like this. Her expression told him what she was thinking, her pride, her satisfaction. And he was glad to have given her that.

* * *

102

Amy looked about the same. Still that mix of tightly-pulled-together professional and surprised little girl look of pleasure as she opened the front door to him.

'Come in, come in. Let's go to the kitchen.'

She didn't wait for an answer, just led him deeper into her house. It seemed to him more feminine now, with light, airy curtains over the windows. He glimpsed a flowered sofa as Amy led him down the hall; the place just had an overall lighter look. So he wondered if she was secretly glad to be rid of her messy, masculine husband. He detected no trace of the late Paul.

'We need to talk about your case.'

'Of course. You talked to the prosecutor.'

'I did.'

'So what's the problem?'

Edward thought, *Other than that they think you're a murderer and a career criminal?* He remembered what he'd learned in private practice, that he much preferred representing someone who knew himself to be a crook, instead of a regular citizen who couldn't believe he'd blundered into the world of criminal law and kept insisting he didn't belong there.

'Your burglaries, Amy. That's the problem. The fact the D.A. has evidence that you've been breaking into houses for years. That's what they think takes you from being an ordinary angry-wife husband-killer to being someone worthy of a death sentence.'

He'd spoken harshly on purpose, to get her out of this confused-suburban-professional act she was pulling on him, but when he saw Amy's face starting to crumple he added quickly, 'Which they don't expect to get, by the way, they don't think there's a chance, so I might be able to talk them out of the idea of trying you for that altogether.'

But it was too late, the damage was done. Her eyes filled with tears that quickly spilled over and ran down her cheeks. Amy brought a hand up to her mouth. He noticed fleetingly that her nails were bitten down.

'What burglaries?' she managed to get out.

He said gently, 'That's what they call it when you go into someone's house without her permission when she's not there. That's what it looks like to a prosecutor, Amy.'

He took her other hand and held it, feeling the warmth grow from the joining of their flesh. In that moment he remembered comforting her as a child when no one else could. When she'd skinned her knee or lost a pet fish, when her parents couldn't do what her big brother could; convince her that things were going to be all right. Bactine and affection had worked wonders for Amy, and no one could apply them like Edward could.

'How do they—?' She quickly skipped that question. Amy pulled her hand away from his, stood up and turned away. He realized she was embarrassed.

'Amy.' He said her name both to draw her back and to reassure her that he didn't condemn her. This was one of a defense lawyer's first jobs, to convince a client that he saw her as a human being, a good one, in spite of whatever charge she was facing, even in spite of whatever guilt she might admit to him. 'We have to talk about this, Amy.'

'OK,' she said with her back to him. Then turned back around and sat, but now with her hands in her lap and her eyes watchful.

'They have one report from one of your friends who actually found you in her house. She decided not to report you at the time, but apparently she's come forward now. This was about three years ago, a woman named—'

'Louise Donaldson.'

'Yes.'

'I went to a party at her house the night before and I'd lost an earring. Didn't discover it until I was home, so the next day I went by to ask her if she'd found it, but nobody was home. I'd been out on her terrace at one point, so I went back there, through her gate, looked around, then tried the back door just for the hell of it and it turned out Louise had left it unlocked. So I went in to look around and she came home and found me.'

Edward just looked at her for a few seconds, then said what he'd say to a regular client. 'That sounds like the cover story you had ready if someone came home while you were in the house.' Amy looked down, so he continued. 'So I assume your friend Louise bought the story, since she didn't call the police.'

Amy shook her head, still looking down. When she answered she was almost whispering. 'No, she didn't. I could tell by the way she looked at me. "I never leave doors unlocked," she kept saying. I said, "Well, you did this time. Or maybe one of the kids came out just before you left for school or whatever." I could tell she didn't buy it. But nothing was missing and I was someone she knew, so she just let it go. But she looked at me differently from then on. I wondered what she told people we knew.'

'Now D.A.'s office investigators have examined the lock and found scratches that indicate it was picked.' Edward said this very quietly, trying not to sound judgmental. He had a sudden urge to show her his own set of lock picks, see if she'd compare, but he hadn't had them for years. 'Which doesn't mean much, this long after the fact. The scratches could have happened any time.' After a pause, for a response from her that didn't come, he asked, 'What were you really looking for?'

Amy continued watching him, her eyes searching his face.

'That's a technique, isn't it?' she said to him. 'Ask a question that assumes the client committed the crime, skip right over that big question and go to other issues like motive or something that also assumes the crime.' Amy continued to study his face for another few seconds, then smiled slightly. 'All right, I'll let your technique work. I didn't know what I was looking for. Just something to know about Louise besides that she was a wonderful hostess who made everything look easy and gracious. Some evidence that she had a child locked in a closet, or masturbated to Victorian porn, or just dropped her used Kleenexes on the floor. That's all it was, Eddie, just a peek backstage.'

'Did you find what you wanted?'

Amy just continued to smile at him. It was her secret, what she had on her friend; she had paid for it. He hadn't.

So he tried another technique. 'That wasn't your first time, was it? How did you get started?'

Amy let enough silence pass to tell him she knew what he was doing but was still going to indulge him.

'I had a boyfriend in college. You never met him. I was a little ashamed of him, actually. He was kind of crazy. But in a fun way, I thought. You know those early romances; you don't quite know what's normal yet, so bad crazy can look a lot like fun crazy?

'Anyway, one time we went to see these friends of ours, who turned out not to be home. But Ben really wanted to get in, he thought there was . . . well, it doesn't matter, but he wanted in, so he took me around the house. It was one of those little houses in Hyde Park in Austin. He went to the back, to a bedroom, looked around, then raised the window. I said, "How did you—?" and he grinned and said, "I unlocked it myself, last time I was here."'

'Was this daytime?'

'Yes, it was a daring daylight break-in. But it was college, nobody had anything worth stealing. Ben looked around . . .'

For pot, Edward assumed.

'. . . but then he just wanted to show me what a thrill it was. I was scared to death. Ben wanted to make out, or more, but I insisted we get out. But, just before we went back out the window,

107

I opened a little wicker bedside table, I don't know why and I found something. The people who lived here were three girls and I thought they were all kind of mean girl bitches, but I opened this drawer of this bedside table and found a Bible. A white Bible like for a child and I opened it and saw an inscription. The girl's grand-mother had given it to her. It made me see her in a different light. See, I'm not just looking for bad stuff, Edward, and certainly not for anything I can use on anybody. Just insights.'

She just wanted to know more about everyone than anyone else did, Edward realized. He who had sat in his office so many times and had people spill their guts certainly understood the urge.

'What did the inscription say?'

Amy paused a minute, then decided to tell him. 'It said: "You need to read this every day."'

'Jesus.'

'Yes. That's what her grandmother told her, that she was worried about her soul. Or maybe she meant it in a nice way. But I didn't think so. I wanted to look around for more clues, but Ben was already outside. But he hooked me, I under-stood. I looked at that girl differently from then on. She had a grandmother who thought she was destined for hell. How would you react to that?

'Then there was just being in the house. Like I said, I was scared to death the whole time, but maybe that was just because . . .'

'It was your first time.'

'Yeah.' She smiled at him. 'My virgin burglary. Too scared to enjoy it. But later I realized it could feel good. Because I had just a touch of that

108

feeling, just before I went out the window, when I could see safety but I was still inside. I felt like I owned the place.'

'So you kept at it.'

'Oh, no. Hell no. I was completely creeped out. I broke up with that boy right after that. I didn't want to see him again. I felt dirty. When I heard his voice I felt worse. It's like . . .' She glanced at him almost shyly. '. . . to continue the analogy, you're so ashamed after the first time that you don't do it again for a long time.'

'So?'

Amy hesitated. This was an interesting, racy conversation they were having, unlike any before, even though he'd thought they had a close relationship. But not a lawyer-client one, this one required her to reveal a deeply hidden side of herself.

'Even though I quit, for a long time, I didn't forget that feeling. After college – remember that year I took off? – I was deciding what I was going to do. Whether I was going to go on to medical school and be daddy's little doctor, or do something else entirely like you did.'

He hadn't known he and his father had been competing role models for her.

'Mainly I was just tired. I'd been working so hard for so long and was so worried about grades, and class rankings, and who loved who and who was mad at who. I needed a break.' She laughed. 'Imagine now thinking that high school and college had been hard work. And just the worry all the time. It didn't seem like that for you, Eddie. Nothing seemed to bother you.'

He smiled slightly, ruefully. But this session wasn't about him. He didn't say anything and Amy resumed.

'So when I came back and did go to medical school, I felt like I was behind. Remember when a year's difference made you feel old as the oceans? I guess I had a little bit of an inferiority complex at that point. One day, I was home for a few days in the summer and went with Mom and Dad to a pool party, at one of their friends' houses. Their daughter had been a friend of mine in high school but, by then, she was already married and pregnant and I felt even farther behind. But I remembered my skills.

'I excused myself, went into the house and went straight to the room where she was staying while she was visiting and I searched her suitcase. Then the parents' medicine cabinet and the mother's bedside table. And came out feeling great, feeling like the image of normality. I just smiled at everybody and relaxed and got a little tipsy and felt great.'

Edward wondered briefly what she'd found: anxiety medications, sex toys, a diary? But it didn't matter, he realized quickly. It was being the holder of secrets again. The secret itself didn't matter much.

'So I took up my second career again. Just once in a great while, Eddie. When I was feeling down, or mad at somebody, or just bored. It was a thrill. It made me feel powerful and less weird myself, to know everybody else's weird hidden business.'

Everyone's weird, Edward thought. It took

some people longer than others to realize that. Some people never did. Maybe most people thought there was a golden adulthood of placid striving and family happiness that nearly everyone reached, except them. He looked around the beautiful kitchen with its white surfaces and pastel accents, like something from a magazine. Almost anyone looking at this room, at Amy's whole house, would think this homeowner had reached that successful, happy plateau of normality.

Amy turned to him. She was wound up now, he saw. She had never told anyone what she was telling him.

'It's addictive, Eddie, finding out about people's secret lives. Getting inside them. It's like performing surgery on them. Even the purest have secrets. Some are ridiculously mundane, some are pathetically weird. But you never look at the person the same way again. And they're not all bad. I found out someone I thought was cold and emotionless loves his children more than his own life. He's sacrificed for them in a way no one else has.'

'How?'

'I'm not going to tell you. I'm going to keep his secret. But usually it was more like revenge. I'd go to a party or a dinner at one of these mansions (like Louise Donaldson's) and the hostess would come down all done up, with a little smile because she was coming from the secret part of the house. All the rest of us got to see was how perfect her life was, no matter what kind of mess she'd left up there. And if she irritated me during the evening I'd think, "Just wait, bitch, I'm going to

111

see your secrets. Even if it's just that her bathroom is disgusting.'"

After a moment Amy added slyly, 'That was my reason for the so-called breaking and entering. I guess other people have other reasons.'

She turned, leaning back against the sink. Edward looked straight at her, his mouth twisted ruefully. Yes, the irony hadn't been lost on him: for years Amy had been committing the conduct that had sent him to prison. The family crime.

She made a small indication with her head and he got up and followed her to the living room. This was a beautiful room too, but colder than the kitchen. They just stared at each other for a long moment, knowing each other better than they had an hour before.

She cleared her throat and said, 'That's what it was all about, just learning people's secrets. And the thrill. I've hidden under a bed while a man and woman made love over my head. And not the man who lived in that house. So I could have popped out from under there and they would have been more scared than I was. But I'd rather hold onto the secret.'

'And you only got caught that one time?'

'Only time.' She said it with pride and smiled at him ironically.

That returned them to the painful subject at hand. When Edward glanced at her, Amy was staring at him. It seemed as if the rapport they'd just developed went both ways. She knew what he was thinking.

'I didn't break into Paul's house,' she said.

'That's how it looks to the D.A., with this background.'

'I didn't have to break in. That was my home. It was my home too.'

'No it wasn't, Amy. He had moved out of your home. You never lived in Paul's house.'

'It felt like I had. I'd spent time there. Nights. Spent the night and got up and went to work the next morning. I had clothes there. A toothbrush.'

This was an aspect of the prosecution's case they had to attack hard, he realized again. Even if Amy did kill her husband, but didn't break into his house, that would be a defense to capital murder. It would mean the difference between life without parole and life with, where Amy could get out in twenty or thirty years, which sounded horrible but beat the hell out of never.

'Did you have a key? Did Paul give you one?'

'No. He kept saying he was going to, but he hadn't gotten around to it. We hadn't gotten back together that long before . . .' She fell silent.

'Amy, let me ask you some things. You started going out with Paul while he was Dad's research assistant, right, when you were both in medical school?'

She shook her head. 'Paul had graduated. And you've got it backwards. Paul and I were already dating when he got the job with Dad.'

'Really?' Edward made a little 'hmm' sound.

'Why? Is that important?'

Maybe. Who knew what was ever important in a case? But it changed the way he remembered their lives. He'd thought Paul had gotten hired on his own merits, because he was a brilliant medical student – he would've had to be, to live up to their father's standards – but instead he'd

113

already had a connection to the family when Dr Hall had hired him. Was that something he'd been grateful for at first, but then had come to resent? Was it one of the problems in their marriage? Did Paul feel like a professional son-in-law, who'd started out his career with a significant leg up, because first he'd gotten into his mentor's daughter's pants?

But he'd asked Amy enough secrets for this one session. And she might not even know the answer to that question. Her husband wouldn't have discussed with her his (theoretical) resentment of her and her father.

'I loved him, Edward. You know that, don't you? You saw it between us. Didn't you?'

Maybe. He really couldn't remember.

His sister was staring at him. Her expression seemed to be asking, *You are going to save me from this, aren't you?*

Jesus. Was he?

Seven

'Any idea why your brother-in-law picked this neighborhood?' Mike asked, driving through an area of southwest Houston not nearly as upscale as the one Paul had left behind.

'None. Maybe just got lucky on an available rental?' Edward asked.

'Maybe. This isn't particularly convenient to the medical center. But he picked it, eight months ago. What was he like? I never laid eyes on the guy.'

'Very earnest guy, Paul. As soon as you started talking to him, you felt like he was really hard-working. He'd work even at a conversation, you know? Leaning in, almost getting spittle in your face from him talking. I don't know how Amy—'

No. Bad remark there about to happen.

'Wow, you really liked the guy, huh?' Mike said, shooting a sidelong glance at him. 'I hope, when I'm gone, you can think of something better to say about me than that I used to spit on people when I talked to them.'

'No, no, that's just the first thing I happened to remember. I was mostly off on my own when Paul and Amy were becoming a couple. And then, you know, away at extended summer camp. He seemed like a good guy. Hard-working, smart. I thought he was good enough for Amy and that was my only concern, so after I decided that I didn't think much about him anymore.'

He sat musing for a minute, as the houses glided by, imagining what he'd missed. In a way, Paul had taken Edward's place in the family, slipping into it just as Edward went off on his state-funded vacation.

'This is it.'

Mike had parked across the street from a wooden frame house with four windows across the front. It was painted a light blue, with white trim around the windows and the eaves.

'Have a key?' Mike asked.

'No. They wouldn't release one to Amy, even though she's his wife, since she's also the prime suspect. Let's take a look around anyway.'

They did. The house seemed watchful as they approached, crossing the front lawn that was growing lush in the Houston spring. They stood in front of the windows on the right hand side and peered in, cupping their hands around their eyes to break the glare. Inside was a living room, furnished in Living Room Standard, with a couch and two chairs. This was the leather furniture Edward remembered, dark and heavy, which accounted for why Amy's seemed new. Edward and Mike proceeded on around the house, Mike's eyes on the ground, Edward's watchfully forward. Around the side of the house, toward the back, was a gate in a chain link fence. Here, a strip of yellow crime scene tape still hung but someone had torn it across, so it just dangled limply, a foot or so of yellow leftover. There was a lock for the gate, but someone had taken it off, hooked it through one of the diamonds of the fence and failed to replace it. What did it matter now?

Next to this gate, was a gate into the backyard of the house next door. Edward glanced into it, worried about a witness, but the slice of yard he could see was empty of human habitation.

So they went in Paul's gate, saw nothing worth investigating in the small backyard and went up to the back door. It was locked, a simple lock in the doorknob. Edward wished again that he still had his lock picks. Instead he and Mike both looked around. Mike felt all around the woodwork of the door and shook his head. Edward noticed one of those tripod barbecue grills, waist-high on its stand. He didn't think of Paul as an outdoor chef kind of guy. Edward ran his hand underneath it and sure enough found a small metal box, the magnetic kind where one hides a spare key. The key fit the back door lock.

'Not very concerned with home security, was he?' Mike said conversationally.

What Edward was thinking was, *Paul had gone to the trouble of having a spare key made, but not one for Amy, in spite of their supposed rapprochement.* Amy had said he just hadn't gotten around to it, but he'd gotten around to making this one.

Edward left the investigator to search and went across the hall to the master bedroom. Edward stepped inside, feeling suddenly skittish, as if he were intruding. A king-sized bed was neatly made, with a deep maroon comforter and over-sized pillows. Beyond it were more windows, with a view of the garage attached to the house next door. This room would be private even with the windows open.

Closer to hand, Edward studied the floor beside

the bed, near his feet. It had been cleaned, leaving it shinier than the area beyond. This was where Paul had fallen. It was his blood that had polished his floor. It had been cleaned well, by a professional, but Edward fancied he could still see the outline of the body there. The empty space made this real for him. Here was where the body of his brother-in-law had lain, his blood spreading across the floor as Amy worked on his chest, trying to restart his heart. Had Paul lived through any of that? Had he felt Amy trying to save his life?

The room had been restored to order, but something about a crime scene remains a crime scene. He stepped carefully around the spot on the floor and tried to look at the room overall. Edward had never been in this house, but could he deduce anything from it?

Against the wall, opposite the foot of the bed, was the door into a closet. He could tell because the door was ajar, revealing clothes on hangers. On the top of the nearby dresser, items were lined up in a neat row: skin cream, sunblock, a box of tissues. He opened the three wide drawers of the dresser one at a time, finding nothing more interesting than briefs, T-shirts and socks. One unopened package of underwear sat on top. Paul had been a man starting over, from the bottom up. The whole room had a starting-over feel. It was simple, with little brought over from his old life.

There was a mirror inside the closet door, a rack of ties just inside the closet, within reach of it. This was where Paul would have stood to put the finishing touches on his appearance, just before he left the room. Amy said he'd been in this room when she'd rushed in, after hearing the gunshot. But he hadn't been almost dressed or he would have been right here, looking at himself in the mirror just before going out. Instead he'd been shot over there nearer the door. Had he been rushing toward the intruder with the gun? Or walking slowly toward someone he knew, possibly his wife, holding out his hands in an attempt to calm? The placement of the body should have told him something, but he wasn't sure what.

'Very neat guy, your brother-in-law. Even after the techs put the kitchen back together, I could tell he had things laid out neatly. Cleaning stuff under the kitchen sink, paper bags folded in a rack inside the pantry door, spices laid out in alphabetical order.'

'Like an operating room,' Edward answered. 'Dad used to say that getting things in order to begin was half the job.'

Mike grunted noncommittally and moved past Edward into the closet. He turned on a light and saw suits lined up on the left, shirts and slacks on the right, shoes lined along the floor.

Mike nodded. 'Yep. Very neat guy.'

'Do you see any women's clothes?' Edward turned toward the closet himself. As he did so he heard a sound behind him, then another sound that was so distinctive that anyone who had ever heard it would recognize it.

The sound of a handgun being cocked.

Eight

Edward froze. His instinct was to move, but instinct didn't tell him which direction. Push Mike deeper into the closet so he'd be safe and hope Mike had come armed? Jump inside the closet himself? Fall down on the floor so the bed blocked him? The urges competed and canceled each other out, so Edward just stood there, as if he hadn't heard anything at all. He raised his hands to show he wasn't armed himself, but was afraid to turn. He knew as soon as he did a bullet would hammer into him and in seconds he would be re-creating his brother-in-law's death scene.

'Turn around slowly,' an unfamiliar voice said.

Edward did so, so slowly he was barely moving at all. His body knew that sight of the person holding the gun would be his last. The gunman wouldn't like Edward's looks, or wouldn't like the fact of not recognizing him, or wouldn't like Edward's seeing the intruder's own face. And he would pull the trigger and that would be that.

But it wasn't a gun*man* at all. As Edward turned, he got a glimpse of the woman in the doorway, then turned to her full face. She was a stranger to him. Edward's gaze moved slowly upward, starting with the gun, which she held as if she knew what she was doing: with both hands, out from her body, the barrel leveled steadily at him. She wore a very light sweater over a tank top that

120

revealed a thin figure with good lines. Her neck was long, strong, unmarred by sagging flesh. She had a straight jawline, full cheeks, a mouth clenched into a tight line and grim dark blue eyes. Her brown hair was disheveled. Through the thin sweater he could see her shoulder bones. She looked stripped down, like a survivor.

'I'm Paul's brother-in-law,' Edward said. Because it was obvious this was no burglar or robber. Her glare told him she mistrusted him for being in this house without permission.

'*Her* brother,' the woman said. The gun didn't drop. Her mouth didn't open into an apologetic smile.

Edward nodded. 'Amy's brother,' he confirmed. 'Edward.'

Her mouth twitched as if she might say something, but then she stopped.

'And I'm an investigator,' came Mike's voice from inside the closet. 'With a gun of my own.'

The woman lowered hers. She still watched Edward with suspicion and something like disgust.

'I saw somebody coming in,' she said. 'Burglarizing the place, I figured. People read about a murder happening, wait a few days for the investigation to be done, then break in to steal what they can. The worst kind of vultures.'

'Is that what people do?' Edward asked, holding out his hands further to show he hadn't taken anything.

'Cops told me about it, said I ought to watch out for that.' She raised her voice. 'You can come out of there now. With or without your gun. Mine's down.'

Mike edged slowly out, saw she was telling the truth and took another step out of the closet.

'How about putting the gun all the way away?' he suggested mildly. 'Those things go off sometimes.'

'How about showing me a badge or some ID or something?'

'I'm private. But how about this?' He handed a framed photograph toward the woman.

She said what Edward was thinking.

'What the hell?' She added, 'What is this, you receiving your license or something? You carry it with you? Framed?'

'Some pictures in the closet on a high shelf,' Mike said to Edward. 'I was just looking through them when we got interrupted.'

Edward watched the woman holding the picture, with no idea what she was seeing.

'The late Paul Shilling's wedding party,' Mike explained to the woman. 'This guy here is in back, behind the bride.'

'Yeah, I see that.' The woman looked up from the picture to Edward, studied him critically.

'I haven't aged well. Tough few years.'

She made an unamused sound, tossed the photo face down onto the bed, and said, 'I still don't think you should be in here. Let's go out.'

A couple of minutes later, they were sitting on the small front porch of Paul's house. It turned out the woman was wearing blue shorts and had nice legs, which Edward hadn't noticed until they were outside. You'd think a man about to die might latch onto a detail like that.

'I live there,' she said, indicating the red brick house next door. 'Valerie Linnett.'

They introduced themselves all around. Mike seemed to know her already. He hitched his chair around so he could look directly at her.

'You're the neighbor who heard the gunshot.'

'Yeah. If you've got a little experience of fire-arms, you recognize that sound right away. It ain't a screen door slamming.'

'So you were the one who called the police?'

She looked at him levelly, indicating she would only be questioned a little bit and no farther.

'Yeah. I almost came over, like I did just now, but not after hearing a shot. Let the professionals do their job.'

'Smart,' Mike said.

Valerie shrugged off the compliment.

'Had you ever seen my sister here?' Edward said.

Valerie's expression softened, apparently remembering Edward was a bereaved family member.

'A couple of times, maybe. I'm not in the habit of spying on my neighbors.'

Edward shrugged. 'It's a neighborhood. You notice your neighbors. Paul had lived here for a few months. You'd met him.'

'Yeah. Just to say hi to, you know, watering the yard, walking to the car. I think once he came over when I'd invited a couple of the other neighbors over for drinks on my patio. I certainly didn't know him.'

'I'm sure he was busy. You are too, probably. Do you mind if I ask—?'

'I'm a pharmacist,' she said. 'Hard work but

123

regular hours. It gets frantic sometimes, but at least I know when I'll be walking out.'

Edward nodded. Pharmacists with enough seniority to schedule their own time made good money, which explained how she could afford the brick house.

'So did you and Paul ever talk shop? He was a doctor,' Edward explained.

'I know he was a doctor,' she snapped at him. 'I knew that much.'

While Edward held up his hands in surrender, Mike took over the conversation. 'Do you mind telling us your story?'

Edward thought she was surely going to refuse, with some remark about their not being cops, when she began. 'It was a Saturday afternoon, you know, getting toward evening. I'd been doing yard work, so I'd just taken a shower and was thinking about having a drink or what I was going to do for dinner. It was a mild day, early March, and I had the front windows open. Heard a car door and I looked out. Like you say, you notice what goes on at your neighbors' houses. It's about watching out for your own, too.'

'Sure,' Mike said.

'I saw her – your sister – on the front porch, about to knock. She didn't look threatening, you know, so I just turned away and started making a drink when I heard the gunshot. Almost dropped my glass and hit the floor. But it obviously wasn't too close by. I ran to the window again and saw she was gone from the front porch. I waited, I had that hesitation I told you about, thinking I should go over, so I waited a couple of minutes to see if anything would happen, but I didn't hear anything else. So then I called the cops. I didn't know what had happened, but better safe, you know?'

Mike nodded. 'Did you go look out the back? Could you see his backyard?'

She shook her head. 'Maybe a few minutes later I did, just to see if I could see anything from another angle. And yes, I can see a slice of his yard from my window. But I didn't see anything. I couldn't see into the house from any angle of mine. When police came I let them in my house, so they could see all I'd been able to see was his porch.'

Mike nodded again. 'Had you seen her before? The woman on the porch?'

'His ex-wife? Yeah, a couple of times.'

Edward began, 'They weren't—'

'Living together,' Mike interrupted him. 'They hadn't been together for a while.'

'I know.' She nodded. 'I mean, it was obvious she was a visitor, not living there.'

'Did you ever see anybody else visit him?'

'Look, I wasn't—'

'Yeah, yeah, you weren't spying on him, I know, we've established that. But we've also established that people notice things. My neighbor's having an affair with the pizza delivery boy. Orders pizza two, three times a week, the kid goes inside.'

Valerie stared at him, then laughed shortly.

Mike shrugged. 'So what about it, other visitors for Dr Paul?'

She let a beat go by, then slowly shook her head. 'Sure. He was a single doctor. I saw him bring home a woman now and again. And a couple of other people came to visit, maybe. I wasn't watching, I didn't have my face pressed to the window. We all want our privacy, right? But there could've been dozens when I wasn't noticing. A gunshot gets your attention.' Then Valerie said, 'Maybe you two should move on before I call the police again.'

Edward stood slowly. 'We'll go, but we'll be back, too. We're not the enemy, you know. We want to solve this murder even more than the police do. He was my brother-in-law.'

'Yes, but she's your sister. You want to save her. That's more important to you than solving the murder.'

There was no response to that. Edward turned and walked away with Mike.

They asked at the other surrounding houses. No one had seen the whole picture. A couple had vaguely noticed Amy arrive, nearly everyone had heard the gunshot, but no one could give a complete timeline, unsurprisingly.

'Thanks,' Mike said to every one of them. 'Here's my card. If you think of anything else . . .'

Walking away from the last house they were going to try, Mike said, 'Two of them have already changed their stories since the first time I talked to them. One of them saw Amy just getting out of her car as the gunshot was going off. Now he says no, he saw her arrive and the gunshot was a minute or two later. Doesn't know if she was still on the porch or inside the house.' He shook his head disgustedly. 'Cops.'

Edward knew what that shorthand meant.

126

Police had begun with a prime suspect, so the questioning of witnesses was suggestive. *Are you sure you didn't hear the shot until later? Are you sure she waited on the porch at all? Well, all the other witnesses are saying* . . . And the story began to bend to the cops' version rather than the original truth. Reality was altering, to one in which Amy was not just suspicious, but guilty as hell.

As they reached the car, Edward remembered something else, from when he was in the murder scene bedroom and heard that gun click. Edward had been exposed, vulnerable. Mike was in the closet, unknown to the intruder. It occurred to Edward that his friend had used him as a shield, waiting to reveal himself until the newcomer had shown her own intentions.

'Thanks for your help with the gun-toting neighbor lady, by the way. If she'd shot me, would you have jumped out and taken her down or just waited for her to go away?'

'You were in the line of fire already,' Mike shrugged, starting the car and taking off. 'Nothing I could do about that. But hey, I spoke up. Took her attention off you. Give me some credit. And be grateful you were in your sister's wedding party,' Mike added.

Edward laughed. 'First time for that.'

Nine

Amy continued to have court appearances, approximately one a month, and Edward kept appearing with her. Every time, he expected someone to point out that he wasn't a lawyer, even to be taken into custody for practicing law without a license, but he continued to go unchallenged. His suits seemed poor disguises for what he was, but they worked. In this building, put an orangutan in a suit and give him a briefcase and he could probably pass. Let him work out a plea bargain and see how well he did, before you decided whether to get a human lawyer.

And Edward still had the briefcase. It was nearly empty, but he carried it as part of the ensemble.

'Come on, man,' Edward continued to say to the trial prosecutor, in increasingly frustrated tones and David continued to hold up his hands, a gesture meaning, *My hands are tied*. Edward needed to work his way up the food chain.

At a late June setting, something out of the ordinary did interrupt the routine. At the end of the session the judge looked at him and said, 'Come see me, please.' He went out the door behind her bench and down the hallway to the court offices. Inside, Cynthia's door was closed.

When he knocked her voice called, 'Come in.'

Edward went in and she waved at him to leave

128

the door open. Cynthia wouldn't want to be seen meeting him behind closed doors.

Cynthia hadn't stood up or extended her hand. She was still wearing her robe, which looked hot and uncomfortable, a black drape in Houston in the summer. Edward suddenly wondered what she was wearing underneath it.

'Why are you smiling?'

'It's just so strange,' Edward said. 'Being back here. Everything the same but everything changed. You on the bench, for one thing.'

She stared at him for a couple of beats, as if he were criticizing her credentials, but then said, 'I know. Crazy, right? But somebody's got to do it. Someone has to make the decisions. And I think we do a pretty good job here.'

'I hear that you do.' Edward sat looking at her, his former partner in crime. Cynthia gave no hint they were anything other than lawyer and judge. No twinkle in the eye, no glint in her smile. He waited for her to do something to acknowledge their past, but Cynthia gave him nothing but a bland smile.

'Edward.' She drew herself up straighter. 'I want to encourage your rehabilitation. I really do. If that means beginning to practice law again, and it happens to be in our court, fine. We will give you every aid we can offer.'

He waited for the *but,* which he knew was coming.

'But this isn't a therapy session, Edward. It's a murder trial. And your own sister. We all know only a fool represents himself. Is it any wiser to represent a family member?'

'No. It's idiotic. I can't believe I'm doing it.'

Cynthia sighed, a sound of relief. 'Good. I was afraid . . . well, it's between you and your sister. But it's in our court. We cannot have you make a spectacle, an appeal to sympathy, or anything outside the law.'

'When have you ever known me to do that?'

It was a deliberate gibe, another attempt to have her acknowledge that they had – one time, one show only, tonight on the big stage, folks – *once* made quite a spectacle together in a courtroom in this building. Cynthia looked down, cleared her throat, then raised her eyes to him again. Her eyes were dark brown, luminous. That one night they had shone a warm light on him strong enough to make him reach for her. But they were cold obsidian now.

'You were a very good trial lawyer, Edward. You've been gone for a while, but that's between you and your client. What I want to emphasize today is the decorum of our court. The court will not allow you to disrupt that. You understand?'

'I do. If that's what you wanted to tell me, it wasn't necessary. I will not make a circus of this case. The D.A.'s office has done that, with this ridiculous capital murder charge. My only interest is in defending my sister. Since I don't intend to keep practicing after this, I'm not concerned with furthering my career with publicity from this trial. All right?'

He had spoken rather harshly. Cynthia stared back as if deciding whether to respond in kind.

But she said mildly, 'Good. We have an understanding.'

'Yes, Your Honor. Is that it?'

She nodded. He rose and walked to the door, when the judge quietly said his name. She twirled her finger, a sign he took to mean to close the door, so he did and stood waiting.

'I'm sorry for what happened to you, Edward,' Cynthia said.

'Good. I didn't know. I never heard from you.'

'It would have been very difficult to get in touch with you.'

'I had a pretty fixed address there for a while. I would have been easy to find.'

'That's not what I mean. It would have been a bad idea to try to reach you, for both of us.'

He'd been in prison, so Edward didn't think his situation could have been worsened. Cynthia meant protecting her own ass, which he'd understood all along. While he'd been going through the legal system, both ends of it, and being shat out the other side, she'd gone on improving her credentials as a trial prosecutor, culminating in being appointed a judge. Yes, it would have been a very bad idea for Cynthia to have any contact with a jailbird former lawyer. Edward couldn't have said how he might have pictured this meeting, but it wasn't like this, with Cynthia's cold refusal to acknowledge there had ever been anything between them.

'I did my best for you, Edward. Believe it or not. The office wanted to come down much harder on you than we did. Much. I talked them out of that.'

'Thanks.'

He stood waiting for some more personal connection.

131

'But this is what I wanted to make clear. We will not speak of this again. Nothing about – your old case – must come up during this trial. And if you took this case because you think I will grant you some special favors in trial—'

'I don't.'

She nodded. 'Good. We needed to be clear on that. I will treat you as I would any other lawyer.'

'That's all I expect.'

'Good. Then let me add one thing and we will not speak of it again.'

'I am grateful to you, Edward. But that cannot be expressed in trial. You understand?'

'Of course.'

'But I am grateful. I pray for forgiveness every day.'

'Not to me.' Almost instantly he regretted the remark, but since she wasn't going to be doing him any favors anyway, it didn't matter. 'I understand, Your Honor,' he added quickly. 'You won't need to remind me. Thank you.'

Cynthia nodded, a dismissal. Had she looked outraged there for a second? Remorseful, angry, any human emotion? If she had, she had suppressed it so quickly he hadn't been able to see it. Edward went out quickly, not looking back.

Out in the courtroom Edward saw a lawyer he used to know. He waited while the man finished talking to his client, one of the prisoners in coveralls sitting in the jury box.

'Hey, Ed,' the other lawyer said as he stood up from his conversation. 'You're back?'

'Apparently.'

132

Gene was tall, already a little stooped even though he was barely into his forties. It made his conversations seem intimate, as he bent toward anyone with whom he was speaking. 'Didn't you have a problem with the bar?' he asked confidentially.

'Yeah. But we patched things up. Can I talk to you for a minute?'

'Sure.' Gene stood listening.

'I haven't seen Cynthia as a judge. What's she like?'

Gene looked around. Even though the bench remained empty he gathered up his briefcase and strode toward the doors with a head gesture at Edward.

Out in the hall Gene said, 'You remember what she was like as a prosecutor?'

Edward nodded, 'Always pushing, always pressing up against the line.'

'Yeah. Well, she won't tolerate that stuff now. Judge Cynthia would slap the shit out of her old self. And don't ever call her anything except Judge or Your Honor. Don't try to pretend the two of you ever knew each other on the other side. She will hurt you if you try.'

'Black robe fever.'

'One of the most virulent cases I've ever seen. No chance of recovery. I can't imagine her home life. Her husband must have to ask permission to approach the bench.'

Edward said, 'Thanks, man.'

Gene nodded. He still stood there, as if he hadn't delivered the punchline yet. So Edward said, 'Anything else?'

'I used to think she bent the rules so hard because she was that tough. Now I'm not sure she ever knew the rules. But she'll rule like she wrote the treatise on evidence. Don't question her. You know how it is. The ones who are shakiest on their knowledge . . .'

Edward nodded. Judges who weren't sure of the law came in two categories, the ones who were willing to listen, read opinions offered by the lawyers and even look up the rules. Cynthia was the worst kind, the one who would stand by her ruling, even if you could show her without doubt that it was wrong. It was painful to practice in front of such a judge. It could be dangerous.

But of all the lawyers in the building, Edward was the one with least to fear of being held in contempt and threatened with jail time.

Edward walked away thoughtfully. In Texas, we don't choose judges at all. Voters make random selections on ballots, knowing nothing about the choices except their parties and genders. Not their experience, age, race. They pick judges without knowing what they look like, or whether they got out of law school five years ago or thirty; where they ranked in school, their legal experience, whether they'd actually tried cases or just sat in an office. So we get the judges we deserve: some capable, some not, some idiots. It is not a system designed to select Learned Hand or Oliver Wendell Holmes to preside over our trials. Good lawyers avoid the whole electoral process, because they have thriving practices they don't want to jeopardize by putting their fates in the hands of ignorant voters. So we end up with judges who are among those who decided to run, who might have the experience or might not, might have wisdom but most probably do not. There's no wisdom test to get on the ballot.

Then they put on the robe. Several things can happen to them after that. Some grow on the job, becoming at least experienced, if not wise. Others stop learning at all at that point, having already reached the pinnacle of the profession, in their minds. They certainly stop learning humility. Now Edward knew the worst kind would be presiding over his sister's trial.

Edward had an appointment to see his father. Yes, an appointment. 4:30 in the afternoon, at the end of the day when Dad would be done with his patients, just the two of them to talk, as if they might have something to say ladies shouldn't hear.

His father's consulting offices were in a high-rise on the edge of the medical center, on the twelfth floor. There had probably been a view when the building first went up, but now just showed other similar buildings. Dr Hall was sitting behind his desk wearing a white shirt and a loosened tie. He had his glasses in his hand, gesturing, talking rather rapidly, so he didn't see his son for a moment. There was someone else there in the visitor's club chair, a man in uniform, whose long neck looked very stiff from behind.

Dr Hall noticed Edward and stood up, causing his visitor to stand too.

'John, this is my son Edward. I've asked him to join us.'

It was news to Edward, that he'd be joining anyone other than his father. 'Hello, son. This is John Dusin. A good friend.'

John Dusin was also a cop, Edward saw when he turned, a high-ranking one. Edward had never learned to read all the insignia on uniforms, but took a guess.

'Hello, Captain.'

'John is fine,' the man said, gripping Edward's hand firmly. He had a tanned, barely lined face composed of strong straight lines and he gave Edward a few seconds' extra scrutiny, as if running through Wanted posters in his mind.

'I asked John to join us,' Dr Hall said, gesturing them into chairs, 'to help us figure out what to do about Amy. John was telling me the investigation isn't even ongoing anymore.'

'I was trying to explain to your father,' the man began. Edward now saw he was in some distress. His eyes made a silent plea to the lawyer son. 'Once we've arrested a suspect, it's no longer a police case. We hand over everything we've got to the D.A.'s office and stop working the case. Like on "Law and Order,"' he added helpfully, turning back to Dr Hall.

Who looked very displeased. 'I just don't understand that. There's still been a crime committed, hasn't there? Isn't it still your department's job to solve it?'

'When we arrest a suspect we feel we have solved it. Now, the D.A.s can keep investigating, they've got investigators on staff.'

'But can't you order your men to continue looking into the case?'

136

'That's not the way it works,' Edward said, feeling himself in the odd position of helping out a police officer. 'Each case gets only one solution, at least from the police department's point of view. They have a lot of cases, they have to move on. It's a court case now, Dad, not a police one. As Captain Dusin says, the D.A.'s office can investigate further, especially if we give them some good reason to do so. And, of course, we've got our own private investigator working for the defense too. In court, police officers' solutions sometimes turn out to be wrong.'

He couldn't help taking that last shot and he felt the officer give him a sidelong look.

But the cop said, 'That's right. And I sincerely hope this is one of those times, Dr Hall.' He stood. 'Now if you don't mind, I've got to get going. I'm still on duty; this was just my break time.'

'Thanks for coming, John. I appreciate it.' But Dr Hall's voice was flat, and he didn't stand up, making it clear that a departing handshake wasn't in order. The police officer seemed to flee gratefully, closing the office door behind him.

'I saved that man's mother's life,' Dr Hall said. 'And do you know why? Because I did further tests and kept looking into her case, after another doctor had made a diagnosis that turned out to be disastrously wrong. You see? Further investigation saved her life. I thought John would understand that.'

'Did you hear anything he and I just said? It's not a police case anymore. It's passed into another bureaucracy. He no longer has any authority over it.'

137

'All right. Then next time I'll have the District Attorney here. I'm sure I've done one of his friends or family members a favor.'

'*Her. Her* family.' Edward was still on his feet, staring at his father. He found this act hard to believe, his father turning into the Godfather, trying to reach his tentacles into the system. 'And it wouldn't work. You'd get yourself into trouble just by trying.'

'Of course it works that way.' Dr Hall still hadn't looked up at his son. His eyes scoured the desktop. 'I've worked in this city for nearly forty years. I've helped a lot of people. Many of them influential now, and when I finally ask for one little thing in return—'

'Little? Dad? Helping someone go free after committing a murder isn't a little thing. You know that. Talk sensibly, please.'

'"Committing?" So now you think she did it too? Your own sister? You think she killed her husband?'

'It doesn't matter what I think. From their point of view that's what they think you're asking, to let her out from under a capital murder charge because they owe you a favor. It's not going to work that way, Dad.'

'I'm not asking that. I'm just asking them to look into it further, because they've obviously got it wrong so far. I'm just asking them to make the system work for Amy. I've got to do something, don't I?'

For the first time, Edward saw his father's distress and that he did understand. He just didn't like what he understood and he felt helpless. A feeling Dr Hall would hate, because he was the closest thing to a god on this earth. He had 'wrested life back from death many times,' as he'd said. His trembling hands showed his agony at not being able to do it again for his own daughter.

Edward sat down. 'You can,' he said gently. 'You can help. Everybody can. Cops came up with the answer they did because they didn't know anybody else involved. Amy's just a suspect to them. They've investigated a lot of murders and they know the spouse or some other family member is always a good bet. Amy is just a peg they fit into a slot. Partly that's because this murder looks very personal. So suggest some possibilities to me, Dad. You knew Paul his whole adult life. First he worked for you, then he was your son-in-law. Tell me why someone would want to kill him.'

Dr Hall shook his head. 'He could be abrasive. He could be abrupt. I saw that with the staff. But to the point of making someone want to kill him? No. And I don't know anything about his personal life since he and Amy separated. I'd barely seen him. Do you think he got involved in something unsavory? Lots of men go crazy when they're getting divorced. I've seen it many times.'

Edward began. 'There are three reasons to commit murder, Dad. Know what they are? I had another prosecutor who taught me this.'

'Hate?'

'Yes. On the list. "I hate this bastard, he's fucked me over one too many times, this bitch doesn't deserve to live, this asshole cut me off in traffic."

That's one. Maybe not the first, but one. Next is expediency.' Edward didn't wait for his father to guess. '"I want this guy's money, if I kill him I can have his job, his wife, his car." Not personal, just someone in your way. And the third, and possibly most popular?'

His father shook his head, unwilling to play this game with him.

'Love. Maybe the number one reason people are in prison for murder. If I can't have you—'

'Nobody will.' Now his father did nod along.

'Yes,' Edward said. 'If it's not the significant other it's children. "I can't make it in this world, but I can't leave you behind to suffer my absence, so I'm going to drown all four of you in the bathtub before I go." And the rest of us are left behind wondering what's wrong with these crazy fucks. So, Dad, given that, and everything you know. Who killed Paul?'

'I have no idea.'

Edward sat and looked at his father. His father stared back at him gravely, with his bushy gray eyebrows, his prominent forehead, his slightly bulging blue eyes. He looked sincere as Robert Frost, and maybe as deep. Edward wondered, was this the first time he'd ever known his father was lying to him?

'Dad? Seriously? If you don't have any idea, who does?'

'I think it was a stranger,' his father said.

'Who came in to . . .?'

'Sell him drugs, maybe, and decided to rob him instead. Didn't the autopsy show cocaine in his system?'

'A drug dealer wouldn't want to kill a good customer for a one-time score.'

Edward changed tactics. 'This award he'd just won. What was it for?'

'He'd had some success in a clinical trial for a new kind of cancer treatment. Or at least a variation on a treatment. Paul promoted it like it was the next to last step to the universal cure everyone's looking for.'

'Was it?'

Dr Hall said with some disgust, 'Paul was better at talking up his projects than he was at the research itself. I read his findings. It wasn't much of a breakthrough and I don't even know that he could reproduce the result.'

Edward was watching his father curiously. 'How do you know so much about it?'

'It was research we started together, actually. Two or three years ago, before he and Amy separated. I decided it was a dead end, but Paul went off on his own and kept at it.'

'Successfully, apparently.'

Dr Hall looked at him with his features turning sardonic, a look familiar to his son.

'One award from a local medical society doesn't make one Jonas Salk. The award was more encouragement, I'd say. "Keep at it," that sort of thing.'

Things kept shifting for Edward. It had all been personal a few minutes ago, trying to think about Paul the person. Now it had turned again into a case, like so many he'd worked on over the years. The dead man had made a success of research he'd taken from this man across the desk. Had his father resented that? It was a motive. Hate, as his father had guessed first, also maybe expediency. If Paul died, could Dr Hall take back the project, become the doctor who cured cancer?

'What?' his father said.

'Nothing. Was he working with anyone else after he left you?'

Dr Hall shrugged. 'He had a team, I think. I'll get you their names.'

The murder's happening on the night of the awards dinner seemed to suggest professional jealousy as a motive. Could his father have gone to argue with his estranged son-in-law and former colleague, then gotten mad enough to shoot him?

Meeting with his father had been unsettling. He couldn't get Dr Hall to admit to understanding the situation and Edward had felt no connection coming back the other way. No confidence in him, no approval.

He drove around the city, something he used to fantasize about when he was in prison. He had only spent two years in confinement, but it had felt like the way the rest of his life would be. The system – the criminal justice system he knew so well – could just pluck him out of his life and give people with no more moral superiority than he, the equivalent of high school principals, the power to put him behind a locked door and tell him he couldn't come out again until they decided. Like a three-year-old placed in time out, but a time out with iron bars and ugly institutional smells, occasionally interrupted by screams of the obviously insane. It had been beyond horrible, it had been humiliating too, that he had fucked up so badly that he gave these people the power to take over his life and tell him what to do every minute of every day. Edward had spent hours on his bunk, sitting up, knees raised, head down between them, hands covering his ears – basically in an upright fetal position – trying to imagine his way out of there. Picturing neighborhoods in Houston, which way he would turn to get to a randomly chosen destination. What the hamburger had tasted like at One's-A-Meal, how the music soared off the walls at Rockefeller's. Some rare people apparently had the ability to deny the prison system authority over their souls, imagining themselves away, but Edward couldn't do it. The wall close to his arm was too real, insisting its way into his consciousness even while his imagination worked its hardest.

So now that he was out he drove for real, wanting to revel in living the fantasy that had been most precious to him. But he kept feeling that wall close beside him, those bars behind his eyelids.

Edward found himself in a familiar neighborhood before he knew it was his destination. He parked in front of the little white frame house with the yellow trim, trying to picture it as home. Trying to imagine this as a routine homecoming at the end of an ordinary day. *Honey, I'm home!* Couldn't quite bring it off. He knocked then opened the door, as Linda had always told him he should do.

Linda was coming into the living room from the kitchen, walking quickly. When she caught

143

sight of him her pace slowed. Her face lit up. Her eyes literally glowed, her cheeks rose and expanded, she even colored a little.

Edward went to meet her and they kissed. He held her longer than she expected. Her lips were soft and yielding, a little cool. After a moment she drew back.

'What brought that on?'

He smiled in turn. 'Love, I'd say.' Her blush deepened. Edward widened his eyes and said, 'Say, I've got an idea.'

'What?' Both anticipation and suspicion in her voice.

'How'd you like to meet my family this weekend?'

The suspicious part of her reaction overtook her face. 'Why? What's changed your mind?'

He shrugged. She was still in his arms, so her arms moved up and down atop his.

Edward said, 'I've been telling you how they are. Now I'd like your opinion.'

'Really?'

He sensed her beginning of regret. *Be careful what you wish for.* 'I could cancel.'

'No. We're going. But I have no idea what to wear.'

In the event, Linda looked both lovely and not fussed over. She wore a simple green dress that displayed her figure without flaunting it and a thin silver necklace, with understated earrings.

In his parents' living room was the family tableau he'd expected; his mother and Amy on the white sofa facing them across the room, Dr Hall at an angle to them on the club chair, all

144

with teacups in their hands like American actors in a bad play trying to appear British. Then the cups clattered down as Dr Hall stood – a lady had just entered the room – and Edward said, 'Mom, Dad, Amy, this is Linda.'

'Edward's secret love,' Dr Hall said heartily, talking over his wife. 'It's a pleasure to meet you, young lady. Miss—?'

'Benson, Dr Hall. But Linda is fine. Hello, Mrs Hall.'

'Hello, my dear. Come sit by me. This is such a delight.'

Linda sat beside Mrs Hall, smiling demurely as she turned down an offer of refreshment. Amy sat on her other side. Edward took his seat to the side; offstage, as he thought of it.

Mrs Hall's gaze looked kindly as she asked Linda, 'And how did you two meet?'

'I'm a paralegal. We met in the course of our jobs. I'd met Edward at our office and then he came to a reception we had when we moved to larger offices. That's when we started talking.'

Dr Hall held out to Linda a silver plate holding tiny cookies. She took one, saying, 'Thank you, Dr Hall.'

'Marshall, remember?'

'I'll try. It's just that you're so distinguished.'

She'd said the secret word, without Edward even prepping her.

Mrs Hall said, 'Don't you look nice, Linda. So you and Edward started dating recently? Since he got out?'

'Yes, it's been a year,' Amy said. 'A secret romance.'

Mrs Hall held Linda's attention. 'I hope I'm not prying too much—'

'No, just enough.'

'Hush, Edward. It can be a trial having a son who thinks he's witty.'

'I know what you mean.' Linda kept smiling and the gentle interrogation continued.

When they left, Amy followed them out onto the porch, closing the door.

'Well, that wasn't too bad,' she announced brightly.

'The clan on its best behavior,' Edward agreed.

Linda looked back and forth between them.

'You two are so jumpy. They're perfectly nice people. What were you afraid might happen?'

Amy and her brother exchanged looks and neither had an answer for her.

Later, at home, having relieved themselves of their clothing, Edward said, 'Go ahead, let me have it: "You were wrong, they're lovely people" or "Oh my God, you didn't half warn me."'

Linda propped herself up on her elbow. 'No, I could see why you were worried. I mean, your mother, she's very sweet and all—'

'Sweet?'

'Yes. She is. But I felt a little like she suspected I was an enemy spy and was trying to get information out of me, testing my disguise at the same time.

'But at the same time she really wanted to know about me, because she cares about you so much, Edward. She does, you know.'

He took her in his arms again and stared at her

in slight wonderment. Edward didn't remember this happening to him before, wanting this much to be with a woman after having her. He almost said it then, he was about to, when Linda rolled over and asked, 'What are we going to do for dinner?'

Later, over pizza, she saw him returning to his thoughts and asked, 'What's the matter?'

He laughed. She saw the humor in it too. Linda put her arms around him and made a soothing sound like she would for a baby.

'It's just Sunday night,' she whispered. 'It makes everything seem overwhelming. In the morning you get up and put one foot in front of the other and you can do whatever you have to do. You know you can.'

And she was right. The next day, in the daylight, he could handle whatever he had to, even when the prosecutor dropped the bomb on him.

Ten

'We just got this,' David Galindo said, tossing a DVD onto the desk in front of Edward. 'Came in the mail, of all things. No return address.'

'Don't slay me with suspense, David. What is it?'

The prosecutor smiled. 'Why don't we watch it together?'

He walked Edward down the hall to a conference room. Around them Edward felt the thrum of people going about their jobs. There was laughter from one office doorway they passed, two women and a man chatting. Another office door was closed and someone could easily have been crying behind it. Edward remembered it all. It was an office with all the intrigues and romances inherent in an environment with four hundred or more mostly young people. But here they worked actively to send people to prison, in between the flirting and pushing upward.

David had a television with an attached DVD player set up in the conference room. David put the DVD into the player, dropped his lanky frame into a chair and picked up the control, pressing play.

It was Paul. The image of his brother-in-law alive was startling. Edward had gotten so used to Paul being in the past tense. The camera was focused fairly tightly on Paul, so it was hard to

148

see much background. Edward was fixed on Paul's face, anyway. Paul looked rather distinguished, his receding hairline making his bony forehead look impressively intelligent.

'My name is Dr Paul Shilling. Today is March fourteenth. Almost the Ides.'

Yes, Paul was one of those who used his title as if it were a given name. But Edward hung on his words.

'I am making this recording because I'm uneasy. It's probably nothing, and I'll just laugh and destroy this in a few months. But right now, I think it's important to say that, if I am found dead, it will be my wife, Dr Amy Shilling, who murdered me.'

Paul stared into the camera as if willing belief into his listeners.

'Amy and I have been separated for some time, going through a divorce. Just lately we've been seeing each other again to talk about those issues. Amy seems to be under the delusion she and I are going to get back together, romantically. I've tried to dampen down those expectations without being rude or mean, but that's getting harder to do. Amy wants to get – amorous. The thought makes me . . .' Paul shook his head. 'Let's just say we have completely, uh, conflicting views on that. I just want to get divorced. I just want to get on with my life. I am afraid that very soon I'm going to have to make this absolutely clear to Amy, and when I do, well, she's subject to fits of anger. More than anger, really. She's attacked me physically in the past. And this is going to be humiliating for her. She's attached such

149

importance to being a doctor's wife – *my* wife, to put it, um – that I don't know how she'll react. Especially if she fin— especially if she thinks of me with another woman. I'm afraid that might push her over the edge.

'So I thought it would be prudent to make this record and give it to a friend, who will mail it to police if I'm murdered. As I said, I'm probably being melodramatic or overly – what's the word? – but at any rate, I wanted to do this. Thank you.'

Then Paul just sat there. After several seconds he directed his stare out of camera range, made an impatient hand gesture and the screen went black.

David got up and turned on the break room lights. Edward hadn't moved from where he'd been standing.

After a moment he said, 'What utter horseshit.'

David's eyebrows lifted.

Edward continued. 'How many murders have you tried, David?'

David shrugged. 'A few.'

'A lot, I think. How many has this office tried? And have you ever had one where the victim told you who killed him?'

'I think I've heard of a couple.'

'Yeah, on TV. "Message from the Grave"? What bullshit.'

'How?'

Edward was pacing now. 'How do I know? I'm no IT guy. Have you had this thing checked? Could it have been spliced together? Or just made up entirely? If John Wayne can be making new

TV commercials, some bright kid could have cobbled up something looking like Paul accusing Amy. Anyway, you'll never get it into evidence.'

David shrugged again. 'Maybe, maybe not. Want to have a pretrial hearing on it?'

Edward absolutely did not. Let this thing go public? No thanks. Forget about trying to pick an impartial jury after that. Every TV station in town – hell, several national television shows – would want to air this footage. **Dead Man Accuses Estranged Wife**. They'd eat it up.

So Edward ignored the question and blustered on.

'Anyway, it's just ridiculous. Who can ever predict his own murder and who the murderer will be?'

'Well, when you leave here I might tell people to keep an eye out for you if something happens to me.'

'Ha ha. Seriously, David, this is ridiculous. What you need to look for is where this came from. This is from someone trying to bury Amy because they don't want any suspicion on themselves.'

'I don't—'

'If it was legitimate, why wouldn't the person who had it bring it to you in person? Just appear at the front desk and say, "I've got some evidence in a murder prosecution your office has going on." Why the secrecy?'

'A lot of people don't want to get involved, you know that.' David glanced at the TV screen as if he wanted to look at the DVD again from the perspective Edward was suggesting.

'Yes, a lot of inadvertent witnesses to a crime

don't want to come forward, for fear of retaliation or whatever, but this came from someone Paul supposedly trusted enough to give them this special assignment. This trust. "Turn this over to police if I'm found dead." Why wouldn't the person do just that? And I mean the day after the murder was on the front page. If this came from someone who actually cared about Paul, he would have shown up with this in hand, so he could answer questions about what else Paul was thinking and the other things that made him suspicious. Instead, they want to hide in the dark while making sure you keep the spotlight trained on Amy. It stinks, David. It stinks like day-old skunk shit.'

Edward could see David thinking. Edward was actually pretty impressed with himself, with his rapid responses to this devastating evidence. He was spinning out theories like a madman, drawing the prosecutor farther and farther from the evidence itself.

No, not like a madman. Like a lawyer.

David seemed to have the same thought himself. He looked at Edward with a little smile and said, 'You're pretty good, old pal.'

'Because you know I'm right.'

David only shrugged.

Edward stepped closer to him, pointing at the television screen. 'Do not release that to the press,' he said carefully and quietly.

David shook his head. 'I won't.'

Edward felt a rush of relief. This DVD was still horribly dangerous to Amy, but there was a good chance Edward could keep it out of evidence at trial. It was, after all, hearsay, and denied him

152

his right to cross-examine a witness, Amy's constitutional right to confront her accuser. You can't
question the dead.

Well, you can, but it's unproductive.

'Thank you,' he said. 'That'll give us both time
to investigate this. You have a copy for me?'

'Back in my office.'

'And if you change your mind about releasing
it you'll let me know first, so I can try to talk
you out of it or we can go to the judge?'

'Sure, Edward.'

'Thank you.' Edward turned and started walking
out. When he'd reached the doorway David cleared
his throat and Edward felt a chill.

'Unless I'm ordered to release it,' the prosecutor
said.

'I have something for you to see,' Edward said
into his cell phone. By the time he got to Amy's
house she was there.

'What's happened, Edward?'

He just looked at her, and she saw it in his face:
something terrible.

'Come in, come in.'

'Thank you. Where's your DVD player?'

While turning on Amy's television a minute
later, Edward suddenly realized how mean this
was. On his already fragile sister, he was about
to spring the sight of her dead husband, suddenly
alive again and accusing her of ushering him
across the veil. Prim little Amy, sitting on the
couch with her knees together and hands folded.
She looked so innocent, like a little girl waiting
for a surprise she'd been promised. Amy was

about to be hurt badly, again, and he was the one doing it. But he wanted very much to see her reaction the first time she saw this, before she could put up defenses.

'Come on,' she said.

'Amy, this is going to be bad. It's Paul. Just prepare yourself, OK?'

He pressed Play on the DVD player and sat beside her, putting his hand over hers, those hands of hers that were twisted as tightly together as barbed wire.

Almost as soon as the DVD started, he realized he'd made another mistake, tactically, by sitting beside his sister. He couldn't see her face. But he felt her reactions through her hands. They loosened when she saw Paul on the screen, alive again, looking at her. From the side, Edward saw his sister smile a little. When Paul began his accusation of her, Amy's hands fell open completely, surprise making her slack. A minute later she leaned forward, concentrating on her late husband as he explained why she would want to murder him. Glancing aside, Edward saw studiousness and intense curiosity in the curve of her back.

Released from her hands, Edward stood up and moved to the side, to where he could see Amy's whole face for the rest of the video. He'd seen the DVD already and he had weeks to study it. Only these few moments allowed him to see his sister's first reaction to it.

Amy stared at the screen thoughtfully now, without apparent emotion. When the DVD came to the most hurtful part of Paul's statement, that his wife wanted them to be 'amorous' again and the thought appeared to make him shudder, Amy didn't flinch. She just watched the conclusion of Paul's performance with apparent nostalgic affection.

'So I thought it would be prudent to make this record and give it to a friend, who will mail it to police if I'm murdered. As I said, I'm probably being melodramatic or overly – what's the word? – but at any rate, I wanted to do this. Thank you.'

Amy nodded when her husband stumbled over the one lost word. She looked up at her brother calmly.

'Where'd this come from?'

'We don't know. Someone mailed it to the D.A.'s office.'

'Mailed it? They didn't bring it in person?' Amy sat back and said, 'Huh.'

'Well?'

'Well what?' she asked, with an actual look of bafflement.

'What about this, Amy? Is it true? Why would Paul have made this? Were you scaring him?'

She was scaring her brother a little, reacting so calmly, with nerves as calm as a professional killer's.

She gave an exasperated expulsion of breath. 'Please. Paul afraid of me? Don't be ridiculous. Attacked him? Can you see that? Me coming at him, with my big claws out?' Amy made her hands into claws for a mocking moment, and he had to admit it looked silly, like a little girl pretending to be a cat. She was at least half a foot shorter than her dead husband and slight by comparison. Edward had never known her to get enraged to the point of violence, not even throwing a cup.

'Then why would he do this?'

'He's drunk,' she said.

'What?'

She waved a hand at the screen as if it were obvious. 'On the DVD. He's drunk on his ass.'

Edward turned to the blank screen. 'I don't think—'

'You have to know Paul really well to be able to see it. He was a very accomplished drinker. You could tell when he'd start feeling it because he got more precise. His language got very careful, even eloquent. Feed him enough scotch and he'd turn into Winston Churchill.'

'Amy, I didn't see any sign of that.'

'Because you didn't know him that well. I've seen it a lot. Like when he said, "I jusht want to get divorced." Did you hear that little slur? We'll watch it again and I'll show you. And then at the end, where he couldn't think of the word he wanted? He was about to pass out, trust me.'

Did he? Did Edward trust what his sister was telling him? How could someone react this coolly to being accused of murder?

'Would anybody else be able to recognize what you're telling me, that he was drunk? Anybody else who knew him well enough?'

'I don't know. Maybe one of his old friends from college or med school. Not Dad. He was always very careful around Mom and Dad.'

Edward shifted tacks. 'But what difference does that make, Amy? Answer my question. Is any of it true?'

'Such as that he still wanted a divorce? I don't know. Maybe he was just leading me on so I'd take it easier on him about the money and such. Maybe he just wanted another bounce with me out of nostalgia, or pride. I don't think so, but maybe. Obviously he was pretty good at hiding things from me. Maybe our little reconciliation would have run its course and we would have still gotten divorced anyway.'

Edward observed, 'You don't seem very upset.'

Amy shrugged. 'I've had a lot of time to think about it. Believe me, I've had my tearful nights, even screaming at him for being dead. But I've had time to move on from the marriage. When he first left I thought I'd die, it's true. I mean, die. I thought I would. But I didn't.' She looked up at her brother a little proudly. 'I got up every day and went about my business and carried on with my job. I even went on a couple of dates, Edward. You didn't know that, did you? I'm very discreet.' She laughed, a brassy sound. 'I saw that there were other possibilities in my life. I still loved Paul, yes, and if I could make it work with him I wanted to. But I wasn't suicidal. Certainly not homicidal.'

It was a great performance, but she'd had time to practice it. He had to admit her reaction wasn't what he'd expected. Paul's accusation hadn't knocked the legs out from under her at all.

As if to demonstrate her poise, Amy stood up. She walked to the television and started the DVD again. This time they talked as they watched it, like the DVD commentary to a TV show. Amy pointed out critically the places where Paul

157

seemed to slur a word slightly. Under her tutelage, Edward began to hear it too.

But that didn't make what Paul was saying lies. *In vino veritas*, as the saying went. Or as James McMurtry put it in a song, 'Whiskey don't make liars, it just makes fools.'

'What about this?' Edward dared to ask this second time around. 'That you wanted to get "amorous" and it almost makes Paul shudder?'

'Oh, please.' Amy actually laughed. 'He wanted it more than I did. That was always true. He came on to me first, Edward. Not subtly, either. One time we were talking, right here, he was sitting next to me at the table, going over our portfolio, of all things, when he leaned over and kissed me and, almost immediately, grabbed my – my breast. I was startled, to say the least. At first I thought it was just, you know, wanting to bag the one that got away.'

'Did you say "bag"?'

'Shut up. You know I'm not a trashmouth like you.' She laughed again. Edward smirked back at her. It was amazing how they could fall that quickly back into their childhood patterns, but the grooves were laid long and deep.

'Anyway, that lingering attraction was completely mutual,' Amy finished.

'Did you know he was seeing other women?'

'My doctor husband going out with other women in the medical community, in which I spend my every working day? No, Edward, that was a complete mystery to me . . . Of course I knew it. He didn't make any secret of it. He wanted to show me how attractive other women found him.'

'Maybe he just wanted the other women.'

Amy looked at him frankly. 'Maybe.'

Which made Edward wonder if his sister had had other outlets herself for those urges. She said she'd had 'dates'. How had they ended? These questions weren't prurient. They were lawyerly. A woman with other men on the side was less likely to get murderous over her husband's having other lovers – at least, theoretically. Edward didn't like it, but he was going to have to question his sister more closely about her personal life. Maybe even have one of her lovers testify at trial, to show the jury she had other irons in the fire, so to speak.

She interrupted his thoughts. 'Here's the important question, Edward. Who's Paul talking to?'

He frowned. 'The future? Police?'

'No.' Amy shook her head impatiently. 'Who's holding the camera? Who's he making that little gesture to at the end to turn it off?'

Edward looked at her with one eyebrow lifted. His sister asked a good question.

Before he left, he told Amy he wanted her to see a psychiatrist.

'You think I have mental health issues?' she asked, cocking her head.

Possibly, he thought. 'Not at all. I want to be able to show the prosecutor, and maybe eventually a jury, that you don't. I want you to have a psychological evaluation. Something objective, on paper, which I can use if I need it.'

She stared at him, looking for his real motive. He understood her suspicion.

Amy asked slowly, 'What if it shows something – that doesn't benefit us?'

'Then we keep it to ourselves. It will be confidential.'

'But then at least you'd know,' Amy concluded, looking him in the eye.

She was so damned smart.

By the end of summer, trial was drawing close. Edward still worked at his day job, but he was spending more and more time on the case. More time with the 'defense team,' Mike and Amy. Those two treated each other like colleagues, not friends, speaking very carefully and politely when the other was present.

In early September they had a court date, a vitally important one, over the DVD, Paul's recording. Edward had filed a motion to suppress that evidence, which brought him back before Judge Cynthia. This time right up at the bench in front of her, with David Galindo close by his side.

'Your Honor, could we have this hearing in chambers?' Edward asked quietly. Behind him, the courtroom was half full of negotiating lawyers and anxious defendants and their families. Maybe even a newspaper reporter, for all Edward knew.

'Why?' the judge asked. The prosecutor stood silent, taking no position.

'The nature of the evidence is so prejudicial, if it got out we wouldn't be able to pick an impartial jury in this county,' Edward said. He looked for anything in Cynthia's expression that said she remembered him as anything more than a lawyer who went wrong and couldn't find it. In spite of her early warning that she'd do nothing

160

to help him, he held out hope for at least a subtle influence on her.

'Why don't you just make a proffer to me of what the evidence is? Can you two agree on that? Is there any reason I actually have to see it?'

Edward and David turned to each other, lifted their eyebrows, shrugged, and nodded.

'Sure,' the prosecutor said. He nodded his head toward Edward.

Edward cleared his throat. 'It is a recording apparently showing the deceased, Your Honor, saying that if he is found murdered it will be my – the defendant in this case who killed him. He doesn't really give a reason—'

'Is whether he gives a reason or not relevant to the legal issue?' Cynthia questioned. 'No? Then let's get on with it. What's your objection to it, counselor?'

Edward began tentatively. 'Well, obviously it's hearsay, Judge. It denies my client her constitutional right to confront and cross-examine her accuser. There are a lot of questions I want to ask about why he would make this recording, questions that would go to his credibility, but I can't.'

Edward's voice got stronger as he talked. Cynthia had put him in a difficult position, springing this hearing on him so suddenly. He had to be careful to make all his legal objections right now, for the record, or lose them for the trial and possible appeal. Preserving error, it was called. He wouldn't be allowed to argue something later that he wasn't telling the judge right now. So his mind raced ahead of his tongue, dodging one way and another, like a frantic student pulling books off shelves, hastily flipping through them, then tossing them aside.

'There's also a question of authenticity, Your Honor. I don't see how the prosecution can authenticate this recording when we don't know who recorded it, how and where it was filmed, or whether it's been altered in any way. Usually, of course, the prosecutor has a witness to say, "I took this video, it hasn't been changed, it looks like what I saw when I was taping it." There can't be such testimony in this case.'

'We can get a witness to say this is the deceased, this is what he looked and sounded like,' David said.

'But not to say this is how he looked on this occasion, which is crucial. It's hearsay, Your Honor, pure and simple.' Edward remembered what his lawyer acquaintance had told him about Judge Cynthia, that maybe she didn't know the law so well after all. 'It's an out of court statement offered for the truth of the matter asserted.'

'Yes, Mr Hall, we're all familiar with the definition of hearsay.'

'But there are very good reasons why it's not admissible in court, Your Honor. Cross-examination is all we have in court, Judge. When a witness makes a bare statement it may sound believable. It's only under questioning that it may become apparent that what he's saying isn't reliable at all. And this isn't just a witness making a statement about something he saw. It's him predicting the future. It's purest speculation. It wouldn't be admissible on that basis alone.'

He felt proud for remembering that word on the fly. 'Speculation.' That was a legal objection. It was a little absurd how quietly happy with himself that made him. The judge made sure he was finished, then with her expression still completely blank, turned to the prosecutor and lifted an eyebrow.

'To begin with, Your Honor, it's a dying declaration,' David Galindo began.

'No, it's not.'

'Please, counselor, I allowed you to make your argument without interruption, please give me the same courtesy.'

Edward wanted to interrupt him again to say that David had in fact interrupted him, but he could hear the childishness of that even before he said it. Instead he just rolled his eyes.

'It's a statement by the victim made in anticipation of his death,' David continued. 'Such dying declarations are specifically admissible as an exception to the hearsay rule. They are deemed reliable because no one knows this information better than the victim. We admit 911 calls from victims saying, "Someone's trying to break in and I think it's my ex-husband. He called earlier and threatened to kill me." As for the defense's other objections, we can produce any number of witnesses to say the person on this DVD is Paul Shilling, the victim. I also anticipate having expert testimony that this recording hasn't been altered from the time it was made.'

'Do you know when it was made?' Cynthia asked quietly. Edward was grateful for her question. It wasn't exactly pertinent, but he didn't mind if the judge focused on the wrong thing, as long as she ruled in his favor. This could be the whole trial in miniature, right here.

'No, Your Honor,' the prosecutor admitted.

'Where?'

'We haven't been able to identify the background, Judge.'

'Who made the recording?'

'I'm afraid we don't know that, either, Your Honor. It was mailed to us anonymously.'

Judge Miles cocked her head, looking at the prosecutor as if he were her subordinate and she wasn't pleased with his performance.

'It's admissible as showing the relationship between the victim and the defendant prior to the crime, which is specifically admissible in a murder trial, Judge.'

Cynthia looked off into space thoughtfully. Edward realized something else. David Galindo was in front of this judge every day. He knew what she liked to hear, knew the arguments that made sense to her. It was one of the many advantages prosecutors enjoy over defense lawyers.

'Through competent evidence, yes,' Edward said hastily. 'Just because the subject matter is relevant doesn't mean you can introduce it through inadmissible evidence.' As Cynthia continued to hesitate, he added, rather lamely, 'And he's drunk on the recording, Judge.'

He was counting on how moralistic Cynthia seemed to have become. Cynthia wouldn't look back at him. She just stared into space. When the prosecutor started to speak again, she waved

164

him to silence. Finally her eyes snapped back down to the level of the lawyers.

'The court is going to reserve ruling at this time,' she said levelly. 'Both sides may submit case law. We will run this objection with the trial. The court will rule at the time the evidence is offered.'

Fuck, Edward thought. He had been prepared to win this or lose this today, forgetting the third option always available to a judge.

'Your Honor,' Edward said hesitantly, 'I was hoping to have a ruling on this so I would know how to prepare a defense . . .'

'Then I guess you need to prepare two ways, don't you, counselor? You are both excused. We will hear this matter again.'

'You were great,' his sister said afterwards. She had watched from the first row of the spectator seats. 'I was right about you.'

'We have a problem.'

'What?' Amy asked, genuinely perplexed. 'You were great, I saw you. You know she'll rule in your favor come trial.'

Come trial.

'I even think the judge may like you. Did you and she ever have a thing?'

Edward stared at his sister.

'This isn't middle school, Amy. Do you understand you're on trial for your life? Here's the problem. She didn't give me a ruling on whether she's going to allow that video into evidence. If she lets it in, we're done. You're in prison. Your ex-husband saying you're going to kill him, when

165

most people would say that's a reasonable hypothesis to begin with? We're as screwed as screwed can get. And Judge Cynthia, with whom you asked if I had "a thing," just said she's not going to make that ruling until we're deep into trial. So it's a little hard to prepare for it.'

Edward turned and looked back at the judge, who was now hearing two other lawyers at the bench. Cynthia must have felt his stare, but she wouldn't glance in his direction. Replaying some of what she'd said in his head, he realized she had become one of those judges who either referred to herself in the third person, as an institution – 'the court will rule' – or in the first person plural. 'We're very grateful to the voters that they chose to keep us in this position from which we try to serve them to the best of our ability.' She never seemed to break character. He'd bet she'd tell her clerks, 'Hold any calls to the court, we're going to the bathroom.'

This loftiness was always a bad sign in a judge, either of insecurity or an enormous ego, or both – a good judge, confident in her authority, doesn't have to keep reminding lawyers that she's the judge – but in this case it seemed particularly dangerous for Edward. Cynthia was so determined to show no sign of favoritism toward him that she might bend the other way.

Eleven

Tracking down other women Paul had dated wasn't hard. He hadn't been secretive about any of it, quite the contrary.

This one seemed quite a catch herself. Laura Martinelli was the director of a charitable foundation, with long legs, eyelashes and neck; she looked a questioner frankly in the eyes, with her own lustrous green ones. She sat behind the rather small desk in her relatively unadorned office – the money should go to the sick kids, not her – and answered every question Edward and Mike had in a low, deeper than average voice that made a man lean toward her.

'How many times did you and Paul go out?' Edward asked. It seemed like a safe, beginner sort of question, but Ms Martinelli turned it back on him, looking at him very directly but speculatively.

'How many dates did the late Paul and I have?' she repeated, sort of. 'I could ask you to define "date," of course, and all sorts of rigmarole, but let's just say five or six, depending on how carefully you define "going out." Sometimes we stayed in.'

Oh good, they were going to have badinage. Edward looked at her and Laura looked back, two honest stares of appraisal. She looked like a rich, beautiful woman at the peak of her appeal.

She was standing atop it, looking at him with ever so slight a smile in her eyes.

Mike interjected himself. 'Did you think it was leading somewhere?' he asked in his quiet, deep voice.

Laura Martinelli gave him a look that should have made him question whether he should have been put into 'special' classes in school.

Inclining her head, she said, 'Yes, I thought I was going to walk down the aisle on my daddy's arm and be happy ever after. Imagine my devastation when I found out I wasn't the only woman in his life. Now you want me to say, "If I couldn't have him no one would," right? Do you have a tape recorder?'

Mike looked like he was gathering his forces for a comeback, but Edward took over.

'So did you ever hear he might be reconciling with his wife? My sister?'

'I always assumed he would,' she said. Even though there was a desk between them, Edward could tell by her change in posture that she had just crossed her legs. He wished the desk weren't there.

'Really?' he said. 'So you weren't—?'

'In it for the long run?' She shrugged. Laura Martinelli blinked. She was doing Edward the honor of considering the question honestly. 'Maybe. If it had worked out that way.' She looked up and the moment of introspection was over. 'We were just getting to know each other and I wasn't sure I even liked him yet. I knew he still had feelings for his wife. They may have been intense, contradictory feelings, I don't know.

If he started talking about her I let him, but then he'd look at me and cut himself off. But it was clear their story wasn't over.' She shrugged again. 'Maybe that would have played itself out and he and I would have had something. But I would have been OK either way.'

I'll bet you would, Edward thought. Laura had a great stare, composed of appraisal, humor, a bit of sexual invitation, but an honesty that down-played that into *let's wait and see.*

'I'll bet you raise a lot of money for charity,' he said, starting to rise.

She just sat there, giving him a little smile that said, *You know I do.*

Laura Martinelli turned out to be the most forth-coming of the lot. The others would acknowledge being seen in public with Paul, because they couldn't deny that, but were more circumspect about what went on in private. No one wanted to claim membership in the conquest-of-the-month club. The most significant of them gave up very little, but what she did say added a telling detail.

Dr Louise Fisher was Paul's research partner. Not a full partner, even she acknowledged that – and there were a couple of associates who claimed she'd been little more than a note-taker – but they had worked closely together every day. She wasn't nearly the obvious catch that Laura Martinelli was, but the fact that Paul had wanted her at all said something about him, or the phase of his life he was enjoying. *No woman can resist me,* he would have been projecting by being seen having drinks or dinner with Dr Fisher.

According to her, that's all it was.

'I knew about the others,' she said. 'I had no intention of being one of them. He'd come to work sometimes with a sly grin and scratches on his neck, like he was in a rough relationship. It was disgusting. But, after he asked me enough times to have a drink after work, it seemed rude to keep saying I had to get home to my cat.'

Edward had met her in the lab, Dr Fisher actually wearing a white lab coat and walking along black-topped tables holding beakers and tubes. She laughed.

'One time he turned that on me and said he'd like to meet my cat.'

'And did he?' Edward asked as non-interrogatively as he could.

She turned and looked at him. She had nice eyes, he noticed for the first time, brown with an indication of depths.

'I think having sex with me might have been superfluous,' she answered the unspoken part of his question. 'He just wanted to be seen as desirable.'

Louise Fisher turned away. It was hard to tell much about her figure in the lab coat, but she walked well, and her hands appeared very competent as she made small adjustments among the lab objects.

He realized she hadn't answered his implied question, about whether she'd slept with her research partner. Maybe the answer she had given was good enough, but Edward needed to know more. Even as objectively as she spoke about his late brother-in-law, that might have been hard-won wisdom from after the fact of falling prey to him. And a woman seduced and abandoned had a classic motive for murder. Edward didn't know if she was a good suspect, he just wanted to have alternative suspects he could throw out for the jury. Show enough people who might have wanted Paul dead and Amy no longer looked so obviously guilty.

'I'm sorry, Dr Fisher, to be so insistent, but you know it's not prurient interest. So after one of these working dinners or drinks, did Paul ever invite you back to his place?'

'Oh no,' she said, turning back to him abruptly. 'No one ever went to Paul's. I don't even know where he was living. No one did.'

'No one?'

'No one I knew. He was secretive about it. A couple of times something would come in that we'd been waiting for, after he'd left for the day, and I'd call him and offer to courier it over to him. He always said no, either he'd come back in to pick up a copy or I could scan it and email it to him. It seemed odd because otherwise he was very secretive about anything involving our research. He wouldn't have liked some important report scanned into the system, but he kept an even tighter lid on where he lived.'

She was watching Edward with those brown eyes, which could turn very studious, as if looking to him for some insight into the man who had been his brother-in-law. Edward had nothing to offer.

A few minutes later he left without knowing for certain whether Paul and his research partner had ever been intimate. Only her cat knew.

Was it infidelity? Was Paul cheating on Amy? What if they were separated, didn't that make it OK? What if she thought they were *un*separating? Wasn't that a classic motive for murder?

But for whom? The wife or the girlfriend(s)?

'OK, so we can interview the other girlfriends, if we can track them down,' Mike said in the coffee shop in which they met to compare notes. 'And maybe they'll have the same story or maybe one of them will seem like a murderous psychopath. I'm not sure I'm qualified to spot that. You?'

Edward shook his head. 'I don't know what people are thinking. I don't even know what I think.' He was picturing his brother-in-law's life, his newfound freedom. Edward didn't know if Paul had really considered his marriage a prison. He'd been courting his ex-wife again . . . or had he just been leading her on while dating women he'd probably fantasized about banging for years?

But now he felt he'd gotten what he needed from Dr Fisher. She had more than one motive. If Paul went back to his wife and to his position in her family, presumably he'd also be taking his research back to the senior Dr Hall, Amy's father, which would represent a double betrayal of Dr Louise Fisher.

'Hey,' Mike interrupted his thoughts. 'I don't see you much around the apartment any more. You and Linda getting ready to make it legal?'

172

He laughed to make it seem not a real question, but his curiosity was obvious.

Edward said, 'Why should I start being law-abiding now?'

This time Mike's laugh was genuine.

Later, this time with Linda herself, who had worked for years in his own profession and had learned a lot, he mulled over the issues about who might be lying. Linda was a good reader of people, he had learned that.

'I started out taking Amy at face value, of course I believed her, but now I don't know anything. I'm trying to evaluate everybody else, what about her?

'What do you think?' Edward said, looking at her. They were sitting on the little porch in the dusk before dinner. The last light of the sun showed him Linda's face. Edward watched her, thinking how many changes he'd seen in her in the relatively brief time they'd been together.

'How would I know?'

'No, really, tell me what you think. Please.' He found he really wanted Linda's opinion on this, because she had only met Amy a few times, had never spent any time alone with her. In other words, she knew her only very little better than jurors would. So her impression was significant.

'How can I answer that?' Linda said. 'I've only seen her in social situations and only a couple of times. I never saw her with Paul, or with any other man. How can I possibly know what she was like in those situations? Was she a jealous lover with a terrible temper? It doesn't seem likely. Sweet little Amy. But we're all different in love.'

'But you must—'

'It seems much more likely to me,' Linda said, giving in, 'that she'd be the type to run away and cry her eyes out rather than grab a gun and blast him. That's all I can tell you.'

'Thanks,' Edward said, and he meant it. Linda had just given him an idea of at least two ways to go at trial. Get the jury to think they knew Amy – 'sweet little Amy,' in Linda's phrase – so they'd never be able to picture her as a wild-eyed jealous murderess. Or keep them from knowing Amy at all, so they still couldn't judge. If they didn't think they knew what she was like at all, they couldn't think her a murderer. Right?

Summer was almost over. The next time he went to court, it would be for trial.

1-800-672-4349

174

Twelve

'Ready,' the prosecutor announced easily, barely bothering to stand before slouching back down in his chair.

Edward stood more slowly and formally. 'The defense is ready, Your Honor.'

He didn't feel that way at all. Amy smiled up at him, putting her hand over his on the counsel table, the woman on trial for her life trying to reassure *him*. But her face also brimmed with confidence in him.

Edward felt none in himself. He stood there waiting for the first prospective juror to come filing in, hoping no one could see him trembling. The judge sat behind the bench, Amy to his right, the prosecutors to his left and, up there, stood the empty witness chair. In this chair they would interview the prospective jurors, eighty or ninety or more strangers, twelve of whom would become the jury that would decide Amy's fate. Edward just needed to find one. The one who would hold out against a guilty sentence, who would question everything the prosecution did. One prospective juror into whose eyes Edward could look and see that promise to be the renegade and, at the same time, fool the prosecutors into letting him or her remain on the jury.

The terror of trial. Edward had never felt it before, certainly not in this virulent a form. As a

175

prosecutor he'd always felt confident of winning. All the prospective jurors who walked into the courtroom would look at the defendant and immediately think, *I wonder what he did.* They'd deny thinking that, but they couldn't help it. The defendant always looked guilty, just by virtue of being the defendant. After all, a police investigation had put him there, hadn't it?

Edward hadn't felt the fear as a defense lawyer, either. In that position he had the opposite comfort. He was expected to lose. The defense always lost. On those rare occasions when a defendant was found not guilty, it was big news that shot around the courthouse quickly, that got reported in the press. A lawyer who could pull that off became a nine days' wonder of a celebrity. There was no pressure on a defense lawyer. If you lost it wasn't your fault, the odds were just too stacked against you, yet there was the enticing, exciting prospect of beating those odds and becoming that minor celebrity. And the stakes were so tiny: the life of some stranger sitting beside you. The client was probably guilty, probably belonged in prison and meant nothing to the defense lawyer anyway.

Amy's hopeful smile as she looked up at him made his trembling worse. He wanted to tell the judge he was a fraud and run screaming out of the courtroom. But he couldn't. Paradoxically, that smile of his sister's that scared him so much also held him in place. He believed what she believed, that he was the best hope of saving her.

Consequently, when they began questioning would-be jurors, Edward did it much more carefully than he ever had before. He stared at each one as he or she answered the prosecutor's questions, looking for a tell that the person was a liar, prejudiced against white people or women or otherwise poison to have on a jury.

'Yes, I saw something about it on TV,' the first one said, a middle-aged Hispanic woman, who listed her profession as 'homemaker.' Did that mean she'd resent a professional woman like Amy?

When it was Edward's turn to question her, he stood formally and said, 'Hello, Mrs Acosta, my name is Edward Hall. This is my sister Amy.'

'Hello, ma'am,' Amy said politely, as if being introduced at a party.

'I'm a lawyer and I'm going to be representing my sister, who as you heard is a medical doctor accused of murdering her husband, who was also a doctor. I'd like Amy to be able to respond to that in her own words.'

He sat and Amy said, 'I loved my husband very much, Mrs Acosta. We were separated, but we'd started seeing each other again and I believed we were going to get back together. I didn't kill him. I would never have done that. I tried to keep him alive after finding him shot.'

It had been Edward's idea for Amy to talk as much as possible during jury selection. Unlike in most trials, he wanted the jurors to have personal conversations with her, feel they'd begun to know her. Sweet little Amy.

Amy sniffed and looked away, as if the pain of losing Paul had just hit her. Edward patted her shoulder without looking at her, wondering if his sister was a much better actress than he'd suspected or if that emotion was genuine.

'Ma'am, the reason I bring this up is to ask you if you think there's anything wrong with a lawyer representing a family member?'

'Of course not,' the lady said almost indignantly. 'Family sticks together.'

'Thank you, ma'am.' Edward continued the conversation, drawing from Mrs Acosta the facts that: she had four children herself, all alive and healthy, thank God; her Catholic faith didn't approve of the taking of human life, even by the legal process and she believed in the presumption of innocence. Edward felt a growing sense of rapport with her. *This is the one,* he thought. There was nothing objectionable about her as a juror, but he felt she related to Amy as a person, and would at least hear the evidence objectively. Relief crept up his back and arms. The first potential juror, and she was golden.

When he passed the lady back to the prosecutor, Mrs Acosta smiled at Edward and at Amy too.

David Galindo didn't ask her another question. Without looking up, writing on his legal pad, he said, 'The state will exercise a peremptory, Your Honor.'

In a capital case, each side had fifteen peremptory challenges – 'strikes,' in legal parlance – it could use to remove someone from the jury panel, even if there was no other legal reason to do so. *No!* Edward wanted to shout. *I want her.* But there was nothing he could do about it. A lawyer had no power to veto the other side's use of a strike.

'I liked her,' Amy whispered as Mrs Acosta departed.

'Me too.' He shot a glower at David, but the prosecutor wouldn't look over at him. Instead David stood and addressed the judge.

'Your Honor, having had to use that strike, I object to the defendant carrying on any more conversations with prospective jurors.'

Even as Edward was rising to his feet to respond, Judge Cynthia frowned at her prosecutor and said, 'What's your objection?'

'She's not entitled to hybrid representation, Your Honor. Ms Hall is represented by a lawyer, he should do the talking for her.'

So Edward continued to his feet. 'She's not representing herself just by exchanging a couple of sentences with a prospective juror, Judge.'

'I agree,' the judge said, continuing to look only at the prosecutor.

David seemed unfazed. 'In effect she's entering a plea prematurely, Your Honor. She's saying she's not guilty before the time in trial for that plea.'

Edward said, 'I think the prosecution's real objection—'

'I can interpret the prosecutor's words for myself, Mr Hall. The court does not recognize a valid objection, so it is overruled.' She did finally look at Edward. 'But keep it brief, Mr Hall.'

'Yes, Your Honor.'

So Amy continued to talk to the potential jurors, making statements about her affection for her husband, trying to draw him or her out. If nothing else, they could tell the polite jurors from the rude ones. The ones who refused to respond to Amy,

179

even to look at her, Edward tried to find ways to challenge and remove from the jury. Cynthia mostly ruled in his favor in those attempts, but not always. Edward had to use two of his precious strikes before the day was over.

Was the judge doing him any favors? He couldn't tell. For the most part she wouldn't look at him, but that might have been just to cover the fact that she was trying to help him out. Cynthia seemed to grow more remote as the day wore on. Even angry. But at whom he couldn't tell.

Edward noticed something else that first day of jury selection. David Galindo wasn't asking any of the prospective jurors any questions about their feelings concerning the death penalty. Every juror had filled out a lengthy question-naire weeks before this process began, so the lawyers had some information in that regard, but in a death penalty case, both sides always explored the jurors' feelings on that subject in person. The death penalty. It was the ultimate topic about which to ask jurors. *Do you believe the government has the right to kill a person? Could you vote for that outcome, for someone to lie gasping on a gurney, while the drugs the govern-ment had put into her system denied her that breath? Do you think there are some people among us so monstrous that we have to end their lives? Do you think this is one of them, sitting right here in front of you?*

It wasn't an annoying squeak in the floor-board; it was the whole room in which they sat. They were all in the guts of the death penalty.

The lawyers had to probe gently into the biggest question of all in any possible criminal trial. *Hi. How ya doin'? How about this weather? You think you could vote to kill this warm, breathing person sitting next to me?*

So you had to ask a lot of futile questions. David Galindo wasn't doing that. This seemed to support what he'd told Edward, that he wasn't genuinely looking for a death sentence. Was David cutting him a break? Or laying some sort of trap? Edward couldn't decide and the doubt made him edgy and nervous. While Edward scrambled all over the field, working his ass off, the prosecutor just asked minimal questions, and said, 'The State accepts this juror, Your Honor.'

By the end of the day, there were two jurors neither the state nor the defense challenged, a white man and an African-American woman. Edward hesitated, taking a long pause before accepting the woman. He thought the prosecution would try to pack the jury with minority members, who might resent the rich white defendant and therefore be more likely to find her guilty. Edward's hesitation wasn't racist. He liked the woman personally, a thirty-eight-year-old married mother of two, who worked as a loan officer in a bank. But racism and reverse racism were facts of life, and nobody ever answered questions about them honestly. In the end, he sighed and took her. The woman grimaced when learning of her selection, which made Edward feel easier. It indicated she didn't have an agenda of trying to get Amy.

So, by the end of the first day they had two

jurors, which was lightning speed for a capital murder trial. Sometimes the jury selection took more than a month of eight-hour days. This one was being streamlined by David Galindo's refusal to talk about the death penalty.

When Cynthia called a halt for the day and hastily left the bench, David turned to Edward for the first time all day.

'You used to be better at this,' he said.

'I'm a little rusty. But I don't think—'

David shook his head.

'You used to have this offhand, kind of lazy charm that seemed to give you a rapport with the jurors, like you were a good host of an interesting party. Now you're so serious I can almost hear you sweating.'

'She's my Goddamned sister, David.'

David shrugged and began packing his brief-case. Edward realized maybe his former colleague had been trying to help him out, give him good advice. But Edward didn't apologize.

That night's dinner with Linda and his family was strained, but not nearly strained enough, in Edward's opinion. His family members were subdued – Linda was the one who mainly kept the conversation going – but the tension wasn't nearly taut enough. It was like the night before one of them left on a trip, or had a big present-ation to make. They still didn't get it, the danger Amy was in, the horror like a trap door on which they were all sitting. Edward wanted to scream at them.

'I like the two jurors we have,' Amy said.

'Yeah, let's invite them to lunch,' Edward responded.

Linda laid her hand over his.

He gave her little finger a squeeze, to say, *Yeah, I know.* 'I like them too,' he said to Amy. 'Especially the woman. But I don't trust either of them, and I'm not going to trust anybody we have on this jury. Jurors lie, Amy. They never, ever tell the truth, except maybe the occasional crazy one and they're easy to spot. Most of them hide their feelings, tell you what they think you want to hear and try to guess the right answers to your questions. It's like a chess match with both sides able to hide their moves. Some people want on the jury and don't want to let you know that. Most want to run screaming out of the room because they don't want the responsibility – and those are probably the ones you want. I've been doing this a while and I don't think I have any insight at all into jury selection. And I've never talked to a lawyer who did.'

After dinner, while everyone else cleared the table and started coffee, Dr Hall cut Edward out of the herd none too subtly and led him to his study. His father acted very uncharacteristically, like a weak actor playing the role of his father, never having met him. He kept looking down or glancing over at his bookshelves or somewhere else. He cleared his throat more than once.

'There's something that – there was an incident some months ago, two months before Paul's death, maybe, and several people know about it, even though it wasn't – it didn't get public attention. But there may have been a police report, so I think I need to tell you this.' Finally Dr Hall looked up at his son.

'You're scaring me, Dad. And I'm already terrified, so if you thought this was going to help, you probably—'

'I know, but you have to know, so they can't spring it on you unawares. As I say, some short time before Paul died, there was a break-in at his lab—'

'Oh my God,' Edward said, understanding instantly. 'Amy? What was she looking for?'

The throat-clearing happened again and now Dr Hall was looking away, too.

'You know that the research, for which Paul was given the award, was started with me. When he was my student he took a couple of ideas of mine and asked if he could develop them. That's how I remember it, though of course Paul would probably—' He remembered that, at this point, Paul couldn't contradict anyone. 'At any rate, we worked on it together at first. Later Paul claimed that when he'd gone out on his own he'd taken a different direction, but I doubted it. I suspected his work was based very directly on my earlier work.'

'So you asked Amy—?' Edward began, thinking, my God, how many people knew about his sister's hobby?

'No,' Dr Hall said. In that one syllable he sounded like his old self, emphatic and in command. 'I never asked your sister to do anything. But I did discuss the idea with her. Especially after she and Paul separated. Then we were sort of allies, Amy and I, with a common cause of mistrusting this man we'd allowed into the family.'

'And into your lab,' Edward said, thinking, *And into your daughter's pants*. He wondered if his father had ever thought that, that maybe Paul had started dating Amy to get to him. It would be a very egotistical thought, but not necessarily wrong.

'So did Amy come to you with some evidence that Paul was ripping off your work?'

'No,' emphatic Dr Hall said quickly. But then the other Dr Hall, the hesitant, reappeared. His eyes stopped meeting Edward's. 'At least, not directly, but some papers appeared here. Right here on this desk. With file-marks on them indicating they came from Paul's lab: some lab notes and one preliminary report Paul wrote for someone. A potential commercial sponsor, I suppose.'

'And did they show he stole from you?' Edward repeated. That 'commercial sponsor' remark demonstrated one aspect of his father's interest. It might be that Paul had been about to become very rich. The doctor or scientist who invented a cure for cancer, even a very narrow, restricted cure only good for one type of cancer, would become a multimillionaire. Edward looked around his father's study and realized what it represented. A nice room in a beautiful house in River Oaks, for God's sake, the richest neighborhood in the biggest city in Texas; did his father want more than this?

But then there was the fame, of course.

Dr Hall shook his head quickly. 'Inconclusive

at best,' he said. 'It did indicate a track I had taken, but other people had pursued the same course. No, she didn't take the right—'

He stopped himself, looking horrified.

'I didn't ask her to do this,' he repeated, this time mumbling. Dr Hall looked down at his own hands or his desk, as if expecting to find something else there. His eyes appeared glazed. To Edward it seemed he had just witnessed his father's descent into old age.

'So you think . . .?' Edward asked gently.

Finally his father looked into his eyes. The older man's were anguished.

'Maybe she did find better evidence that Paul had stolen from me. But she kept it, and as she studied it she thought, if Paul was out of the way, *I* could resume the research. Maybe even with Amy as my assistant.'

From which position, Edward thought, *she could feed her father back the other stuff she had stolen. She could help him become even more famed and honored, rather than let her cheating ex-husband get that credit.*

He and his father were going to stop talking now. They were probably thinking the same thing, but neither was going to speak that thought aloud. The ideas could be denied life if they remained unspoken, if they never hung in the air of this cloistered, sacred room.

Edward rose, saying, 'Thanks for letting me know this, Dad. Like you say, I would have hated to have it sprung on me by the opposition.'

Dr Hall just nodded, his head down again. Edward left the room quickly. He had another thought, one not to be shared with his father, and he wanted to get out of the study before his father could read it on his face. It would probably come to Dad, though, maybe already had, because it was pretty obvious.

This information didn't create a motive for murder only for Amy.

Thirteen

By the next morning's jury selection, Edward had added a new layer to that thought. His father must have known Edward would think that. Maybe Dr Hall had been offering himself up as an alternative perpetrator. That's why he had told Edward the story. Maybe Dr Hall had been offering to sacrifice himself for his little girl.

'Are you paying attention to this man?' Amy whispered.

Edward nodded. The man in the witness stand was tall and fair, with a solid, slightly rectangular head and a clear, straightforward gaze. Amy had her laptop open in front of her, with the man's Facebook page pulled up on the screen. In the information open to the public, he had a picture of himself with his wife and four children, all dressed as if for church, and a link to the church itself – a megachurch for prosperous Houstonians, the minister of which assured them they were going to Heaven for the same reason they were well off, because God loved them.

Amy pointed to another section of links, to Republican office-holders of the extremely conservative variety, all of whom the potential juror 'liked.'

When it was Edward's turn to question the potential juror, he said very politely, 'Thank you for being here, Mr Simmons. Let me ask you first, will you be financially inconvenienced by having to serve on this jury?'

Mr Simmons grimaced slightly. 'It won't help, but I've hired good people in my department. They can handle things for a while and I'll be available to them at breaks and in the evenings.'

'Good. Excellent. I see from your questionnaire the company of which you're vice president, but you list your wife's profession as "homemaker." Has she ever worked outside the home?'

'Oh yes. I wasn't sure what to put there, actually. It's only been since the birth of our younger two that Irene gave up her job as a pharmaceutical rep. And she'll probably go back to that once Susie and Pete are in school. She'd better, if we hope to put all four through college.'

He chuckled, joined by everyone else in the courtroom. No one wanted to offend someone who might end up on the jury. But Edward needed to probe a little deeper.

'But she's all right for now with her stay-at-home mom role?'

'Oh yes. It was something we discussed from the beginning, before we even had children. Irene was raised in a traditional family household and she very much enjoys fulfilling that role now.'

Edward wondered if that was true and wondered if Mr Simmons believed it himself. Edward looked at him closely, as if he could see through to his thoughts. This was the most crucial decision of trial – whom to let on your jury – and it was always done blindly. It was too bad you couldn't look into someone's eyes and see his soul.

'Thank you, Mr Simmons,' Edward said, and

stood to address the judge. 'The defense will accept this juror.'

Amy was tugging at his sleeve as he sat. She was pointing to the information on her screen. This was exactly the kind of sanctimonious man who might resent a woman like Amy, who not only worked but was a highly educated professional. Edward leaned over to whisper to her very quietly.

'There are such things as sincere Christians, Amy, even ones who vote Republican. Or if he's as smug and obnoxious as you think, that will come out during deliberations and there's a good chance he'll piss off our Juror Number Two.' The African-American professional woman. As their jury was growing, so were Edward's concerns about its composition. Now he not only wanted his kind of jurors in the jury box, he wanted a mix of people who wouldn't be able to agree unanimously on a guilty verdict. Jury selection now was like a game of Risk, each juror an army Edward was moving around the board, sometimes allied with other armies, sometimes at war with each other.

'State?' the judge said impatiently.

David shook off his second chair, a young woman Edward didn't know, and stood. 'We will . . . accept Mr Simmons.'

Edward was glad of the hesitation. So the other side wasn't sure either. That was the best he could hope for at this point.

So it went, day by day, juror by juror. Edward had fallen into trial mode. He'd talk to Amy at lunch, during breaks and at the end of every day, but was more or less ignoring his family. Both his families. He was spending nights back in Mike's apartment, because Mike was still working on the case and they'd compare notes at the end of the day. Linda claimed she understood and didn't feel rejected, but Edward sensed in her voice a hurt quality, which he interpreted to mean she thought he didn't think she was smart enough to help in this crisis. But that wasn't it. He needed to concentrate and Mike was actually a member of the defense team. Sometimes Amy was there fairly late into the night too, finally starting to take this prosecution seriously.

'That Laura Martinelli, much as you liked her, wasn't entirely forthright with you,' Mike said, sitting back in his easy chair.

'I never said I liked her.'

'Yeah, I guess that was a different vibe I was feeling in the room when you were staring into each other's eyes. At any rate, she said she only went out with Paul, what, half a dozen times? According to other sources, it was significantly more than that, even just counting the public occasions. In fact, a woman from the banquet organizers said Ms Martinelli was originally slated to accompany Paul to that awards dinner, until about a week beforehand when her name got crossed out and Amy's penciled in.'

'What?' Now Amy's stare was entirely on the former cop. 'She was going in my place? Or I took her place, or what the fuck ever?'

Amy swore so rarely, this one sounded like a

bomb going off in the room. Her faced was deeply flushed that quickly.

'Yes, ma'am,' Mike answered matter-of-factly.

'I guess it would make sense to take a colleague of sorts to the dinner,' Edward said. 'And maybe Ms Martinelli's foundation was one of the beneficiaries of the dinner?'

'Plus there's the added benefit that you could fuck her afterwards,' Amy said. She stood up and paced across the room and back, quickly.

'You knew he had other lovers,' Edward said. 'And you said it didn't bother you.'

'Not until you rubbed my nose in one of them. Laura Martinelli.' Amy made a disgusted snort.

'It's good you're getting this out of your system now,' Mike said. 'Because seeing you like this right now, *I'd* vote guilty.'

She sat and crossed her arms. 'All right, so good work, Mike. But what good does it do us?'

'It shows they had a closer relationship than she'd let on—'

'And I love the fact she lied about it,' Edward interjected.

Mike nodded and continued. 'So Ms Martinelli may have had some hopes for the future, as far as Dr Paul was concerned. Then he dumped her for you, Amy, maybe at the last minute.'

'You said her name got crossed out a week earlier.'

'That doesn't tell us when Paul told her. Maybe it wasn't until the day he was killed.'

'Does she have an alibi?' Edward asked.

'Yeah, the same one as half the women in Houston on a Saturday afternoon; she claims she was

192

shopping. Even showed me a couple of receipts, but they were from earlier in the afternoon.'

If, instead of the cool, detached, dater-of-many-lover-of-none, Laura Martinelli had appeared for them, she had actually been a jealous lover; she could easily have followed Paul home some time, so she knew where he lived.

'And if she did go over there, she was already thinking of murder,' Edward continued, getting excited.

'How do you know?' Amy asked.

Mike answered. 'Because she parked her car somewhere else, where the neighbors didn't notice it. Maybe she was even deliberately trying to frame Amy, given the timing. Laura certainly knew what time the awards banquet was going to be, what time Paul would be leaving or his date arriving.'

Edward said to Mike, 'But when you say it would have been natural for him to take a professional colleague to the dinner, why not his partner in the research itself? Surely Dr Fisher would have been the most natural choice. Especially since they'd, you know . . .'

'Slept together?' Amy said. Her arms were still crossed, but her face wasn't so red. 'You can say it in front of me, I'm all right now.' Then added, to the open air, 'Louise too? Really, Paul?'

Edward and Mike exchanged a glance. Yeah, Amy was obviously fine.

'Here's another thought,' Edward said quickly. 'Maybe Louise Fisher knew Laura Martinelli was scheduled to accompany her partner then got replaced at the last minute by Amy. Then if Louise killed Paul either Laura or Amy would get blamed for it.'

'And Dr Fisher would inherit the research too,' Mike agreed. 'She could kill three birds with one shot.'

Amy was looking back and forth between the two of them.

'Wow, it's just like Perry Mason. You two come up with great theories. Except, oh, wait, there's no evidence of any of this.'

Mike smiled indulgently. Edward took his sister's hand.

'Amy, here's something I guess I should have told you a long time ago. Perry Mason is bullshit. I'm a defense lawyer, not a detective.' Amy looked puzzled. 'We don't have to solve the mystery, babe. We just need to make it look like the police didn't solve it either. We don't have to prove a case against any of these people. We just have to keep the prosecution from proving theirs against you.'

Amy sat back, light dawning. 'Oh. You're right.'

Mike chimed in, 'So the more suspects we parade in front of the jury the better. Then your brother here will just say to the jury in final argument, "Reasonable doubt, reasonable doubt, reasonable doubt . . ."'

'In slightly more clever phrasing than that, I hope,' Edward said.

'Yeah, yeah, I said I got it. I get it.' Amy looked almost happy again. 'So you two aren't so much detectives as you are—'

'Bullshit artists,' Mike agreed cheerfully. Edward nodded.

Then Mike sobered. 'But I really will start looking into these two women more.' Turning to Edward, he added, 'Any other links between them, people who've seen them. You know. And try to find out about other women the late Paul was dating, but these two look the most closely involved.'

'Yes,' Edward said deliberately.

Amy just sat back, arms folded, not being taken in.

Edward was happy when the long week in court ended, but he didn't get weekends off. Not now that trial had begun. He had a nagging doubt he needed to resolve for his own satisfaction and that meant a return to Paul's house.

This time he made sure to have the visit approved by the watchful, gun-toting next-door neighbor.

Valerie Linnett shrugged, standing in her doorway. It was late October, but that said nothing about the weather in Houston. It was a warm Saturday morning, with only a slight hint of coolness, and Ms Linnett was dressed accordingly: shorts and a T-shirt. She apparently liked shorts, based on his earlier meeting with her and today, and shorts liked her, too. Her hair, now fully gray – was that how it had been before? – was cut short and she wore no makeup, but her legs belied the old-lady look.

She stood there barefoot and said, 'Sure, what do I care?' She turned away and he thought she was done with him, but her voice floated back. 'Mind if I watch?'

Edward had a key from the management

company and imagined that extra was still under the barbecue grill, but what could he say?

'Sure.'

Edward did a walk-through of Paul's house like a prospective tenant, the neighbor lady following in his wake. He wanted to engage her in conversation, but she was giving him minimal responses.

'You said you saw several women coming and going here.'

'Uh huh.'

'Do you think you could identify any of them?' If they could contradict Laura Martinelli's claim that she didn't know where Paul had lived, that would make her an even better suspect.

But Valerie wasn't going to help. 'I didn't study them. They were women. All had two legs and tits. They just passed through my peripheral vision.'

'Could they have been hookers?' Maybe that was why Paul hadn't wanted other women coming to his house.

'If they were they were damned expensive ones. Nicely dressed, with nice cars.'

Edward heard something in her voice and turned to face her. 'Did *you* ever go out with Paul?'

Valerie stared at him. After a moment she said, 'I don't have to answer your questions.'

'Not here,' Edward agreed cheerfully. 'If you'd rather wait until you're on the witness stand under oath, with a judge *ordering* you to answer me, that's fine.'

He just kept looking at her with an open, pleasant expression on his face. This wasn't hostile at all, but they were on his turf now, metaphorically

196

speaking. She didn't have her gun and he had the whole legal system behind him.

'It's embarrassing,' Valerie finally said, ducking her head to demonstrate. 'Yes, Paul and I went out one time. Like I told you before, we were neighborly at first, until he finally asked me out and I thought OK, what the hell. We had things in common – pharmacist, doctor – but, very early on in the evening, it became clear to me that all he cared about was getting into my pants. He ordered me a drink and a bottle of wine for us to share and just sat back in the booth staring and smiling at me, clearly imagining me naked. He couldn't have repeated back one thing I said, I can guarantee that.'

Edward was doing his best to look at her straightforwardly and not like a man imagining her without her clothes.

'And you weren't, uh . . .'

'Receptive? Look, Mr Hall, this is none of your damned business and I'll be very grateful if you won't ask me about it in court, because it's got nothing to do with anything, OK?'

He nodded.

Valerie crossed her arms, looking embarrassed.

'I won't say I'm above having sex for its own sake or just a good time, but I don't want to be a number on a checklist. Dr I'm-Getting-Divorced clearly had an agenda. He probably hit on the waitress while I was in the ladies room. He just wanted to run up a score. I didn't want to play. That's why I quit trying to be neighborly after that. I'd seen all the way through him and there was nothing there except a tongue hanging out.'

197

Wow, Edward very nearly said. Others had implied something like this about Paul, but no one had put it so plainly. He felt dirty and wanted to apologize for his whole gender. Would it help, he thought for a second, to say, *I promise I have absolutely no desire to have sex with you?*

Before the moment could grow any more awkward, if that were possible, there was a knock at the front door and they heard it open.

'I asked my sister to meet me here,' Edward said quickly. 'I need to ask her a couple of things about Paul's belongings. Hi, Amy. Valerie, this is my sister Amy.'

Valerie and Amy exchanged polite greetings, then everyone stood there awkwardly, until the neighbor realized they were waiting for her to leave. She walked stiffly out, taking care not to brush against Amy in the doorway.

'Who was that?' Amy asked.

'Lady next door. She's been watching the place since – you know. Cops told her people might try to break in. Neighborhood busybody, apparently. Told me she didn't remember what women coming to see Paul looked like, but then described their clothes and cars. Come back here, OK?' Edward asked, and went out the door into the short hallway to the master bedroom.

He stood inside it for a few seconds, next to the spot where Paul had died, before Amy joined him, her feet dragging and arms still crossed.

She seemed reluctant to cross the threshold. 'What?'

'You said you'd started keeping a few clothes

198

here. Could you show me? I've looked in the closet, but—'

'Oh.' Amy seemed relieved. She turned and hurried out of the room. Edward followed in surprise. 'Not in there,' she said over her shoulder. 'Paul had it pretty well packed with his stuff. Mine was in here.'

She led him across the hall to the room that had a daybed and a desk, the home office. Amy went straight to the closet and slid its door back. She seemed glad to get out of Paul's bedroom.

Sure enough, a few dresses hung in the closet. Also a handful of blouses and a couple of skirts.

'There's a little built-in dresser in here with a couple of pairs of – of underwear. And so forth. An old pair of slippers and tennies. Just in case I, you know . . .'

'Yeah.' He walked over to the closet and looked at the dresses. A couple were simple, what might at one time have been called frocks, but another three were evening dresses. He'd learned what he wanted: Amy actually did keep clothes here at her estranged husband's house. Giving credence to the idea they'd been in the process of reuniting.

He pulled out a long deep blue evening dress with a slit up the side and deep cleavage.

Amy was blushing again. 'Yes, I got that one after we separated. Planning to wear it for a night out on the town after our reconciliation was official. But unfortunately . . .' She sniffed suddenly. 'Can we go?'

A crying woman generally gets her way. Amy hurried out of the room.

Edward stopped for just a few seconds at the closet door and picked out the beautiful evening dress. He held it up, close to him.

Amy was five feet four inches. He knew exactly where she came to him, just slightly above his shoulder. Edward held the dress up and realized that he, at five feet eleven inches, could have almost worn it himself.

Why would Amy have claimed that dress, which clearly didn't fit her, was hers? Had she seen it in the closet before and known she wasn't the only woman in her estranged husband's life?

This was a terrible thought on the eve of trial.

Fourteen

The following week, as Cynthia came striding out in her black robe, the bailiff said, 'All rise.' Edward wondered about her perspective as she sat and looked out at the packed courtroom, which included a television camera at the back.

'Please sit,' Cynthia said. 'Announcements?'

As usual, it seemed as if it had taken forever to get to this moment and as if it had come much too fast. Luckily, he was the defense. He didn't have to have a case prepared yet, he just had to counterpunch. David Galindo let his second chair stand and announce that the State was ready for trial.

Then Edward stood slowly and said, 'Edward Hall for the defense, Your Honor. We're ready.'

That felt like a lie. He didn't feel remotely ready to put on a defense for Amy, because he didn't have one.

But that wasn't the main reason for his hesitation before making an announcement. It was because at that moment of proclaiming in the courtroom, in front of everyone, that he was representing the defendant, Edward irrevocably embarked on practicing law without a license. That crime that would get his parole revoked if nothing else. But he still felt no one else could do it better. Amy put her hand over his and smiled at him.

The courtroom was full of dozens of people, closely packed. The jurors obviously felt intimidated by the attention, which was all to the good. Edward wanted them to take their jobs very seriously, because the State's case, while fairly strong, had a few holes, such as no eyewitness to the shooting.

On the other hand, the jurors probably also knew what was expected of them at the end of a trial: to come back with a guilty verdict.

The prosecutor read the simple indictment to the jury: after entering Paul Shilling's home without his consent, Amy Hall did intentionally cause his death by the use of a deadly weapon, i.e., a firearm.

Then the judge asked, 'How do you plead?'

Edward was standing with Amy. She looked over at the jurors and said, 'I am not guilty.' She sounded convincing.

Then Cynthia lifted her neutral eyes to the prosecution table and said, 'Does the State wish to make an opening statement?'

'Yes, Your Honor,' David said, and walked toward the jury box, buttoning his suit jacket. 'Good morning,' he said. 'We believe the facts will be simple. The victim, Dr Paul Shilling, a well-known Houston physician, was living alone in a house on the southwest side because he had been separated from his wife for several months. That would be the defendant, Dr Amy Hall Shilling.'

Edward felt Amy stiffen beside him. This was that moment when all eyes turned on her and she felt suddenly she had to look the epitome of innocence. But what did that look like? A gentle smile? A look of mourning, with one teardrop slowly trickling down the cheek? Amy opted for a very serious expression and a direct stare back into the jury box, which was about all one could do.

'Yes, the defendant is a doctor too,' David continued to the jury. 'And the defendant comes from a prominent Houston family, including her father Dr Marshall Hall, a very well-respected diagnostician, and her attorney brother Edward, who is sitting next to her there.'

Edward didn't like having his family brought forward to the center. In the prosecutor's apparently laudatory introduction of the Halls, Edward heard undertones of *rich, privileged, arrogant, spoiled.* It showed Amy as a little rich girl who thought she could get away with anything.

'Now, Dr Shilling, the deceased, appeared to be going through a very happy time of his life, in spite of his separation. Or maybe because of it. He was about to receive a major award for his research and he seemed to feel a sense of long-delayed freedom. By that I mean he was dating, more than one woman, and apparently enjoying it very much. In other words, he was moving on with his life.

'But the other Dr Shilling, Amy, was not. I believe you will hear evidence that she wanted to reconcile with her husband, wanted that badly. You will also hear evidence that for Paul, what his wife considered romantic dates were just business meetings, over how to divide their property and end their marriage. Amicably, he hoped, so he didn't let her know about the other women in his life. But we believe you can make the reasonable inference that, in her mind, she found out that her husband had just been toying with her. Yes, this trial is about jealousy and what the defendant perceived as infidelity, in a way that seemed to mock her. The usual elements of a domestic murder, in other words.'

Oh, Edward could imagine this prosecution's view of the evidence playing well both with the jury and all those people on the other end of that television feed: *When it comes right down to it, the rich and powerful are just like the rest of us, down in the dirt like everyone else.*

'A classically simple case,' David continued, 'when you strip it right down. What I think you will hear is that, on a day when Paul was going to have a major professional triumph and definitively separate himself from his wife forever, she appeared and shot him dead. Period. In the end, this will be a very easy guilty verdict for you. Thank you.'

Edward stood quickly and started talking while advancing toward the jurors. 'Well, yes. That's what the prosecution usually wants, for you to believe the simplest version of events, because that's what police usually seize on.'

'Objection, Your Honor.' David Galindo hadn't even sat back down. 'This isn't an opening statement, this is argument.'

'Sustained. Mr Hall—'

'Yes, Your Honor. I understand.' He turned his back on her, his eyes on the jurors. 'The evidence will show that the police found Amy bending

204

over her dying husband's body, because she was trying to save his life. That she had called 911. That even though, yes, she was on his front porch when the gun was fired, it wasn't her gun. She didn't bring a gun. The evidence will show that police could not take the trouble to investigate thoroughly enough to come up with other suspects – of whom there are many – so they arrested the easy one: the estranged wife, with blood on her hands.

'You will also hear, and this is not bragging about my little sister, this is the simple truth, that Dr Amy Shilling is a very smart person, graduating with honors from both college and medical school. You will hear that she is not the kind of person to commit so stupid a crime. To let herself be seen entering the house, leaving her car plainly visible in the driveway, knowing what attention it would draw immediately after a gun was fired, and then remain at the scene just waiting to be arrested. No. I believe the evidence will show a much murkier world than the prosecution wants to present, with several suspects who have reason to dislike Dr Paul Shilling extremely, to the point of murder.'

He ran his gaze down the two rows of eyes again, then turned and walked back to his table.

'State, call your first witness,' Judge Miles blandly intoned. She would not return Edward's look. Hanging over the trial was still that DVD of Paul accusing Amy of his murder, and the fact Cynthia hadn't ruled on its admissibility yet. If she let it come into evidence, this trial would become what the prosecution had predicted, very simple.

Edward almost felt as if he were being black-mailed. But for what? What did the judge want from him?

The theory of trying a case that Edward had been taught as a young prosecutor was that you started a trial dramatically, with your second strongest witness, and saved the best one for a big finish.

David instead started slowly, with a patrol officer who testified to being dispatched to the house at nearly 6 p.m. on Saturday and what he'd found there. The same things he'd found at other locations, in similar circumstances: a bleeding body on the floor, a distraught family member bending over him, blood on the floor, a gun nearby, within reach. Then he had escorted Amy out but detained her, started putting up crime scene tape, waited for the paramedics and cleared a space for them to remove the victim.

The officer was an African-American man in his early twenties, with only a couple of years on the force. His uniform was crisp, his hair cut neatly and his eyes alert.

When Edward's turn came to question him, Edward frowned and said, 'Let's clarify a couple of key points, officer. You were the first officer through the bedroom door, correct?'

'Yes, sir.'

'What was Amy doing when you first walked in?' Normally Edward would refer to the person next to him as 'my client,' or 'the defendant,' but he had decided that in this trial Amy would be called by her own name.

'She was down on the floor, sir, doing chest compressions on the victim.'

'Have you been trained in CPR, officer?'

'Yes, sir. Of course, sir.'

'Did she appear to be doing it correctly?'

'Yes, sir, she did. She was compressing the victim's chest with both hands instead of the old-fashioned mouth-to-mouth, which is considered outmoded now.'

'Yes. Did you take over for her?'

'No, sir. I put a hand on her shoulder and she said quickly, "I'm a doctor. This is my husband." And since, as I said, she appeared to be doing it well, I just let her continue.'

'Could you tell if Paul was still alive? I'm referring to the injured man.'

'It's hard for me to say, sir. I think so. His eyes were open. He was gasping air in and out as she compressed his chest, so I would have to say yes.'

'Did he say anything?'

'No, nothing.' The officer shook his head for emphasis.

'All right, officer, so Amy was down on her knees on the hardwood floor doing chest compressions on her husband. Did it appear to you she was trying to save his life?'

'Yes, sir, that's how it seemed to me, sir.'

Edward passed the witness, with satisfaction that he had wrung as much as possible from this State's witness with minimal knowledge of the facts.

David Galindo said, 'Officer, had you been dispatched to other murder scenes prior to this one?'

Edward was almost on his feet, but the witness was too fast for him. 'Yes, sir. A few.'

'Have you seen other instances where someone, who later turned out to be the murderer, was apparently trying to save the victim's life when you got there?'

This time Edward was faster. 'Objection, Your Honor. What he may have observed in other cases is irrelevant to this one.'

'It's about his observations based on experience, Judge, just like the defense asked about.'

Edward frowned at Cynthia's hesitation, and said, 'Your Honor, there are a great many appellate opinions saying what happened in other cases is not relevant to the case on trial.'

The only effect of his expanded objection was that it had given Cynthia time to make up her mind.

'That objection is overruled.'

Edward remained on his feet a moment longer, staring at the judge. His objection had been perfectly valid, in fact, so well-established it should have been sustained without a thought. Cynthia became aware of Edward's stare and turned her dark eyes back to his. Hers gave nothing away, didn't even reflect back the light.

David Galindo was asking, 'Do you remember the question, officer?'

'Yes, sir. Yes, I've been to other crime scenes where the murderer appeared remorseful and was trying to revive the deceased.'

That completely ruined the tiny advantage Edward had won during his cross-examination. He sat slumped, glaring at the judge.

David continued, 'Officer, you're the one who found the gun, correct?'

'Yes sir. The victim obviously had a gunshot wound, so for officer safety I wanted to make sure the suspect wasn't still armed.'

'Where did you find it?'

'Under the bed, maybe five feet from the defendant.'

When the officer was passed back to him, Edward asked, 'Was that the first place you looked?'

'After visually inspecting the flooring that was visible, yes, I checked under the bed next.'

'So the gun was in the place most likely for someone to find it?'

'Objection, Your Honor. Again, that calls for speculation.'

Edward said crisply, 'No, it's a question of fact, Your Honor. This officer was looking, so he knows the most obvious places he'd look.'

Cynthia actually answered him. 'To which he's already testified. He can't know where another searcher might have looked first. Sustained.'

'What's going on?' Amy whispered, after her brother passed the witness and sat glaring at the judge. Edward only shrugged.

The next witness was Paul's next-door neighbor Valerie Linnett. She wore a nondescript pastel dress, loose enough to give no indication of her figure. Her gray hair, shot with a few strands of brown, hung straight and she wore no makeup. She wore small, round glasses from another era. Edward frowned. Valerie so obviously didn't want to be here she'd apparently tried to make herself invisible. She looked around as if surprised to find the courtroom so crowded.

David quickly established who she was, what she did for a living, and her house's immediate proximity to Paul's.

'Had you met the deceased?'

'Yes, several times. He'd only lived there a few months, but I made a point of going over and welcoming him to the neighborhood. So did other neighbors, I think and we visited back and forth a few times early on.'

'But that stopped?'

'We didn't have a disagreement or anything like that. It just seemed clear we weren't going to become great friends and we were both busy with our own lives.'

'Let's go to the day of the shooting,' the prosecutor continued. 'Do you remember that day?'

'Of course. It was a Saturday, late in the afternoon.'

'Do you remember what you were doing?'

'Yes. I'd been working in the yard and I was about to take a shower, but I decided to have a drink first.'

'Do you know the defendant, Dr Amy Shilling?'

'We've met once, now.' Valerie bobbed her head in Amy's direction.

'Did you know her that day?'

'No, I'd never seen her before.'

Edward frowned. Was that what she'd told him, or Mike? It seemed to him she'd said she had seen Amy once or twice at the house.

'Did you see her that day?'

'Yes. I happened to be looking out my window

and I saw her car pull into the driveway and saw her go up on the porch.'

'Did she enter the house?'

'Yes. She knocked and then it looked like she just went in without waiting for an answer.'

Now Edward sat up. Was that what she'd said? He looked through his witness notes as the questioning continued.

'Then what happened?'

'Nothing for a few minutes. I was getting ready for my shower when I heard a gunshot.'

'Were you sure that's what it was?'

'Oh yes. My father used to take us kids out into the woods to shoot. It's a very distinctive sound. You don't forget it.'

'How much time would you say passed between when the defendant entered the house and you heard the gunshot?'

'A few minutes, like I said. I wasn't timing it. Maybe ten minutes tops?'

Now Edward felt panic setting in. This wasn't what she'd told him. He couldn't be sure – he and Mike had questioned so many neighbors, and none of their stories matched up perfectly, of course – but then he found the statement Valerie Linnett had given Mike.

When the witness was passed to him, Edward waited until he had her full attention. Her eyes widened slightly behind her small round frames, almost as if she was afraid of him. Her thin dress made her look very vulnerable, almost frail.

'Good morning, Ms Linnett. I'm Edward Hall, Amy's brother.'

'Yes, I know, Mr Hall. Good morning.'

'Yes, in fact, you and I have talked before this, right?'

'Yes,' she said, hesitantly.

'You also talked to my investigator.' This time the witness only nodded. 'And you told us a somewhat different version of this story, didn't you?'

'I guess somewhat. I wouldn't use the same words every time.' She looked puzzled.

'No, this is a very significant detail that you've changed. You told me, and my investigator, that Amy was still on the front porch when you heard the gunshot. Isn't that correct?'

'I don't think so. Maybe. I'm not sure what I said to him.'

Edward held in his hand so the witness could see Mike's summary of what she had told him. Edward said slowly, 'Or in fact you said she was just going in when you heard the gunshot. Correct?'

Valerie Linnett, a good-sized woman, had begun to shrink into herself, hunching her shoulders. 'I think – yes, I do think that's what I told you.'

'Now you're saying she went in and you didn't hear the gunshot until "a few minutes" after that. Correct?'

'Yes.' Ms Linnett nodded her head vigorously.

'What's happened to make you change your mind?'

'I've had time to think about it. Knowing this trial was coming up, that I'd be testifying, I thought very hard about what I actually saw and I realized it must have been longer than what I told you. Because I saw her on the porch, saw her go in, then I went and made my drink. That must have taken a few minutes.' More slowly,

212

thoughtfully, she said, 'So looking back, I think more time must have passed than I originally thought.'

That was an explanation, though not a good one. Edward wanted something more sinister. Leaning back, staring at the witness for a few seconds before he spoke, he said, 'Did you talk to police before you changed your mind?'

'Well, of course, police officers have questioned me a couple of times. Being the closest neighbor, I assume that's natural. I even let them come in and see the view from my window.'

'And did police suggest to you that you should change your story?'

'No.' She shook her head for emphasis.

'They didn't tell you your neighbors had said something different from you?'

She started to shake her head again, then stopped and inclined her head thoughtfully. 'Well, the second one did say another neighbor said your sister had been in the house a while before the gunshot.'

'Did he ask you to think about it some more?'

'He asked me to please be sure of what I'd seen.'

'Do you realize that's an interview technique designed to plant a different version of events in your mind?'

'Objection,' David Galindo said quickly. 'This witness hasn't been qualified as an expert in interviewing witnesses or any psychological—'

'Sustained,' Cynthia said. 'Don't answer the question,' she instructed the witness, who nodded meekly.

That was OK, Edward hadn't expected an answer,

he'd just wanted to ask the question, to plant the idea in the jurors' minds.

'Don't you think you would have a better memory of what happened, when your memory of the event was fresher, right after it happened, rather than months later? Well after your memory's been tainted by hearing what other people might or might not have said?'

'No. When I saw the – your sister on the porch next door I didn't attach any significance to it. I wasn't concentrating. It was only later, after thinking about it, that I remembered more clearly what I saw. Right after it happened I was so confused I didn't have time to sort out what had happened.'

'Did you hear anything else between Amy's appearance on the porch and the gunshot? A scream, the sound of raised voices, anything?'

'No, nothing like that.' Ms Linnett's shoulders widened out a little. She stopped looking attacked.

'Did you ever go look out into the backyards, Ms Linnett?'

'At some point I did, but not right after the shot was fired. I was still staring at the front porch.' She was sitting very still in the witness chair.

'Can you see into Paul's backyard from inside your house?'

'Part of it. There's a privacy fence, so I can't see it all.'

'What's behind your backyard and Paul's? Is it someone else's yard?'

'No. There's an alley.' Her answers went along with her stiff posture, growing more clipped.

Edward nodded again. 'And do you have a gate into the alley?'

'Yes. That's where the trash is picked up.'

'Do you keep that gate locked?'

'There is a lock, but I don't have it locked half the time, because I go in and out that way to put trash in the trash cans.'

'Do you know if Paul's house has a gate into the alley?'

'I assume so. The yards are all alike.'

'Pass the witness,' he said.

'Ms Linnett,' David asked quickly, 'did you see or hear any sign of anyone else being in Paul Shilling's house that afternoon? I'm talking about at the time you heard the gun go off.'

'No sir. Nothing.'

'Pass the witness.'

Edward said quickly, 'Are you sure about that last answer, Ms Linnett? Remember how confused you said you were right after the gunshot? In your confusion did you perhaps miss signs of someone else going into the house?'

'No, I don't think so.'

'An unfamiliar car parked a few houses down, perhaps?'

She sat up straighter. 'No, I didn't see anything like that. In fact, I looked a few minutes later when I thought of it, but there was nothing.'

'When you first talked to my investigator you remembered seeing Amy on the porch when the gun was fired. So is it possible you saw two different women, one who went in a few minutes earlier and then Amy on the porch when the shot was fired?'

Ms Linnett frowned at him, not in anger, in concentration. Then she shook her head. 'No. There was only one woman. That one there.'

'How can you be sure?'

'I just am.'

Edward sat looking at her, hoping the jury would sense and absorb his disbelief in what she was saying.

Finally he asked, 'You said the trash is picked up in the alley, so there's room for a car to park back there?'

'Yes. Of course.'

'No more questions, Your Honor.'

The prosecutor asked immediately, 'Did you hear the sound of a car starting and leaving after the gunshot, ma'am? From the alley or anywhere else?'

'No. I didn't hear anything like that.'

'No further questions.'

No other witness had heard a car in the alley either. Edward knew that from his witness statements. He turned to watch Ms Linnett walk out past him. As she walked stiffly up the aisle, Edward's gaze shifted. His mother and father were on the front row. Linda sat toward the back of the spectator seats, looking back at him. She smiled encouragingly.

The judge looked over the spectators' heads at the clock on the back wall. It was only 11:30, but she turned to the jurors and said, 'We're going to break for lunch now. Please do not discuss the case with each other or with anyone else. Be back in the jury room by one, please. All rise for the jury.'

Edward watched the jurors file out, then turned back toward the bench, but Cynthia had fled.

The Halls went out together. Along the way Edward said hi to Linda.

'Thanks for coming.'

'Sure.' She smiled.

He followed his family down the hall, then looked back, expecting to see Linda coming along, but saw her turning the other way, toward the elevators.

'Just a minute,' he told his family, and hurried after her. He caught up to Linda, touched her shoulder. She turned and looked surprised.

'Aren't you coming to lunch with us?'

'Oh.' Linda looked past him in the direction of his family. 'Uh, no. Y'all need to talk about the trial and I need to get back to the office. We're having a deposition over lunch. I'll see you later.'

'But—' he said, as the elevator doors opened and she rushed in.

'That old lady was an outrageous liar,' Mrs Hall said at lunch in the little courthouse cafeteria.

'Outrageous,' Dr Hall echoed. 'Can you get her charged with perjury after this is over?'

'Why would she lie about me?' Amy asked, turning toward her lawyer.

'You don't know what police can do when they question a witness like that,' Edward said. 'They interview witnesses initially and when they already have a most likely suspect – you, in this case – their questions are informed by that. Deliberately or not, they try to make their own

217

jobs easier, trying to nudge people out of their stories, move the playing pieces just a little bit, make the puzzle pieces fit better in the picture they've already got in their minds. Then, when they come back with a follow-up interview, they can sound like they're accusing a witness who isn't falling into line with the answers they want. By the second interview there's a strong subtext of *You're in trouble but I can help you.* The witness feels accused if he or she doesn't say what the cops want. It's a powerful technique.'

'What can you do about it?' his mother asked, leaning forward toward him. Amy sat stiffly at his left side.

'Nothing now. The damage is done, unfortunately. We're going to be stuck with what the witnesses think they remember now.'

The lunchroom featured industrial white walls and acoustic tiles on the ceiling. Around them the scuffed linoleum floors showed the passage of many feet. Edward thought he could hear a murmuring substratum of old conversations, speakers long since gone, some to prison, some to the morgue. Their voices lingered as if stuck to the tables and walls like flies in amber, straining to pull free.

When they returned to the courtroom they separated. Dr and Mrs Hall resumed their seats on the front row, while Amy and Edward passed through the gate in the railing. Edward used to feel privileged to go through that barrier into the front of the courtroom, an area reserved for lawyers. Now he realized forcefully that it also separated the accused from their supporters. It was the entrance

218

to a cattle chute that would guide his sister inevitably to prison.

David Galindo looked up from the adjacent table. Edward couldn't read what the prosecutor's eyes were saying. This trial was also different for David from his usual trials, when he dispassionately tried to convict a stranger and win from the jury as many years of imprisonment as he could manage. He didn't know Amy, but he knew how much she meant to Edward and Edward sensed a sort of secret sympathy from the longtime prosecutor, his former rival. But even if that were true, there was no way for David's sympathy to express itself. He had his assigned role to play.

The afternoon brought more of Paul's neighbors. Only one was nearly as positive in his memory as Valerie Linnett. Howard Lewis was a burly-shouldered man who drove a truck for a local produce company. He wore a plaid sports coat over a blue shirt. His house was directly across the street from Paul's. Mr Lewis shifted uncomfortably in his chair after every answer, but those answers were loud and forthright.

'I was passing by my front windows about six-ish that afternoon and I seen her, that lady there. Her car was in the doctor's driveway and she was standing on the front porch, knocking, it looked like. I was just passing by; I didn't stop to study her. But after I went to the kitchen I heard the gunshot. I ran back to the living room and, on the way, I thought I heard another smaller bang, like a door slamming. When I got back to my front window she was gone from the porch,

219

but the door was just bouncing back closed, like she'd run in right after—'

'Thank you, Mr Lewis,' the prosecutor said smoothly. 'Let's not speculate, please. At any rate, Amy Shilling was gone from the porch by the time you got back.'

'Yeah.' The witness kept watching Amy. 'For me it was just, I saw a lady on the porch, then the next time I looked she was gone. I thought the second sound could've been the sound of the door slamming behind her when she went in.'

'Are you sure about the timing of what you saw and heard, Mr Lewis? Is it possible that in fact—?'

'Yeah, I'm sure,' the witness said, as if the prosecutor wasn't the first to try to budge him off his story. 'If she went in before the gunshot it was only by a few seconds. I think she was still—'

'Thank you, Mr Lewis. I'll pass the witness.'

Edward smiled at him pleasantly. 'What were you saying when the prosecutor interrupted, sir? You think she was still—?'

'Objection to speculation,' David Galindo said so quickly Edward hadn't even noticed him rising to his feet.

'Sustained,' the judge said blandly.

Edward stood up too. 'Your Honor, this isn't speculation. This is based on the witness's observations and memory. He can draw conclusions from his own perceptions. Any witness has to be allowed—'

'I've made my ruling, Mr Hall,' Cynthia cut him off.

220

Resuming his seat, Edward asked, 'Had you ever seen Amy at that house before, Mr Lewis?'

'Maybe once.'

'On this other occasion when you saw Amy, was it the same way? Standing on the porch, knocking at the door?'

'Yes, sir. One time when I was mowing my front yard I saw her pull up to the curb, get out and go up to the porch. She knocked and waited and the doctor came to the door and let her in.'

'Thank you, sir. I notice you keep calling your neighbor "the doctor." Did you know him by name?'

'Yeah, we met a couple of times. One time we were both outside and I went over and shook hands with him. Welcome to the neighborhood, that sort of thing. Another time his next-door neighbor was having a few of us over for drinks and he dropped by.'

'Was that Ms Linnett? Valerie?'

'Yeah. She had a nice deck in her backyard. When it was still a little cool – back in the fall, after the doctor had just moved in – she had people over.'

Edward sat staring at the witness, wondering what he knew and could say that would turn the case in Amy's favor. There was something, he felt sure. As Edward sat there he was struck forcefully by the fact that this man had been there, within sight and hearing, when the crime happened. He hadn't been able to see inside the house, but there must have been some other hint. Edward pictured the scene, Amy knocking, then a gunshot, either with her still on the porch or

221

just after she entered. And if there really was another person inside who'd killed Paul, how could this neighbor have told?

'The gunshot drew your attention, Mr Lewis?'

'Yes. Of course.'

'So after that you kept watching and listening?'

'Sure.'

'Do you remember hearing anything else after the gunshot?'

'Her scream. I remember that.'

'How did Amy look when you saw her standing on the porch, sir?'

'Look? She was just standing there, knocking.'

'Well, was she knocking as if in a hurry for the person inside to open up?' Edward demonstrated with a series of rapid, angry knocks on the counsel table.

'No, not like that. Just a simple knock, three or four times.' Mr Lewis was watching the lawyer intently.

'OK, fair enough. Did you see anything in her hands?'

'Purse, maybe. I don't remember anything else.'

'Certainly not a gun, right? You would have remembered that.'

'No sir. No gun.'

'Thank you, sir. Thank you for coming down, Mr Lewis.'

So the truck driver neighbor trudged away. As he passed the defense table, he gave Amy a sympathetic look.

Cynthia took a break in mid-afternoon. Edward thought about following her into her office to confront her, but that would be useless. He knew she was ruling against him more than she should, but had no idea what was behind that: just trying to look fair to both sides? To balance out doing him a huge favor over Paul's DVD? Or maybe, as the other lawyer had told him, she just really didn't know the rules of evidence. A judge who didn't know the law was scary, unpredictable.

During the break, while the jury was out of the room, Amy said to Edward,

'How do you think it's going?'

'Please don't ask me that every time we take a break, OK? I need to stay focused on the individual witnesses; I can't be taking the temperature of the case every few minutes.'

He'd snapped that out automatically, then realized it was exactly wrong. He did need constantly to evaluate the progress of the prosecution. Not as if watching over a sick patient, instead as if making small adjustments while sailing. If the wind changed, he needed to be aware of it and do something about it.

'Sorry.' He turned to her. 'How do *you* think it's going?'

Amy's eyes were wide and tear-filled.

'Amy. Amy.' He pulled her close and hugged her. She was a bundle of sticks. 'What's the matter? Relax, darling. It's fine, things are fine.'

He pulled back and saw those huge eyes still staring at him. The hug had worked as well as throwing gasoline on a flame.

'Edward,' she said, and it sounded as if her voice was coming out of those huge eyes. 'I can't – this

– this is—'And she started sobbing, right there in the middle of the still-crowded courtroom.

Edward just stared at her. He wanted to hold her again, but that was obviously worthless. Amy had just had *The Realization*. Yes, this was going forward. This trial wasn't a game of Clue, it was about her. *Her*. Her life and how it was going to be every day from now on. Either she would go back to her wonderful life as a successful doctor from a prosperous, well-known family, or she would be thrown into a black hole in the ground, from which she could never crawl out. From looking at her, it was clear Amy hadn't grasped it before. Edward remembered her first days in the courtroom, when it had all seemed like a game to her. Clearly, she had gotten over that.

'Amy?'

She gasped and took a deep breath. 'It's OK,' she said, and sniffled.

'Can I get you—?'

Amy said, 'No, I'll—' Then she suddenly stopped talking, as if she couldn't any more. Her throat went stiff, veins standing out, and she put her head back and screamed.

Screamed. Right in the courtroom, Amy lifted her head like a wolf and screamed. High-pitched but not weak, full-throated, a scream of pain and fear that wrapped the courtroom in what she was feeling. Edward felt it down his spine and along his arms, all his nerves responding. He wanted to reach for her but couldn't. That scream held him at bay like a wall between them. He reached out futile, trembling hands, but didn't touch her.

A bailiff started toward them, but he was a ways away. Amy dropped her head and started sobbing.

Ten minutes later it was an ordinary courtroom again, one in which nothing unusual seemed to have happened. The judge's empty bench loomed in Edward's view. Cynthia must have heard Amy's scream but the judge hadn't budged from her quarters. Was she just not interested?

Oh, they were going to have a talk about this, Edward and Cynthia. *Mano a mano*, felon to judge, equal to equal. He just wasn't sure when, or whether his sister would be on her way to prison by then.

'Amy,' he said calmly. 'Let me just clear up some information from these last couple of witnesses. OK?'

She nodded eagerly, a woman hanging on by her breaking nails.

'True you were empty-handed or almost when you knocked?'

She nodded. 'I was carrying a little clutch purse with my car keys in it, but I'd left my big purse in the car. Why?'

'It's a good detail. It means you weren't carrying a gun.'

Paul had been shot with his own gun, indicating a spontaneous murder. And those usually took longer to happen than the short time between when Amy knocked and when the gunfire was heard. For Amy and Paul, there had been no time for an argument to develop, for horrible, finalistic words to be exchanged.

225

'Edward?' Amy's voice was high still, dropping back to a little girl's. 'Eddie? We're going to win this, right?'

He looked into her big, round, terrified eyes.

Wrapping up the afternoon was the medical examiner who'd performed the autopsy; always gruesome testimony, a human broken down into parts, those parts disrupted by violence. Amy sat forward for this, staring at the woman as she listened to the medical details. Occasionally Amy nodded, sometimes a crease appeared between her brows.

Edward didn't see what could be won from this witness. Paul was unquestionably dead and a bullet had certainly accomplished that. But Amy listened as if she could unravel some mystery that might bring him back.

The prosecutor (this time David Galindo's young assistant) asked, 'Dr Skinner, what was the most obvious finding of your autopsy?'

The M.E. was young-looking, slender and had large glasses that magnified her brown eyes. The question startled her; lawyers didn't usually cut to the chase like this.

After a moment of reflection she said, 'Well, obviously, the bullet hole and its entry into the body.'

'Where was the entry wound?'

Edward looked over at the young prosecutor, liking her against his will. He admired her jumping right into the meat, so to speak, of the testimony.

'The bullet entered from the back, almost

under his shoulder, so it went through the ribs and the lung.'

'Can you describe more fully "from the back," Dr Skinner?'

'Yes. The back of his left side. More nearly his side, actually, the bullet hit a rib, nicked one of the ventricles of the heart, and, as I said, went into the lung.'

Amy's study of the doctor was no longer intent and clinical. She sat back with her hand to her mouth, tears starting from her eyes.

'Was that a fatal wound, doctor?'

'Oh yes. It would have been impossible to restart the heart' – she glanced over at Amy, her medical colleague, who had attempted the life-saving procedure, as if to comfort her in her failure – 'after a wound like that. The heart simply wouldn't perform its function. It was emptying of blood even as it filled and the lung was collapsed. He was . . .' She gave Amy another long look. Edward had never seen anything like this in a courtroom. Amy just stared back, but not hostilely, just as if she had given the M.E. permission to finish her sentence. The witness went on, 'He was lost as soon as the bullet went through him.'

'Were there any other injuries?'

The doctor frowned at her report. 'Some healing scratches on the back of one hand that seemed unrelated. And a healing scratch on his neck as well. But they had nothing to do with the cause of death.'

Edward remembered what Louise Fisher had said about Paul coming in scratched a couple of

227

times, as if he was in a volatile relationship and enjoying it.

Soon after that the young prosecutor said, 'Pass the witness.'

Edward took his time starting in. He sat there looking as if he was thinking, a tactic he had often used in court, but this time he really was thinking. Then he abruptly stood up and twisted his torso, reaching his right hand up under his left shoulder. 'So you're saying Paul was shot about here, Dr Skinner?'

'Yes. Slightly farther back, actually. Just under the latissimus dorsi muscle, if you know what that means. You can see it on my chart.'

'Yes. The near back of the ribcage, sort of.'

'I guess you could put it that way.'

Edward walked toward her, continuing to twist himself.

'So, doctor, if Paul was facing someone with a gun, who fired at him, what would he have to do – what would they both have to do – for him to be wounded in that way, if the person with the gun fired at him?'

'He would have . . .' Dr Skinner was twisting in her seat.

'You can stand and show us,' Edward said. He didn't even look at Cynthia.

The young medical examiner came down the couple of steps from the witness stand. She turned out to be almost a head shorter than Edward. He stepped back, looked at her unlined face and wide brown eyes, and saw that she was waiting for his direction.

Edward said, 'All right, you be the shooter, Dr

Skinner. I'll be Paul. Direct me. Tell me what I'd have to do for the bullet to enter where it did. How about if I started out facing you, for example?'

'Well, you'd have to turn away from me. Pivot on your right foot, turning toward your right, almost all the way around but not quite. There. Stop.'

Edward felt uncomfortable, barely balanced with most of his weight on his right foot, his torso twisted. He was facing away from the jury box now, toward his sister at their counsel table. Edward almost had his back completely turned away from the M.E. but not quite.

'Like this?'

'Yes. Approximately. Within a couple of inches, I'd say.'

Edward looked back over his left shoulder at her and saw that Dr Skinner, consciously or otherwise, had fashioned her right hand into a gun in the classic childhood manner, her index finger pointing toward him.

'And from your examination of the body, would the shooter have been firing the gun from about the position where your hand is now?'

The doctor looked down, as if suddenly aware that she'd armed herself.

'Um. No. The bullet entered the body at a less sharp angle than this would produce. She raised her hand about six inches, holding it awkwardly higher than a person naturally would. The natural inclination would be just to lift the forearm at the elbow, keeping the upper arm hanging straight down. The way Dr Skinner stood looked very awkward.

'Is that about right, doctor?'

She looked down at the angle of her finger and across to Edward. 'Yes. About like this.'

'This feels very uncomfortable,' Edward said, his voice showing the strain of his unusual posture.

'Object to counsel testifying,' the young prosecutor said quickly, but Edward ignored her, not even hearing Cynthia's ruling. He assumed she'd sustained the objection, but that was insignificant. He'd said what he had to say, and the jury could see it. Edward broke the pose and walked back toward his witness.

'Just a minute, please, doctor. Hold that pose for a moment, would you. How does that feel? Natural?'

'No. It feels awkward. I couldn't hold this pose for very long. It's straining my arm.'

'All right. Drop it then, Dr Skinner. Thank you.' He waved her back toward the witness stand. As Edward walked back toward his table he said, 'How tall are you, Dr Skinner?'

'Five four,' she said as she settled in her seat.

Edward nodded as he sat too. 'And I'm five eleven, about the same—'

'Objection,' the prosecutor said, more quickly this time.

'Sustained,' the judge said forcefully.

'About the same height as the deceased,' Edward finished.

Before he could ask another question, the judge said sharply, 'Counsel approach the bench.' Edward and both prosecutors went up to her, Edward strolling, the other two walking more quickly, their heads already bowed slightly in deference. When they all got close, Cynthia leaned across the bench and said, 'Mr Hall, you will not ignore the court's rulings and talk past them. If you do so again I will hold you in contempt and punish you with jail time. Do you understand?'

'I do, Your Honor.' He answered coolly, staring back at her. Then he remembered she still had a very significant ruling hanging over Amy's head and he recovered himself. 'I apologize to the court,' he added, trying to sound both humble and remorseful. 'I got caught up in the moment. It won't happen again, Your Honor.'

She nodded, perhaps mollified. Cynthia's glare was a powerful thing. He could see it retreat even while she continued to look at him. Then she nodded, dismissing them all.

Edward resumed his seat, wondering what he was doing. He'd known a handful of lawyers who openly battled with judges when in trial. Edward had always thought such lawyers were idiots. Why antagonize the one person with the most power over what evidence the jury got to hear or not? But now he could understand. If Cynthia wasn't going to do anything but damage his case anyway, why defer to her? Let the jury see how bad a judge he thought she was.

But there was still her ruling on the late Paul's DVD accusation to come. That was too crucial to get into these petty confrontations with the judge. He drew a deep breath and tried to settle down.

In the meantime, the prosecutor was asking the witness, 'Doctor, you said the way you were holding the gun felt awkward. But it only takes a moment to fire a gun, doesn't it?'

'So I understand. I've never fired one.'

'And a person can fire a gun while raising it, correct?'

'Objection, Your Honor. Calls for speculation. She just said she's never fired a gun.'

Edward had kept his voice quiet and respectful. Cynthia looked at him, nodded and said, 'Sustained.'

'And Mr Hall said the way he was standing felt uncomfortable. But it's not your testimony that the deceased was standing that way, posed like a statue when he was shot, is it, doctor?'

'Objection, Your Honor. This witness certainly wasn't at the scene. She can't possibly answer that question.'

'Sustained,' Cynthia said, this time still staring off over the lawyers' heads. Apparently Edward had accomplished what he'd wanted with his fake apology.

Both sides passed the witness and she was excused. As the doctor walked out she looked at Edward and gave him a little nod as she passed him.

Amy leaned over to whisper, 'Was the prosecution witness just flirting with you?'

'You know how those pretty women doctors are,' he whispered back. 'They can't help themselves.' It was a relief to hear Amy regain her normal tone of voice. She couldn't stay as clenched as she'd been right after lunch. Her personality was reasserting itself.

When the judge told David Galindo to call his next witness he asked instead to approach the bench.

There he said, 'Judge, it's after four thirty and

we need to have a brief hearing outside the jury's presence. We only have a handful of more witnesses to present. Could we excuse the jury now and do that hearing?'

Cynthia turned toward the jurors and smiled.

'Ladies and gentlemen, we'll make this first day a short one for you. Please remember the court's instructions. Don't watch or listen to any media coverage, and don't allow anyone to talk to you about this case. Have a good evening.'

Amy stood and watched them, but the jurors left with their heads down, none of them looking at her.

Then the lawyers turned back to the judge.

'Your Honor,' David began, 'as I said, the State only has a few more witnesses. This is a very straightforward case. We wanted to alert the defense to that first of all, that we will probably be resting our case tomorrow. Maybe by lunch time. But in that regard, Your Honor, we need the court's ruling on the admissibility of our crucial piece of evidence; the recording Dr Shilling made accusing the defendant of his murder.'

'Before it happened or before anyone knew it might,' Edward pointed out.

'Yes, I've already heard the arguments from both sides, Mr Hall.'

'Your Honor, they don't even have a witness to authenticate that DVD, anyone to say it hasn't been tampered with. I can bring the court a photograph with Paul Photoshopped into it to make it look like he's sitting in the audience during this murder trial. That wouldn't be evidence and neither is this. There are any number of ways—'

David interrupted, 'We can put on any of several witnesses to identify Dr Shilling on the DVD. We can—'

'I *said*,' Cynthia snapped, then recovered herself, 'the court has already heard both sides' arguments and reviewed your case law. I understand your need for a ruling at this point and I think both sides deserve one. Very well.'

Edward felt a calm settle over him. Winning this issue would feel like a triumph, no matter how the rest of the trial went. At least he'd be assured that no other lawyer could have done a better job for Amy than he had. And in that moment he felt sure he had read Cynthia correctly. She'd been ruling against him on almost everything else so far, so she wouldn't look biased in his favor when she awarded him this one. It would appear to be a just and impartial ruling.

'None of the cases presented to the court address this issue precisely.' She held up her hand as both lawyers started trying to speak again. 'But certain principles do emerge. Here is the court's ruling: State, if you can produce an expert to say the recording hasn't been altered in any way and another to identify the deceased on that recording, it will be admitted.'

'*What?!*' Edward almost screamed. 'But that doesn't address the content at all, Judge. It's hearsay. There's no way on earth it's admissible. No appellate court—'

But he was talking to himself. Cynthia had

234

pulled a judge's favorite trick, rising and turning in one motion as soon as she'd made her ruling, disappearing out her back door in a swirl of robe.

Edward turned and stared at his sister, feeling his own face draining of blood just like Amy's was.

Fifteen

When Edward arrived at Linda's house it was dark and he felt like a creature of the night, a vampire or a ghost haunting this world. He couldn't feel blood pumping through his body. He barely managed to trudge to the door.

They were screwed. His sister was headed for death row. That recording of Paul looking into the camera and saying if anyone killed him it would be Amy, no matter how much Edward could discredit it, no matter how much doubt he could cast on it, was devastating. Who wouldn't believe a man saying he knew who was going to kill him? Tomorrow the jurors were going to look into Paul's eyes, hear him telling them the answers to any questions they might have and they were going to believe. There was no possibility they wouldn't.

He knocked. Seconds went by. Half a minute. His hand was raised to knock again when the door opened. Linda looked out, appearing startled.

'Jesus. Edward. I wasn't expecting you.'

'Really? You didn't think I'd come home?'

Linda looked at him, a long steady stare.

'Come on in,' she said finally.

When she opened the door fully, he saw she had damp hair and was wearing shorts and a T-shirt.

'I'm surprised to see you,' she repeated. 'I thought

236

you'd be with Mike and Amy, or with all your family.'

'I was. We had a lot to talk about.'

Linda made no response, not by word or posture or gesture. He reached for her, hugged her, laid his head on her shoulder. God, he was glad to see her. Linda meant so much to him, to be able to see her, to come home to her like this, to always have her waiting.

'It's so great to see you.'

She cocked one eyebrow. 'Thank you.' She sounded a little surprised.

'Yeah, of course. I thought you'd come to lunch with us today. I wanted to ask you what you thought about that one witness. Valerie Linnett. The next-door neighbor. She—'

'Edward. I don't have any advice.'

'Oh. OK, well, I didn't think you'd have any specific advice, but if we talked about it like we do—'

'Edward.'

He didn't like the way she kept stopping him with his own name, seemed a bad sign. Linda looked down, shook her head as if sighing, then raised her eyes and crossed her arms.

Oh, shit, he thought. *Crossed arms.*

'Edward, if you had asked me to take the day off to watch your first day of trial I would have. I would have taken a leave of absence from my job for the last month, for two months, so I could have helped you prepare and be there every day making notes. But I just dropped by for a few minutes on the short lunch break I had. I don't have any insight to give you. I watched that woman, but just like anybody else in the audience. I don't know what to tell you. Seemed to me to be telling the truth but who knows? If I had more to go on maybe I'd have a suggestion, but what I've heard about her has just been hit or miss.'

'Linda,' he began, and then she did something very hard. She just stood there silently, looking right at him, listening to how he'd finish that aborted sentence.

And he had nothing. Nothing to say. He knew what she was about to say and he had no answer for it.

After a few seconds, she took pity on him and started talking again. Her voice was odd, quiet but strong, forceful without being shrill. It seemed like Linda, her strong, solid, practical essence simmered down into that soft, authoritative voice.

'If you had ever, at any point in this case, asked for my help I would have dropped everything else to do whatever little pitiful thing I could have done for you and Amy. I hoped you knew that, but I've never been able to tell. You just come and go, and when there's a really important war council it's you going over to meet with Mike, or Mike and Amy, or Amy and all your family.'

'I brought you into my family, I thought.'

'Oh for Christ's sake, please.' She dropped her folded arms and stared at him as if he'd said something completely off the point. 'You're not serious, are you? *You* brought me into your family? I wormed my way in; I practically had to blackmail you. You didn't ever want me to meet them.'

'I've told you why—'

She held up a hand and he stopped talking. Linda was in complete charge.

'You didn't bring me into your family. You didn't let me into your *life*. That was all me, Edward. I'm sorry. I'm afraid maybe I . . . took advantage of you.' She shook her head. 'But whatever. I'm not your assistant; I'm not even your girlfriend. I'm just some girl you used to know slightly who threw herself at you at a low point in your life.'

He had no answer to that, because it was the simple truth. There had been times he'd had dark thoughts exactly like what she'd just said. He could say he was glad to have her in his life now, but he hadn't demonstrated that lately. Linda, hearing his silence, gave him a wry smile.

'Yeah. I'm sorry, Edward. I wanted to save this until after the trial, but I've been rehearsing that speech and you set it off.'

He reached for her. Linda let him touch her arms, but she didn't lean forward for a hug. Edward dropped his hands back to his sides.

'I've tried to be supportive,' she continued, looking down. 'I know what you're going through. You and Amy. But you don't need my support. You don't need me. Just go do what you have to do.'

He reached for her again and this time Linda turned away, back toward the open door of the house. Edward followed and stepped outside. 'Please go away now. I'm not going to change my mind.'

'Linda—'

She turned back and looked at him. An ironic smile didn't hide the tears in her eyes. She stood there waiting, letting him say whatever he wanted.

And again he had nothing. Linda had latched onto him so quickly, as soon as he'd walked out the prison doors, there hadn't been time for him to examine how he felt about her. Just being with her had felt so comfortable. Comforting. When that door closed with Linda on the other side, it was going to feel like he'd just been kicked out of his home.

'I'm sorry,' he said. 'Sorry I didn't make you feel wanted. Sorry I got so distracted with this case I forgot to tell you how grateful I am for everything you've done.'

She started crying, with one sharp sob that sounded jerked out of her, then with a steady flow of tears and her shoulders gently shaking. Edward reached to comfort her and she shrugged off his hand. '"Grateful,"' she said.

'I mean—'

'You mean what you said. Thank you for your expression of gratitude,' she added, trying to sound ironic, but Linda had too much sincerity for that. He heard exactly what she meant and how deeply he had hurt her.

'Good luck,' she said in a low voice, then raised her head. 'I mean that. Good luck to you and Amy in this trial. You'll win it. You know that. You're the best.'

She turned quickly and closed the door. Edward stood staring at it for long seconds, hoping for a change of heart on the other side, but it didn't come. Linda had spoken with the slow, resigned voice of a woman who had spent a long time thinking about what she was saying. He wouldn't be able to change her mind.

Edward turned away, took a few steps along the porch, then turned and looked back at the closed door.

Yes, it felt exactly as if he'd just been kicked out of his home.

He sat there for a few minutes on the porch, hoping she'd regret her decision and come out. He looked at his car in the driveway, the lights in the houses across the way. If he lived here, there might be a fight going on inside, or at least entreaty. But, instead, he was here on the porch because he'd arrived from somewhere else. If he'd run over there'd be no sign he was even here, except for him sitting on the porch.

The problem was that she wasn't wrong about anything. Linda was very perceptive. Smart emotionally rather than intellectually. She read people very well. Edward just hadn't realized she'd been reading him all this time. He'd been so distracted by other events – finding a job, readjusting to being outside the walls, then Amy's arrest – that he'd taken Linda and his relationship with her for granted. She was his girlfriend because she was the only woman he was dating. Edward had taken that part of his life at what he thought was face value. Now he realized Linda hadn't been distracted, not like he thought. *She'd* been paying attention to him; *he'd* been taking her for granted. That must have hurt her like hell, for her to break up with him now, during the biggest crisis of his life. He wanted to go back and replay every scene with her. But it was too late for that because, unfortunately, she understood everything, with her emotional brilliance.

'Are you OK?'

'No, Amy, I am not OK. I'm extremely pissed off at this judge for letting in this piece of evidence, I'm pissed off at the prosecutor for even offering it and I'm trying to think damage control and coming up with nothing. So no, not OK.'

They were sitting at their table in court – *that* had started to feel like home – waiting for the jurors to come in. Edward hadn't told Amy about Linda. He didn't want his sister to think he was distracted.

He sat up straight, looked down at his notes and tried actually not to be distracted. OK. The devastating DVD was going to come into evidence. What do you do about that? Think about how to counter it. Even use it to advantage, if there was any possible way. No possible way to do that in this case. What was the other thing, then? He tried to remember his training.

Suddenly the judge entered, walking briskly to her bench at almost the same time as the jurors started into the room, from another door in the corner. Edward didn't even bother to glare at her.

'Call your next witness, State,' Cynthia said.

Surprisingly, the name the prosecutor said when he stood up was, 'Dr Louise Fisher.' Paul's research partner.

She entered quickly. Edward turned to watch her come up the aisle. It was hard for him to remember what she looked like out of a white lab coat. Today, Dr Fisher had chosen a simple dress in a muted blue color. It looked vaguely professional and also vaguely frumpy. He understood. She didn't want to appear as Paul's lover, just his colleague.

She sat in the witness chair and took the oath without looking at the counsel tables. David quickly established her credentials and familiarity. Then he held up a DVD – *the* DVD – in a sleeve marked with a tag and identified it as State's Exhibit 68.

'Do you recognize this, Dr Fisher?'

'Yes. I've seen it once in your office and then again this morning.'

'Can you tell us who appears on this recording?'

'Dr Paul Shilling.'

'The man you shared offices with for how many years?'

'Seven.'

'Any doubt in your mind of the identity of the person on this DVD?'

'No sir. None.'

'Does anyone else appear on this recording?'

'No. Just Paul.'

'Thank you, Dr Fisher. Pass the witness.'

There was no point to asking her any questions. She couldn't help him, not with this part of trial. All she had done was identify a man on a recording – accurately, as Edward knew very well.

'Hello, Dr Fisher. Just a few questions now.'

She clutched her purse. Her face looked pale and vulnerable.

'Do you recognize the background in this recording?'

She gulped, frowned, tried to think. 'I didn't really notice it. It's a paneled wall, nothing on it. No, I didn't recognize it.'

'Is it Paul's house?'

'I've never been to the house where he was living when he – when he died.'

'No? But didn't you see each other socially as well as professionally?'

'Yes, but he – Paul – wouldn't tell people where he lived.'

'Or at least not you?'

'Yes.'

'Let's go back to that paneled wall. Is it his office?'

'No. That's completely different material and he has diplomas and professional certificates and photos on his office wall. No, I've never seen this place before.'

'You said you've seen this DVD all the way through. Does Paul appear to be his normal self on it?'

Dr Fisher frowned, leaning forward in the witness stand. 'What do you mean "normal?"'

'Does he seem the same as he usually did? Such as at a day at the office.'

'Well, he's—' She checked herself and thought.

'Would you like to see it again?'

'No. I actually have very good visual memory,' she said distractedly. 'I'm just playing it back in my mind.'

As he waited, Edward looked at the jurors. They seemed to watch her as respectfully as Edward, quiet as spectators at a surgery. Dr Fisher came out of her mini trance and said, 'I certainly can't say he appeared as he did every day. Certainly he's much more intense on the recording than he usually is.'

'Is that the only difference?'

'He—' she began, then shrugged. 'I don't know what you're looking for.'

'You saw Paul socially as well as professionally, didn't you, doctor?'

She stared at him and it seemed she wouldn't answer, but then she did. 'Yes. A handful of times.'

'Did you see him when he'd been drinking?'

She went back to staring at him so directly it seemed like a glare, except that her face retained almost no expression. *Oh yes,* Edward thought, *for this woman and Paul to have any chance of engaging like human beings, alcohol would have had to be applied. Liberally.*

'Yes. Not to excess, but a few drinks, yes.'

'Based on that experience, would you say he'd been drinking when he made this recording?'

'We weren't drinking buddies,' she snapped. 'I haven't studied him for signs of intoxication.'

'That's too bad,' Edward said. 'You might have made a more helpful witness.'

'Objection,' David Galindo said, on his feet. There was a pause, and Edward realized David must be doing what Edward himself was, thinking of what exactly was objectionable about Edward's last remark. *Defense counsel is being a smartass* should cover it.

'Argumentative,' David finally blurted.

Cynthia immediately said, 'Sustained,' which

245

clearly would have been her response no matter what the prosecutor said.

Edward almost felt he could ignore the judge. Her rulings no longer had significance for him. She had already dropped the atom bomb on him. He didn't have to worry about her sniper fire.

Besides, he had remembered his training. How to use this witness.

'Let me ask you about your social relationship with Paul. When did you begin—'

'Objection,' the prosecutor said again. 'This exceeds the scope of the direct examination. I only asked her to identify a person on a recording.'

Edward was standing too before David finished talking.

'Your Honor, we enjoy in Texas what is known as "wide open cross." Once you put a witness on the stand, that witness may be cross-examined on any relevant subject. I'm sure the court is familiar with this concept, having used it many times as a very successful prosecutor. It means when a witness—'

'Counselor, you may stop the law school lecture.' Cynthia was looking at him directly, her unlined face curious. 'I'll allow it.'

Edward sat quickly. 'When did you begin dating your colleague, Dr Fisher?'

She wrinkled her nose in obvious distaste. 'We went out together a handful of times. I'm not sure when it began.'

'Well, let's narrow it down. Was it before or after Paul separated from his wife?'

Her eyes widened as she looked at Amy, shaking her head. 'After, of course. Long after.'

'How did it happen?'

Louise Fisher shifted uncomfortably on her chair. The jurors were no longer slumping, all of them watching her.

'Casually, I suppose. One day we were finishing up rather later than usual, and he asked me if I'd like to go have a drink with him and maybe dinner. I didn't see any reason to refuse.'

'Where did you go?'

She named a well-known local seafood restaurant. Edward remembered it from his prior life. Expensive, dark, with booths that were completely private and separate from each other.

'How nice. What were you drinking?'

'I had a gin and tonic, maybe two, then we ordered dinner and Paul ordered a bottle of wine.'

'Did you have your share of it?'

'At least. Later it seemed to me Paul hadn't been drinking as much.'

'How did that evening end?'

Louise Fisher shifted in her chair again. Very few witnesses realize how they reveal themselves in their body language as they testify. The jurors were a few feet from her. Every little hesitation, cough, clearing of the throat, shifting of the eyes, registered with those people in the jury box, who had been charged with paying the most attention they'd ever paid in their lives to any event. Most jurors take that very seriously. These saw the witness shift, look down, and decide whether she was going to answer the question truthfully. It was very obvious.

She lifted her head and looked straight at her interlocutor.

'Paul offered to drive me home and, after the drinks and the wine, that seemed prudent. He said he'd come back in the morning and pick me up. Then when we got to my house he suggested maybe it would be easier if he just spent the night there. That took me by surprise.'

'Was he suggesting sleeping on your couch or in your guest room?' Edward asked in a very neutral voice. Nevertheless, Louise looked at him sharply.

'No. Right after he said it he kissed me.'

'Hmm,' Edward said, then just sat there musing, as if he'd been as taken by surprise by her answer as Louise had obviously been by the kiss. She was blushing, looking down at her hands, twisting in the chair. She couldn't look at Amy any more.

'Did he spend that night with you?'

'Objection to relevance,' David Galindo said. 'This isn't about this witness's love life.'

'No, it's about the deceased's,' Edward responded quickly. 'The State has suggested he was killed in a crime of passion. It's certainly relevant to inquire into who else might have had similar feelings.'

'Overruled,' Cynthia said. 'But only so far, Mr Hall. I don't want you needlessly embarrassing this witness.'

'Yes, Your Honor.' As if he cared. 'That means you need to answer the question, Dr Fisher. Did Paul spend that night with you?'

'No,' she said in a tiny voice. Then she added just as quietly, 'Not that night.'

'So you did go out again.'

'Yes.' She suddenly looked up and appealed to him. 'They were separated. They had filed for divorce. He didn't seem to me like a married man anymore.'

'I understand. So tell me about the relationship, please.'

'We did one more drink-after-work occasion. That time I kissed him back when he dropped me off. The next time was an actual date. Paul picked me up on a Saturday night, we went to dinner again, walked around a little, talking, then back to my place. This time it was sort of understood that he would stay.'

'So you had sex.'

She nodded, eyes downcast again.

'How long did that relationship continue?' Edward asked gently.

'Not long.' Louise's blush had deepened. 'Maybe two or three occasions. It seemed—' She stopped herself.

Edward waited, then asked quietly, 'It seemed like what?'

Louise looked up, straight at Amy this time, and said, 'It seemed like Paul had gotten what he wanted.'

She wanted his wife to know it hadn't been her fault, she hadn't been the seductress; she'd been the victim.

'But the sexual aspect of the relationship did continue for at least a brief while, from what you've said. Yet you said Paul wouldn't let you know where he lived?'

'No. I asked, he avoided the question. After we'd stopped the . . . the dating relationship, it seemed to me he hadn't wanted me to be able to find him and make a scene. He had a refuge to escape to.'

'Did you believe he had other women when he was with you?'

'I knew he did. That's one of the things that made me feel' – she gulped but continued – '*used*. He lost interest quickly and I felt like a fool.'

'But you continued working with him?'

'Yes. I didn't feel I had much choice about that. The research was important. It was important in and of itself and it was important to both our careers. I didn't want to jeopardize that.'

'Did you feel jealous when you thought about him and the other women?'

Louise shook her head, no longer making eye contact with anyone.

'I'm sorry, Dr Fisher, but you have to answer out loud.'

'No, I wasn't jealous. Not the least bit. I just felt – sullied.'

'Do you know the names of other women he dated, Dr Fisher?'

She named three names, one of them Laura Martinelli.

'Were you jealous because you knew about those women? Did he flaunt them in front of you?'

Louise Fisher looked up, eyes making perfect circles, to match her mouth. 'Oh no. Oh no. I felt sorry for them. I wanted to tell them . . .'

'What did you want to tell them, Louise? These other women Paul dated?'

She raised her head suddenly, stared at him and said loudly, 'I wanted to tell them, *Run away! Don't do it. He just – He just wants to use you.*'

'No more questions,' Edward said very quietly.

Then he noticed the silence. The prosecutors were whispering, heads bent together. Edward took the opportunity to look at the jurors, whose eyes were all over the place. A few still stared at Louise Fisher with evaluating looks and Edward suddenly wondered if he'd just ruined his own case. If he'd just proved the deceased was a lying asshole scoundrel, didn't that give his sister sitting beside him more of a motive for killing the bastard?

'No more questions,' he suddenly heard from the prosecutor. Poor broken Louise looked around, wondering what she was supposed to do now.

David ignored her and said, 'Your Honor, we have a very brief witness to testify to the authenticity of this next exhibit.' He held Paul's DVD in his hand. 'Then we'll be playing that for the jury. Should we proceed, or—?'

'How long is the recording, counselor?'

'Relatively brief, Your Honor. Ten minutes or so.'

Judge Cynthia looked over at the jurors, who looked back at her noncommittally.

'I think this jury deserves a break first. Bailiff?'

The bailiff led the jurors out through the door up near the judge's bench. Cynthia exited out her own private door. Louise Fisher sat forgotten on the witness stand, looking confused about what to do next.

Then someone appeared at her elbow. It was Amy, up there standing next to Louise, offering her an arm. Louise looked at her with a mixture of gratitude and apprehension, and sweet little Amy patted her hand.

One juror, looking back, saw this exchange. Only one.

Edward stayed at counsel table with Amy during the break. The prosecutors were gone, so the front of the room was actually a little private.

'Listen, Amy, they're going to be playing Paul's video during this next part. How you watch it is very important. Don't sit there and look pissed off – it's the worst thing you can do. That's like you're sullen because you've been caught and don't sit there shaking your head. That looks annoyed and guilty. Like you're mad that this evidence got found instead of, you know . . .'

'Mournful and sad because I'm seeing my beloved husband for maybe the last time?'

He looked at her, startled. It was the most cynical remark he'd ever heard his sister make.

'I meant that actually is how I'm going to feel, Edward.' She crossed her arms under her breasts. 'Any other advice? Make-up tips?'

'Amy, this is important. This could be the whole ballgame.'

'I know. I know.' He could hear the tears at the back of her throat. 'This is me being found guilty. I understand, Edward. What expression of mine can change that?'

Edward didn't know. He didn't even know what face she could wear to convince him of her innocence.

* * *

Some electronics nerd testified for the State that the DVD had not been altered, then David offered the recording.

Edward rattled off a string of objections, ending with, 'But most of all, Judge, this completely deprives my client of her right to cross-examine witnesses against her. There's no way I can question this supposed "witness" about what he's saying. And I have a lot of questions for him, Your Honor. Starting with why would you—?'

'I will allow you to make a bill of exceptions about those, counselor. Anything else?'

'It's just not fair,' Edward said, and heard himself whining like a child at bedtime. 'We don't know anything about this recording. If he was drunk, if there was someone out of camera range holding a gun on him, if—'

'I get it, Mr Hall. Overruled. Mr Galindo, the exhibit is admitted and you may publish it for the jury.'

A television on a rolling cart had been set up directly across from the jury box. It seemed a wave went across the spectators as they all turned more or less in unison. David's second chair pressed play on the remote control.

Paul came onto the screen abruptly, as if he'd leaped into the television. He sat there for the beat of a few seconds, staring straight into the camera. Did he look drunk? Wasn't that the stare of a drunken man trying to concentrate?

But he spoke very well. 'My name is Dr Paul Shilling. Today is March fourteenth. Almost the Ides. I am making this recording because I'm uneasy. It's probably nothing, and I'll just laugh

253

and destroy this in a few months. But right now, I think it's important to say that, if I am found dead, it will be my wife, Dr Amy Shilling, who murdered me.' He continued, looking fixedly into the camera.

Edward shifted his study from Paul to the room behind him, not much of it was visible. Paul sat in a low chair. The camera showed him at medium range, from about the waist up. Paul leaned toward it as if trying to convince the camera of his sincerity. The wall behind him was paneled in medium brown wide planks. There was nothing on the wall except a couple of small objects that caught the light. Edward concentrated and saw that they were hooks.

He had seen this short recording half a dozen times, but for the first time he noted a drop of sweat on Paul's forehead. Edward looked intently at him, listened hard. Yes, he heard it now, the slight slur to some of Paul's words. Speaking about Amy wanting to reconcile with him, he was saying, 'Let's just say we have completely, uh, conflicting views on that. I just want to get divorced.' And Edward heard, 'Lesh jusht say . . .' and 'I jusht want . . .' But Paul's next words were very clear, perhaps from overcompensating.

'I just want to get on with my life. I am afraid that very soon I'm going to have to make this absolutely clear to Amy, and when I do, well, she's subject to fits of anger. More than anger, really. She's attacked me physically in the past. And this is going to be humiliating for her. She's attached such importance to being a doctor's wife – *my* wife, to put it, um – that I don't know how

254

she'll react. Especially if she fin – especially if she thinks of me with another woman.'

Edward heard that Paul had been about to say '. . . if she *finds* me with another woman.' Acknowledging there were others. But they already knew that.

'I'm afraid that might push her over the edge. So I thought it would be prudent to make this record and give it to a friend, who will mail it to police if I'm murdered. As I said, I'm probably being melodramatic or overly – what's the word? – but at any rate, I wanted to do this. Thank you.'

The screen went dark.

'Pass the witness,' David said, which was hilarious. The witness still on the stand was the technician who'd testified to the accuracy of the recording, but there was nothing to cross-examine him about. The real witness had been Paul, and as Edward had pointed out to the judge multiple times, he was beyond questioning.

Edward turned and looked at his sister for the first time since the recording had started playing. Amy sat there with a hand up to her mouth, a tear streak running down her cheek. She looked devastated, trying hard to hold herself up. She had found the right expression for watching her late husband accuse her. Amy just looked unbearably sad, as if her heart had been pierced by seeing the man she loved one last time, with him unable to respond or know she was near.

Edward stood up and said to the judge, 'I can't cross-examine the witness who just testified, Paul Shilling. I can't ask him why he made that recording or how he came to that wrong conclusion. I can't question the person who was holding the camera. Can't ask Paul how much he'd had to drink before he—'

'Objection, objection,' David Galindo said. 'Object to counsel testifying.'

'Sustained,' the judge said, looking sternly at him.

Edward turned and looked at his opponent, David Galindo. Edward's former rival in the D.A.'s office, but that was a long time ago. David had far surpassed whatever Edward had accomplished as a prosecutor. And he was a decent guy, or so Edward thought. But a lot of lawyers take on trial personalities that are different from their day to day ones. Even opposing lawyers who were good friends in real life couldn't necessarily trust each other in the courtroom. *That wasn't me, that was my evil trial twin.*

Edward decided to take the chance.

He said, 'Let the record reflect that the effect of that completely inadmissible evidence was devastating. The jurors were riveted. One woman on the jury began crying. They were sneaking looks at the defendant, obviously thinking: *How could you do this?* There is no way for the defense to recover from this piece of evidence.' Turning to the prosecutor, he says, 'Mr Galindo, do you disagree with anything I've said for the record?'

After a long pause the prosecutor said, 'No. No, I don't disagree about the effect of the evidence. Only about its admissibility.'

'I have no more questions of this witness,' Edward said.

David rose slowly, because it's a terrible moment,

frightening to give up control and said, 'The State rests, Your Honor.'

Cynthia turned. 'Does the defense have witnesses to present, Mr Hall?'

'You bet we do, Your Honor.'

She glanced at the clock on the back wall.

'We'll begin the defense case after lunch. Be back at one thirty, ladies and gentlemen.'

Sixteen

Amy turned quickly to Edward. 'Put me on first.'

He shook his head. Even if the defendant testi-fied, it wasn't until last. Amy would have the advantage of hearing all the other trial witnesses first; she could tailor her testimony to address all the evidence of trial. It was one of the very few defense advantages.

'Yes,' she insisted. 'Now while that recording is fresh in their minds. Let me explain it for them. Let me point out what's wrong with Paul. Let me tell my story before we put on the others. Yes, Edward. That way what I know and what I tell the jurors is the background for everything else we put on.'

He had two other witnesses waiting in the hall. Edward was ready to start his case today. But Amy made a good point.

'It's not a fight with the prosecutors, Amy. Looking mad is the worst thing you can do. If the jurors see you angry they can picture what you—'

'Do I look mad? Do I sound angry?'

He had to admit her voice was calm, her gaze steady.

'I just want to tell my story, Edward. I'm ready.'

He shrugged. 'OK. Let's go to lunch just you and me. I want to go over the main points again.'

Amy smiled. 'I thought you said you didn't want me to be over-rehearsed.'

Edward stood up. 'Lawyers say a lot of bullshit.'

'Please identify yourself.'

Amy turned to the jurors. 'I'm Amy Shilling.'

'It's Dr Shilling, correct?' Edward asked.

'Yes, I'm a pediatrician.'

'How old are you, Amy?'

'Thirty-two.'

'You were married to Dr Paul Shilling?'

'Yes.'

'For how long?'

'Two years. A little longer.'

Amy was composed on the stand but not blood-less. She moved easily in the hard chair when she turned, but didn't fidget. For some answers she looked directly at the jury. For some she paid close attention to her lawyer.

'How did you and Paul meet?'

'In medical school. Paul was ahead of me, already doing a residency in the hospital when I started. He asked me out not long after the first time we met.' She smiled, obviously still flattered.

'Did you work together?'

She shook her head. 'No. Never. We were in different fields. Paul was an internist and a researcher. He worked with my father, but not with me.'

'Who is your father?' Edward corrected himself. 'Our father.'

'Dr Marshall Hall. He's a well-known diagnostician. Paul began working with him after Paul and I started dating.'

Again, hearing her say that, Edward thought Paul sounded like an opportunist. He didn't want to hit that note very hard. Amy didn't seem to hear the implication of what she'd just said, which was good. Thinking her husband had taken advantage of her would be another motive for murder. In his peripheral vision, Edward saw both prosecutors bent over their legal pads making rapid notes.

'Tell me about Paul, about your relationship.'

Edward asked the broad, open-ended question and sat back. At first Amy kept looking down. Then she raised her head and smiled.

'He was a wonderful man. Driven, focused on what he was doing, which didn't just include his work. When he turned those brown eyes on me he still had that same focus. It could make you feel like a research subject, but then they would soften so much when he smiled and he had the gentlest touch.' She looked up and sniffed, then turned toward the jury. 'He was a good listener. The best. If I said his name he'd look up and put down whatever he'd been doing, the newspaper or tying a fishing fly. Look right at me and listen. We had such great weekends. Just us. Taking a little trip or just staying in. He had a gift for shutting out the world, wherever we were.'

To Edward it sounded as if she was talking about, at least in part, bed. Those intense weekends of not leaving the house, looking into his eyes. That would best be done from a supine position. He shied away from that subject. Passion begat passion. That was why he told himself not to ask. But the real reason was that he just couldn't ask his little sister to describe for strangers what a great lay her husband had been. Edward didn't want to hear it himself.

'Yet you were separated at the time of his death. Why?'

'Paul's idea,' Amy's eyes fluttered. 'We had only been married for two years, yes, but we'd been together much longer than that. It was like a very early seven-year itch for Paul. He was becoming well-known for the breakthroughs that were rumored about his cancer research, he was getting attention and I sensed he felt tied down.'

'"Sensed"?'

'Yes. He didn't say that, but I thought that was the reason. He told me other reasons – I was smothering him, he needed time apart, things like that – but I thought he felt restricted by being married. His behavior after we separated confirmed that for me.'

'So you knew about the other women in his life?'

Amy grimaced. 'Of course. The medical community in Houston is a small town. A small gossipy town. Of course I heard about Paul's social life.'

'What did you think about that?'

She looked at the jurors. 'I thought, at least he was honest enough to leave me first instead of having affairs. Later I thought, I guess he needed to get this out of his system.'

'Did you go out yourself?'

'I went out a handful of times. Very unsatisfactory for my dates, I'm sure. I was still in love with Paul.'

'What was the status of your relationship at the time Paul died?'

261

'We were reconciling. He'd spent a couple of nights back at the house; I'd been to his two or three times. I even started keeping clothes there. It seemed to me that Paul had had the fling he needed – flings – and discovered he still loved me and still wanted to be married to me. We'd even talked about getting pregnant.' She actually blushed. 'I think he was on the verge of coming back. We were going out that night to the dinner where he was going to receive his award. It was going to be a kind of a coming-out occasion for us; our first public reappearance.'

Edward was studying the jury as covertly as he could. A couple of them were leaning toward Amy ever so subtly. More than that still hung back in attitudes of skepticism – eyes hooded, hands covering mouths – but all of them studying her closely.

'So how were you feeling towards Paul as you stood on his porch that Saturday night?'

'In love. More than ever. Happy. Excited we were going out together. Happy for him about his award. Just happy. Standing there, I was happy.'

'Did you have anything in your hands?'

'Just a little clutch bag for my car keys. I'd left my purse in the car.'

'Amy, let's watch this DVD that Paul made again.' Without asking the judge's permission, Edward strode toward the television. He turned to his sister. 'Ready?'

She nodded. The jurors turned their lines of sight in Edward's direction, there was such a tight collective focus he could feel it. He turned on the television, picked up the remote control and pressed Play.

Edward stepped aside and talked over the first few words. 'What did you notice about this the first time you saw it, Amy?'

'That Paul was drunk when he made this.'

There were actually a couple of gasps from the audience. The jurors' faces changed too, frowning in concentration. Edward hit Pause. Paul stopped talking in mid-word, his mouth focused in a little o.

'How can you tell?'

'Paul wasn't much of a public drinker. Not many people had seen him intoxicated, I think. But I had. He drank more in the couple of months before he left me. I learned his pattern.'

'Such as what?'

'He'd start speaking more precisely, as he does here. Listen. "If-I-am-found-murd-ered," he's hitting the consonants very distinctly.'

Edward hit Play long enough for the jurors to hear that. Yes, he did sound like a man taking elocution lessons. But these jurors had no basis for comparison.

'What else?' he said over the still-playing DVD.

'At the same time,' Amy said, 'no matter how hard he tried, he'd still slur his words a little. There. Hear it? "Lesh jusht say . . ." He couldn't help himself. See him frown? He heard it himself. Now he'll try even harder for the next sentence or two to sound like Laurence Olivier.'

They all listened very hard to Paul trying very hard to sound sober and reliable. This time Edward let it play to the end. With Amy's commentary, they could all hear Paul stumble occasionally.

When it ended and Paul was frozen on the screen, Amy said, 'I could tell there at the end, too. When he can't find the word he was wanting? Paul was never at a loss for words. He sometimes sounded as if someone had written his lines for him ahead of time and he'd memorized them perfectly. If he was going to make something like this, something so supposedly important, he would have known what he was going to say. Here he was stumbling along, making it up as he went.'

'You heard the part where he said you had attacked him physically in the past.'

She made a sound between a laugh and a snort.

'Was that true?' Edward asked.

'No. It's ridiculous. I've never attacked anyone in my life, least of all Paul.'

'Amy, stand up, please. Come down off the witness stand.' She did, right in front of the jurors. Edward walked toward her.

'How tall are you?'

'Five four.'

'How tall was Paul?' By the time Edward asked that he was standing right in front of her, looking down. He couldn't help smiling at her, his little sister.

'About six feet, a little taller than you.'

At that moment, Edward seemed to soar over her. He'd told her to wear flats today.

Without being asked, she added, 'And he worked out, too. He worked out and ran, even more so since we'd separated. I would have been crazy to try to assault him.'

That wasn't a very good remark. The answer to it was: *That's why you used a gun.*

Amy went back to the witness stand.

'Amy, how were you feeling when you arrived at Paul's that day?'

'Happy. Paul and I were getting back together, I had a new dress and I was expecting a beautiful evening.'

'Did you ring the doorbell or knock or just go on in?'

'Both, sort of. I rang the bell, knocked, then started reaching for the doorknob.'

'And what happened?'

'I heard the shot.' Amy's voice had changed again. Her eyes were open and suddenly tearful. Edward looked at the jurors. He thought he had them then. Or rather, Amy did. It was very clear she was reliving the moment and on her face the jurors seemed to be too.

'What did you do?'

'I hesitated, I'm ashamed to say. It was a gunshot, it was dangerous. I thought about running back to my car for my phone and calling police. But then I thought it must have been an accident and maybe Paul was hurt. So I ran inside, calling his name.'

'Where was he?'

'In the bedroom. I ran back there and immediately saw him on the floor. He was lying on his back like he'd slumped forward onto the bed then slid down to the floor. The gun was on the floor. I kicked it out of the way as I ran to Paul and I immediately started trying to apply CPR. His phone was on the nightstand, and I called 911 and talked to the operator while I worked on him and kept telling them to hurry, hurry.'

'Was Paul – gone?'

'No. Not entirely. He was looking at me. I stopped for a couple of seconds to see if he could talk, but he just stared at me. Then his eyes got wider. I kept working, telling him to breathe. *Breathe, damn it.* But he couldn't. His eyes got wider, like I said, then they changed. Paul just – left. Suddenly, just like that, he was there then he wasn't. I started trying to keep oxygen going to his brain, so he wouldn't suffer brain damage if he could be revived, by doing chest compressions. I was still doing that when the paramedics arrived and took him. Then the police took me.'

She sounded and looked tired. In the short space of her testimony, Amy had relived the event and, aside from everything else, it had been hard physical work trying to keep her husband alive.

'Did you see any sign of anyone else when you went into the house?'

'No. But I wasn't looking for any. I thought I heard the bang of the back door closing, but I was focused only on Paul.'

Edward asked a few more questions, but he was done. He had never seen a more sincere-seeming witness than Amy had been, but maybe he was biased. Most of the jurors were looking at her sympathetically.

But Edward knew what was wrong with his case. That's why he was reluctant to stop questioning Amy, to turn her over to the opposition. Finally there was no choice, though.

'Pass the witness.'

'That was very selfless of you, Dr Shilling,

running into that house in spite of the personal danger to you.' Yes, David Galindo knew the problem with Edward's case too. It just wasn't believable, the timing.

'Well, as I said, I did hesitate. I'm ashamed of myself for that. But I thought Paul might be injured. I knew he had that pistol and I was afraid there'd been an accident with it.'

'So you knew about the gun?' David slouched back in his chair, watching Amy.

'Yes. He bought it a few years ago, for protection of the house, he said. Sometime after he left I noticed he'd taken it with him.'

'You went looking for the gun at your house?'

Amy understood where he was going. 'No. I was looking for something else in the drawer where I knew he kept it and saw it was gone.'

'Why did you look?'

'I was worried about Paul. He acted so strange in those days just before we separated, I was afraid he might, might be going to hurt himself. Plus he wouldn't tell me where he was living at first and when I saw he'd taken the gun I was afraid he might be in some dangerous neighborhood. I worried about him.'

They were reasonable answers Amy gave, but the prosecutor had accomplished something else with this line of questioning. Amy no longer looked tearful and sympathetic. She was staring at David, dueling with him. Very quietly, but still, her precise answers made her look careful rather than spontaneous as she'd seemed under Edward's guidance. Edward cleared his throat, trying to send her a signal, but Amy didn't glance his way.

267

'Did you see any other car when you parked in front of Paul's house?'

'No.'

'As you stood there on your estranged husband's porch—'

'Objection to fact not in evidence,' Edward said quickly. 'They weren't estranged, they were reconciling.'

'Quibbling over semantics, Your Honor. They remained separated.'

'Overruled.'

Edward remained on his feet for a second, staring at his sister. She finally glanced at him and understood from his slight frown what he was trying to convey. She didn't nod, but she inhaled a little raggedly and let out a long breath.

'As you stood there on your estranged husband's porch, did you hear raised voices?'

Amy sniffed again as she shook her head. 'No.'

'Any sounds at all from within the house?'

'Nothing I can recall.'

'You said you might have heard the back door banging shut as you ran in. You know no other witness we've heard from heard that?'

'I don't know that any of them were in a position to hear it.'

'Did you hear a car engine start in the alley?'

'No. By that time I was so busy with Paul all I could hear was my own pulse in my—'

'I'm sure. But a car starting is a pretty noticeable sound, isn't it?'

She nodded. David waited, making her speak. The prosecutor was hoping, Edward knew from experience, to make Amy glare at him. Nothing a prosecutor likes better than a murder defendant looking mad. It's almost as good as putting the gun in her hand. Amy didn't, though. She looked down at her own hands, then up again as if surprised David was still waiting. 'I suppose,' she said quietly.

'So you just happened to be standing on the porch at the exact time a fatal argument going on between your husband and someone else reached its climax. Is that your version of events, Dr Shilling?'

Still quiet, Amy said, 'No. I don't have a version. I'm just relating what I saw and heard.'

'Uh huh. OK, let's go over a few other things, ma'am.'

For half an hour he took her back through the facts of her marriage breaking up, her half-hearted dating of two or three other men (showing she was still emotionally attached to her husband), her knowledge of Paul's active social life (demonstrating the strong possibility of growing jealousy), the fact that she was the only person who'd heard that she and Paul might be reconciling.

Finally David turned to his assistant, whispered to her, and she handed him a large shopping bag. 'May I, Your Honor?'

The judge nodded to him. Her expression was completely neutral. She wouldn't look at Edward.

As David stood up with the bag, he said, 'This was identified by an earlier detective as items found hanging in your husband's spare bedroom closet. State's Exhibit 36. Would you step down, please, Dr Shilling?'

Amy did so, bringing her closer to the jury. David stood a couple of steps in front of her. The prosecutor was also much taller than Amy, Edward was glad to see, making her look small and harmless. As Amy looked up at him, David rummaged in the large bag and drew out a blue dress.

'Do you recognize this, Dr Shilling?'

Edward did. It was the evening dress from Paul's closet that Amy had claimed was hers.

'I'm not sure,' Amy said. 'It looks familiar.'

'As I said, it was in your husband's closet. Would you mind slipping it on, please? Just over what you're wearing.'

Amy looked at Edward for rescue, but there was no objection he could make that would be upheld. The prosecution was entitled to such a demonstration. Edward just sat there helplessly.

'Your Honor?' David said.

'Please put on the dress, Dr Shilling,' Cynthia told her.

So Amy did. The dress was made to be tight, but it did fit over the dress she was wearing. When the dress fell into place, it was obvious it was too big for Amy in the bust and thighs. It hung on her. And it hung to the ground.

'I guess you weren't the only woman to keep clothes at your husband's house, were you, Dr Shilling?' David said, turning and walking back to his table. Amy had no answer. 'Had you seen that dress, hanging in the closet with your own clothes?'

Amy struggled for moments, then said, 'Not that I remember.'

'Uh huh,' David said, resuming his seat, leaving Amy standing there in, what was for her, the hopelessly misshapen dress.

'Pass the witness.'

Seventeen

The defense's second best witness was probably Laura Martinelli. Although as it turned out, not so good as Edward hoped.

As she took the stand, she was not nearly the femme fatale she had been playing with Edward in her office. But she didn't try to downplay her sexuality either. She wore a business suit, grey pinstripe, very conservative, but with a thin, sheer blouse underneath. Maybe this was the most conservative outfit she had, who knew?

As she took the stand, Laura knew the score. Edward was going to present her as an alternate suspect. Laura understood that. She stared back at him from the witness stand, neither hostile nor intimidated. Her dark hair was luxurious, spilling down her neck. Her tongue flicked out, wetting her lips, which didn't need it. After a summer in Houston, her skin was pale, but lustrous. There was blood pulsing under the white skin.

'Please state your name.'

'Laura Martinelli.'

'Please tell us what you do, ma'am. And also your marital status, if you don't mind.'

'I am the executive director of a charitable foundation that raises money for abused children. And I am happily single.'

'Do you know my sister here next to me, Ms Martinelli?'

'No. I've never had the pleasure. I've heard of her, of course. Much of my work is done with the medical community in Houston.' Laura turned her eyes on Amy, then trained them back on Edward.

'But you knew her husband, Dr Paul Shilling, correct?'

'Yes, I knew Paul. In a casual way for years, because of my work, then a little more personally for a brief period before he died.'

'How shortly before he died?'

She leaned back, remembering. Even her neck was lovely. Edward glanced over at the jury, saw women looking at her enviously, men with another emotion. 'I'm not sure. When was that? When he died, I mean.'

'Last March. Almost a year ago.'

'I'm really not sure, then. Paul and I dated briefly, a handful of times, early in the spring. I remember it was always hot when we were together.'

There was nothing Edward could do with that answer except let it stand. He looked down at his notes, giving that answer a few seconds to breathe on its own.

'Did you break up?'

'You know, I've been trying to remember, knowing I'd probably be called as a witness in this trial. And the truth is, I just really can't remember. We didn't have a fight, I know that. It just seems like the relationship ran its course in a fairly short time.'

'No acrimony, no bitterness?'

She crossed her legs and folded her hands on top of her knees. 'No.'

'Didn't you tell me it became clear to you he was still in love with his wife?'

'I may have. I really don't remember now.'

Edward raised his voice. 'Laura. Ms Martinelli. Was there any emotion at all involved in this affair for you?'

She frowned, mildly. 'I wouldn't even call it an affair. A few dates. A handful, really. We realized pretty quickly we weren't meant for each other. I'm in a wonderful relationship now, with a man who—'

'Yes, I'm sure he's a lucky man. Let me ask you this, Ms Martinelli. Were you supposed to go to the awards dinner with Paul?'

She raised her eyes to the ceiling, trying to remember something incredibly trivial. 'At some point we may have talked about it . . .?' she said vaguely.

Edward stood up abruptly. 'Your Honor, may I approach the witness?' he asked, while doing so. He didn't even hear Cynthia's answer.

He rummaged through the exhibits at the front of the courtroom, and pulled out the long blue evening dress David had used earlier. Edward held it up in all its beauty. It shimmered, hanging from his hand, as if he was spewing blue flame like a sorcerer.

'Do you recognize this, Ms Martinelli?'

She stared at it in a disinterested way, as if she were shopping and Edward was the inept clerk. Then she looked up.

'No.'

Edward turned to his longtime acquaintance

and former (very briefly) lover. 'Your Honor, may the witness please be ordered to try on this dress?'

Cynthia stared back at him unimpressed. 'Why, Mr Hall?'

Edward was taken aback. 'Because it was found in the deceased's home and obviously any woman it would fit would be a suspect, Your Honor.'

Edward held out the dress to Laura Martinelli. She sighed, looked at it, stood up.

'You can just put it on over the clothes you're wearing.'

Laura held the dress up next to her. It looked very slim next to her voluptuous curves. 'I don't think so,' she said.

This was good. The dress would fit her well, tightly but well, unlike Amy. It would prove another woman was intimately involved in Paul's life, who would be offended – fatally, maybe – by his returning to his wife.

Edward looked up at the judge. 'Your Honor?'

Cynthia looked at Edward, looked at the blue dress, the witness, finally at the prosecutor, hoping he would save her by objection. But David sat there blandly, looking back at her with a slight smile. Everybody likes a drama.

Cynthia turned to the side. 'Bailiff. Open the door to the holding cell. The witness can change in there.'

'Cell?' Laura Martinelli said rather loudly. 'I don't think so.'

The judge looked at her. Laura looked back. A judge can make witnesses do many things: speak, give blood samples, have their fingerprints

275

taken, even partially undress in court. It would be very difficult to order a woman to go into a room and change clothes if she didn't want to do so.

Cynthia sighed. 'Very well. You can use the court's chambers. We will take a brief recess.'

She stood. The judge walked out and Laura followed her, carrying the dress. They jostled each other briefly in the doorway to the back.

Laura Martinelli returned to court after the recess with a blank-faced female bailiff walking closely in front of her. Laura was indeed wearing the blue dress, but over it she wore the bailiff's jacket. She didn't resume her seat but stood near it.

'The witness will take the witness stand,' Judge Miles said.

'I can't,' Laura said tightly.

'Ms Martinelli, the court is ordering you—'

'She actually can't, Your Honor,' the bailiff interjected.

'I can't sit in this dress,' Laura said stiffly.

The judge looked to the bailiff, who nodded affirmation.

'But it fits,' Edward pointed out. 'Your Honor, please let the record reflect that the witness is wearing the dress.'

He turned to the prosecutor, who shrugged. 'Acknowledged,' he said.

'Now, Ms Martinelli,' Edward resumed his questioning and his seat, 'would you please take off the jacket so the jurors can see the full dress?'

'I'd rather not.' Laura held her head so high she was looking over everyone's heads.

'Ma'am,' the judge interrupted. Laura looked at her. 'Please?' Cynthia said calmly.

Laura sighed, then shrugged out of the jacket itself. Then they could see the problem. The dress fit her, all right, the way an aging beauty's skin fits her face after too many cosmetic surgeries; so she can no longer express human emotion. The zipper in back wasn't all the way to the top and it seemed to be straining to retreat downward.

The dress fit very tight and low across Laura's bosom, and equally tightly across her hips. In the back, it looked sprayed on her naked body. The faint clicks of cell phone cameras could be heard in the courtroom.

She could walk in the dress, maybe dance in it. No one could make her try to sit if she said she couldn't. It would have been possible for her to go out for the evening in this dress. It would draw stares and comments, but that was what some women wanted at a big event, wasn't it? And there were men who would want that woman on their arms.

'Thank you, ma'am. Would you like to change back before you continue your testimony?'

'If you want me to be able to talk in a normal tone of voice, yes.'

'Judge?'

'Go ahead, ma'am.'

As Laura left, observed by all observers, the bailiff hurriedly followed. Cynthia looked at the jurors. 'This time let's just all stay here. Jurors, if you want to stand and stretch, please do.'

Edward whispered to Amy. 'What do you think?'

'I think, if that's her dress, Paul was letting himself have quite a bachelor life.'

'You don't think that's to his taste?'

'Are you talking about the dress or the woman in it?'

Edward nodded. Amy shrugged. 'Not when we were together. At least he'd never suggest I wear anything like that.'

Edward looked questioningly at his sister.

She blushed.

'Shut up,' she whispered.

'I'm sorry for putting you through that demonstration, Ms Martinelli,' Edward said. 'I didn't mean to embarrass you. I only have a few more questions. You said you went on several dates with the late Paul Shilling?'

'Yes.'

'Was drinking involved?'

'I assume you mean alcohol. Yes, sometimes.'

The slight facetiousness or edge Laura Martinelli had displayed during the first part of her testimony was gone now. She was all business.

'Did you ever see him intoxicated?'

'Yes. I suppose. I didn't pause and try to estimate how drunk he was at the time.'

'Did you notice any change in his behavior at those times?'

'Of course. That's why we drink, isn't it? He'd loosen up. He'd be fun.'

'Ms Martinelli, I'd like to show you a recording and ask your opinion of Dr Shilling's state of sobriety at the time he made it. David?'

As the television was being pushed back into

place, Amy tugged at Edward's elbow. 'You're going to show that damned thing again?'

'Yes. Shh.'

As the recording played again, Edward watched the jurors and the witness. This time he could see the jurors appeared less affected by the recording. A few looked at it closely, perhaps for the clues Edward and Amy had suggested. A couple didn't seem to be paying attention at all. Repeated viewings had dulled the video's edge.

Laura Martinelli, on the other hand, seeing it for the first time, leaned forward and didn't appear to blink, studying her late lover's face.

When it was over Edward turned off the television. 'Well?'

Laura frowned, looking down. 'I can't be sure. He had been drinking when he recorded that, yes.'

'How can you tell?'

'I'm trying to think. Honestly, Paul and I didn't spend that much time together. What are the signs?' she asked herself.

'Did you hear him grope for a word there at the end? Did he ever do that sober?'

'Not that I recall. No, generally Paul was very glib. And now that I think about it, what's telling in that video is how – clipped? Is that the word I want? – how tight his voice became.'

'Precise?'

'Maybe that's the word.' She shrugged and looked at Edward, wearing an expression as if she really wanted to help. 'Like I said, I didn't study him for how he behaved at various levels of intoxication.'

'I understand.'

She volunteered, 'But as controlled as he looked in that video, he seemed nervous to me.'

'Really?'

'Yes. Paul always had this easy confidence about him, drunk or sober. It was one of the things that made him attractive. He always seemed to be in control of whatever was going to happen. On that recording, though, he seemed—' She shook her head. 'I don't know how to describe it, but he didn't appear to me to have that self-assurance I always saw in him. His shoulders, the way his hands were clenching each other. I never saw him act like that.'

Edward didn't know what to make of that. It made him silent for a moment. Out of the corner of his eye, he saw his sister nodding.

'No more questions,' he finally said.

David huddled with his second chair, then stood to say he had nothing more to ask the witness.

Laura Martinelli walked out between the counsel tables without glancing to either side.

'Call your next witness, defense.'

'Your Honor, my next witness is standing by nearby, but not in the building. Given the difficulty of this building's elevators, it might take a while for him to get up here.'

Cynthia pondered, looking up at the clock on the courtroom wall. It was after four o'clock on a Friday. Trial clearly wasn't going to finish today.

'All right. We will resume Monday morning at nine thirty. Jurors, please remember the court's instructions. Do not talk to anyone about this case, do not . . .'

Edward slumped in his chair, glad to have the weekend to think.

David Galindo leaned across the aisle and said to him, 'We have to talk. But I have to clear it with my administration first. Come to my office in about half an hour, OK?'

'Sure. Talk about what?'

David, gathering up files, didn't look at him or answer.

Eighteen

So Edward had half an hour to kill. Downstairs in the district clerk's office he filled out a request form for a piece of evidence from an old case. He handed it to the clerk, who frowned at being asked to do her job this late before the weekend. She brought the case up on her computer screen.

'This case name is your name,' she said accusingly.

'That's right.'

'I thought you were a lawyer.'

'That's right too. Inconceivable, isn't it?'

'If we've still got it, it will be archived,' the clerk said, all business now. 'Check back here Tuesday.'

'I will, thank you.'

David beckoned him inside the DA's offices.

'What's going on?' Edward asked, but David just shook his head until they came to his private office and David shut the door behind him. This looked like the office of someone in the middle of a big trial. There were three boxes against the wall under the windows, other files on David's desk.

'I've just had a battle,' David said as he seated himself. David wouldn't look at him and he kept moving things around on his desk unnecessarily.

'Are you about to propose to me?' Edward asked.

In a sense.

David looked directly at him and said, 'Here's the deal. Literally. Your sister can plead to straight murder and thirty years. We're taking the death penalty and life without parole off the table.'

Edward sat wide-eyed. He heard his mouth automatically negotiating.

'*Cap* of thirty. I can ask the judge for less.'

David shook his head. 'Thirty. You know what I had to do to get Admin to agree to that?'

'No, what? Seriously, this comes out of nowhere. What?'

'Not out of nowhere. It's that damned DVD of the fucking victim talking right into the camera and what you said on the record after it was played.'

About the devastating effect on the jury of Paul's accusation.

'Cynthia should never have let that in,' David said, annoyed.

'You argued strenuously for its admittance.'

'Oh, tell me you never did that, Edward, when you were on my side of the desk. You push for everything you can get and more. Maybe our appeals section can still get the case affirmed on appeal, but I told Admin I doubt it. That was a devastating piece of evidence and there was really no basis for admitting it.'

'Then why'd you offer it?'

David gave him a look and Edward let him off the hook. Obviously the prosecutor had had his orders. The D.A.'s office had to fight to get its strongest piece of evidence into evidence, so they could later tell reporters: 'We tried. It was the judge. She wouldn't let it in.' But even as he argued, David had been assuming Cynthia would do the right thing.

'I hate being in front of a judge who doesn't know the law,' he muttered. 'So that's the offer,' David said, standing up. 'On the table 'til Monday.'

'This is going to be a tough sell, David. Make it easier for me. Cap of thirty.'

David hesitated, which told Edward he was already authorized to make this backup offer.

'Fine. Cap of thirty. Cynthia'll give you the max she can anyway.'

'Maybe. That's my worry. Hey. David.' Edward stood and held out his hand. 'Thanks, man.'

David took it.

As they stood there, Edward said, 'This is still going to be tough for me to sell to Amy, not to mention my parents.'

'Well, luckily you've got the weekend to do it.'

'Yeah, isn't that swell.'

To go from a potential death sentence to thirty years, parole in fifteen probably, was a win for the defense. Every lawyer he knew would celebrate that. It was the difference between having a life and not. With a death sentence or life without parole, Amy would never see the outside of prison walls again. She would go in someone, a doctor, a daughter, beloved sister and friend and colleague, and in a remarkably short time become no one; a cautionary tale about a woman who lost it all when she shot her husband in a fit of jealousy. *What was her name? You know, we used to see her every day.* Edward had felt that happening to him in only two years.

284

But with this sentence, Amy would get out. She'd emerge. She was a young woman, she'd be out before she was fifty, she'd still have years of life. She'd have a life as opposed to death or living death.

This was a major triumph for Edward, especially given how long he'd been out of the game.

But he still had a strong feeling Amy wouldn't see it the same way.

'So what did he say?' Amy asked. 'Edward. Out with it. They made an offer. What does that even mean, if not dismissing the case?'

They were at her house, where he'd kept her waiting while he drove around.

'OK. Here's the thing, Amy. Usually before trial both sides negotiate to see if they can reach an agreement.'

'Sure. That just never seemed to be a factor here because I didn't do it.'

'Being guilty isn't the only reason for taking a plea bargain, Amy. It's because you look at the evidence and see if you think the prosecution can make you look guilty anyway. Believe me, there are innocent people in prison because they wouldn't take offers because they just didn't do it.'

In his mind that last phrase was ironic, because almost every client he'd ever had had claimed to be innocent. He stared at Amy, wondering if she was.

'You've been in the courtroom, Amy. Analyze. What do you think are the chances that jury's going to find you guilty?'

She wasn't angry, so she didn't overreact or snap back.

'I looked them all in the eyes while I was testifying,' she said. 'They believed me. I'm sure of it.'

'Maybe. And then they saw a recording of your husband saying you killed him.'

'You said that would never come into evidence.'

'I said it shouldn't. In a better judge's court it wouldn't have. But in the world we're actually living in now it did. That's what we have to deal with.'

'Doesn't that mean the case will get reversed on appeal even if they do find me guilty?'

'Maybe. You can't count on anything on appeal. And if they get a capital murder conviction *and* a death sentence on you, Amy, the highest criminal court in this state is very reluctant to reverse those cases. They find ways around doing it. But even if we did win, it would just mean a new trial, with you already in prison for the two or three years the appeal would probably take. And in the second trial a judge won't make the same mistake and let that recording in. It's only because of that that the prosecutor has made me the offer he did today.'

She sighed, her shoulders slumped, and Amy returned her gaze to him. 'OK, tell me this great offer.'

Edward ignored her sarcasm, going into salesman mode. Quiet but earnest. 'They agreed to let you plead to murder. Just murder. That's taking both a death sentence and life without parole out of the realm of possibility. It means someday you'd get paroled. You'd live through your prison sentence and get out.'

'No guarantee of that. But enough suspense, Edward. What did—?'

'Thirty years. I know how awful that sounds, Amy. But it wouldn't really be thirty years. Not even close in your case. Let me give this some context. A regular life sentence, not life without parole, is the equivalent of sixty years. That's how they treat it for calculating parole eligibility. Even after serving half that sentence so you're eligible for parole, it's been thirty years. In reality that's a death sentence for almost anybody. Even if it's not, you come out into a world you don't understand and where nobody remembers you.

'But thirty. With a thirty year sentence, when you're paroled, you still have years of life ahead of you. And most of the people you ever knew still waiting for you when you get out. Years of life . . .'

Amy's face and voice remained calm. 'So when would I get out with a thirty year sentence? Eight? Nine? Do they count good conduct—?'

'Because it's murder with a deadly weapon, you wouldn't become eligible to be considered for parole until you'd done half the sentence.'

He watched his sister. Amy didn't seem to have heard at first, but when she turned the lamplight caught a streak down her cheek, a tear.

'I know it sounds terrible, Amy, but I did two years inside. You find out it's a routine like anything else. Like high school, you find your group, avoid the others. There's free time. I got a lot of reading done.'

'Great. Except mine will be like going through

high school four times. If I even get out then . . .' She closed her eyes, drew a deep breath, opened them again, and looked at him intently. 'Edward. I'm not some idiot. Listen to me, I'm evaluating this. I'm not rejecting it automatically.'

'Thank you.'

'Shut up. But I don't have enough information. I can't do the—' She held her hands in front of her cupped palms upward, moving one up and one down. Edward nodded. 'So help me. Tell me honestly, I can take it. Am I going to be found guilty?'

'You're asking me to tell you the future, Amy. You know I can't. I predicted the judge wouldn't let in Paul's DVD. Clearly I'm no prophet. Now you're asking me to predict twelve people instead of one. But I know what you're saying. I have more experience at this than you do. So I'll do my best. Here's the calculation for me. On your side, you look sweet and innocent and you testified as sincerely as anyone I've ever heard. You did great.'

'That's because I'm really—'

'Yeah, I know. Please don't use that word again. In this analysis it has no weight at all. Zero. That's on your side. Great testimony, great face. Plus the gunshot happened so fast after people say you went in, it's hard to believe the gun was out and a fatal argument ensued that quickly.'

She smiled and nodded. He wished she wouldn't.

'Here's the other side. You're the estranged wife, the most likely suspect. He cheated on you, he dumped you and was about to be celebrated and famous – and you wouldn't be part of it. Maybe you were starting to get back together but,

288

even if you were, it looks like – from the dress in the closet – he was still seeing other women. And you probably knew that. You were undoubtedly there when he was killed and at least one witness put you already inside the house when the shot was fired, not out on the porch.'

He had to take a breath to continue. 'And finally, the recording of Paul saying you killed him. Maybe he doesn't give good reasons, maybe he was drunk, but that doesn't make him a liar. This is your husband talking, the one person in the world besides you who knows you best and knows your relationship best. And he says you killed him.'

Amy's chin was down now. She stared up at him through half-closed eyes.

'And finally, Amy, I hate this but it's true. Juries nearly always convict. That's the unspoken extra factor on the prosecution's side. No matter what jurors say about believing in the presumption of innocence, when they first come in and look at the defendant they think: *I wonder what she did.* They can't help it. They figure the police and the prosecution did their jobs. Sometimes they overcome that and I thought for a while they would in this trial. But now I'd have to say that my best professional estimate is that the verdict is what they are in the vast majority of trials. Guilty. I'm sorry, but that's what I think.'

'I thought we were going to beat that.'

'Me too.'

She stood. 'All right. Go away now.'

'Amy.'

'I know. I need to sleep on it. Thanks, Eddie.'

* * *

He drove, thinking, but to no effect. Edward felt homeless, his car inclining toward Linda's house, but he went to Mike's and fell onto the couch face down. He barely slept that night, but woke up clear-headed, pulled himself together, and headed back to Amy's.

When she opened her door she said, 'I've made up my mind.'

'I know,' Edward said. Amy looked at him but didn't have to ask a question. He could tell by looking at her that she'd decided. She could tell from a quick study of his face that he knew what she'd decided.

'Taking the offer is the smart thing to do,' she said gently.

'Yep.'

'But I can't do it.'

'I know.'

'I can't stand up there and say I'm guilty, that I killed my husband. Because I didn't.'

'I know. And I know you can't take the deal.'

Amy tilted her head as she looked at him. 'What's happened to you? What do you know now that you didn't know last night?'

'Nothing. That's a problem.'

'What are you going to do?' Amy asked.

'I've got work to do.'

Nineteen

Mike met him at Paul's house late Saturday morning. Edward had seen the DVD of Paul's accusation several times by now and was sure he'd recognize the room in the background; it had wood paneling on the walls and blank spots where pictures or decorations had been taken off. But there was no matching wall in Paul's house. A quick check confirmed all the walls were drywall painted shades of beige.

Back in the hall, Edward was looking up at a dangling string attached to a door in the ceiling for the attic access. He pulled and it turned out there was a built-in ladder. Edward climbed into darkness, hoping there was a light switch above – a light for a large finished-out room with wood paneling. When he stuck his head through the opening it was too dark to see anything and his groping hands discovered no light switch.

'Here,' Mike said below him, handing up a flashlight. Edward pointed the flashlight toward the center of the room and turned it on.

'Anything?' Mike asked.

'Nothing. Damn it.' Edward shone the light all around. Just an unfinished attic, not even with a floor, just beams with cheap Sheetrock underneath. His foot would go right through it if he tried to walk up here. 'There're some boxes and stuff, but no paneled wall. Damn it, this was a smart idea. Why isn't it working?'

'He just recorded it somewhere else that we don't know about, that's all.'

Edward came back down the ladder. 'He was drunk, so it was probably spur of the moment to make that. Should be at home. He wouldn't be comfortable making that recording where he might be seen or overheard.'

Mike peered up at the ceiling, remembering the recording. 'Could be a cheap motel somewhere, he got a private room just to make that, maybe?'

'Don't forget the next question: who's holding the camera?'

'The woman he was having an affair with? Fits my motel theory.'

'Then we're screwed. We'll never find that.'

'Maybe credit card records,' Mike said. 'I'll see what I can find the rest of the weekend. But what if we do find it? What does it prove?'

'I just hoped it would lead somewhere. Tell us who he was with. We could question that person. Create a new suspect, maybe.'

He crossed the hall to the living room. Same view, slightly different angle. From a side window he looked at the house next door, the one belonging to Valerie Linnett. He could see a slice of her living room too, so she could easily have seen Amy on the front porch as she claimed. She didn't have paneled walls either. Must not have been a feature of this neighborhood.

The only other thing he could do over the weekend was work on his closing argument. 'Sweet little

Amy' was the subtext, but he needed something more logical. 'Police just didn't do their jobs' sounded like a theme, but it would be nice if he could suggest an alternative suspect. Paul had made someone mad enough to kill him. Edward wasn't even sure he'd seen that person in court. They'd all seemed so composed. Valerie Linnett, who'd seen through Paul and stopped seeing him after only one or two dates. Louise Fisher looked a better bet, with her potential personal and professional jealousies, but no one had ever seen her at the house. Ditto Laura Martinelli, who was so self-possessed and self-confident it was hard to imagine Paul getting under her skin enough to make her want to kill him. These women seemed too emotionally remote for the role of jealous, murderess mistress.

Then who? It didn't have to be the real killer, just someone Edward could make look like one. As he and Mike had cheerfully told Amy, they weren't detectives, they were bullshit artists.

There could have been a car in the alley and a man as the killer instead of a woman. But again, who? The truth was, no one looked as good a suspect as sweet little Amy.

By Sunday afternoon he gave up thinking about it all and drove to Linda's.

He'd called ahead, Linda opened the door immediately to his knock. She'd put on lipstick. Her face seemed thinner than the last time he'd seen her, which was only a couple of weeks ago. She wore a T-shirt and blue jean shorts.

'Hi.'

'Hello, Edward. Come in.'

She led him into the living room. Her legs looked good. She looked good all over, in fact. If he said anything to that effect she'd probably answer that he must be lonely.

'You've lost weight.' Seemed a less provocative way to put it.

Linda turned to face him and shrugged. 'I've had more time to exercise.'

'I haven't. Could we go for a walk?'

'What is it, Edward? Do you want to talk about something? Ask me something?'

He shook his head. 'I didn't come with a plan, or a speech. Just want to take a walk.'

She studied his face for a minute while he tried to look sincere. 'OK. Just let me get shoes.'

It was a beautiful fall afternoon. Edward had been so caught up in trial he'd been indoors all day every day and had barely noticed the weather changing. Suddenly he wished this was his life, walking with Linda through a peaceful world, with the prospect of a pleasant evening and bedtime ahead of them.

'How have you been?' he asked.

'You know. The job is always there. Same people around me but new clients to deal with. Do that, come home. Do it again the next day. It's nice.'

He hadn't thought that's how that recitation was going to end, but as Linda said it, it did sound like a nice life.

'I know how you've been doing from the news. How's Amy?'

'Holding up. My parents are there most of the time. Would you mind taking a day off and coming to watch?'

They walked on in silence for several seconds. Linda touched his arm, but only lightly and briefly. 'What is it that you want, Edward?'

Linda looked at him, an open, unlined face, her eyes clear and curious. And loving? Still? He couldn't tell. She didn't look hostile at all, but not particularly affectionate either. Just curious, like a detached bystander.

'You think this is what I came over here to say, and it isn't. My subconscious just kicked this up on me. I'd like you there. I'd like your insight. Evaluating the jury, the judge. I think Amy would like to have you there too.'

Linda smiled, which changed her face, broadened her cheeks, made her lips fuller. 'That's pretty chickenshit, using your sister to try to get to me.'

'I know, and her on trial for her life, too. I'm starting to sound desperate.'

Linda turned and started walking again. 'I'll have to think about that.'

Edward said, 'Me too. We're all such thinkers now.'

'You always have been, babe. But I liked you in spite of it. Edward. Do you even know what you want?'

That was an excellent question. They continued in silence, side by side. It was nice.

Twenty

'Did both sides have time to look at my proposed charge over the weekend?' Judge Cynthia asked from the bench. Her black robe was zipped so high and tight on her neck it was impossible to tell if she wore anything underneath it. Her face was as blank and expressionless as the robe.

'Yes, Your Honor,' Edward and David answered at the same time.

'I'm giving a charge on the lesser offense of murder, since there was testimony that your client was there by invitation, Mr Hall. Do you have any objections?'

'No, Your Honor.'

'All right, then. We'll bring the jury in and you can call your next witness, Mr Hall.'

Edward said, 'No, Your Honor. The defense will rest as soon as the jury returns.' Then he turned and looked out into the filled spectator seats. For the first time he noticed someone near the back. 'One moment, Your Honor,' he said offhandedly over his shoulder and strode through the gate in the railing.

'Hi,' he said to Linda a moment later. 'Thanks for coming.'

She just nodded, looking up at him. She was dressed nicely, in a business suit he hadn't seen before. He was struck again by the smoothness of her reddish pale skin, beginning to crinkle slightly beneath her eyes. They smiled at each other. 'Anything?' he asked.

'I watched the jury before they went out. The two women on the front row really like Amy, but they also look like subservient types. The grumpy old white guy on the second row is your toughest sell. Don't waste your time on him. He's ready to vote for death, maybe for all women. If you can turn the younger man two over from him, he might carry the rest along. He's studying everybody so hard, I don't think he's decided either way yet. The rest I don't know. Could go either way. Your best bet is to let them look at Amy as much as possible.'

'Thanks, Linda.' He leaned down close. 'Thanks for being here.'

'One other thing,' she said. 'The judge hates you. I mean deep-seated hate. Is she afraid of you for some reason? What have you been doing to her since I've been gone?'

'Nothing. She's not my concern. Thanks again.'

He squeezed her hand, then turned and walked quickly back up the aisle.

'Ready, Your Honor,' he said briskly, as if everyone else had been holding up the proceedings.

The young woman led off jury argument for the prosecution, after Cynthia had read her instructions to the jury.

'Margaret Posner for the State. Good morning.'

She got no responses. It was not a good morning. He was glad jurors didn't think so.

'I want to talk to you briefly about one element of this prosecution. Murder you certainly understand.

Intentionally causing the death of another human being. But this trial is over something bigger. *Capital* murder. As we talked about during jury selection, capital murder is murder plus something else. In this case we've alleged murder in the course of burglary. Now where do we get that? The defendant wasn't breaking into her estranged husband's house. She didn't use a lock pick or wear a mask, carrying a bag over her shoulder labeled 'Loot.'

'Well, that's not what a burglary has to be. It doesn't have to be your classic cartoon burglar breaking into someone's house in the dead of night. The judge's instructions tell you that burglary just means entering a residence without the consent of the homeowner, while intending to commit another crime once she gets inside. What crime would that be? That's easy. Amy Shilling entered that home without her husband's consent with the intention of murdering him. That's burglary. That's capital murder.'

Ms Posner paced up and down in front of the jurors, not using notes.

'Your other question might be, how can you know that she entered the home with the intention of murdering him? Here's how. The timing. The neighbors who saw her go in, before the gunshot, say that was no more than a minute before they heard the shot. Not time for an argument to develop, not time for her to get mad at her husband. She had to be mad when she went in. She had to be in a killing rage already. So she either pulled out his gun that she'd already taken on a previous occasion, or she grabbed it from the hiding place she knew, and she shot him, almost as soon as she went inside. She must have gone in with that intention.

'And how do we know she entered without Paul's consent? Again, that one's easy. Because of where he was. In the bedroom. Just getting dressed. He didn't walk to the front door in response to any knock. He didn't even start in that direction, as anyone would when he hears a knock or a door-bell ring. He was standing several feet inside his bedroom door, still getting dressed, when his wife came in and shot him.

'Why? Well, David will talk to you about that. Maybe Amy had found the other woman's dress on an earlier occasion. Maybe she'd realized her soon-to-be-ex-husband had just been leading her on. Maybe she didn't want him having a happy life and leaving her behind. Whatever. What I want to make clear to you is that when she entered that home without permission, with the intention of killing her husband, she was committing capital murder. If you believe it was murder, then you believe she intended to kill him, which means you believe she committed capital murder. Please have the courage of that conviction.'

She nodded to the jurors and walked briskly back to her table.

Edward sat impressed. It was good logic. As he rose himself he glanced at Amy. She looked back at him, her face a study in composure. She even smiled. Her smile struck him as almost smug, certain her big brother was going to get her off. That smile gave him pause. Were the prosecutors right about his sister?

'That was a good argument,' he began, standing close to the jurors. 'If she committed murder then it was capital murder. That's an excellent exercise in logic.

'But it's flawed and I think you all see how. Nothing has refuted Amy's claim that she was at Paul's house by invitation. He was expecting her, they were going out together. This didn't look like a classic burglary because it wasn't a burglary. No burglar walks into someone's unlocked front door in broad daylight in view of any witnesses who happen to be watching. The fact that the front door was unlocked shows that Paul was expecting Amy. He remained in the bedroom because when he heard Amy's knock or the doorbell rang he simply called out. 'Come in!' Who hasn't done that when you're expecting someone?

'And the fact that he was expecting Amy demonstrates that she didn't kill him. What motive did she have for doing that? The prosecutor suggested some scenarios, but there isn't any evidence to back up any of them.'

He ran his eyes slowly along the jurors, almost all their eyes looking back at him. He paused briefly as he looked at the two women on the front row Linda had mentioned. They did appear to be listening sympathetically but, like all jurors, they also tried to give no signals to their thoughts. *Can I get a nod?* No.

'What the evidence has shown, which I told you during jury selection, is that my sister is not an idiot. She is a very smart, accomplished woman. If she was mad at her husband, she'd had six months to cool off while they'd been separated.

If she was furious enough to kill him, she wouldn't have gone about it in this ridiculous, obvious way. If nothing else, she would have parked with her car out of sight and gone in more subtly. Think how easy it would have been for her to get away with that. Park in the alley or the next block, go in through the back gate or over the back fence. Paul's neighbor Valerie Linnett's back gate wasn't locked. She said so. A smart killer would have gone in that way, crossed her backyard, gone out Ms Linnett's side gate, through Paul's side gate, which *was* unlocked and into his backyard that way. Everyone who heard the gunshot went to look out their front doors, so the murderer could easily have gone out the back door of Paul's house and gotten away. Which is what happened.

'Yes!' Edward said, building. 'I am going to tell you the real killer was already in the house and went out the back door while Amy was distracted. Someone who had planned this killing. Someone who knew what a big night this was for Dr Paul Shilling and wanted to deny him that. Someone who hated him.

'Who might that have been? Well, pick your suspect. The research partner who hated him because he was stealing their joint research project from her and, on top of that, had rejected her sexually after a couple of dates? The next-door neighbor who ditto thought he was an asshole? Laura Martinelli – we'll come back to her – who was supposed to be his original date for that big night?

'I don't know.' Edward paused, looking over the jurors individually, taking at least a full minute to do so. The women on the front row looked back at him, the grumpy old bastard on the back row – why did Edward always leave one of those on the jury? – glared at him with folded arms, everyone else sat looking attentive.

'Maybe some woman we don't even know about, as secretive as Paul was about his liaisons. I can't tell you. It's not my job to know,' Edward said. This was material from his jury stump speech, his greatest hits medley. 'It's theirs.' He pointed to the prosecutors. 'It's the cops.'

'Remember the police testimony?' He shrugged theatrically. 'What investigation did the police do? They came into the murder scene, saw my sister desperately trying to save her husband's life—' He turned and pointed to Amy, as he should have been doing all along. *Isn't she great, folks? She's too cute to be a murderess.* Amy did her part, looking serious and concerned, her eyes going along the row of jurors. 'And the cops' job was done, as far as they were concerned: "Ah hah, we've got our crime solved!" What did they do after that to try to solve it?'

One of those women on the front row almost raised her hand and he saw what she was thinking. His answer.

'Nothing. They did nothing. Once they learned Amy was the estranged wife, the murder weapon was a few feet away and there was blood on her hands – never mind that it got there from her attempts to save her husband's life – they thought: "Our work here is done."'

'So once the actual murderer stepped out the back door, she was golden. No one was going to follow her, no one was going to sweep the bedroom or the house for her fingerprints. No one was going to check for tire prints in the alley. She was gone like a ghost. She didn't even have to have an alibi she'd faked.'

He stopped, put his fists on his hips and looked them over again.

'Even as unlikely as it seems that the murder could have happened with this close timing, doesn't what I've said make more sense? Amy's not this dumb, to kill the victim like this. The other women Paul was involved with, all smart, accomplished women themselves, maybe they were smart enough to pull this off without ever even getting questioned by police.

'For example.' He stopped again, looked them all over. It seemed he had their attention. 'Laura Martinelli. Oh my God. I fell in love with her myself. I wanted to ask her out right here in the courtroom, right, guys? And she was supposed to be Paul's date that night. Originally he was going to the awards banquet with her. They would have made a lovely couple, don't you think?

'And then he called her up and dumped her. Can you imagine, being *Laura Martinelli* and having someone break a date with you because he was reconciling with his wife?' He turned and gestured at Amy. He didn't want to say, *She's pretty but she ain't no Laura Martinelli*, so the gesture would have to suffice.

'This was probably the first time this ever happened to Laura, who'd pictured herself becoming the new wife of a man going places. Laura knew how big a deal Paul was about to become – and remember her, wouldn't she be fabulous as the wife of a very big deal? What a power couple. She testified she's moved on, she has someone else now. Of course she does. But that doesn't mean she wasn't mad as hell when Paul broke up with her that abruptly, ending that big a dream for her.'

It had been years since Edward had given a jury argument; he had been falling back on his tried and true material. But now he was into it, he was branching out, riffing from his prepared notes.

'Now if I were in your position and had your huge responsibility, the next thing I would wonder is, well, was Laura Martinelli the kind of person who could do this? Did she have anything like a history of violence?' He turned toward the prosecution table. 'Well, did she?'

After a few beats of silence, he turned back to the jury.

'They don't know. They didn't investigate her or any other potential suspect. The police didn't. The police are paid to do a job – some of them have years of experience at it – but none of them performed that job in this case. The detectives didn't detect.

'The one person you know they did investigate was Amy, because she was their only suspect. And did they uncover anything to suggest she was capable of committing this kind of crime? Specifically did they bring you any evidence that in the years of their relationship, even during their supposedly bitter break-up, Amy did anything violent toward him? Did they even have a screaming fight?

'They want you to believe she was so furious at this man she went over there planning to murder him. She must have had this in mind for a while, to have taken his gun and hidden it or mapped out this plan. Then she marched right into the house, this first-time murderer, and carried out her plan instantly, right there on the spot. She would have had to be enraged and stayed that way for days. Have they brought you any evidence to suggest that?'

Edward turned and looked at his sister. 'Amy, will you stand up, please?'

'Objection, Your Honor,' David Galindo was on his feet to say. That was good, because he towered over Amy. 'The evidence is closed. He can't re-enact some scene or ask her to testify again.'

'The defendant is always on display throughout the whole trial,' Edward responded. 'She's been used as essentially an exhibit during trial and either party can always call the jury's attention to a particular piece of evidence during jury argument.'

'That's a novel argument,' Judge Cynthia began. 'I'll allow it.'

In the meantime, Amy had stood up anyway. She had been a very obedient client for her lawyer brother. She stood silent, looking at the jury with a level, liquid gaze. She was wearing flats today and looked rather slight. Edward went and stood close to her to emphasize that.

'Do you think she could have done this? That's the question for you today. You know she couldn't. You know they haven't proven she's capable of murder.

'Yes, someone was furious at Paul Shilling. The philanderer. The arrogant heartbreaker. The police investigated Amy thoroughly and didn't find any evidence she had ever, in her whole life, done anything remotely like this. They didn't investigate any of the other people, who had reason to be furious at the victim, at all.'

He walked back to the jury and stood right in front of them, but at one end of the jury box so he didn't block their view of Amy.

'That's the definition of reasonable doubt, folks. It's all right to rely on your impressions. Your instincts. But to convict someone of murder, you have to have evidence. The prosecution has only brought you very slight evidence Amy was even inside the house when the gunshot was fired – one witness's testimony – as opposed to others who said she was still outside. That's not enough. Not for this serious a crime. Not to ruin this life. You can sort through the evidence all you like and you won't find enough to convict. Take your time. Take your job very seriously. Thank you.'

He hated to stop talking. He hated to let them out of his hands. But he felt confident he'd found a convincing argument. Edward walked back to the defense table and sat, along with his sister, who took his hand and squeezed it gratefully.

David Galindo stood slowly and stayed in his place beside the counsel table. 'The defense has the same right as the prosecution to subpoena witnesses and records. They have the right and the ability to investigate—'

'Objection,' Edward said quickly, having antici-pated this argument. 'The prosecutor is attempting

306

to shift the burden of proof to the defense. That burden is always on the State.'

Cynthia said flatly, 'Overruled. But be careful, Mr Galindo.'

'The defense can investigate people too. Nobody obstructs them. They can search police records.'

'Objection!' Edward said, this time sincerely. 'That is absolutely not true. We don't have the power the State does to search criminal histories under the control of the police.'

'That's not—'

'Sustained,' the judge ruled this time. 'Move on, Mr Galindo.'

'They put on evidence,' David said quietly. 'They presented you with a defense. But nothing to suggest one of these other people committed this murder. No one saw them, no one heard any sign of anyone else out of place in this neighborhood. Only this one person, the one on trial today.'

David spoke with little emotion. He was going to be the precise analytical lawyer.

'The defendant's lawyer, her brother, has said she's too smart to have committed such an obvious crime. Two answers for that. The first is that someone mad enough to commit murder, in a murderous rage, isn't thinking straight. It's an irrational act, killing someone. Almost by definition, Dr Amy Shilling wasn't thinking straight.

'The other answer is sitting at that table. The defendant is the sister of someone who's been one of the best criminal defense lawyers in this city for years.'

'Objection,' Edward said, this time on his feet. 'First, there's been absolutely no evidence of

307

that. Thank you, but there hasn't been. Second, may we approach the bench?'

After studying him briefly, Cynthia simply nodded. Edward and David went up to the bench right in front of her. Edward kept his head turned from the jury and his voice low but urgent.

'This is invading attorney-client privilege, Your Honor. I believe the prosecutor is suggesting I helped her plan this, which is outrageous to begin with. But if I gave any advice to my client, that subject is untouchable in court.'

'That's not what I'm suggesting.' David glanced at Edward as if that suggestion itself was out of line. 'Helping a client plan a crime is beyond a lawyer's duties and not protected by attorney-client privilege, which is not what I'm suggesting.' He held up his hands as Edward turned toward him furiously.

'He's trying to use against her the fact that she has a lawyer in the family, which isn't a crime. I object, Your Honor.'

The judge looked back at him blandly, apparently unfazed by either lawyer's emotions.

'I don't see any sign of an attorney-client relationship being established before a crime was committed and there was occasion for her to hire a lawyer. Overruled.' She made a brushing away motion as Edward stared at her.

He continued to stare in that direction as he took his seat. The prosecutor was going on about how having a lawyer in the family had probably given her an insight into planning crimes, plans that worked and plans that failed. But Edward watched the judge. She wouldn't look at him, though once Cynthia did shoot him a sharp sideways glance. It might have been a questioning look, it might have been sullen. It was too quick to tell. It certainly hadn't said *Come hither.*

But what Edward thought he'd seen in that brief glimpse was fear.

David continued. 'Well-planned crimes have a lot of ways to fail and, when they do, the perpetrator looks obviously guilty for having come up with such an elaborate scheme. While criminals get away with spur-of-the-moment, poorly-thought-out crimes of passion.

'Mr Hall has suggested that the defendant knew where Dr Shilling kept his gun. Probably the same place he'd kept it at the family home, in the nightstand. Who knows what might have set her off when she went into his house, the house he'd left her to find freedom in? Maybe, when she went to get her evening gown, she saw the other dress in the closet, the one obviously not her size. So she ran to his room, grabbed his gun and shot him in a murderous rage. Then, as so often happens with murderers, she instantly regretted it and tried futilely to revive him. Which doesn't mean . . .'

Edward continued to watch the judge. When all this had started, he had hoped Cynthia would do him some hidden favors, at least give him a break in her trial rulings, given the huge, secret debt she owed him. Instead she had ruled against him at every turn. What was in her mind?

Maybe she was saving up for one big favor for him. Then she'd be able to point to the record to say she'd shown him no favoritism. But what would that big favor be?

Boy, he was really looking for the pony in the room.

Edward felt a slight pressure on his hand that took him by surprise. He looked down to see that Amy had slipped her hand into his. Looking aside, he saw it was because she was scared to death. The skin of her face was tight and very pale. Her lips invisible as she tried to keep her chin from trembling. She gave him a little smile when she felt his stare, but there were tears in the corners of her eyes.

He'd never had to sympathize with a client before. They were just defendants. Almost always guilty, usually deserving whatever was going to happen to them. But this was Amy. For the first time in his life Edward felt his life bound up with his client's. If he lost this trial, Amy's life would be over and his would be too. He would never stop blaming himself.

'Finally I want to return to something my partner talked to you about,' David Galindo said quietly. 'The evidence shows planning on the part of the defendant. In spite of what I said about something inside setting her off, the more probable, almost certain fact is that she went into that house with the intention of murdering her husband. There just wasn't time for any other interpretation. She must have already been furious when she went in.

'Which means she didn't stop to ring the door-bell or knock. She just went up on the porch and went in, which means she entered the victim's home without his consent. Do you think he would ever have let her in if he knew what she was planning? No, she just went in. She entered a habitation without the consent of the owner, with the intention of committing a felony. The felony she then committed. Murder. But because it was in the course of burglary it was capital murder.

'And her victim knew how furious she was. Don't forget Dr Shilling's recording. He knew. He knew his wife was catching on to him. He knew her simmering rage. He'd felt it before. He did his best to protect himself from her. Please don't let his effort have been in vain.'

David set down the DVD he'd been holding up and slowly sat down, watching the jurors. Those twelve, though, wouldn't look at the lawyers at all. Almost in unison they turned toward the judge.

'The bailiff will now escort you to the jury room to begin your deliberations. All rise for the jury, please.'

Edward stood up and took his sister's arm. She leaned against him so heavily he knew she'd fall over if he weren't there. Amy held up her chin and smiled bravely at the jurors, who all kept their faces resolutely turned away from her – except one of those women from the front row who shot a quick glance at her. Very good sign, that, or at least Edward tried to think so.

Then they were gone and the courtroom had that strange empty feeling actors must feel, as the last audience members troupe out while the actors are still left on the stage. Edward and David Galindo blinked at each other. Edward saw

David's impulse to reach across the distance between their tables and shake his hand, also saw him decide the gesture wouldn't be appropriate this time.

Then they both turned to see the judge still sitting on her high bench. This was uncharacteristic of Cynthia, who usually darted out of the room as quickly as she could. She stared at Edward. Again, like an actress who could show her true emotions now that the audience was gone. Cynthia looked at Edward with her lips pressed into a tight, straight line.

Then she rose and did leave the room, quickly, not looking back.

'Man, what did you do to her?' David asked Edward, as he gathered up his papers, not waiting for an answer.

Edward wondered himself. He turned to Amy. 'It could be hours, Amy. Go with Mom and Dad. Leave the building if you want. I'll get word to you when they have a verdict.'

'Where should we go?' she asked wonderingly, as if surprised still to be free.

'I'll show you,' a voice said and Linda reached to take Amy's hand. Linda smiled at Edward and it seemed to him he'd been waiting a long time for someone to do that, give him a warm smile.

'Good job,' she murmured, softly enough for only him to hear.

He mouthed thanks.

'Aren't you coming?'

'I'll meet you.' He headed for those damned elevators and downstairs to the clerk's office.

They had the DVD he'd ordered and allowed him to check it out with only his signature and the number from his bar card, which the clerk couldn't tell was just ornamental by this time.

Twenty-One

The jury took hours. They were out for the rest of the day. Later, Edward couldn't believe what they'd been arguing about.

The Halls spent an uncomfortable couple of hours in a coffee shop near the courthouse, then, when it became clear the verdict wasn't going to happen any time soon, retired to Dr and Mrs Hall's house. Linda joined them. Amy clung to her hand so tightly Linda didn't have much choice. They drove their separate cars to the house, but as soon as Linda entered the hall, Amy walked quickly to her, wrapped her arms around and touched foreheads with Linda, as if they could communicate telepathically.

They had picked up takeout Chinese on the way. The warm noodles felt like worms in Edward's mouth. He put down his fork and didn't pick it up again. When he looked up they were all looking at him, his parents quizzically, Amy nodding her approval, Linda – Linda placed her hand over his briefly and he realized he'd felt terribly cold until then. Her warmth traveled up his arm into his chest.

He stood up, suddenly needing to pace, and for a moment saw them all looking at him; his parents questioningly, as if there were anything more he could tell them. As if he had the one secret about the justice system he'd saved until now, the one that could save Amy from all this. Amy looked encouragingly, which was ironic, and Linda – What was her expression? Affectionate, he thought, but also with some sort of question.

'I need to make a call,' he said and went to call Mike.

Linda thought Amy shouldn't be alone, so offered to spend the night with her, which Amy gratefully accepted. Edward volunteered to go pick up clothes for Linda. Before he left, he managed to get Linda alone for a few seconds, and hugged her tightly.

'Thank you, thank you.'

'You're welcome,' Linda answered, smiling.

Edward's errand was legitimate, he needed clothes, but mainly he wanted some time to himself, to try to think and to be alone with a DVD player. He picked up clothes from Linda's. It felt strange for him to be in the house where he used to more or less live, intimately choosing her blouse and underwear and shoes. For moments he felt so much like the man of the house, but it wasn't his house. He could have been a burglar, one with fetishes.

He went on to Mike's to get clothes for himself. Mike was there, on the phone, with very little to report. Edward would have preferred to watch the DVD alone, but he could hardly ask his land-lord to leave, so the two of them watched it. It was a copy of the security footage from the courthouse that had been part of the case against Edward. The prosecution had clearly only requested a certain time period, the one coinciding with the security guard's report.

The camera showed a long shot down the back hallway behind the courtroom. After a minute of nothing happening there was movement and the security guard appeared. He walked up to the door of the judge's chambers, jiggled the doorknob, appeared to listen to something within, then opened the door and went in. A few seconds later Edward appeared, darting out the door and down the hall, carrying most of his clothes. He ran fast – 'like a thief,' was the appropriate expression – disappearing down the hall. It looked like he was going to get away.

Then the security guard came out and ran down the hall himself. There was no audio on the security footage, so they couldn't hear the sounds of pursuit, and the chase never returned this direction. In Edward's mind, he could picture how it went, through the courtroom, out another way, rapidly getting partly dressed while on the run, out into the nighttime corridor again, then almost, almost free, standing there in front of those damned intractable elevator doors.

He realized now that even if he'd gotten away, he probably would have gotten caught by this recording itself, showing him running out of the supposedly empty offices with its much diminished store of cocaine evidence.

Mike reached for the control to stop it, but Edward shook his head. They kept watching, fast forwarding.

It was possible no one had ever watched this DVD. The prosecution had preserved it for trial, but there hadn't been a trial, Edward had ended up pleading guilty. If anyone had watched it, it

316

would have been in a desultory way, just to see the part Edward and Mike had just watched, the part showing the defendant's guilt. Almost undoubtedly, no one had watched the whole thing. It would have been incredibly tedious, staring at three or four hours of mostly empty corridor or of people coming and going on legitimate business before the courthouse closed for the night. No one would have put in that effort until the case was going to trial and it never did.

Certainly no one before now had watched the recording to the end. That became very apparent as Edward and Mike kept watching.

'Hmmh,' Mike said when it happened. He stared intently at the screen.

'Yep.' Edward nodded, took out the DVD very carefully and left it in Mike's keeping, as he headed back to Amy's house, carrying his domestic burden of clothes.

Amy drank wine at her house until she was very sleepy and Linda took her off to bed. Linda was going to stay in the guest room. There was no hint of an invitation for Edward to join her. She did give him a hug and a kiss before she left, but it just felt like encouragement.

Edward wanted to stay up by himself for a while anyway, thinking. He fell asleep on the sofa, but was still the first one up in the morning, making coffee then getting in the shower. When he emerged Linda was standing there, his cell phone in her hand. 'The court called,' she said. 'The jury's back.'

*   *   *

'Have you reached a verdict?' the judge was saying to the presiding juror an hour later.

'We have, Your Honor,' said the woman standing at the corner of the jury box nearest the judge. She wasn't one of the two women Linda had said were on Amy's side.

Wait, wait, wait! Edward wanted to shout. *This should take more time, there should be more build-up. If nothing else, this should be delayed. Someone should come running in with a surprise announcement, something should slow this process, halt this screaming engine bound for—*

'And is that verdict unanimous?'

'It is, Your Honor.'

'Hand it to the bailiff, please.'

Cynthia was one of those judges – Edward would have bet on this – who wanted to see the verdict before anyone else except the jurors. The bailiff formally took the jury verdict and carried it to the judge still folded over, so no one but the judge could see. Cynthia opened the page, looked at it, paused, shot a look at Edward he couldn't decipher and handed the pages back to her bailiff, who returned them to the juror.

The juror opened the pages to the verdict form. She read out the verdict in a strong voice.

'On the charge of capital murder, we find the defendant not guilty.'

The presiding juror looked up briefly at Amy, who grabbed her brother's arm with both hands, a strong grip.

'Wait,' Edward whispered. 'Just wait.'

The juror looked down again. 'On the charge

318

of murder in the first degree, we find the defendant guilty.'

Amy's grip continued cutting off the blood flow in Edward's arm, as if her hands had frozen in place. He couldn't look at her. He kept watching the juror, who closed the pages and stared sympathetically across the room. Edward studied all the jurors now. Most of them looked this way, with almost hopeful expressions on their faces, as if asking whether they'd gotten it right. They wanted their work graded.

Finally Edward turned to look at his sister. Amy stood frozen, her expression trapped between that hopeful joy – that was there when she'd heard the words 'not guilty' – and the expression that would come next but wasn't quite here yet. One of horror would appear as she saw her future hurtling toward her, like a monster coming to consume the rest of her life.

Behind him, the sounds of the courtroom came into focus, the murmurs of a room full of people, one sob, the rising babble of voices. Up on the bench, Cynthia banged the gavel.

Then she turned to the jurors and said formally, 'Thank you for your work in reaching a verdict, jurors. I'll ask you to retire back to the jury room now. We will call you out soon.'

They filed out in the silence that had filled the courtroom now, so the rustle of their clothes as they moved was the only sound. As soon as the door closed behind them, the judge looked coolly at the lawyers.

'Are you ready to begin the punishment phase, Mr Galindo?'

'Your Honor, in light of these developments, may I have a few minutes to confer with defense counsel?'

'Very well. We will take a fifteen minute break.'

She departed in her usual hurried fashion, while Edward turned curiously to the prosecutor. David started to speak, glanced at Amy, and gestured Edward aside. They went and stood in front of the now-empty jury box, affording them some privacy. Edward saw his mother emerge from the audience and put her arms around Amy, who sobbed on her shoulder. In the audience, Linda stared at Edward. He had no gesture to give back to her.

The prosecutor said, 'Now that the death penalty and life without parole are off the table, I'm reinstating my offer, Edward. Thirty years.'

'I think I can do better than that with the jury,' Edward said by rote, negotiating on autopilot.

'Not after I put on that army of witnesses about the burglaries your sister has committed over the years. The jury'll be wishing they had the option of capital murder again.'

After a moment of silence while he thought, Edward said, 'Let me talk to her.'

'You know how a jury feels betrayed, once they learn the defendant isn't who she pretended to be in the first phase of trial. Once they find out sweet little Amy is actually a serial criminal . . .'

'I said I'll talk to her.'

The prosecutor was right about that, Edward thought as he walked toward his sister. He had seen it lots of times, a jury give a defendant a break by finding him guilty of the lesser offense, then in punishment giving the maximum sentence for that lesser. Especially, as David had said, when the State had good punishment evidence.

'Amy.'

His saying her name had no effect. Amy was still crying, still hugging their mother. Dr Hall had joined them now, although he just stood staring at his son, obviously having no idea what to do. Edward gave him a curious look. It seemed his father was about to speak, but he didn't. Linda hovered out in the audience. Edward waved her forward.

'Amy, I have to talk to you. We don't have much time.'

'Apparently I'm going to have a lot of time.'

Edward pulled her aside. He didn't want to make this sales pitch to his whole family. From the corner of his eye, he saw Linda stop just outside the gate in the bar, but he motioned her forward.

'The prosecution's made an offer, Amy. Now that the jury's found you guilty of murder, the punishment range is five to ninety-nine years, or life. Any sentence of sixty years and up is treated as sixty years for parole purposes.'

'Parole,' Amy said flatly. Linda had joined them now, putting her hand on Amy's arm and looking at Edward uncertainly.

'Yes, parole. That's what you've got to think about now, Amy. I've seen this happen lots of times, where you think you've caught a lucky break by being found guilty of the lower offense, but then getting a high sentence for that one.'

'He's right,' Linda said, realizing her role. 'It happens all the time.'

'Maybe they'll give me probation,' Amy said wanly. 'After all, I'm a perfect candidate. I still have a lot to offer—'

'No Houston jury's going to give probation for murder,' Linda said as kindly as possible.

'No,' Edward said. 'Doesn't happen.'

'So what are you asking me to do?'

'If you get a sentence of sixty years or life, with a finding by the jury that you used a deadly weapon – and that's a certainty – you wouldn't be eligible for parole for thirty years.'

'I understand. We had this discussion before. So what's their offer?'

'He's reinstated his offer of thirty years.'

'That means you'd be eligible for parole in half as long,' Linda added quickly. 'Fifteen years as opposed to thirty.'

'Thirty years,' Amy said flatly. 'It's still a thirty year sentence. I could have to be in prison that long.'

Edward leaned over her and took her hands.

'Not someone like you, Amy. You'd make parole the first time you came up for it. Almost positively. I mean, I did, and you're much more likable.'

His joke fell completely flat.

'Do I have to decide right this second?'

Edward shrugged. 'The judge gave us fifteen minutes and we've used about half of it.'

Amy went completely still, even her eyes didn't blink. Edward could almost see her thoughts running across the screen of her forehead of the life she wouldn't have: treating patients; new romance; children; being a neighborhood mom;

leaving her children with her parents while Amy and her husband went out to nice dinners and concerts; her house; her furniture. All that life was disappearing a piece at a time, as if movers were coming in and emptying her cabinets, her silverware drawer, her closets. The other future, the one that was actually going to happen now, was just a blank stone wall. He knew Amy couldn't imagine it at all.

Edward thought harder than he ever had in his life, but there was no solution.

'Just a minute,' he said and returned to David Galindo.

'Twenty,' Edward said. 'Give me twenty.'

David was shaking his head before Edward's second sentence. 'No chance, man. I'd lose my job.'

'No, you won't. Call and run it by them.'

'We only have a few—'

'Fuck Cynthia, David. What can she do if we don't start her precious trial on time? I'll stall her if need be.'

David hesitated. Edward felt sure David would make the offer on his own, but he doubted he could sell it to his powers that be.

Edward started talking again. 'I might be able to get probation from this jury, David. I know you said it couldn't happen, but this is a very sympathetic defendant, with a victim who treated her and a bunch of other women like shit. I can hang them up if nothing else. I know, I know, you're going to prove that Amy broke into people's houses for years. And then did nothing. Didn't destroy anything, didn't take anything. You're going to prove she's a serial trespasser.

323

Big deal. She's a curious person. She cares about people. I'm going to parade in a bunch of children she's cured and their grateful parents. In fact, screw your twenty years. I'm ready—'

'I'll call the office,' David said, then gave Edward another look to say he hadn't been fooled by Edward's speech.

But Edward had fooled himself, a little bit. Maybe he was giving away the future Amy could still have. Even if she'd killed her husband, she was still his sister. And she was an actual productive member of society, more so than this criminal courtroom had ever seen. Was it possible to get probation for murder? Even in Houston, with its traditionally hard-hearted juries? Edward was afraid now David's superiors would say yes.

He turned back to his family, including Linda. They gave him those damned hopeful stares, still expecting him to pull off a miracle, even after he had perfectly demonstrated he couldn't.

David, talking on his cell phone, shook his head at Edward, not finding whomever he needed. Edward looked at the clock. More than ten minutes had passed since the judge had given them fifteen.

David clicked off and said, 'Bobby said I have to run it by the D.A. herself and she's at some conference. They're trying to track her down.'

They could tell the judge the circumstances; they were negotiating to try to spare her having to hold any more trial. But Edward could well imagine Cynthia making them start the punishment phase anyway, while they waited for an answer, just to show she could.

Edward walked toward Amy and took her arm.

'You have my cell number?' he said to David. 'Good. My sister and I are going for a walk.'

They took those elevators all the way down to the ground. That would buy them time. No one had ever managed a return to the world above in less than twenty minutes. Edward could imagine Cynthia fuming as she was told Elvis had left the building.

It was twenty minutes later when David called him. Edward and Amy had spent that time walking around the block. They were deep into November now. Downtown Houston was not the place to go to breathe in the crisp air, but even here they could feel the season and could smell the bright funk of decay. The breeze stirred their hair and reddened their cheeks.

'How far do you think I'd get if I just made a run for it?' Amy asked. She wasn't looking at him; she was staring off at the long vista of another possible future. He couldn't tell how serious she was. Before he could answer, Edward's phone buzzed in his pocket.

He barely had time to get out the word hello.

'OK. Twenty,' David Galindo said.

'Thanks. Tell the nice judge we're heading up.'

He turned to Amy and she could see in his eyes what had happened. Her own widened. Now she had to make the most terrible decision of her life. Edward just looked at her. He could see her thoughts again. The movers had stopped packing her future into boxes. They looked up, interrupted at their job. Parole in ten years. Amy was

325

thirty-two. Now a child became a possibility again. Practicing medicine, too. She was smart as hell, she could catch up on developments in ten years. She could stay in touch with the profession in prison. Ten years. It was an awful future, but ten years ago she had been twenty-two and she could remember that clearly. Ten years.

'My God, Edward, what should I say?'

Thirty minutes later they stood before the judge, alongside David Galindo.

'So you've reached agreement?' the judge said, looking from face to face and lingering on Edward's, her dark eyes flat and unblinking.

'Yes, Your Honor,' they said in chorus and David Galindo handed her the short, simple, terrible agreement. 'We've all signed it.'

And Amy had dropped one tear on the page. Cynthia didn't seem to notice as her eyes ran down the paper to the bottom line.

'Twenty years?' She looked up. 'Twenty?' she said to the prosecutor. David just nodded.

'And you agree to this, Dr Shilling?' This time Cynthia's stare slid past Edward quickly.

'Yes, Your Honor,' Amy said meekly. Edward had explained to her what would happen next and she feared the reality of it. The transition was the worst part: the cold bite of handcuffs around your wrists; turning to see your family watching you taken into custody; changing in that moment into someone other than the person they'd always known; transforming into a criminal just as if she stood and undressed in public.

Cynthia seemed perturbed by the agreement.

But whatever made her resist, the judge suddenly overcame it.

'Very well. Is there any legal reason why I should not assess sentence now?'

'No, Your Honor,' Edward said, standing with his arm around Amy.

Cynthia did so, saying the formal words that took away a big chunk of Amy's life. When it was done she concluded, 'Bailiff, take the defendant into custody.'

The bailiff was already standing behind Amy and did it quickly, even with a hint of gentleness. Amy gave Edward one startled look and disappeared behind the metal door of the holding cell attached to the courtroom. It happened so fast Edward didn't have a chance to say anything, though what he could have said he didn't know. He felt exactly as if he had just betrayed his sister into slavery.

Rustling began throughout the courtroom. The show was over. People in the audience were standing, raggedly rather than uniformly, like when the lights come up in a movie theater.

But wait, there was an encore.

'We will have to bring the jury out and dismiss them,' Judge Cynthia said to the lawyers, who were the only people left standing in front of her.

Edward started to turn away.

'But first we have another order of business,' the judge continued.

Edward turned back to her. Now he was the sole recipient of her attention. She stared at him as if her eyes could devour him, as if she could pull him to her with only the force of her stare.

327

It could have been lust in her expression as her stare consumed Edward, her lips shaping themselves into something like a leer.

'Mr Hall, the court has been growing increasingly suspicious as you tried this case. How did you overcome so quickly the stigma of conviction and time in prison? How did you get back into the good graces of the state bar of Texas so easily?'

Oh, shit. This was what she'd been saving up for. This explained some of her attention toward him. Edward stopped breathing.

'Yes, I can see you know where I'm going with this. And where you're going, I suspect, is back to prison. I checked with the state bar five days ago. I didn't want to interrupt the trial, but I know the truth now. Your license to practice law hasn't been reinstated, Mr Hall. You haven't even applied for it.'

Edward looked back at her, trying to read her. The only question was how long? How long had she been waiting to get him?

'Which means,' Cynthia said, standing up and motioning the other bailiff over, 'that you have been practicing law without a license. In my court. That is a felony, Mr Hall. It is certainly a reason to revoke your parole. Bailiff, take him into custody.'

And then it was all re-enacted: the handcuffs, the stares, the feeling of one's identity circling the drain and gurgling down. Edward wondered fleetingly if being arrested would be easier this time, his second time.

It wasn't.

Twenty-Two

Well, this was all familiar. The holding cell, tiny and narrow. The way the bailiffs now treated him like furniture to be moved rather than a person. Ironically, Edward and Amy rode to jail on the same bus, but he couldn't talk to her. She was up front with the couple of other women and he was in back with the men.

Evening found him in his newly-assigned cell. Edward lay on the thin mattress of his metal bunk waiting for his cellmate to return, which was when the ordeal would begin. The guy would be pissed off at having a new roomie before anyone told him. Edward was taking up some of his precious space, so they would start off on bad terms. But the main question was who the cellmate would be. Maybe an embezzling accountant, that would be wonderful. But, much more likely, a weightlifter who was here because of anger management issues. Edward waited tensely for footfalls, not even thinking past the next few minutes. That was how one survived inside.

But, as no one arrived, his thoughts began to drift. Eyes closed, he could have been at home on his own couch. He could disappear inside his head. What he saw in there was his brother-in-law's face. He could imagine how happy Paul would have appeared in the last months of his life, occasionally arriving at work late with the smug smile of someone freshly glowing with sex. Even more occasionally with scratches, demonstrating the volatility of his relationships. Where was he finding these women? He wasn't bringing them home, according to his neighbors. But no one had been keeping track of Paul's whereabouts during his apparently wild bachelor nights. Had he been afraid of Amy finding out about that life, once they started seeing each other again? No, Paul hadn't been thinking that way until shortly before his death. No, his behavior had been more the opposite, trying to rub his estranged wife's face in his new lifestyle.

Louise Fisher would have seen him in person, nearly every day. If she were the jealous type at all, that might have sent her over the edge. Edward should have had her investigated more thoroughly. Laura Martinelli too. She was the only person who'd said her relationship with Paul had ended. There was no way to prove the opposite, certainly not from inside this cell.

When the footsteps did come, they were the measured stride of legs in uniform pants. Edward opened his eyes, all thoughts driven away as he stood on the razor blades of readiness for what came next.

Sure enough, the same deputy who'd escorted him here was back, unlocking the cell and saying, 'Come on.'

Hoping he'd been reassigned to some white collar criminal section, Edward hurried after him. The deputy led him back toward the booking area, toward the exit, in other words.

330

Edward mustered up the courage to say, 'What's happened?'

The deputy said tersely, 'Somebody made your bail, of course.'

Edward actually stopped for a moment. 'Bail?'

It was Mike waiting for him, of course. Mike would know how to make a bond; Edward's family would not. But who had set a bond anyway? Cynthia would never have—

'Several people talked her into it, actually,' Mike told him as they walked out thirty minutes later. 'A little group of lawyers. They said they could go to any judge to have a bond granted and anybody would release you on personal recognizance. A whole group talked her into setting a bail amount. Guys you've known for a long time.' Mike started naming names, of people Edward had tried cases against and drunk with.

'Actually, I think David Galindo was the main one,' Mike said casually. 'That's kind of what won her over.'

But Edward didn't have time to think about that. He turned around and looked back at the jail.

'Do you think they'd let me visit Amy?'

Mike looked at him as if he was crazy, but then shrugged. 'You're still her lawyer.'

It took an hour. When she finally came to him on the other side of the thick plastic of the attorney visiting booth, she looked terrible. She'd obviously been crying, her hair was disheveled and orange was not her color.

But she also carried herself well, shoulders and

head high – already beginning, he could see, to steel herself for the years ahead.

He wanted to say encouraging words to her, but it would be unfair. He didn't want to give her hope. He hadn't come to talk to her about legal matters. His questions were more of the opposite variety.

'Amy? Listen to me. Here's what I want to know. Do you still have your lock picks? If so, where are they?'

'I need you to help me tomorrow. Can you do that, please?' Edward held the phone tightly, listening to the silence.

Finally Linda sighed. 'Sure. What do you need me to do?'

'I'll pick you up in the morning, about ten. I'll call when I'm on my way. It won't take long, I hope. Linda.'

'Yes.' He tried to hear the shades of cool in her voice, couldn't decipher them all. But maybe there was nothing layered to her tone. Maybe it was just the tone of a love that had cooled to room temperature over the course of time.

'This may not be entirely legal, what I need to do tomorrow.'

Linda didn't hesitate either. 'It's for Amy, isn't it?'

'Yes.'

'All right then. I'll see you in the morning. Good night, Edward.'

She hung up in the middle of his thanking her.

It was a weekday morning in wintry, sunny Houston. Edward parked boldly in Paul's driveway. He and

332

Linda stood in the front yard, scanning as much of the neighborhood as they could see. It was a Wednesday morning, everyone should be at work or school. Both Edward and Linda ended up staring at the house next door. Valerie Linnett was a pharmacist, a job she said she'd taken because the hours were more regular than working in a hospital. The house looked empty, but they couldn't see into the garage.

'What are you thinking?' Edward asked.

'Nothing in particular. What are you?'

'I wanted you to look over Paul's house with me, look for any sign of a woman I might have missed. But I had a feeling we might end up over there.'

'In the neighbor's house?'

'Yes. Instead of looking for signs of a woman in Paul's house—'

'Look for signs of him in hers.'

Edward nodded. 'I realize it's a bad idea,' he continued, 'but I'm kind of at the end of my rope. I need something for a motion for new trial, some new evidence . . .'

Linda stared at the house next door. 'What made you think of Ms Linnett?'

'She's closest.'

Still watching the house next door, her eyes rising, Linda mused, 'Everyone said Paul was so secretive about his home address and wouldn't bring women here, until Amy. But there was one he'd dated right next door.'

'Yeah. That made me wonder if he was hiding his newer women from the early one.'

'Well, here's something. You said you checked

Paul's house all over looking for a place he might have made that recording. But his attic wasn't it.'

'No. It was just studs and insulation.'

'Hers isn't. Hers is finished out.'

'How do you—?' Edward began, then looked where Linda was. Above the first floor of the house next door was a dormer window, with curtains hanging in the window.

'You wait out here,' Edward said. 'Be my lookout.'

Linda shook her head. 'You wanted a woman's eyes. Let me in, then you stay out here and be *my* lookout.'

He refused that, so they ended up doing the stupidest thing. They stood at Valerie Linnett's back door, Edward looking for wires or other signs of a security system. Finally he gave up, looked closely at Linda, who nodded, and he easily opened the lock with Amy's lock picks.

'You're a natural,' Linda said in a neutral tone.

He opened the door quickly. There was no sound. That didn't mean no alarm, but they felt momentarily reassured. Edward stepped inside. Linda closely followed. Closing and locking the door behind themselves, they stepped hurriedly through the kitchen. If Valerie had had anything to do with his killing, she would surely have gotten rid of the obvious signs of his presence long ago. She had never been a suspect; police had never asked to search her house, though at trial they'd mentioned her letting them in to see the view from her window.

One door from the kitchen led to the living

room. They took the other door that opened to a hallway. To the right seemed to be the master bedroom, if this house more or less matched Paul's. Linda led the way that direction. Edward was trying to look at everything – photographs on the walls, the carpet runner over a hardwood floor – while listening intently for the sound of a car. Linda just hurried ahead, into the bedroom. Edward ran after her in as light-footed a way as he could manage. They hadn't even checked the garage, for all they knew Valerie Linnett might be asleep in her bed after a late night.

But the bedroom was empty, the bed neatly made. Former nurse. Hospital corners. Not only did Edward see no obvious sign of a man's presence, he saw no indication that a person lived here. Not a hairbrush on the dresser, a book on the nightstand. It looked like a bedroom in a model home, except that realtors usually added a couple of personal touches. The bedspread was flowered, the curtains white and airy. The blades of the white ceiling fan looked dust-free.

Linda was already at the closet. She emerged with a plaid robe that looked very much like a man's.

'*Paul's?*' she mouthed.

Edward shrugged. The robe looked very generic. Valerie could claim it had been her father's, or that she herself preferred men's robes. Linda shook her head, indicating no other clue. She put the robe back and they stood looking at each other for a moment. There was one other place they had to look, but that didn't mean they both needed to go up there. They stared at each other, having a silent debate, until Linda brushed past him and started toward the hall.

'You stay down here, then,' she said in a normal tone of voice. 'I'll go up, you can warn me if you hear something.'

'Like hell.'

But Linda wouldn't be dissuaded. She was already in the hall, pulling the cord that lowered the attic stairs. They came down silently.

'Well-oiled,' Linda commented, and immediately started up the stairs. Her hips looked well-oiled for that matter, moving quickly. 'I feel that stare,' she said offhandedly.

'What should I do about it, blush and look guilty?'

While bantering he was hurrying up after her. They clambered out onto a painted wooden floor, cheap but effective. Linda started to say something else, then just sucked in her breath and stood silent.

The attic was furnished: a desk, a plush chair over close to the window. Here were the personal touches missing from the bedroom below. A bookcase half-filled, with mostly what looked like novels, some self-help tomes, even a few children's books – maybe beloved leftovers of Ms Linnett's childhood.

But Linda was staring across the room at the wall opposite the desk. It was paneled in a moderately dark, cheap-looking paneling. There were pictures hanging on the wall. It was easy to imagine the pictures removed, leaving only the bare hooks that had been on the wall behind Paul's back, when he'd said earnestly into the

336

camera that if he was found dead it was his wife who'd murdered him.

Edward wheeled the desk chair over in front of that wall and did remove the pictures that were right behind it. And they were staring at the stage set for Paul's DVD.

'Perfect,' Linda muttered. She snapped a picture with her phone.

The scene made Edward remember the video, which he'd watched so many times. Paul had been drunk, Amy had said, and after that Edward could see it. He'd stammered a couple of times; he'd seemed the teeniest bit confused. For someone of Paul's intellect, that was significant. But viewing the scene, picturing Valerie Linnett holding the camera, Edward remembered something else.

Stammering didn't just indicate drunkenness. Paul had been afraid. He'd risked letting his girlfriend, the one right next door, see that he was seeing his wife again. He must have put Valerie off with some explanation: that he was going over the divorce settlement with Amy, something like that. But in the explanation Paul had pissed off his girlfriend, who could sometimes be violent. And she knew how to handle a gun. She'd held one on Edward.

'Look at these,' Linda said, studying the pictures on the wall a few feet away. There were only a few, but they were good: Paul and Valerie at dinner, staring into the camera and holding hands and Paul and Valerie in a hotel room, in a selfie in which they were clearly changing clothes.

'Wow,' said Linda. 'The frumpy old lady next door cleans up pretty good.'

Because this was a very different-looking Valerie Linnett. Instead of her short gray hair she had long, luxuriant brown hair. Her eyes were lustrous. And they could see she'd lost weight in the time since Paul's death, see it in her figure from a year ago, which was striking in the bra and panties she wore in the selfie. In that one she and Paul were both grinning drunkenly.

'She said they'd stopped seeing each other,' Linda said. 'But that wasn't necessarily so. They could come and go through their back gates and backyards and nobody would ever know.'

Edward nodded. 'Not just that. Maybe it was no coincidence Paul was living here in the first place. Valerie used to work in a hospital. Paul had hospital privileges. I'll bet if we check—'

Linda was jumping ahead of him. 'So he left his marriage and moved in next door to his girl-friend so he'd have ready access to her but not have to admit to the affair. Because he didn't want anything coming out that might hurt him in the divorce. Then he discovered he might be a hot commodity on the dating market. That took some juggling, all that dating he was doing on the sly. The girlfriend must have been getting suspicious, then seeing his wife appear at his house was the last straw.'

'So he told her he didn't love Amy, he hated her and feared her. Then made that DVD to appease his jealous girlfriend.'

Linda had continued to take pictures with her phone, moving across the room to put it all in context. Her path had taken her to the window.

Suddenly she said, 'Shit. Edward.'

'She's here?'

'Looks like she's just been to the grocery store or something. Quick, let's—'

Edward jumped to the head of the attic stairs. He reached down; looking for a handhold to pull the stairs up, but that couldn't be done from up here. The stairs were more like a ladder that folded in half to rise into the ceiling. That folding could only be done from below.

There was no choice. He couldn't bluff his way out of this. Edward rushed down the ladder, moving as quietly as he could. He looked back up for Linda, but she didn't appear.

Then he heard the back door open.

Edward folded the ladder and pushed it up on its springs. Thank God for its good oiling. The ladder folded smoothly away and back up into its hiding place.

Leaving Edward standing exposed and Linda trapped above. He started backing away, toward the living room, hoping he could go out the front door while Ms Linnett was coming in the back.

There was a small sound behind him. Edward turned. Valerie Linnett was staring at him. She'd circled around.

'What the hell?'

'We need to talk,' he said quickly, moving toward her. She stepped back.

Edward pressed his small advantage. 'My investigator is on his way here. We need an explanation about something.'

'What are you doing in here? How did you get in my house?'

Edward waved away the question with a

339

gesture. He was still moving toward her, hoping just to get close enough that he could dart past her to the front door. He fell back on the only tool he had, a lawyer's weapon: his tongue.

'I was going to wait on your front porch, but it's cold, so I tried the knob and it was unlocked. You should be more careful. I'm pretty sure your neighbor across the street saw me come in. I just got here. Listen, you know my sister got convicted, right? Well, you said something at trial we need to talk about. You said you thought Paul might have brought another couple of women to his house without anyone noticing. What made you—?'

'What the hell do you want here?' Valerie Linnett wasn't buying his act. Her eyes were sharp as they glared at him. She clutched her purse against her side as if trying to strangle it and Edward knew the purse was a stand-in for him. Involuntarily, he took a step back.

'You didn't come here to talk and I don't leave my door unlocked. Ever. You broke in. Looking for what?'

Edward tried to look innocent. That hadn't worked for him in how long? 'What would I be looking for? No, I came to talk to you. My investigator . . .'

Valerie shot a look over his head, in the direction of the attic access. For just a second, Edward's gaze followed hers. When he looked back down she was staring at him again. Her eyes had narrowed and hardened even further. She didn't accuse him, so he had no opportunity to deny anything. Valerie knew. Anger made her look older. Wrinkles creased her forehead and aimed arrows

340

at her eyes. Edward could sense the front door behind him. He could turn now and there was nothing she could do to stop his escape. Maybe she'd follow him. He still had to figure out a way to rescue Linda. Maybe she'd . . .

Valerie reached into her purse, then let it fall to the ground, leaving only her hand holding the pistol. It was a semi-automatic like Paul's, elegantly silver, but no lady's gun. When she pointed the bore at him it looked big enough to blow half his chest away. Edward lifted his hands.

'Listen—'

She shook her head. 'No more listening. You're a Goddamned burglar. You broke into my house. I know the law. I'm within my rights to—'

'I'm going to turn and run to the front door now. You'll have to shoot me in the back. It will look like murder.'

'Good. That makes my story that I didn't know who you were look more plausible. Goodbye.'

But she didn't fire. Edward was now sure that she'd shot Paul, but that had been the result of careful planning and timing – Paul probably hadn't seen her as he turned toward her. Shooting a man while looking him in the face was a different proposition. Valerie was still going over her story in her mind, wanting to make sure she had it right. Spontaneous murder was harder.

'It doesn't matter what you found,' Valerie said slowly. 'You won't be around to tell anyone.'

Then they heard noises. Not just one sound, a series of thuds from over their heads. Valerie involuntarily looked up.

That was Edward's chance, but he wasn't an

action hero. He too looked upward. When their eyes both lowered, they were looking at each other with different expressions. To her questioning look Edward nodded knowingly.

'Who—?' Valerie began, then her nostrils flared again. 'It's your damned sister up there, isn't it? It's not enough she – She has to break into my house too? God damn you both, I'll—' She suddenly turned the gun upward and fired through her ceiling.

Edward shrieked. Just screeched, like a banshee. This crazy bitch was willing to take the chance of shooting anyone who was up there. But it wasn't just anyone, it was Linda. Edward dove toward Valerie Linnett and before she could lower the pistol's barrel again he was on her, knocking her back, scrabbling at her hands. As they went down his head butted her chin.

He heard her say, 'Oof,' then a bigger noise of air being expelled as they hit the ground, Valerie underneath him. He also heard the sound of the handgun firing again. Only once, before the back of her head hit the hardwood floor and the gun dropped nervelessly from her hand – he vaguely heard it clatter.

For just a moment he lay there on top of her. It was weirdly intimate. They could have been lovers, locked in a passionate embrace or snuggling in the aftermath. The woman was clearly unconscious, but that could have been the result of great lovemaking too, instead of hitting the back of her head on the floor.

Edward stood up, slipping on something. Valerie lay there helpless, but the gun was close by her hand, reminding him that she had tried to shoot the woman he loved. He wanted to kick her in the head, just for good measure.

When he pulled back his right leg, though, he realized he had no strength in his other leg. It crumpled under him. On the floor, he realized why he had slipped a minute ago. There was a streak of blood underfoot.

Edward saved his strength to head toward the attic access, but he didn't make it. The blood, he realized now, was streaming down his leg. Just as he understood this, he heard another, louder thump, this time from outside. He turned to see Linda scramble to her feet out there. A moment later she was peering in one of the front windows, holding up her phone like a weapon. She cupped her hands around her eyes to block the glare, then those eyes widened. As she darted from the window, Edward started in that direction, then slipped again. This time he fell.

Linda was holding him then, raising his head, crying. Edward just stared up at her.

'You have beautiful eyes,' he said.

She lowered him gently and he felt her unfastening his belt. Beginning to slip away, he thought, *She wants to make love now? Here?*

'I'll give it a try,' he said aloud. 'But I—'

Then he was gone.

Twenty-Three

He woke alone, in white light. Edward felt light-headed. Light-bodied, too, in fact. He lifted his hand and saw that it was white too, pale as paper, emerging from a white sleeve.

'Shit,' he said.

He was dead, just when he'd finally had a plan. He'd known just what to do to fix everything. But he hadn't told anyone, so he'd taken that secret to the grave. Maybe someone else would figure it out. But he'd also wanted to tell Linda his revelation about her. About them. He hoped more than anything that she would figure that out.

At least he seemed to be in Heaven. He must have done more good in his life than he could remember. Then he realized the first word he'd said in Heaven was 'shit.'

The light diminished somewhat as if he was being sent to the other place. Edward turned his head and saw a burly black man in green scrubs closing the blinds at the window. The room remained pretty bright, but now it was obviously a hospital room. Edward had just been momentarily sunlight-addled as the room glowed with light just as he'd opened his eyes.

'Not people's usual reaction when they find out they're alive,' the nurse or doctor or orderly at the window said of Edward's first word. 'You got a lot of debts or something?'

He smiled. Edward shook his head, then reconsidered.

'Maybe. Yes.'

He heard the door open, and Linda entered from the hallway carrying a pink plastic pitcher.

'Ah,' she said when she saw he was awake. 'Here, water.'

'Here's your chance to thank the woman who saved your life,' the man at the window said. Edward decided he was a doctor. 'If she hadn't stopped the blood flow with your belt, you would have bled out before the EMS got there.'

'Oh. I thought she was just trying to get me naked one last time before I went.'

'Idiot,' Linda said, shaking her head. But she was smiling.

The man came over and looked at the readings on the instruments that were connected to Edward. He nodded his head gravely. 'You'll be OK. Just don't go jogging for a while and eat a lot of red meat.'

'Wow. Medical advice I've always wanted.' Edward reached for Linda's hand. She came closer, still smiling.

'Well,' the man said, looking at the joined hands. 'I'll see you later.'

'Thanks,' Edward said. When he was gone Edward and Linda started talking at the same time, but Edward prevailed.

'I realized something when that crazy woman shot up into the ceiling. You were up there and I had to stop her. I wanted to kill her, because you're the most important person in the world to me. I love you, Linda.'

She just looked at him for a while. She really looked beautiful this morning, her pale skin accented by full red lips and long, dark eyelashes.

Finally she said, 'You don't have to say that.'

'I do, because it's true and I hadn't said it and somebody might try to shoot me again any minute before I get another chance.'

He tugged gently at her hand and she bent over and kissed him. 'How about getting in here with me?' he whispered.

'The doctor said you should take it easy for a while.'

'He only specified jogging. But I just want to hold you.'

Carefully, she lay on the bed full length next to him, their heads close.

After quite a while, Edward said, 'It sounded to me like he said I can get out of here now.'

'I don't think that's what he said. You need to rest.'

'No rest for the weary. I've got some heavy blackmailing to do.'

Edward's plan had several steps to it, as the best ones do. Some people say the simplest plans are the best but, in his experience, simple plans didn't take care of enough problems or look far enough ahead. Simple plans like, say, breaking into a court reporter's office and taking some of the cocaine she had stored away. That plan should have had way more steps to it.

Two days later, Edward limped into Judge Cynthia Miles' courtroom, using the cane Linda had bought him. He'd automatically tried to reject

346

the idea of using it, but in fact he rather liked it. It gave him a sort of jaunty air, while at the same time adding *gravitas* to his persona. A man wounded in the line of duty obviously had more depth than some people might have thought.

He was wearing a black suit too, still in his lawyer's disguise. He stopped in a back corner of the courtroom to survey the room. Cynthia was on the bench, listening to two lawyers talk at her. It didn't appear she liked what either of them was saying. She glanced up, her gaze swept the room and passed him, then the judge did a double take at sight of Edward. He didn't nod or wave, just stood there. Then he heard Cynthia snap something about taking it under advisement. She rose quickly and left the bench in a swirl of robe.

After she exited through the back door, Edward limped forward and through the side gate in the railing. No one glanced at him. As Edward kept walking, he remembered something a friend of his had told him when Edward left the D.A.'s office. It was an older lawyer who'd been around for quite a while.

What he'd said was, 'Try to enjoy yourself instead of trying to do important work. Because the one thing I've learned, from being in this courthouse all these years, is this: no matter how important you think you are, the day after you walk out of this building for the last time, life in the courthouse will go on exactly the same as if you'd never been born.'

Edward had gotten to see actual proof of that, having been gone for a while.

He found Cynthia in her chambers, pretending to

read something, pretending she hadn't been waiting for him.

'Hi,' he said casually.

She gave him a flat, dark stare. 'I'm surprised to see you here.'

'You set my bail.'

'That's not what I mean.'

'I know. Me neither.' He went back and closed her door.

'We should not be having an *ex parte* communication,' Cynthia said stiffly. She remained sitting, but her hands were on the arms of her chair, her back straight and he knew her legs were bent under her, ready to spring up. Did she think he was going to attack her?

'Well, those are between a judge and a lawyer,' Edward said easily, 'and, as you pointed out in court, I'm not a lawyer anymore.'

'You'll never practice law again. You're going back to prison.'

Cynthia appeared to relax as she said that, which fit Edward's theory that she'd known much earlier than she let on that he hadn't regained his law license.

'I've been trying to figure you out from the first time I walked into your courtroom. Once we were in trial, I kept waiting for you to shade your rulings in my favor because of the huge debt you owe me. But you didn't. When you came down on me as hard as you could, once I was in jail – again – I figured it out. You don't hate me. You're afraid of me. You're terrified of me.'

'I'm not—' she began, but her posture was quite otherwise.

348

'I'm the one person who can expose you as a criminal, who can ruin your good life. So you needed to destroy me, specifically destroy any credibility I might have if I decided to tell our story, so that if I did no one would believe me. And ideally I'd be back in prison and no one would listen to me anyway.

'By the way, I'm not going back to prison. You didn't talk to anybody when you found out I was still disbarred, did you, Cynthia? You should have. You were never that good at the legal side of things, were you? You were an excellent trial lawyer and you picked up enough law to be a good judge, but practicing law without a license is a very unusual crime. It has elements you probably aren't familiar with; that it has to be done with the intent to deceive and for remuneration. But Amy will testify that she knew I was still disbarred and that I never charged her anything for appearing with her in court. I was just her representative, not her lawyer. You should read a statute some time, Cynthia.'

'That's Judge Miles to you.' She stood up now, her eyes smoldering again. 'You need to remove yourself from my sight, now.'

'Well, it wasn't Judge Miles when we started, was it, Cynthia?' Edward slowly and carefully removed a DVD in a sleeve from his suit coat pocket. 'This is an exhibit that was prepared to be introduced at my trial and was introduced as proof of my guilt when I pled no contest. It's a copy of the security camera footage from our night of – how shall I put it – personal examination of the evidence in the cocaine trial. But because I chose not to contest my case, nobody ever watched it to the end. They knew I was on it, leaving the court chambers, and that's where they stopped, if anyone watched it at all. The security guard caught me dead to rights, so all they needed was his testimony. But someone took that security footage right away, the day after I got arrested, because they knew those things get erased and reused pretty quickly. So the evidence sat there and nobody reviewed it or, if they did, they didn't see it all or they didn't tell anybody they did.

'Was that because you were the prosecutor, Cynthia? You told me you removed yourself from the case, but since you let me swing all by myself for our mutual crime, I don't have much faith in your word.'

Edward had sat in one of the visitor chairs by now. Cynthia remained standing in her robe. She stood very rigidly, fists on her desk, her face darkening.

'Well, I finally got it and watched it to the end. And made a few copies. Want to see? Oh, look, you have a television all set up for reviewing evidence.'

He stood up, turned on the flat screen and inserted his disc.

'Don't worry, there's no sound. See, here I am exiting the court's chambers. And a few seconds later, here comes the security guard, in hot pursuit. I didn't reappear in that hallway; I led him as far away as I could. For you. Anyone would have stopped watching at this point, because there was no more drama. Just a door standing ajar.' Then he began fast-forwarding.

The counter on the screen showed ten minutes pass. Twelve. Then the door moved a little, and a woman emerged from the offices. Cynthia. Anyone who knew her would recognize the figure on the screen. She glanced both ways, tilted her head to listen, then tiptoed toward the camera and out of sight. As a prosecutor, Cynthia had probably had a key card that would let her use the stairwells and Edward knew that she had gotten out of the building without being seen. There was no telling how she'd managed her escape, but she had.

Edward turned off the television, removed the disc from its player and laid it on Cynthia's desk. She was still standing rigidly glaring at him, but there was something behind her glare now. She seemed to have physically shrunk a little.

Folding her arms, Cynthia said, 'Now you're going to add blackmailing to your list of crimes?'

Edward shook his head. 'I'm not asking you for anything. I'm not threatening you with anything. That's what I came to tell you. You've always thought I was going to give you up as my partner in crime, but I never have, have I? Not when I was first arrested, not when plea bargaining for my freedom, not when I got out of prison. Not even, for God's sake, when you had me arrested *again*! If I didn't do it then, what makes you think I will? I won't, Cynthia.'

'And what do you want from me in exchange?' The tone of Cynthia's voice had changed. She may have thought it was still harsh and commanding, but to Edward's ear a slight pleading tone had crept into it. There is no curiosity so intense as curiosity about one's own future.

351

Cynthia's control was pretty tight, but her voice and now her eyes revealed her anxiety.

He stared back. 'I just want you to give me a fair break. Judge Miles.'

Edward turned quickly and left without looking back.

David Galindo was in the outer office when Edward emerged.

'What were you doing?' he asked idly.

'*Ex parte*ing the judge. Your turn now.'

David looked at the closed door. 'I don't talk to her if I can help it.'

'Good. Walk with me instead.'

When they arrived at David's office he was just finishing reading the last page of the document Edward had handed him, glanced at the heading again – *Motion for New Trial* – and dropped it on his desk.

'Pretty detailed affidavit you attached. It does seem to leave out a few key details, though.'

'Those will come out at the hearing.'

'Yeah, yeah,' David said. 'Has Cynthia seen your motion?'

'I didn't give her a copy personally. I imagine her clerks have given it to her by now, though. Why?'

'Because you know she'll never grant it, no matter what.'

'No, I'm not sure of that. I think she'll give it serious consideration.'

'No judge ever wants to grant a new trial,' David said. 'And especially with a big case like this, she doesn't want it back on her docket to be tried again. Clogs up the process.'

'I know. Those innocent defendants who get convicted are a bitch, aren't they?'

David turned and looked at him for what seemed the first time during this visit. 'You really believe that?' he said quietly.

'I know it, David. If you could have seen that woman's eyes, Valerie Linnett's, you'd know she was capable of murder. Hell, she shot me.'

David shrugged, acknowledging a good point.

'What about her finished attic? It's obviously where Paul made that DVD. Look at it again knowing that, knowing the background. Look at how scared he was. And that dress in his closet that wouldn't fit Laura Martinelli. It will fit Valerie Linnett, trust me. I think she left it there on purpose to try to drive any competition away. Covering the place with her own scent.'

'What would killing him get her?'

'I don't understand these love triangle killings any better than you do. But that's clearly what it was, even though Amy didn't know it. Valerie and Paul had a relationship. They could go back and forth without anyone ever seeing a strange car in either one's driveway. He probably thought he had a brilliant set-up there, until he decided he was quite a catch and wanted to start dating around. And that's why Paul was so skittish about letting a woman know where he lived once he did start seeing other women. He didn't want his extremely jealous next-door-neighbor girlfriend knowing about it.'

'"Extremely jealous"?'

'Remember the scratches people saw on Paul a couple of times? He was in a violent relationship.

353

Maybe that felt fun at first, but I think he knew what Valerie was capable of.'

David considered, and kept his thoughts to himself.

Twenty-Four

Two weeks later, Edward woke up with the love of his life in his arms, smiled and opened his eyes as he felt Linda's lips.

'Hello to you too,' he murmured. They lingered for a while in bed, but it was a working day.

Motions for new trial were usually hopeless. Not usually: almost always. Two hours later, sitting beside Amy in court, Edward reflected on how much different this felt than sitting at counsel table at the start of a trial. Before trial began, there was always optimism that something unexpected could go right. Now it felt as if they were starting out on a trip they already knew ended in disaster.

Amy looked good. She wore a blue skirt suit that brought out her eyes. Being dressed like a normal person had also made her lose that jail flatness. Her eyes darted around as her hands clenched each other. She looked hopeful and scared. Perfect.

Judge Miles called the court to order.

'I have read the motion for new trial with its attached affidavits,' she announced immediately. 'Are both sides ready to proceed?'

'Ready, Your Honor,' Edward said, standing.

David Galindo echoed him.

'You are still acting as your sister's representative, Mr Hall?' Judge Miles asked with little evident surprise.

'Exactly that, Your Honor. Not her lawyer, just standing by her.'

The judge addressed Amy directly. 'And that's what you want, Ms Hall, knowing everything you know now?'

Amy stood too. 'I knew it all along, Your Honor. Yes, I want Edward representing me.'

The judge shrugged. 'Then let's begin. Call your first witness, Mr Hall.'

First Edward called Mike, whose testimony was brief. He had gotten a certified copy of a deed record showing Paul's rent house was owned by his next-door neighbor, Valerie Linnett. Edward also introduced an affidavit that had been on file long enough to qualify as a business record. It was copies of bank records showing Paul's rent checks going to a management company and the company's records showing, in turn, a similar amount (minus fees) being paid to Ms Linnett. David Galindo had no questions about any of it.

The next witness was a woman who had worked at United Presbyterian Hospital for ten years. She too brought business records.

Edward, dispensing with formality, asked her, 'What do those records show, Mrs Arbison?'

Harriett Arbison was a little shorter than average and a little heavier, with small, efficient hands. Courtroom lights glittered off her glasses as she said,

'These are business records showing that Valerie Linnett worked as the hospital pharmacist for four years.'

'Ending when?'

'Not long ago, April before last.'

Only a few months before Paul had moved out of his house, into the one next door to Valerie.

'Do you have other records?' Edward asked blandly.

'Yes. These concern Dr Paul Shilling.'

'Was he also affiliated with your hospital?'

'Yes. Dr Shilling had admitting privileges at United Presbyterian.'

He certainly had.

'Do your records show him ordering prescriptions from your pharmacy?'

'Yes. Quite a few over two or three years.'

'And he would have ordered those through Valerie Linnett?'

'Yes sir.'

Edward had fallen quickly into the ease of being a trial lawyer, sitting back in his chair as he asked questions.

'Do you have any personal memories of seeing Dr Paul Shilling with pharmacist Valerie Linnett?'

'Yes.' Through her glinting glasses, he couldn't tell if she was rolling her eyes or looking askance.

'Could you elaborate, please?'

'Well, I saw him consulting with her a few times, which isn't unusual, of course. Except that a handful of those times they didn't have a patient's chart between them, which was a little odd. Once I walked by one of those consultations and they both stopped talking as I went by. Dr Paul smiled at me and Valerie just looked impatient, like I wasn't passing them fast enough.'

'Any other time?'

'Once I saw them in the coffee shop together, just looking at each other. Staring into each other's eyes, you might say.'

One might.

'Do you remember when that was?'

'I do, because it was shortly before Valerie left the hospital. She looked at me again that day and, when she quit a little later, I wondered if she left her hospital job at least partly to get away from being watched.'

'Was Dr Paul Shilling still married at that time?'

'Yes.' Mrs Arbison looked surprised for the first time. 'I thought he was married until he died, wasn't he?'

Technically yes.

'But on the occasion you're talking about, when you saw him with Ms Linnett, he was still living with his wife?'

'Oh yes. I'd see Dr Amy at the hospital sometimes too. She also had admitting privileges there.'

Another good reason Valerie Linnett would want to leave that crossroads of the medical community and go to a private pharmacy.

Edward walked to the witness and handed her a photograph, one from Valerie's attic wall.

'Do you recognize the person in this picture, ma'am?'

'Yes. That's Valerie.'

'Is that the way she looked on the day you saw her in the coffee shop with Dr Paul Shilling?'

'Yes. You can tell she's dressed to go out in this photo, but those last days when she worked at the hospital she was always pretty nicely made up too.'

'Thank you, Mrs Arbison. I have no more questions for you.'

He handed the photo to the judge, who glanced at it and set it aside.

'State?' the judge asked blandly.

'No, Your Honor,' David said.

Edward shot a look at him. Was David letting him take a free shot? No, the prosecutor was obviously alert and there were at least a page of notes on the legal pad in front of him. There was just no apparent damage control to be done with this witness and David was a good enough lawyer not to look foolish by wasting court time with irrelevant questions.

The judge was making notes too. 'Next?' she said, without looking up.

'Oliver Bennett, Your Honor.'

Who? David mouthed at Edward as the bailiff went out into the hall to call the witness.

Edward just shrugged.

'State your name for the court, please.'

'Oliver Bennett. People call me Ollie.'

The witness was a tall, slim African-American man with an expressive face. After his first remark he glanced at the judge and she smiled back at him.

'What is your occupation, Mr Bennett?'

'I'm a server at Houston's on Westheimer.'

Houston's was an upscale, but not over the top, restaurant not far from the neighborhood where both Paul and Valerie Linnett had lived. Paul had been cautious in some ways about his private life, but from everything that had come out lately he'd been going through a reckless time of life.

359

'Mr Bennett, let me get right to it. Have you ever seen these two people?' Edward walked to the witness stand and showed him two photographs of Paul and Valerie. The witness had already been shown similar photos days ago by Mike.

'Yes. I was their server at least once. Maybe more than once.'

'Is there a particular occasion you remember serving them at Houston's?'

'Yes. The last time. They came in about mid-evening on a weeknight.'

'Do you remember when this was?'

'Last winter. February.' Shortly before Paul's death.

'Why do you remember that occasion, Mr Bennett?' Edward had resumed his seat by now, leaning forward on the counsel table.

'They made it memorable. It was a slow night, the place wasn't crowded, and every time I went to the table they'd either ignore me or look up like I was annoying them. Most people like attentive service, but these two seemed like they wanted to be left alone. I wondered why they'd come to a restaurant.'

'What do you remember about their appearance, if anything?'

'Well, they'd been drinking already. I don't mean they were drunk, nothing like that, but, you know, the way some people get.'

'How is that?' Edward asked curiously.

The witness sat back and looked over the spectators' heads thoughtfully.

'Heightened emotions, I guess you'd say.

360

Experienced servers know what that looks like. They were talking steadily, in low voices that they'd shut off abruptly when I went by to check on them, but I could tell it was pretty intense. She was doing most of the talking, mostly leaning toward him. Sometimes he sat back and folded his arms, as if he was trying to back away as far as he could.'

'Could you hear anything they said?'

'Not much. Like I say, they'd stop when I got close. I just heard little phrases. The one I remember is her saying, "If you think," you know, as if she was saying, "If you think I'm going to—"'

'Object to speculation,' David Galindo said quickly.

The judge looked down at the witness, who looked back at her.

'I don't think so,' the judge mused. 'Good servers have a lot of experience of knowing how conversations are going without hearing every word. I'm going to allow it.'

Mr Bennett nodded as if complimented. David Galindo let his gaze linger on the judge.

The server continued. 'It sounded like she was saying something like, "If you think I'm going to let you get away with this you've got another think coming." Something like that. That's how her face looked.'

Edward wrote a long note about that, letting the testimony sink in. It was obvious the judge was paying close attention.

'Did you see anything else that night that seems important, Mr Bennett?'

'Just one little thing.' The server crossed his

legs and laced long-fingered hands across his knee. 'Things changed toward the end. The man was leaning toward her, looking, looking . . .'

'Looking how, sir?'

'I'm trying to think. Nervous, I guess, but that doesn't say it enough. *Afraid* would be too much. But it was like it was sinking in to him how serious their conversation was. He was leaning toward her, like he was apologizing. By then she was the one sitting back, looking aloof like. But then just when I thought it was going to end she leaned forward and put her hand over his, but not like holding hands. I didn't realize it until I went over to take them the check; she'd been digging her nails into the back of his hand. There were deep red marks on the back of that hand. He saw me look and jerked his hand under the table.'

Which accounted for the scratches the medical examiner had mentioned on the back of one of Paul's hands. Edward moved to the television that remained in the courtroom.

From there he said, 'Let me show you something, please.' Edward turned on the television. The DVD was keyed to the beginning. Paul's face came on the screen. 'Did he look like this that night, Mr Bennett?'

The witness studied the shot. Edward wondered what everyone else saw. Paul looked very different to him now than he had the first time Edward had seen this. Now he could see traces of the drunkenness Amy had claimed, as well as something else. Something a little beyond nervousness, as the witness had said.

362

'Yes, that's how he looked that night.' Mr Bennett pointed. 'See that little mark on his white shirt pocket? That's a wine stain from a little he spilled when I was waiting on him. I remember that.'

Edward wished Paul would show the backs of his hands on the DVD, but he kept them carefully out of sight.

Edward paused it and said, 'Pass the witness.'

'You have a remarkable memory, Mr Bennett,' David Galindo began.

'Thank you. I observe people. That's one of the perks of being a server, being a people-watcher. And that was a slow night, like I said.'

'How is it the defense didn't find you until after the trial, Mr Bennett?'

'I found them. I was out of town when this trial started, but when I got back I saw a front page story about Amy Shilling being convicted and it reprised the whole trial. There was a picture of her deceased husband and I realized I'd seen him. So I got in touch with the defense.'

It happened that way sometimes, a witness not knowing about the case until it was in trial. It was both a blessing and a curse to get such evidence after the trial had ended. It was potentially valuable evidence, but it was also too late.

David looked at the man for a few seconds, then apparently decided it was too dangerous to ask him anything else.

'No more questions.'

Edward said, 'The prosecutor made me think of one more, Mr Bennett. Had you seen this couple in your restaurant before?'

'At least one other time, but it seemed like it was way earlier. Months earlier. They came in a couple of times then stopped. At least that's all I remember of them.'

Which fit Valerie's testimony that she and Paul had dated, then stopped. That's when their relationship had gone subterranean, in Edward's theory.

'No more questions,' he said.

The judge made a few rapid notes, then looked up. 'Next?'

'The defense calls Valerie Linnett, Your Honor.'

A murmur ran through the audience. The defense had spent the entire hearing setting Ms Linnett up as a suspect. Why call her to let her deny it?

Valerie Linnett came down the side aisle of the courtroom, head held stiffly. Edward knew she'd been in the hallway accompanied by a bailiff. Edward had had her served with a subpoena to ensure her presence here today and he'd also called her to say if she didn't appear he'd have her attached – meaning arrested and brought to court. She'd hung up on him. But here she was.

She wore slacks and a dark blouse. She had on no apparent makeup and her hair was longer, but showed more gray than it had when she'd testified at trial. Her movements appeared stiff.

The judge was looking back and forth from the witness to the photograph of her in his hand. Edward gave her time to examine both, then began.

'Hello again, Ms Linnett. Let's get right to it. Is there anything you wish to change about your trial testimony?'

'No.' Her voice was as stiff as her spine.

364

'Let me show you a photograph.' He crossed quickly to her and did so. 'Is that a picture of your side gate and Paul Shilling's side gate?'

She didn't even glance at the picture. 'I can't tell.'

'Your side gates are right next to each other, aren't they?'

'Yes.'

Edward showed the picture to David.

'Will the prosecution stipulate that this is a picture of what I described? I can recall my investigator if necessary.'

David gave it more than a cursory glance, then said, 'So stipulated.'

Next Edward called Ms Linnett's attention to the television, with Paul still frozen on its screen.

He started it again and said, 'Is this your attic, Ms Linnett?'

Again she refused to look. 'On the advice of counsel I refuse to answer any more questions.'

'What?' Edward's attention shot back to her. 'What was that?'

'I have consulted an attorney who advised me not to answer any questions.'

'Do you mean you're asserting your Fifth Amendment privilege?'

'Yes.'

'Against incriminating yourself?'

She finally looked at him, a glare she quickly tried to dim just to a stare.

'I believe it's the right to remain silent. At any rate, I'm asserting it.'

'All right.' He had hoped for this. Her refusal to testify couldn't be held against her in court, in fact in a regular trial the jury wouldn't even be allowed to know she'd asserted the privilege, but the judge had heard it. What the law allows and the assumptions people naturally make have very little to do with each other.

'Ms Linnett, were you and Paul Shilling having an affair?'

She leaned forward and said, 'Same answer.'

'Just to be clear for the record, do you mean you're again asserting your right not to incriminate yourself?'

This time the prosecutor stood. 'I object to characterizing her testimony that way, Your Honor.'

Judge Miles looked at him with evident curiosity. 'What's your objection, counselor?'

'It's prejudicial, Your Honor. He knows he can't burden her exercise of her privilege by referring to it.'

'That's true in front of a jury, counselor, but right now I'm the fact-finder. You can trust the court not to consider inadmissible evidence.'

'I do, Your Honor, absolutely. But I still have to object.'

'You've done so,' Cynthia said curtly. 'Go ahead, Mr Hall.'

David resumed his seat, staring at the judge. She had changed since trial.

'Are you the reason Dr Shilling didn't want other women to know his address, Ms Linnett, because he knew how jealous you were?'

Now not bothering to disguise her glaring daggers, she said, 'Again, I refuse to answer.'

'And we all know why. Well, then let me show you something, ma'am.'

As Edward stood, he caught a glimpse of Amy. She was staring at Valerie Linnett as if she'd never seen her before, this woman who'd been having an affair with her husband, not only since the separation but before. Perhaps she was the cause of the separation . . . Amy didn't even look angry, just befuddled, as if waking up to find a stranger in bed with her.

Edward picked up another one of the trial exhibits from his counsel table. It was the dress that had been hanging in Paul's closet, the one that hadn't fit Amy and had fit Laura Martinelli like skin. He carried it toward the witness stand.

'Would you just go back into the court offices and try this on, please, Ms Linnett, then come out and show us how it fits?'

'I will not.' She sounded as if he'd asked her to strip naked in the courtroom.

David Galindo sat silent. He knew the law. Edward looked at the judge and shrugged.

Kindly, Judge Miles leaned toward the witness and explained.

'Ma'am, you have a privilege not to testify if you choose. But you cannot refuse to be displayed yourself, like taking your fingerprints. I can order you to do that. I am ordering you to put on this dress.'

Valerie sat there staring straight ahead as if she hadn't heard her. There were two bailiffs in the courtroom, a male one at a desk and a female one standing close to Amy, guarding her. At a look from the judge the man stood up and the woman started walking toward the witness. Still without looking at anyone, Valerie abruptly stood up, turned and marched out the back door of the courtroom, behind the judge's bench. The woman bailiff hurried after her, grabbing the dress from Edward in passing.

They all waited stiffly. Edward turned and saw his family in the front row of the spectator seats. His mother was in tears, his father frowning. Linda wasn't with them. Edward turned his attention to Amy, who gazed back at him. Now she looked scared, more so than he'd seen her through this whole ordeal. Her face was the least bearable in the courtroom. Edward turned back to face the judge.

No more than five minutes passed, though it seemed much longer, before the bailiff returned. Valerie Linnett walked in behind her, wearing the blue dress. She had tried to bunch it around her hips, but as she walked it slipped down. The dress hung on her just slightly – Edward had noticed she appeared thinner today than when he'd first met her months earlier – but it fit. The dress showed enough cleavage to be interesting but not enough to be vulgar. It showed off her figure without being provocative. And it was just the right length for an evening sheath, coming halfway down her calves. With the right pair of heels and perhaps a smile on the face of its wearer, the dress could have been stunning.

Valerie turned stiffly toward Judge Miles, not looking remotely like a runway model. After a moment, Cynthia nodded and then inclined her head, giving her permission to leave again. Valerie walked out as stiffly as she'd entered.

'Is this going to be your final witness, Mr Hall?' the judge asked in her absence.

'Only one more, Your Honor. She'll be brief.'

'Dr Shilling? Because I've heard her testimony. Unless she has something new to add—'

'No, Your Honor, not the defendant. We'll rely on her trial testimony.'

The judge nodded and they waited until Valerie Linnett returned, in her slacks and blouse again.

Edward started to pass her, then said, 'The dress fit you very well, didn't it, Ms Linnett?'

'Not really. I found it very uncomfortable.'

I'll bet. 'Do you have an explanation for how it came to be in Paul's closet?'

'Since it's not mine, no.'

'Were you expecting to wear it to the awards dinner that evening? Was that going to be your coming-out-in-public occasion?'

She leaned forward and spoke into the microphone.

'Again, it's not my dress. So no to all that.'

'Pass the witness.'

David Galindo hesitated a long time, looking at Valerie. She didn't look back, keeping her eyes downcast.

David finally said, 'No questions.'

The judge excused the witness, who took a seat in the audience, staring.

'The defense's final witness is Linda Benson, Your Honor.'

Linda wore a dark gray skirt and a green blouse that brought out the color of her eyes. She sat comfortably in the witness chair and looked straight at Edward.

'Linda, you and I recently entered Valerie Linnett's house when she wasn't there. Did you take pictures of the walls in her attic?'

'I did.' They introduced the five photos. When Edward passed them to Judge Miles, the judge looked at them and then at the television screen, which still showed Paul and the wall behind him. One of the pictures even showed a bare hook, just like one behind Paul's shoulder.

'What happened next, Linda, after you took the pictures?'

'You saved my life.'

That they hadn't rehearsed. Edward felt himself reddening under her serene stare.

'Well, I think . . . It was more a case of . . . Just tell the judge what happened, please.'

She did, unable to keep the tension out of her voice as she recounted their realizing they were about to be discovered. Linda's eyes grew moist as she described being alone in the attic, waiting, until suddenly she heard shots and bullets came through the floor close to her. She had practically flung herself out the window then, slid down the roof and landed in the front yard just after Edward himself got shot.

Edward felt the collective silence around her words, the courtroom hushed as everyone stared at Linda. She told about discovering that Edward had already knocked Valerie unconscious. Then she told the part of the story Edward hadn't known, the unbearably long wait for the ambulance while he continued to bleed in spite of her best efforts.

'I couldn't seem to get the belt tight enough,'

she said through tears, looking at the judge. 'I held it in place and held it tight, but there still seemed to be a trickle of blood. The puddle of blood was getting bigger. I thought he was going to die.'

'But I didn't,' Edward said. 'Here I am. Thank you, Linda. I pass the witness.'

David looked at her over his steepled fingers and said, 'Thank you, ma'am. No more questions.'

Edward stood and said, 'Your Honor, the court has my affidavit attached to the motion. I just want to say here that every word of it is true, including that Valerie Linnett said to me, "It doesn't matter what you found, you won't be around to tell anyone." Then she shot me.'

She nodded at him.

More frightened than he'd ever been at ending a court presentation, Edward said, 'We rest, Your Honor.'

'State?'

'We rest as well, Your Honor.'

'Your Honor,' Edward began quickly, as Linda walked past him toward the audience.

Edward continued, 'I'd say trying to shoot the witness in her attic, knowing what we'd discovered, was an admission in itself. Ms Linnett was obviously acting out of a guilty—'

'I didn't invite argument, counsel,' Judge Miles said, not unkindly. 'I've heard enough. I can't believe this wasn't presented during trial. I can't understand why the defense didn't discover this past and current connection between Ms Linnett and the deceased in time to present it in defense. Clearly this is evidence the jury should have heard,' Judge Miles continued, as if having a chat.

'But I'm not sure it qualifies as newly discovered evidence, since it was available before trial, if the defense had only discovered it. The deed and bank records, for example.'

'But not her admissions, Your Honor, and her shooting me. Those didn't happen until after trial.'

'I grant you that.'

Edward was losing feeling in his legs and his hands were shaking. Was the judge deliberately trying to do that to him, raising his hopes then dashing them almost in the same sentence? He felt something cold and looked down to see that Amy had taken his hand.

Judge Miles turned to David.

'Mr Prosecutor, do you believe you heard enough to obtain an arrest warrant?'

Oh my God. Was this going to happen again, Edward being arrested for burglary, this time accompanied by Linda? He stared at Cynthia. She wouldn't look back at him.

'Yes, ma'am. I believe the defense has established probable cause, when a suspect in a shooting murder shoots someone else. Yes, I think we could arrest on that.'

'I agree. Bring me a warrant and I'll sign it. Just a moment, Ms Linnett.' Edward turned to see Valerie standing in the aisle. A bailiff hurried toward her. Valerie's eyes and mouth were open wide.

A minute later, there were two women in handcuffs in the courtroom. Valerie Linnett sat in the jury box looking stunned.

The judge addressed the one standing next to Edward.

'I'm sure you had the most well-meaning defense in the world, Dr Shilling. But you should have gotten a real lawyer. I'm granting the motion for new trial,' Cynthia said brusquely. 'I find the defendant received ineffective assistance of counsel, and I find there is new evidence that tends to negate her guilt.' She turned to the bailiff. 'Release her. Here. Now.'

Cynthia rose quickly. But then she stopped to give David Galindo a hard look. 'I don't expect to see this case again, Mr Prosecutor.'

She left the room quickly, never looking back at Edward. No one would be able to say she'd tended to favor him.

Amy leaned her head against Edward's shoulder. 'I had a great lawyer,' she whispered.

Edward drew a deep breath and had to sit down, relief flooding his system.

The bailiff led Amy over to his desk and Edward turned to the prosecutor, who remained slumped down in his chair.

'Thanks, David.'

David snorted. 'You know I had no choice.'

Edward continued, 'So what are you going to do now?'

'You heard the judge. When my office asks me I'll say I agree. When they ask me to evaluate it, I'll say I think a second trial against Amy is unwinnable.'

The knot in Edward's stomach unwound. He felt quite sure that David would make a compelling case within his office no matter what his official status.

He nodded toward the arrestee in the jury box. 'What about Valerie Linnett?'

'Given your testimony' – David gave Edward a look – 'I feel pretty sure I can convict her.' Then he stood, again not offering to shake hands, and walked away, fading into the spectators like a ghost.

Edward turned and saw his family in the front row, all smiling at him. But Linda wasn't there. Scanning the crowd, he saw her just outside the side gate in the railing. She was beaming at him.

Edward stood and felt Amy back at his shoulder, now free of handcuffs. He turned and they smiled at each other, the secret crooked smiles they'd always saved for each other.

'I'll never forget you, Edward.'

'Of course not. I'm your brother.'

Amy socked him in the arm. 'You know what I mean. Thank you.'

'You're welcome,' he said seriously.

Then Amy gestured him closer and when he leaned in she whispered, 'And I want my lock picks back.'

They touched their heads together and laughed, then turned to embrace their incoming families.

THE END

Author's Note

The courtroom action in this novel takes place in the Harris County Criminal Justice Center, which was inundated by Hurricane Harvey to the extent that at this writing it is inoperable and needing extensive repair. So this novel has become a slight period piece. But I prefer to think of it as set in the near future, when Houston will be back stronger than ever.

Acknowledgments

Heartfelt thanks to Ann Collette, who as soon as she began representing me found me a great home. Sincere thanks also to Holly Domney, who has made the editing of this book the most pleasant of my writing life, and to everyone at Severn House, which sounds to my American ears like a place the Sorting Hat would send me, and in my case it made a great choice. I must also thank my lifelong friend Robert Morrow for sharing his insights into the practice of criminal law in Houston and life in the Harris County Criminal Justice Center. And I totally stole from him the line about 'the day after you walk out of this courthouse for the last time . . .' What else are best friends for?